WRITTEN OR EDITED BY KURT SINGER

The World's Greatest Women Spies
Women Spies
Gentlemen Spies
The Men in the Trojan Horse
Spies and Traitors of World War II
3000 Years of Espionage
Duel for the Northland
White Book of the Church of Norway
Niemöller—Soldier of God
Göering—A Biography
Carl von Ossietzky, A Biography
Ossietzky Speaks
Europe's Dictators
Generals of Tomorrow
The Coming War
Story of a Hypnotist
Europe's Prisons
Compulsory Sterilisation in Germany
Europe's Rearmament
Hitler's Olympic Games
Spies and Traitors
The World's Greatest Spy Stories
The Charles Laughton Story
More Spy Stories
Spies over Asia
My Greatest Crime Story
My Strangest Case
The Danny Kaye Story
Spy Omnibus
Spies for Democracy
Spies Who Changed History
Great Adventures in Crime
Kurt Singer's Ghost Book
Horror Omnibus
Lyndon Baines Johnson—Man of Reason
Albert Schweitzer—Medical Missionary
Great Adventures in Crime
Ernest Hemingway—Man of Courage
Heiman
Mata Hari—Goddess of Sin
Weird Tales of the Supernatural
Tales of Terror
Tales of the Uncanny
Tales from the Unknown

Tales from the Unknown

KURT SINGER

LONDON W. H. ALLEN 1970

PRINTED AND BOUND IN GREAT BRITAIN BY
THE GARDEN CITY PRESS LIMITED
LETCHWORTH, HERTFORDSHIRE
FOR THE PUBLISHERS
W. H. ALLEN & CO. LTD.
ESSEX STREET, LONDON, WC2 R 3JG
ISBN 0 491 00115 0

The stories in this book are reprinted by arrangement with B. P. Singer Features, Anaheim, California.

CONTENTS

INTRODUCTION

Tales Of The Unknown may appear to be so unbelievably fantastic as to suggest that the events recorded within are really the creation of minds no longer able to apprehend the limitations imposed by the unities and verities of reality. This is a very superficial judgement and does not take into reckoning the scrupulous research made by responsible investigators into psychic phenomena and the strange experiences that befall men and women all over the world who are made startlingly aware of the presence of the unknown.

Just as one cannot expect a sightless person to come away from an art gallery enthused, so one must be prepared for the cynicism of those who have closed their minds against any possibility of the existence of the supernatural, despite the powerful evidence garnered over the centuries. We know of the fascination and awe with which the subject was regarded by peoples of the ancient civilizations and of the beliefs that exist today concerning eternal life, reincarnation and communication with those who have died. Extrasensory perception is no longer regarded as an hallucination and thought transference has become an accepted scientific fact.

Many famous novelists and writers have acknowledged their interest in the occult through their work and I believe that the present collection has been greatly enhanced by the inclusion of a number of stories, of both fact and fiction, by authors whose names are familiar to everybody.

With the advent of the space age, and the realization that the mysteries of the universe are now within reach of human enquiry, is not the prospect tremendously exciting? Who knows what cosmic revelation may yet be disclosed to man—the corroboration that death is a transition to eternal life or the harsh truth that existence everywhere is an unending struggle between Good and Evil.

KURT SINGER

THE HAUNTED AND THE HAUNTERS;
or, The House and the Brain

by LORD LYTTON

A FRIEND of mine, who is a man of letters and a philosopher, said to me one day, as if between jest and earnest: "Fancy! since we last met, I have discovered a haunted house in the midst of London."

"Really haunted?—and by what?—ghosts?"

"Well, I can't answer that question; all I know is this: six weeks ago my wife and I were in search of a furnished apartment. Passing a quiet street, we saw on the window of one of the houses a bill, 'Apartments, Furnished'. The situation suited us: we entered the house—liked the rooms—engaged them by the week—and left them the third day. No power on earth could have reconciled my wife to stay longer; and I don't wonder at it."

"What did you see?"

"Excuse me—I have no desire to be ridiculed as a superstitious dreamer—nor, on the other hand, could I ask you to accept on my affirmation what you would hold to be incredible without the evidence of your own senses. Let me say only this, it was not so much what we saw or heard (in which you might fairly suppose that we were the dupes of our own excited fancy, or the victims of imposture in others) that drove us away, as it was an undefinable terror which seized both of us whenever we passed by the door of a certain unfurnished room, in which we neither saw nor heard anything. And the strangest marvel of all was, that for once in my life I agreed with my wife, silly woman though she be—and allowed, after the third night, that it was impossible to stay a fourth in that house. Accordingly, on the fourth morning I summoned the woman who kept the house and attended on us, and told her that the rooms did not quite suit us, and we would not stay out our week. She said dryly: 'I know why; you have stayed longer than any other lodger. Few ever stayed a second night; none before you a third. But I take it they have been very kind to you.'

" 'They—who?' I asked, affecting to smile.

" 'Why, they who haunt the house, whoever they are. I don't mind them; I remember them many years ago, when I lived in this house, not as a servant; but I know they will be the death of me some day. I don't care—I'm old, and must die soon anyhow; and then I shall be with them, and in this house still.' The woman spoke with so dreamy a calmness, that really it was a sort of awe that prevented my conversing with her further. I paid for my week, and too happy were my wife and I to get off so cheaply."

"You excite my curiosity," said I; "nothing I should like better than to a sleep in a haunted house. Pray give me the address of the one which you left so ignominiously."

My friend gave me the address; and when we parted, I walked straight towards the house thus indicated.

It is situated on the north side of Oxford Street, in a dull but respectable thoroughfare. I found the house shut up—no bill at the window, and no response to my knock. As I was turning away, a beer-boy, collecting pewter pots at the neighbouring areas, said to me: "Do you want anyone at that house, sir?"

"Yes, I heard it was to be let."

"Let!—why, the woman who kept it is dead—has been dead these three weeks, and no one can be found to stay there, though Mr. J— offered ever so much. He offered mother, who chars for him, a pound a week just to open and shut the windows, and she would not."

"Would not!—and why?"

"The house is haunted; and the old woman who kept it was found dead in her bed, with her eyes wide open. They say the devil strangled her."

"Pooh!—you speak of Mr. J—. Is he the owner of the house?"

"Yes."

"Where does he live?"

"In G— Street, number —."

"What is he?—in any business?"

"No, sir—nothing particular; a single gentleman."

I gave the pot-boy the gratuity earned by his liberal information, and proceeded to Mr. J—, in G— Street, which was close by the street that boasted the haunted house. I was lucky enough to find Mr. J— at home—an elderly man, with intelligent countenance and prepossessing manners.

I communicated my name and my business frankly. I said I heard the house was considered to be haunted—that I had a strong desire to examine the house with so equivocal a reputation—that I should be greatly obliged if he would allow me to hire it, though only for a night. I was willing to pay for that privilege whatever he might be inclined to ask. "Sir," said Mr. J—, with great courtesy, "the house is at your service, for as short or as long a time as you please. Rent is out of the question—the obligation will be on my side should you be able to discover the cause of the strange phenomena which at present deprive it of all value. I cannot let it, for I cannot even get a servant to keep it in order or answer the door. Unluckily the house is haunted, if I may use that expression, not only by night, but by day; though at night the disturbances are of a more unpleasant and sometimes of a more alarming character. The poor old woman who died in it three weeks ago was a pauper whom I took out of the workhouse, for in her childhood she had been known to some of my family, and had once been in such good circumstances that she had rented that house of my uncle. She was a woman of superior education and strong mind, and was the only person I could ever induce to remain in the house. Indeed, since her death, which was sudden, and the coroner's inquest, which gave it a notoriety in the neighbourhood, I have so despaired of finding any person to take charge of the house, much more a tenant, that I would willingly let it rent free for a year to anyone who would pay its rates and taxes."

"How long is it since the house acquired this sinister character?"

"That I can scarcely tell you, but very many years since. The old woman I spoke of said it was haunted when she rented it between thirty and forty years ago. The fact is, that my life has been spent in the East Indies, and in the civil service of the Company. I returned to England last year, on inheriting the fortune of an uncle, among whose possessions was the house in question. I found it shut up and uninhabited. I was told that it was haunted, that no one would inhabit it. I smiled at what seemed to me so idle a story. I spent some money in repairing it—added to its old-fashioned furniture a few modern articles—advertised it, and obtained a lodger for a year. He was a colonel on half-pay. He came in with his family, a son and a daughter, and four or five servants: they all left the house the next day; and, although each of them declared that he had seen something different from that which had scared the others, a something still was equally terrible to all. I really could not in conscience sue, nor even blame, the colonel for breach of agreement. Then I put in the old woman I have spoken of, and she was empowered to let the house in apartments. I never had one lodger who stayed more than three days. I do not tell you their stories—to no two lodgers have there been exactly the same phenomena repeated. It is better that you should judge for yourself, than enter the house with an imagination influenced by previous narratives; only be prepared to see and to hear something or other, and take whatever precautions you yourself please."

"Have you never had a curiosity yourself to pass a night in that house?"

"Yes, I passed not a night, but three hours in broad daylight in that house. My curiosity is not satisfied, but is quenched. I have no desire to renew the experiment. You cannot complain, you see, sir, that I am not sufficiently candid; and unless your interest be exceedingly eager and your nerves unusually strong, I honestly add, that I advise you *not* to pass a night in that house."

"My interest *is* exceedingly keen," said I, "and though only a coward will boast of his nerves in situations wholly unfamiliar to him, yet my nerves have been seasoned in such variety of danger that I have the right to rely on them—even in a haunted house."

Mr. J— said very little more; he took the keys of the house out of his bureau, gave them to me—and, thanking him cordially for his frankness, and his urbane concession to my wish, I carried off my prize.

Impatient for the experiment, as soon as I reached home, I summoned my confidential servant—a young man of gay spirits, fearless temper, and as free from superstitious prejudice as anyone I could think of.

"F—," said I, "you remember in Germany how disappointed we were at not finding a ghost in that old castle, which was said to be haunted by a headless apparition? Well, I have heard of a house in London which, I have reason to hope, is decidedly haunted. I mean to sleep there tonight. From what I hear, there is no doubt that something will allow itself to be seen or to be heard—something, perhaps, excessively horrible. Do you think, if I take you with me, I may rely on your presence of mind, whatever may happen?"

"Oh, sir! pray trust me," answered F—, grinning with delight.

"Very well; then here are the keys of the house—this is the address. Go now—select for me any bedroom you please; and since the house has not been inhabited for weeks, make up a good fire—air the bed well—see, of course, that there are candles as well as fuel. Take with you my revolver and my dagger—so much for my weapons—arm yourself equally well; and if we are not a match for a dozen ghosts, we shall be but a sorry couple of Englishmen."

I was engaged for the rest of the day on business so urgent that I had no leisure to think much on the nocturnal adventure to which I had plighted my honour. I dined alone, and very late, and while dining, read, as is my habit. I selected one of the volumes of Macaulay's essays. I thought to myself that I would take the book with me; there was so much of healthfulness in the style, and practical life in the subjects, that it would serve as an antidote against the influences of superstitious fancy.

Accordingly, about half-past nine, I put the book into my pocket, and strolled leisurely towards the haunted house. I took with me a favourite dog—an exceedingly sharp, bold, and vigilant bull-terrier—a dog fond of prowling about strange ghostly corners and passages at night in search of rats—a dog of dogs for a ghost.

It was a summer night, but chilly, the sky somewhat gloomy and overcast. Still there was a moon—faint and sickly, but still a moon—and if the clouds permitted, after midnight it would be brighter.

I reached the house, knocked, and my servant opened with a cheerful smile.

"All right, sir, and very comfortable."

"Oh!" said I, rather disappointed; "have you not seen or heard anything remarkable?"

"Well, sir, I must own I have heard something queer."

"What?—what?"

"The sound of feet pattering behind me; and once or twice small noises like whispers close at my ear—nothing more."

"You are not at all frightened?"

"I! not a bit of it, sir," and the man's bold look reassured me on one point—viz., that happen what might, he would not desert me.

We were in the hall, the street-door closed, and my attention was now drawn to my dog. He had at first run in eagerly enough, but had sneaked back to the door, and was scratching and whining to get out. After patting him on the head, and encouraging him gently, the dog seemed to reconcile himself to the situation, and followed me and F— through the house, but keeping close at my heels instead of hurrying inquisitively in advance, which was his usual and normal habit in all strange places. We first visited the subterranean apartments, the kitchen and other offices, and especially the cellars, in which last there were two or three bottles of wine still left in the bin, covered with cobwebs, and evidently, by their appearance, undisturbed for many years. It was clear that the ghosts were not wine-bibbers. For the rest we discovered nothing of interest. There was a gloomy little backyard, with very high walls. The stones of this yard were very damp; and what with the damp, and what with the dust and smoke-grime on the pavement, our feet left a slight impression where we passed. And now appeared the first strange phenomenon witnessed by myself in this strange abode. I saw, just before me, the print of a foot suddenly form itself, as it were. I stopped, caught hold of my servant, and pointed to it. In advance of that footprint as suddenly dropped another. We both saw it. I advanced quickly to the place; the footprints kept advancing before me, a small footprint—the foot of a child: the impression was too faint thoroughly to distinguish the shape, but it seemed to us both that it was the print of a naked foot. This phenomenon ceased when we arrived at the opposite wall, nor did it repeat itself on returning. We remounted the stairs, and entered the rooms on the ground floor, a dining parlour, a small back-parlour, and a still smaller third room that had been probably appropriated to a footman—all still as death. We then visited the drawing-rooms, which seemed fresh and new. In the front room I seated myself in an arm-chair. F— placed on the table the candlestick with which he had lighted us. I told him to shut the door. As he turned to do so, a chair opposite to me moved from the wall quickly and noiselessly, and dropped itself about a yard from my own chair, immediately fronting it.

"Why, this is better than the turning-tables," said I, with a half-laugh; and as I laughed, my dog put back his head and howled.

F—, coming back, had not observed the movement of the chair. He employed himself now in stilling the dog. I continued to gaze on the chair, and fancied I saw on it a pale blue misty outline of a human figure, but an outline so indistinct that I could only distrust my own vision. The dog was now quiet.

"Put back that chair opposite to me," said I to F—; "put it back to the wall."

F— obeyed. "Was that you, sir," said he, turning abruptly.

"I !—what?"

"Why, something struck me. I felt it sharply on the shoulder—just here."

"No," said I. "But we have jugglers present, and though we may not discover their tricks, we shall catch *them* before they frighten *us*."

We did not stay long in the drawing-rooms—in fact, they felt so damp and so chilly that I was glad to get to the fire upstairs. We locked the doors of the drawing-rooms—a precaution which, I should observe, we had taken with all the rooms we had searched below. The bedroom my servant had selected for me was the best on the floor—a large one, with two windows fronting the street. The four-posted bed, which took up no inconsiderable space, was opposite to the fire, which burnt clear and bright; a door in the wall to the left, between the bed and the window, communicated with the room which my servant appropriated to himself. This last was a small room with a sofa-bed, and had no communication with the landing-place—no other door but that which conducted to the bedroom I was to occupy. On either side of my fireplace was a cupboard, without locks, flush with the wall, and covered with the same dull-brown paper. We examined these cupboards—only hooks to suspend female dresses—nothing else; we sounded the walls—evidently solid—the outer walls of the building. Having finished the survey of these apartments, warmed myself a few moments, and lighted my cigar, I then, still accompanied by F—, went forth to complete my reconnoitre. In the landing-place there was another door; it was closed firmly. "Sir," said my servant, in surprise, "I unlocked this door with all the others when I first came; it cannot have got locked from the inside, for—"

Before he had finished his sentence, the door, which neither of us then was touching, opened quietly of itself. We looked at each other a single instant. The same thought seized both—some human agency might be detected here. I rushed in first, my servant followed. A small, blank, dreary room without furniture—a few empty boxes and hampers in a corner—a small window—the shutters closed—not even a fireplace—no other door but that by which we had entered—no carpet on the floor, and the floor seemed very old, uneven, worm-eaten, mended here and there, as was shown by the whiter patches on the woods; but no living being, and no visible place in which a living being could have hidden. As we stood gazing round, the door by which we had entered closed as quietly as it had before opened: we were imprisoned.

For the first time I felt a creep of undefinable horror. Not so my servant. "Why, they don't think to trap us, sir; I could break that trumpery door with a kick of my foot."

"Try first if it will open to your hand," said I, shaking off the vague apprehension that had seized me, "while I unclose the shutters and see what is without."

I unbarred the shutters—the window looked on the little backyard I have before described; there was no ledge without—nothing to break the sheer descent of the wall. No man getting out of that window would have found any footing till he had fallen on the stones below.

F—, meanwhile, was vainly attempting to open the door. He now turned round to me and asked my permission to use force. And I should here state, in justice to the servant, that, far from evincing any superstitious terrors, his nerve, composure, and even gaiety amidst circumstances so extraordinary, compelled my admiration, and made me congratulate myself on having secured a companion in every way fitted to the occasion. I willingly gave him the permission he required. But though he was a remarkably strong man, his force was as idle as his milder efforts; the door did not even shake to his stoutest kick. Breathless and panting, he desisted. I then tried the door myself, equally in vain. As I ceased from the effort, again that creep of horror came over me; but this time it was more cold and stubborn. I felt as if some strange and ghastly exhalation were rising up from the chinks of that rugged floor, and filling the atmosphere with a venomous influence hostile to human life. The door now very slowly and quietly opened as of its own accord. We precipitated ourselves into the landing-place. We both saw a large pale light—as large as the human figure, but shapeless and unsubstantial—move before us, and ascend the stairs that led from the landing into the attics. I followed the light, and my servant followed me. It entered to the right of the landing a small garret, of which the door stood open. I entered in the same instant. The light then collapsed into a small globule, exceedingly brilliant and vivid : rested a moment on a bed in the corner, quivered, and vanished. We approached the bed and examined it—a half-tester, such as is commonly found in attics devoted to servants. On the drawers that stood near it we perceived an old faded silk kerchief, with the needle still left in a rent half repaired. The kerchief was covered with dust; probably it had belonged to the old woman who had last died in that house, and this might have been her sleeping-room. I had sufficient curiosity to open the drawers : there were a few odds and ends of female dress, and two letters tied round with a narrow ribbon of faded yellow. I took the liberty to possess myself of the letters. We found nothing else in the room worth noticing—nor did the light reappear; but we distinctly heard, as we turned to go, a pattering footfall on the floor—just before us. We went through the other attics (in all four), the footfall still preceding us. Nothing to be seen—nothing but the footfall heard. I had the letters in my hand : just as I was descending the stairs I distinctly felt my wrist seized, and a faint soft effort made to draw the letters from my clasp. I only held them the more tightly, and the effort ceased.

We regained the bed-chamber appropriated to myself, and I then remarked that my dog had not followed us when we had left it. He was thrusting himself close to the fire, and trembling. I was impatient to examine the letters; and while I read them, my servant opened a little box in which he had deposited the weapons I had ordered him to bring; took them out, placed them on a table close at my bed-head, and then occupied himself in soothing the dog, who, however, seemed to heed him very little.

The letters were short—they were dated; the dates exactly thirty-five years ago. They were evidently from a lover to his mistress, or a husband to some young wife. Not only the terms of expression, but a distinct reference to a former voyage, indicated the writer to have been a seafarer. The spelling and hand-writing were those of a man imperfectly educated, but still the language itself was forcible. In the expressions of endearment there was a kind of rough, wild love; but here and there were dark, unintelligible hints at some secret not of love—some secret that seemed of crime. "We ought to love each other," was one of the sentences I remember, "for how everyone else would execrate us if all was known." Again : "Don't let anyone be in the same room with you at night—you talk in your sleep." And again: "What's done can't be undone; and I tell you there's nothing against us unless the dead could come to life." Here there was underlined in a better handwriting (a female's), "They do!" At the end of the letter latest in date the same female hand had written these words: "Lost at sea the 4th of June, the same day as ——."

I put down the letters, and began to muse over their contents. Fearing, however that the train of thought into which I fell might unsteady my nerves, I fully determined to keep my mind in a fit state to cope with whatever of the Marvellous the advancing night might bring forth. I roused myself—laid the letters on the table—stirred up the fire, which was still bright and cheering, and opened my volume of Macaulay. I read quietly enough till about half past eleven. I then threw myself dressed upon the bed, and told my servant he might retire to his own room, but must keep himself awake. I bade him leave open the door between the two rooms. Thus alone, I kept two candles burning on the table by my bed-head. I placed my watch beside the weapons, and calmly resumed my Macaulay. Opposite to me the fire burned clear; and on the hearth-rug, seemingly asleep, lay the dog. In about twenty minutes I felt an exceedingly cold air pass my cheek, like a sudden draught. I fancied the door to my right, communicating with the landing-place, must have got open; but no—it was closed. I then turned my glance to my left, and saw the flame of the candles violently swayed as by a wind. At the same moment the watch beside the revolver softly slid from the table—softly, softly—no visible hand—it was gone. I sprang up, seizing the revolver with the one hand, the dagger with the other: I was not willing that my weapons should share the fate of the watch. Thus armed, I looked round the floor—no sign of the watch. Three slow, loud, distinct knocks were now heard at the bed-head; my servant called out, "Is that you, sir?"

"No; be on your guard."

The dog now roused himself and sat on his haunches, his ears moving quickly backwards and forwards. He kept his eyes fixed on me with a look so strange that he concentrated all my attention on himself. Slowly, he rose up, all his hair bristling, and stood perfectly rigid, and with the same wild stare. I had no time, however, to examine the dog. Presently my servant emerged from his room; and if ever I saw horror in the human face, it was then.

I should not have recognized him had we met in the street, so altered was every lineament. He passed by me quickly, saying in a whisper that seemed scarcely to come from his lips, "Run-run! it is after me!" He gained the door to the landing, pulled it open, and rushed forth. I followed him into the landing involuntarily, calling him to stop; but, without heeding me, he bounded down the stairs, clinging to the balusters, and taking several steps at a time. I heard, where I stood, the street door open—heard it again clap to. I was left alone in the haunted house.

It was but for a moment that I remained undecided whether or not to follow my servant; pride and curiosity alike forbade so dastardly a flight. I re-entered my room, closing the door after me, and proceeded cautiously into the interior chamber. I encountered nothing to justify my servant's terror. I again carefully examined the walls, to see if there were any concealed door. I could find no trace of one—not even a seam in the dull-brown paper with which the room was hung. How, then, had the THING, whatever it was, which had so scared him, obtained ingress except through my own chamber? I returned to my room, shut and locked the door that opened upon the interior one, and stood on the hearth, expectant and prepared. I now perceived that the dog had slunk into an angle of the wall, and was pressing himself close against it, as if literally striving to force his way into it. I approached the animal and spoke to it; the poor brute was evidently beside itself with terror. It showed all its teeth, the slaver dropped from its jaws, and would certainly have bitten me if I had touched it. It did not seem to recognize me. Whoever has seen at the Zoological Gardens a rabbit, fascinated by a serpent, cowering in a corner, may form some idea of the anguish which the dog exhibited. Finding all efforts to soothe the animal in vain, and fearing that his bite might be as venomous in that state as in the madness of hydrophobia, I left him alone, placed my weapons on the table beside the fire, seated myself, and recommenced my Macaulay.

Perhaps, in order not to appear seeking credit for a courage, or rather a coolness which the reader may conceive I exaggerate, I may be pardoned if I pause to indulge in one or two egotistical remarks.

As I hold presence of mind, or what is called courage, to be precisely proportioned to familiarity with the circumstances that lead to it, so I should say that I had been long sufficiently familiar with all experiments that appertain to the Marvellous. I had witnessed many very extraordinary phenomena in various parts of the world—phenomena that would be either totally disbelieved if I stated them, or ascribed to supernatural agencies. Now, my theory is that the Supernatural is the Impossible, and that what is called supernatural is only a something in the laws of nature of which we have been hitherto ignorant. Therefore, if a ghost rises before me, I have not the right to say, "So, then, the supernatural is possible", but rather, "So, then, the apparition of a ghost is, contrary to received opinion, within the laws of nature—i.e., not supernatural".

Now, in all that I hitherto witnessed, and indeed in all the wonders which the amateurs of mystery in our age record as facts, a material living agency is always required. On the Continent you will find still magicians who assert that they can raise spirits. Assume for the moment that they assert truly, still the living material form of the magician is present; and he is the material agency by which, from some constitutional peculiarities, certain strange phenomena are represented to your natural senses.

Accept, again, as truthful, the tales of Spirit Manifestation in America—musical or other sounds—writings on paper, produced by no discernible hand—articles of furniture moved without apparent human agency—or the actual sight and touch of hands, to which no bodies seem to belong—still there must be found the MEDIUM or living being, with constitutional peculiarities capable of obtaining these signs. In fine, in all such marvels, supposing even that there is no imposture, there must be a human being like ourselves by whom, or through whom, the effects presented to human beings are produced. It is so with the now familiar phenomena of mesmerism or electro-biology; the mind of the person operated on is affected through a material living agent. Nor, supposing it true that a mesmerized patient can respond to the will or passes of a mesmerizer a hundred miles distant, is the response less occasioned by a material being; it may be through a material fluid—call it Electric, call it Odic, call it what you will—which has the power of traversing space and passing obstacles, that the material effect is communicated from one to the other. Hence all that I had hitherto witnessed, or expected to witness, in this strange house, I believed to be occasioned through some agency or medium as mortal as myself; and this idea necessarily prevented the awe with which those who regard as supernatural things that are not within the ordinary operations of nature, might have been impressed by the adventures of that memorable night.

As, then, it was my conjecture that all that was presented, or would be presented to my senses, must originate in some human being gifted by constitution with the power so to present them, and having some motive so to do, I felt an interest in my theory which, in its way, was rather philosophical than superstitious. And I can sincerely say that I was in as tranquil a temper for observation as any practical experimentalist could be in awaiting the effects of some rare, though perhaps perilous, chemical combination. Of course, the more I kept my mind detached from fancy, the more the temper fitted for observation would be obtained; and I therefore riveted eye and thought on the strong daylight sense in the page of my Macaulay.

I now became aware that something interposed between the page and the light—the page was overshadowed: I looked up, and I saw what I shall find it very difficult, perhaps impossible, to describe.

It was Darkness shaping itself forth from the air in very undefined outline. I cannot say it was of a human form, and yet it had more resemblance to a human form, or rather shadow, than to anything else. As it stood, wholly apart and distinct from the air and the light around it, its dimensions seemed gigantic, the summit nearly touching the ceiling. While I gazed, a feeling of intense cold seized me. An iceberg before me could not more have chilled me; nor could the cold of an iceberg have been more purely physical. I feel convinced that it was not the cold caused by fear. As I continued to gaze, I thought—but this I cannot say with precision—that I distinguished two eyes looking down on me from the height. One moment I fancied that I distinguished them clearly, the next they seemed gone; but still two rays of a pale-blue light frequently shot through the darkness, as from the height on which I half believed half doubted, that I had encountered the eyes.

I strove to speak—my voice utterly failed me; I could only think to myself, "Is this fear? it is *not* fear!" I strove to rise—in vain; I felt as if weighed down by an irresistible force. Indeed, my impression was that of an immense and overwhelming Power opposed to my volition; that sense of utter inadequacy to cope with a force beyond men's, which one may feel *physically* in a storm at sea, in a conflagration, or when confronting some terrible wild beast, or rather, perhaps, the shark of the ocean, I felt *morally*. Opposed to my will was another will, as far superior to its strength as storm, fire, and shark are superior in material force to the force of man.

And now, as this impression grew on me—now came, at last, horror—horror to a degree that no words can convey. Still I retained pride, if not courage; and in my own mind I said: "This is horror, but it is not fear; unless I fear I cannot be harmed; my reason rejects this thing; it is an illusion—I do not fear." With a violent effort I succeeded at last in stretching out my hand towards the weapon on the table: as I did so, on the arm and shoulder I received a strange shock, and my arm fell to my side powerless. And now, to add to my horror, the light began slowly to wane from the candles—they were not, as it were, extinguished, but their flame seemed very gradually withdrawn: it was the same with the fire—the light extracted from the fuel; in a few minutes the room was in utter darkness. The dread that came over me, to be thus in the dark with that dark Thing, whose power was so intensely felt, brought a reaction of nerve. In fact, terror had reached that climax, that either my senses must have deserted me, or I must have burst through the spell. I did burst through it. I found voice, though the voice was a shriek. I remember that I broke forth with words like these: "I do not fear, my soul does not fear"; and at the same time I found strength to rise. Still in that profound gloom I rushed to one of the windows—tore aside the curtain—flung open the shutters; my first thought was—LIGHT. And when I saw the moon high, clear, and calm, I felt a joy that almost compensated for the previous terror. There was the moon, there was also the light from the gas-lamps in the deserted slumberous street. I turned to look back into the room; the moon penetrated its shadow very palely and partially—but still there was light. The dark Thing, whatever it might be, was gone—except that I could yet see a dim shadow, which seemed the shadow of that shade, against the opposite wall.

My eye now rested on the table, and from under the table (which was without cloth or cover—an old mahogany round table) there rose a Hand, visible as far as the wrist. It was a hand, seemingly, as much of flesh and blood as my own, but the hand of an aged person—lean, wrinkled, small too—a woman's hand. That hand very softly closed on the two letters that lay on the table:

hand and letters both vanished. There then came the same three loud measured knocks I had heard at the bed-head before this extraordinary drama had commenced.

As those sounds slowly ceased, I felt the whole room vibrate sensibly; and at the far end there rose, as from the floor, sparks or globules like bubbles of light, many-coloured—green, yellow, fire-red, azure. Up and down, to and fro, hither, thither, as tiny will-o'-the-wisps, the sparks moved, slow or swift, each at its own caprice. A chair (as in the drawing-room below) was now advanced from the wall without apparent agency, and placed at the opposite side of the table. Suddenly, as forth from the chair, there grew a shape —a woman's shape. It was distinct as a shape of life—ghastly as a shape of death. The face was that of youth, with a strange mournful beauty; the throat and shoulders were bare, the rest of the form in a loose robe of cloudy white. It began sleeking its long yellow hair, which fell over its shoulders; its eyes were not turned towards me, but to the door; it seemed listening, watching, waiting. The shadow of the shade in the background grew darker; and again I thought I beheld the eyes gleaming out from the summit of the shadow—eyes fixed upon that shape.

As if from the door, as though it did not open, there grew out another shape, equally distinct, equally ghastly—a man's shape—a young man's. It was in the dress of the last century, or rather in a likeness of such dress (for both the male shape and the female, though defined, were evidently unsubstantial, impalpable—simulacra—phantasms); and there was something incongruous, grotesque, yet fearful, in the contrast between the elaborate finery, the courtly precision of that old-fashioned garb, with its ruffles and lace and buckles, and the corpse-like aspect and ghost-like stillness of the flitting wearer. Just as the male shape approached the female, the dark Shadow started from the wall, all three for a moment wrapped in darkness. When the pale light returned, the two phantoms were as if in the grasp of the Shadow that towered between them; and there was a blood-stain on the breast of the female; and the phantom male was leaning on its phantom sword, and blood seemed trickling fast from the ruffles, from the lace; and the darkness of the intermediate Shadow swallowed them up—they were gone. And again the bubbles of light shot, and sailed, and undulated, growing thicker and thicker and more wildly confused in their movements.

The closet door to the right of the fireplace now opened, and from the aperture there came the form of an aged woman. In her hand she held letters—the very letters over which I had seen *the* Hand close; and behind her I heard a footstep. She turned round as if to listen, and then she opened the letters and seemed to read; and over her shoulder I saw a livid face, the face as of a man long drowned—bloated, bleached—seaweed tangled in its dripping hair; and at her feet lay a form as of a corpse, and beside the corpse there cowered a child, a miserable squalid child, with famine in its cheeks and fear in its eyes. And as I looked in the old woman's face, the wrinkles and lines vanished, and it became a face of youth —hard-eyed, stony, but still youth; and the Shadow darted forth, and darkened over those phantoms as it had darkened over the last.

Nothing now was left but the Shadow, and on that my eyes were intently fixed, till again eyes grew out of the Shadow—malignant, serpent eyes. And the bubbles of light again rose and fell, and in their disordered, irregular, turbulent maze, mingled with the wan moonlight. And now from these globules themselves, as from the shell of an egg, monstrous things burst out; the air grew filled with them; larvae so bloodless and so hideous that I can in no way describe them except to remind the reader of the swarming life which a solar microscope brings before his eyes in a drop of water —things transparent, supple, agile, chasing each other, devouring each other—forms like nought ever beheld by the naked eye. As the shapes were without symmetry, so their movements were without order. In their very vagrancies there was no sport; they came round me and round, thicker and faster and swifter, swarming over my head, crawling over my right arm, which was outstretched in involuntary command against all evil beings. Sometimes I felt myself touched, but not by them; invisible hands touched me. Once I felt the clutch as of cold, soft fingers at my throat. I was still equally conscious that if I gave way to fear I should be in bodily peril; and I concentrated all my faculties in the single focus of resisting, stubborn will. And I turned my sight from the Shadow— above all, from those strange serpent eyes—eyes that had now become distinctly visible. For there, though in nought else around me, I was aware that there was a Will, and a will of intense, creative, working evil, which might crush down my own.

The pale atmosphere in the room began now to redden as if in the air of some near conflagration. The larvae grew lurid as things that live in fire. Again the room vibrated; again were heard the three measured knocks; and again all things were swallowed up in the darkness of the dark Shadow, as if out of that darkness all had come, into that darkness all returned.

As the gloom receded, the Shadow was wholly gone. Slowly, as it had been withdrawn, the flame grew again into the candles on the table, again into the fuel in the grate. The whole room came once more calmly, healthfully into sight.

The two doors were still closed, the door communicating with the servant's room still locked. In the corner of the wall, into which he had so convulsively niched himself, lay the dog. I called to him—no movement; I approached—the animal was dead; his eyes protruded; his tongue out of his mouth; the froth gathered round his jaws. I took him in my arms; I brought him to the fire; I felt acute grief for the loss of my poor favourite—acute self-reproach; I accused myself of his death; I imagined he had died of fright. But what was my surprise on finding that his neck was actually broken. Had this been done in the dark?—must it not have been by a hand human as mine?—must there not have been a human agency all the while in that room? Good cause to suspect it. I cannot tell. I cannot do more than state the fact fairly; the reader may draw his own inference.

Another surprising circumstance—my watch was restored to the table from which it had been so mysteriously withdrawn; but it had stopped at the very moment it was so withdrawn; nor, despite all the skill of the watchmaker, has it ever gone since—that is, it will go in a strange erratic way for a few hours, and then come to a dead stop—it is worthless.

Nothing more chanced for the rest of the night. Nor, indeed, had I long to wait before the dawn broke. Nor till it was broad daylight did I quit the haunted house. Before I did so, I revisited the little blind room in which my servant and myself had been for a time imprisoned. I had a strong impression—for which I could not account—that from that room had originated the mechanism of the phenomena—if I may use the term—which had been experienced in my chamber. And though I entered it now in the clear day, with the sun peering through the filmy window, I still felt, as I stood on its floors, the creep of the horror which I had first there experienced the night before, and which had been so aggravated by what had passed in my own chamber. I could not, indeed, bear to stay more than half a minute within those walls. I descended the stairs, and again I heard the footfall before me; and when I opened the street door, I thought I could distinguish a very low laugh. I gained my own home, expecting to find my runaway servant there. But he had not presented himself, nor did I hear more of him for three days, when I received a letter from him, dated from Liverpool, to this effect:

> Honoured Sir:
>
> I humbly entreat your pardon, though I can scarcely hope that you will think that I deserve it, unless—which Heaven forbid!—you saw what I did. I feel that it will be years before I can recover myself; and as to being fit for service, it is out of the question. I am therefore going to my brother-in-law at Melbourne. The ship sails tomorrow. Perhaps the long voyage may set me up. I do nothing now but start and tremble, and fancy IT is behind me. I humbly beg you, honoured sir, to order my clothes, and whatever wages are due to me, to be sent to my mother's, at Walworth—John knows her address.

The letter ended with additional apologies, somewhat incoherent, and explanatory details as to effect that had been under the writer's charge.

This flight may perhaps warrant a suspicion that the man wished to go to Australia, and had been somehow or other fraudulently mixed up with the events of the night. I say nothing in refutation of that conjecture; rather, I suggest it as one that would seem to many persons the most probable solution of improbable occurrences. My belief in my own theory remained unshaken. I returned in the evening to the house, to bring away in a hack cab the things I had left there, with my poor dog's body. In this task I was not disturbed, nor did any incident worth note befall me, except that still, on ascending and descending the stairs, I heard the same footfall in advance. On leaving the house, I went to Mr. J—'s. He was at home. I returned him the keys, told him that my curiosity was sufficiently gratified, and was about to relate quickly what had passed, when he stopped me, and said, though with much politeness, that he had no longer any interest in a mystery which none had ever solved.

I determined at least to tell him of the two letters I had read, as well as of the extraordinary manner in which they had disappeared, and I then inquired if he thought they had been addressed to the woman who had died in the house, and if there were anything in her early history which could possibly confirm the dark suspicions to which the letters gave rise. Mr. J— seemed startled, and, after musing a few moments, answered: "I am but little acquainted with the woman's earlier history, except, as I before told you, that her family were known to mine. But you revive some vague reminiscences to her prejudice. I will make inquiries, and inform you of their result. Still, even if we could admit the popular superstition that a person who had been either the perpetrator or the victim of dark crimes in life could revisit, as a restless spirit, the scene in which those crimes had been committed, I should observe that the house was infested by strange sights and sounds before the old woman died—you smile—what would you say?"

"I would say this, that I am convinced, if we could get to the bottom of these mysteries, we should find a living human agency."

"What! you believe it is all an imposture? for what object?"

"Not an imposture in the ordinary sense of the word. If suddenly I were to sink into a deep sleep, from which you could not awake me, but in that sleep could answer questions with an accuracy which I could not pretend to when awake—tell you what money you had in your pocket—nay, describe your very thoughts—it is not necessarily an imposture, any more that it is necessarily supernatural. I should be, unconsciously to myself, under a mesmeric influence, conveyed to me from a distance by a human being who had acquired power over me by previous *rapport*."

"But if a mesmerizer could so affect another living being, can you suppose that a mesmerizer could also affect inanimate objects: move chairs—open and shut doors?"

"Or impress our senses with the belief in such effects—we never having been *en rapport* with the person acting on us? No. What is commonly called mesmerism could not do this; but there may be a power akin to mesmerism and superior to it—the power that in the old days was called Magic. That such a power may extend to all inanimate objects of matter, I do not say; but if so, it would not be against nature—it would only be a rare power in nature which might be given to constitutions with certain peculiarities, and cultivated by practise to an extraordinary degree. That such a power might extend over the dead—that is, over certain thoughts and memories that the dead may still retain—and compel, not that which ought properly to be called the SOUL, and which is far beyond human reach, but rather a phantom of what has been most earth-stained on earth to make itself apparent to our senses—is a very ancient though obsolete theory, upon which I will hazard no opinion. But I do not conceive the power would be supernatural. Let me illustrate what I mean from an experiment which Paracelsus describes as not difficult, and which the author of the *Curiosities of Literature* cites as credible: A flower perishes; you burn it. Whatever were the elements of that flower while it lived are gone, dispersed, you know not whither; you can never discover nor re-collect them. But you can, by chemistry, out of the burnt dust of that flower, raise a spectrum of the flower, just as it seemed in life. It may be the same with the human being. The soul has as much escaped you as the essence or elements of the flower. Still you may make a spectrum of it. And this phantom, though in the popular superstition it is held to be the soul of the departed, must not be confounded with the true soul; it is but the eidolon of the dead form. Hence, like the best attested stories of ghosts or spirits, the thing that most strikes us is the absence of what we hold to be the soul; that is, of superior emancipated intelligence. These apparitions come for little or no object—they seldom speak when they do come; if they speak, they utter no ideas above those of an ordinary person on earth. American spirit-seers have published volumes of communications, in prose and verse, which they assert to be given in the names of the most illustrious dead—Shakespeare, Bacon—Heaven knows whom. Those communications, taking the best, are certainly not a whit of higher order than would be communications from living persons of fair talent and education; they are wondrously inferior to what Bacon, Shakespeare, and Plato said and wrote when on earth. Nor, what is more noticeable, do they ever contain an idea that was not on earth before. Wonderful, therefore, as such phenomena may be (granting them to be truthful), I see much that philosophy may question, nothing that it is incumbent on philosophy to deny—viz., nothing supernatural. They are but ideas conveyed somehow or other (we have not yet discovered the means) from one mortal brain to another. Whether, in so doing, tables walk of their own accord, or fiend-like shapes appear in a magic circle, or bodyless hands rise and remove material objects, or a Thing of Darkness, such as presented itself to me, freeze our blood—still am I persuaded that these are but agencies conveyed, as by electric wires, to my own brain from the brain of another. In some constitutions there is a natural chemistry, and those constitutions may produce chemic wonders—in others a natural fluid, call it electricity, and these may produce electric wonders. But the wonders differ from Normal Science in this—they are alike objectless, purposeless, puerile, frivolous. They lead on to no grand results; and therefore the world does not heed, and true sages have not cultivated them. But sure I am, that of all I saw or heard, a man, human as myself, was the remote originator; and I believe unconsciously to himself as to the exact effects produced, for this reason: no two persons, you say, have ever told you that they experienced exactly the same thing. Well, observe, no two persons ever experienced exactly the same dream. If this were an ordinary imposture, the machinery would be arranged for results that would but little vary; if it were a super-natural agency permitted by the Almighty, it would surely be for some definite end. These phenomena belong to neither class; my persuasion is that they originate in some brain now far distant; that that brain had no distinct volition in anything that occurred; that what does occur reflects but its devious, motley, ever-shifting, half-formed thoughts; in short, that it has been but the dreams of such a brain put into action and invested with a semi-substance. That this brain is of immense power, that it can set matter into movement, that it is malignant and destructive, I believe; some material force must have killed my dog; the same force might, for aught I know, have sufficed to kill myself, had I been as subjugated by terror as the dog—had my intellect or my spirit given me no countervailing resistance in my will."

"It killed your dog! that is fearful! indeed it is strange that no animal can be induced to stay in that house; not even a cat. Rats and mice are never found in it."

"The instincts of the brute creation detect influences deadly to their existence. Man's reason has a sense less subtle, because it has a resisting power more supreme. But enough; do you comprehend my theory?"

"Yes, though imperfectly—and I accept any crotchet (pardon the word), however odd, rather than embrace at once the notion of ghosts and hobgoblins we imbibed in our nurseries. Still, to my unfortunate house the evil is the same. What on earth can I do with the house?"

"I will tell you what I would do. I am convinced from my own internal feelings that the small unfurnished room at right angles to the door of the bedroom which I occupied forms a starting-point or receptacle for the influences which haunt the house; and I strongly advise you to have the walls opened, the floor removed—nay, the whole room pulled down. I observe that it is detached from the body of the house, built over the small backyard, and could be removed without injury to the rest of the building."

"And you think, if I did that—"

"You would cut off the telegraph wires. Try it. I am so persuaded that I am right, that I will pay half the expense if you will allow me to direct the operations."

"Nay, I am well able to afford the cost; for the rest, allow me to write to you."

About ten days after, I received a letter from Mr. J—, telling me that he had visited the house since I had seen him; that he had found the two letters I had described, replaced in the drawer from which I had taken them; that he had read them with misgivings like my own; that he had instituted a cautious inquiry about the woman to whom I rigidly conjectured they had been written. It seemed that thirty-six years ago (a year before the date of the letters) she had married, against the wish of her relations, an American of very suspicious character; in fact, he was generally believed to have been a pirate. She herself was the daughter of very respectable tradespeople, and had served in the capacity of a nursery governess before her marriage. She had a brother, a widower, who was considered wealthy, and who had one child of about six years old. A month after the marriage, the body of this brother was found in the Thames, near London Bridge; there seemed some marks of violence about his throat, but they were not deemed sufficient to warrant the inquest in any other verdict than that of "found drowned".

The American and his wife took charge of the little boy, the deceased brother having by his will left his sister the guardian of his only child—and in the event of the child's death, the sister inherited. The child died about six months afterwards—it was supposed to have been neglected and ill-treated. The neighbours deposed to have heard it shriek at night. The surgeon who had examined it after death said that it was emaciated as if from want of nourishment, and the body was covered with livid bruises. It seemed that one winter night the child had sought to escape—crept out into the backyard—tried to scale the wall—fallen back exhausted, and been found at morning on the stones in a dying state. But through there was some evidence of cruelty, there was none of murder; and the aunt and her husband had sought to palliate cruelty by alleging the exceeding stubbornness and perversity of the child, who was declared to be half-witted. Be that as it may, at the orphan's death the aunt inherited her brother's fortune. Before the first wedded year was out, the American quitted England abruptly, and never returned to it. He obtained a cruising vessel, which was lost in the Atlantic two years afterwards. The widow was left in affluence: but reverses of various kinds had befallen her: a bank broke—an investment failed—she went into a small business and became insolvent—then she entered into service, sinking lower and lower, from housekeeper down to maid-of-all-work—never long retaining a place, though nothing decided against her character was ever alleged. She was considered sober, honest, and peculiarly quiet in her ways; still nothing prospered with her. And so she had dropped into the workhouse, from which Mr. J— had taken her, to be placed in charge of the very house which she had rented as mistress in the first year of her wedded life.

Mr. J— added that he had passed an hour alone in the unfurnished room which I had urged him to destroy, and that his impressions of dread while there were so great, though he had neither heard nor seen anything, that he was eager to have the walls bared and the floors removed as I had suggested. He had engaged persons for the work, and would commence any day I would name.

The day was accordingly fixed. I repaired to the haunted house—we went into the blind, dreary room, took up the skirting, and then the floors. Under the rafters, covered with rubbish, was found a trap-door, quite large enough to admit a man. It was closely nailed down, with clamps and rivets of iron. On removing these we descended into a room below, the existence of which has never been suspected. In this room there had been a window and a flue, but they had been bricked over, evidently for many years. By the help of candles we examined this place; it still retained some mouldering furniture—three chairs, an oak settle, a table—all of the fashion of about eighty years ago. There was a chest of drawers against the wall, in which we found, half-rotted away, old-fashioned articles of a man's dress, such as might have been worn eighty or a hundred years ago by a gentleman of some rank—costly steel buckles and buttons, like those yet worn in court dresses, a handsome court sword. In a waistcoat which had once been rich with gold lace, but which was now blackened and foul with damp, we found five guineas, a few silver coins, and an ivory ticket, probably for some place of entertainment long since passed away. But our main discovery was in a kind of iron safe fixed to the wall, the lock of which it cost us much trouble to get picked.

In this safe were three shelves, and two small drawers. Ranged on the shelves were several small bottles of crystal, hermetically stopped. They contained colourless volatile essences, of the nature of which I shall only say that they were not poisons—phosphor and ammonia entered into some of them. There were also some very curious glass tubes, and a small pointed rod of iron, with a large lump of rock-crystal, and another of amber—also a loadstone of great power.

In one of the drawers we found a miniature portrait set in gold, and retaining the freshness of its colours most remarkably, considering the length of time it had probably been there. The portrait was that of a man who might be somewhat advanced in middle life, perhaps forty-seven or forty-eight.

It was a remarkable face—a most impressive face. If you could fancy some mighty serpent transformed into man, preserving in the human lineaments the old servant type, you would have a better idea of that countenance than long descriptions can convey: the width and flatness of frontal—the tapering elegance of contour disguising the strength of the deadly jaw—the long, large, terrible eye, glittering and green as the emerald—and withal a certain ruthless calm, as if from the consciousness of an immense power.

Mechanically I turned round the miniature to examine the back of it, and on the back was engraved a pentacle; in the middle of the pentacle a ladder, and the third step of the ladder was formed by the date 1765. Examining still more minutely, I detected a spring; this, on being pressed, opened the back of the miniature as a lid. Withinside the lid was engraved "Marianna to thee—Be faithful in life and in death to—." Here follows a name that I will not mention, but it was not unfamiliar to me. I had heard it spoken of by old men in my childhood as the name borne by a dazzling charlatan who had made a great sensation in London for a year or so, and had fled the country on the charge of a double murder within his own house—that of his mistress and his rival. I said nothing of this to Mr. J—, to whom reluctantly I resigned the miniature.

We had found no difficulty in opening the first drawer within the iron safe; we found great difficulty in opening the second: it was not locked, but it resisted all efforts, till we inserted in the chinks the edge of a chisel. When we had thus drawn it forth, we found a very singular apparatus in the nicest order. Upon a small thin book, or rather tablet, was placed a saucer of crystal; this saucer was filled with a clear liquid—on that liquid floated a kind of compass, with a needle shifting rapidly round; but instead of the usual points of a compass were seven strange characters, not very unlike those used by astrologers to denote the planets. A peculiar, but not strong nor displeasing odour, came from this drawer, which was lined with a wood that we afterwards discovered to be hazel. Whatever the cause of this odour, it produced a material effect on the nerves. We all felt it, even the two workmen who were in the room—a creeping tingling sensation from the tips of the fingers to the roots of the hair. Impatient to examine the tablet, I removed the saucer. As I did so the needle of the compass went round and round with exceeding swiftness, and I felt a shock that ran through my whole frame, so that I dropped the saucer on the floor. The liquid was spilt—the saucer was broken—the compass rolled to the end of the room—and at that instant the walls shook to and fro, as if a giant had swayed and rocked them.

The two workmen were so frightened that they ran up the ladder by which we had descended from the trap-door; but seeing that nothing more happened, they were easily induced to return.

Meanwhile I had opened the tablet: it was bound in plain red leather, with a silver clasp; it contained but one sheet of thick vellum, and on that sheet were inscribed, within a double pentacle, words in old monkish Latin, which are literally to be translated thus: "On all that it can reach within these walls—sentient or inanimate, living or dead—as moves the needle, so work my will! Accursed be the house, and restless be the dwellers therein."

We found no more. Mr J— burnt the tablet and its anathema. He razed to the foundations the part of the building containing the secret room with the chamber over it. He had then the courage to inhabit the house himself for a month, and a quieter, better-conditioned house could not be found in all London. Subsequently he let it to advantage, and his tenant has made no complaints.

PSYCHIC ALERT SAVED FILM STAR

by FRANK STEVENS

IN RECENT years, some of the best known public figures have shown a deep interest in the occult and in mystic phenomena, and some have been caught up in events related to the world of occult.

Jackie Kennedy's prediction of the assassination of her brother-in-law, Senator Robert Kennedy, is an example of the latter. The action of film director, Federico Fellini of *La Dolce Vita* fame, who abandoned a movie he had already started after being advised to do so by his astrologer, is another instance of the former.

Brigitte Bardot and her husband, Gunther Sachs, both consult astrologers before making important decisions in their lives. The late singer, Edith Piaf, was a firm believer in seers, mediums, and the possibility of contacting lost ones from beyond the grave. Singer Jane Morgan is convinced that her house in Kennebunkport, Maine, is inhabited by two irritable but harmless ghosts.

But of all the celebrities of our time who have good reason to believe in the reality of the forces of the occult, movie star Elke Sommer stands first.

Elke believes she has been saved from a horrible death twice in the past two years by the intervention of supernormal forces.

On March 13, 1967, Elke and her husband, writer and columnist Joe Hyams, escaped from a fire which caused extensive damage to their Hollywood house. Had not Elke been awakened by a "spirit" which warned her of the danger, they would have been burned to death.

Two months earlier, a medium warned Elke to cancel a trip to her home town near Hamburg, Germany. Elke cancelled the trip—and escaped being kidnapped by an insane mass murderer named Klaus Gossman, who had already worked out detailed plans for kidnapping the actress and murdering her.

Elke, the long-limbed strawberry blonde from Germany who first gained fame by her appearance in the film *The Victors*, has not always been interested in psychic forces and the world of the occult.

In July, 1964, Elke and her husband, Joe Hyams, moved into a large house in Benedict Canyon, Los Angeles. The previous tenant hinted that the house was inhabited by a spirit—a man wearing a black jacket—but both Elke and Joe took the story as a joke.

Before a month passed, they no longer considered it funny. At night, lying in bed, they were bothered by the sounds of footsteps in the hall and downstairs, though no one else was in the house. Sounds of chairs scraping and scuffling against the floor in the dining room downstairs were also audible.

Doors and windows which had been firmly locked were found open an hour later though no one had touched them. Lights went on and off for no discoverable reason.

Finally, Elke, Joe and their guests got repeated glimpses of a stranger—a man in a black jacket—who disappeared minutes after they saw him and could be identified by no one who was nearby.

Hyams, disturbed and intrigued, looked at blueprints of the house to see if there might be a secret chamber somewhere, where an uninvited lodger might be staying. There was not.

He installed electronic sound detection and photographic equipment, and hired termite inspectors to search out every possible hidden nook and cranny in the structure of the house. Again, nothing was found.

By this time, many other people besides Elke and Joe had seen the "ghost" or felt its presence. Mrs. "Red" Buttons came to inspect the house with a view to subletting it one summer. She walked up the steps, stopped, turned white, and refused to enter.

"This house has an evil aura," she exclaimed. "I've never felt this way about a place before."

Harry Kantor, a businessman from New York City, actually did sublet the house in the summer of 1966. In the middle of a party he was giving, the lights went out and a heavy candelabra over the dining room table fell from the ceiling with a tremendous crash.

The lights were not controlled by a master switch—but by separate fuses. Investigation showed that the candelabra had been securely fastened.

Finally, Joe Hyams became so intrigued with the ghost in his house that he wrote a book about it. Before doing so, he called in

"Something impelled me to turn the page back to the account of the 'High Noon' killer. As I did, I saw the photograph of Elke Sommer superimposed on the article about his crimes.

"There was an aura about the superimposed photograph, an aura of evil and horror. It seemed to have a dark glow.

"I felt a foreboding which I knew was not a casual hunch, but a genuine psychic premonition : Elke Sommer was in danger at the hands of the 'High Noon' killer, if she carried out her plans to visit her mother."

Immediately, Frau Bratter sat down at her desk and wrote a short note to Elke Sommer. She told the actress that her psychic powers had warned her of mortal danger if she visited the area of Nuremberg, and urged Elke to cancel the trip.

Four days later, Elke, convinced of the reality of psychic phenomena through her own contact with them at home, did cancel her trip. She was never to regret it.

A week later, the "High Noon" killer struck again, shooting a man who tried to stop him after he had snatched a woman's purse in a department store. This time, he was surrounded and captured.

When police broke into his apartment shortly after his capture, they found a diary recording his plans and criminal ideas.

On the last page of the blue leather diary was scribbled this notation in large block letters : *"Elke Sommer—kidnap her!"*

After intensive questioning by police, Gossman told them that he had read in a local newspaper that Elke was scheduled to visit her mother in the area soon. He had planned to kidnap the actress and ask a huge ransom for her return.

But the police did not believe him. They were convinced that Gossman intended to murder Elke after kidnapping her. In his apartment they discovered proof of this intention.

Among an armoury of weapons—including several rifles, a Sten gun, three hand grenades, four knives, a pistol with a silencer, and a .45 calibre revolver—was found a pistol clearly marked for Gossman's next murder.

On the butt was scratched clearly and deeply the words : X "For Elke."

Had Elke carried out her plan for a visit, in spite of the advice of Frau Bratter, Gossman would have made her his next victim, rather than the man in the department store.

Ironically, Gossman was later tried and after being found guilty, sentenced to the maximum punishment in West Germany, life imprisonment—with the judge handing down his sentence at exactly high noon.

Two years later, on March 13, 1967, a message from the spirit world once again saved Elke's life and that of her husband's also. This time, the message came from the spirit which haunted their Los Angeles home.

On March 20, 1966, Joe Hyams had contacted the well known psychic-sensitive Jacqueline Eastlund, and asked her to help solve the mystery of their haunted house. Joe had left the telephone on a table, and remained off the line while Mrs. Eastlund listened to the aura of the house and collected her impressions.

She told Hyams "I see this house in flames six months from now—be cautious—I also hear a sound like a lot of rain and a sort of tapping."

It wasn't six months, but a year later that Elke woke around six a.m. with a feeling of vague unease. It was raining heavily. As she lay awake, Elke suddenly heard sounds—sounds from downstairs.

For a while she tried to pass them off as more pranks from their mischievous ghost. But this time she felt a sense of anxiety, dread and an inexplicable compulsion to move around.

Finally, she woke her husband. Just as she was telling him about the sounds downstairs and her feeling of dread, a new noise started.

A loud and frantic pounding sounded on their door, as if someone or something were desperately attempting to wake them.

Joe sprang to the door and opened it—to be met by a thick, hot cloud of black smoke. The house was in flames, and their access to the hall was cut off.

Quickly shutting the door again, Hyams called the fire department. Then he and Elke looked around for a means of escape.

Again, the sound of pounding came. This time it came from a window. When Elke ran to look out, she saw why. By climbing through this window she and Joe could drop a few feet to the roof of their garage, and from there easily drop to the ground and safety.

They did, and a quarter of an hour later they were helping the firemen. The fire caused damage estimated at 25,000 dollars.

If the mysterious sounds had not awakened Elke, and if there had been no pounding, Joe and Elke would have perished in the blaze.

Again, Elke had a psychic message to thank for saving her life, which served to reinforce her newly acquired belief in the reality of the world Beyond.

A few months after the fire, Elke happened to be dining in a restaurant in Rome when she was joined by friends. Among them was the beautiful Italian actress, Sophia Loren.

Sophia told the gathering she had just visited one of Europe's most famous mediums, the French seer, Rose Stoller, and that Madame Stoller, after reading a crystal ball, had warned her that someone was about to steal some of her most valuable jewels.

Sophia had ignored the advice. Now, she told her friends, she had just heard that thieves had broken into her Rome apartment and stolen jewels valued at 50,000 dollars.

By listening to and heeding the psychic messages she received, Elke had saved something far more valuable than her jewels—her life.

THE "OUANGA" CHARM

by W. B. SEABROOK

"GO BRING me a humming bird," said Maman Célie, "and we'll see what can be done."

She was talking to her tall grandson, Paul, Emanuel's boy, who had been moping about the habitation for days because a young, high-breasted black damsel down by the spring, who seemed to him more desirable than all the other young black damsels on the mountain, had tossed her crinkly head and sent him about his business.

It was through this idyllic episode of the humming bird that I discovered Maman Célie to be a sorceress, as well as a priestess of Voodoo. The two functions do not necessarily concur.

It seemed to me, however, that she had set her grandson a somewhat difficult task. I had seen humming birds occasionally down yonder among the tropical flowers and fig-banana groves, tiny, fragile, iridescent, darting sprites, as incorporeal as soap-bubbles, as swift to disappear at a threatened touch. To catch one of them seemed almost as difficult as trapping a sunbeam. I knew vaguely that naturalists made use of delicate and cunningly constructed nets, and I had heard with equal vagueness of tiny shotguns spraying microscopic pellets, but Paul was equipped only with his natural wits.

Next day he returned with the humming bird. He had trapped it with a sort of birdlime made of a sticky, gummy sap. It was already dead and Maman Célie hung it up to dry in the sunshine. Meanwhile she persuaded Paul to show me, reluctantly, a former love-charm she had fabricated for him, but which apparently had failed of its purpose, though he still wore it next to his skin in a little sack strung round his neck. She explained its construction and use. Two needles of equal length are stood upright, side by side, baptized with suitable incantations, and are given the names of the youth and his unwilling girl. The two in this particular case were called Paul and Ti-Marie. The needles are then left side by side, parallel but reversed, so that the point of each presses against the eye of the other. The point is symbolic of the phallus and the eye symbolic of the vulva. The reverse doubling simply increases the potency of the charm; it has no perverse significance. The needles are placed between twigs from the roots of the *bois chica* tree, whittled smooth and straight, and then wound round with thread. Like all charms of every sort in Haiti, it was called a *ouanga*. There are love-*ouangas*, hate-*ouangas*, birth-*ouangas*, protective-*ouangas*, and murder-*ouangas*. Sometimes they work, and sometimes they don't. Apparently this one hadn't worked, and Paul now centred all his hopes in the humming bird.

Aware of my curiosity about these matters, Maman Célie permitted me to see her make the new *ouanga*. It was a less weird, less cabalistic business than one might guess, though midnight and moonlight were in it, as she crouched, crooning her incantations, but there was nothing mysteriously dreadful. In a little wooden mortar, which they call *pilon*, she ground the dried body of the humming bird into a dustlike powder, droning, "Wood of the woods, bird of the woods, woman you were created by God. Bird of the woods, fly into her heart. I command you in the name of the three Marys and in Ayida's name. *Dolor, Dolori, passa.*" There was much more of it, untranslatable and cryptic. And with the dried powder of the humming bird she mixed a few dried drops of her grandson's blood, also of his semen, likewise the pollen of jungle flowers.

When all this had been duly ground together into dustlike fineness, she transferred it to a leather pouch made (as Spanish shepherds often do to hold their love-charms) from the scrotum of a he-goat, and gave it to Paul next day.

I was told, for I did not see it, that on the following Saturday evening, at the *danse Congo*, as Ti-Marie swayed past him laughing, he threw the dust full in her face, and that half blinded, with the dust in her eyes and nostrils and mouth, she spat like a young wildcat, and cried out that she would kill him—but she lay with him that night in the forest, and on Monday morning he fetched her home. Doubtless a deeper magic than Maman Célie's was also at work, but I think it would be a mistake to assume *a priori* that without Maman Célie's incantations and the humming bird, Ti-Marie would have yielded.

There were two other occasions when I saw her magic work effectively. I saw her, by processes which she considered magical, cure a dying girl and catch a thief. She said and believed that it was magic. Words are merely labels, and we do not always explain the inner essence of things by rejecting the old labels and inventing new ones. The Lady of Shalott gazed in her crystal mirror to behold scenes far away, and that was sorcery; now we experiment with television, and that is science. The Witch of Endor was a witch, but Svengali is a hypnotist. Old Nostradamus working over his crucibles called it alchemy when he sought to transform lead to gold, but now the Germans are engaged in the same experiment and call it advanced chemistry. I realize that there is a flaw in these parallels. But the scientific-minded Carrel, after his long stay at Lourdes, came away convinced that there were invisible powers unknown to any science at work there, and that the probable power of immaterial emanations to produce constructive or destructive changes in material substances, for instance the human body, was a thing which saints still knew more about than savants. When such things occur at holy shrines, they are called miracles; when they occur in a psychological laboratory, they are called science; when they occur in the Haitian jungle, they are called Voodoo magic. These words are all tags, labels, nothing more. Life and the forces of life remain shrouded in eternal mystery.

Maman Célie's sorcery was principally benevolent, as when she presently began gathering materials for the construction of a *ouanga* packet for me—it seemed that I was to have one of my very own, like that of Louis, which was the first I had ever seen, down in my back yard at Port-au-Prince—and that it was to preserve me safe from all harm amid these mountains. It was to be used also, she told me, in the special ceremonial that would occur when I was finally led into the *houmfort* to face certain of the ultimate Voodoo mysteries. I would need it then, she assured me earnestly.

How much I believed in that *ouanga* packet, and in what manner I believed what I did believe, are questions difficult to answer. I suspect that generally in such matters it is easier to believe in things which are sinister, perhaps dangerous, than it is to believe in things which are benevolent. It is always easier to fear ghosts, hobgoblins, and demons than it is to feel the hovering presence of guardian spirits. How many millions of people have been terrorized by ghosts and sworn trembling afterwards to their reality, compared with the few score in the history of the world who, like Saint Augustine and Joan of Arc, have conversed with angels. I knew that certain other *ouanga* packets in this Voodoo sorcery, horridly devised, were sometimes as definitely deadly as the murderer's knife or poison. There is no question about that. Every white man who has lived long enough with primitive peoples, no matter what his hard scientific background, no matter how rational the texture of his mind, has come finally to an often reluctant admission of the fact. One may find the semi-scientific explanation of how so-called black magic can kill, in the fifteen volumes, more or less, of Frazer's *Golden Bough*; the condensed edition in two volumes has been emasculated. But if one has ever lived, I mean geographically, outside the limits of our well-ordered rule-of-thumb world where every effect is politely assumed to trace back to respectably explicable causes, it will scarcely be necessary to read Frazer to understand that I am not treating here of superstition. Superstition would have had naught to do with my fleeing from that mountain if word had come to my ears that these people were secretly contriving for me the black death-*ouanga*, and even fleeing I might not have been safe. White men have died in London—and the records are in Scotland Yard—because some monk in the mountains of Tibet marked them to die, and sat droning in his far-off cell among the Himalayas. A subtle poison leaving no trace? Who knows? How can one be ever sure?

But the *ouanga* packet they were now preparing to make for me was to be bright-coloured, friendly and protective, and for those very reasons I found it more difficult to view it seriously, to separate it from obvious elements which were merely superstition. Yet had I not accepted it seriously I should have been wrong, for into its making went something more than aromatic leaves and powders; into it went also the imponderable will-to-protect of a community, so that whatever it was or was not magically, it not only deserved respect but had an actual potency-value as the sacred symbol and earnest of their protection.

It was the realization of this, I think, that enabled me to see, somewhat with their eyes, as more than mummery, the ceremony of this *ouanga* packet's making.

In a small, bare room inside Maman Célie's dwelling-house, from which a sleeping-pallet and other common household gear had been removed, a large cowhide was spread, hairy side upward, on the earthern floor, and around it in a circle sat solemnly a dozen negroes whom I knew, mostly of our immediate household. There were eight men and four women. It was night time. The only light flickered upward on their faces from small candles arranged as a geometric pentagram on the cowhide. Barring the doorsill were two crossed machetes, their broad, naked blades inscribed with white chalk symbols, the swirling serpent, the phallic staff, the enmeshed triangles.

Spread in the centre of the candle pentagram, on the cowhide, was a square red cloth, like a napkin, which was to be the covering of my *ouanga* packet. Bright ribbons, red and yellow, lay beside it, and also feathers brilliantly dyed. In little, separated piles upon the cowhide were balsam leaves, leaves of the castor-bean plant, roots of the lime tree; a saucer of flour, a saucer of ashes, a bottle of *clairin*, a bottle of perfume, a tiny iron crucifix.

Maman Célie and I sat on one side in the circle, Papa Théodore facing us. While they chanted almost in undertones, "*Papa Legba, ouvri barrière pour lie; tout Mystère 'gider lie*" (Legba, open the gate for him and every Mystery protect him), old Théodore took some of the roots and leaves, mixed them in a brazier, charred them over a fire now kindled on a plate before him, then pounded them together in a mortar. The two machetes were taken from the doorsill and planted upright in the ground, flanking him on each side. A *bocor* (magician) filled his mouth with *clairin* and sprayed it, sputtering, over all the paraphernalia on the cowhide, to drive away evil spirits. While Papa Théodore continued rhythmically pounding his materials in the mortar, the *bocor* began picking up balsam leaves and castor-bean leaves, one by one, marking each with a chalked cross and depositing it on the napkin, until a new pile was made there. Atop these leaves he now laid the crucifix, also a tuft of hair (tied together with thread) which had been cut previously from the central crown of my head; a paring from my right thumb-nail, and a small square cut from a shirt which had been worn next to my skin. Something of this sort runs through all primitive magic, whether the purpose be benevolent or evil. Articles intimately connected with the individual to be affected, a part of his own body such as hair or nail-paring if it can be procured, or a piece of clothing saturated with his perspiration or grease, are used variously as a substitution for himself. One of the most dreaded forms of Haitian-African magic includes the dressing of a corpse in a garment of the person marked for vengeance and then exposing it to rot away in some secret place in the jungle. Men have gone stark mad seeking that jungle-hidden horror, and others have died hopelessly, searching. Fear, hunger, thirst, jungle-terror, one may say. Names again, tags, labels. But marked for death by the Voodoo curse, they died. In the case of the death-*ouanga* packet, poisonous leaves are used with other corroding and defiling substances. Frazer contends that for magic of this sort to operate fatally without supplementary human agency the victim must *know* and *believe*. Probably this is true. But in the case of unbelievers they sometimes make use of appallingly pragmatic methods to instil faith. I am told that when some years ago "Bank" Williams, the saturnine, cynical, fearless Yankee manager of the bank which is Haiti's treasury, was thus marked for death, on one occasion a dog died in agony lapping pure water from the seemingly innocent clean bowl in which his morning coffee might have been poured had not the bowl been suspected, and on another occasion, deadly poison was found inside an egg whose shell had apparently never been broken. He survived, I am told, because he fought the devil with fire; for weeks, until definite events made his death no longer desired, every particle of food that passed his lips, every garment that touched his skin, first went through the hands of an old wrinkled woman from Martinique who knew every trick of black magic and served him with single-hearted fidelity.

So there was an additional element beyond anything that could be connected with credulity, superstition, or a belief in supernormal agencies that caused in me this knowledge that Voodoo magic was pragmatically effective, whether for good or evil; that caused me to believe in a definite sense that this bright, protective charm which they were engaged in preparing for me now constituted a real and actual protection. There is a queer point involved here which I find difficulty in putting into words. It will doubtless seem to many readers superstitious when I aver that I actually believe the protective virtue would have been destroyed in this charm unless I myself had faith in it. But, suppose I had sat there deeming their whole performance, well, say—silly, or funny? Suppose I had viewed it as futile, childish charlatanism? I do not mean, "Suppose I had laughed or sneered in their faces." I do not mean anything as clearly defined as that. These people were intuitively sensitized to shades of unexpressed feeling, almost like animals. Is it sure that if I had felt a humorous or contemptuous scorn, even secret and unexpressed, I should have been as well protected by this *ouanga*, as safe thereafter among these people in the mountain? I tell you that my believing gave it power. And connected with this truth are many deep collateral truths concerning the power of all magic, miracles, and prayer.

When Papa Théodore had finished pounding the charred aromatic herbs, the *bocor* took a pinch of the substance between his fingers and sprinkled it, muttering incantations, on the pile of green leaves surmounted by the crucifix and the objects which had been a part of myself, of my living body. All arose, and slowly circling, took similarly a pinch of the charred mixture and sprinkled it. I, last of all, was instructed to do likewise. When we were reseated, the *bocor*, with a small glowing brand from the fire, touched off successively three little piles of gunpowder on the cowhide to drive away evil spirits. Then he and Papa Théodore drew the two cabalistically marked machetes from the earth and clashed them violently together above all our heads.

Maman Célie handed me a copper coin and instructed me to place it on the packet. And now, before it was tied up, she told me to make a prayer (wish). I hesitated, then stood with both arms stretched straight out before me, palms downward, as I had seen them do and said in English:

"May Papa Legba, Maîtresse Ezilée and the Serpent protect me from misrepresenting these people, and give me power to write honestly of their mysterious religion, for all living faiths are sacred."

On the afternoon of the Friday set for my blood baptism, more than fifty friends and relatives gathered at the habitation of Maman Célie. There was no reason to suppose that we might be disturbed, but as an extra precaution a gay *danse Congo* was immediately organized to cover the real purpose of our congregation. Maman Célie had told me that I would get no sleep that night; so despite the noise I napped until after sunset, when she awakened me and led me across the compound to the *houmfort*.

Through its outer door, which Emanuel stood guarding like a sentinel and unlocked for us, we entered a dim, windowless, cell-like anteroom in which were tethered the sacrificial beasts, a he-goat, two red rocks and two black, an enormous white turkey, and a pair of doves. Huddled there in a corner also was the girl Catherine, Maman Célie's youngest unmarried daughter; why she was there I did not know, and it is needless to say that I wondered.

From this dim, somewhat sinister antechamber we passed through an open doorway into the long, rectangular mystery room, the temple proper, which was lighted with candles and primitive oil lamps that flickered like torches. Its clay walls were elaborately painted with crude serpent symbols and anthropomorphic figures. Papa Legba, guardian of the gates, god of the crossroads, was represented as a venerable old black farmer with a pipe between his teeth; Ogoun Badagris, the bloody warrior, appeared as an old-time Haitian revolutionary general in uniform with a sword; Wangol, master of the land, drove a yoke of oxen; Agoué, master of the seas, puffed out his cheeks to blow a wind and held in the hollow of his hand a tiny boat; the serpent symbols stood for the great Damballa Oueddo, almighty Jove of the Voodoo pantheon, and his consort Ayida Oueddo.

At the near end of the room, close to the doorway through which we had entered, was the wide, low altar, spread over with a white lace tablecloth. In its centre was a small wooden serpent, elevated horizontally on a little pole as Moses lifted up the serpent in the wilderness; around this symbol, which was ancient before the Exodus, were grouped thunderstones, Christian crucifixes made in France or Germany, necklaces on which were strung snake vertebrae, others from which hung little medallions of the Virgin Mary. On the corner of the altar nearest me, my *ouanga* had been placed. Grouped also on the altar were earthen jugs containing wine, water, oil; platters of vegetables and fruits, plates containing common bread, and plates containing elaborate sweet fancy cakes, bought days before down in the plain. There were bottles of expensive French-labelled grenadine and orgeat, a bottle of rum, kola-champagne, etc. There were also three cigars, not of the rough sort the peasants smoke, but fat and smooth in their red-gilt bands. With a naïve but justifiable rationality, these worshippers, whose gods were vitally, utterly real, saw no anachronism in offering to their deities the best of everything that could be procured. Maman Célie herself, accompanied by Papa Théodore, had gone by narrow trails across mountains and valleys, leading a donkey down to the modern city, shopping there for their celestial guests and returning with the donkey's panniers heavy laden.

On the altar also was a cone-like mound of cornmeal surmounted by an egg, and before the altar candles were burning, and wicks floating in cocoanut shells of oil. At the left were the three *Rada* drums, at the right was a low wooden stool placed for me.

At the other end of the mystery room, so that a ten-foot open space was left before the altar, were seated on the ground the eighteen or twenty people, all close relatives or trusted friends, who were to witness the ceremony. When I entered, they were swaying and singing:

Papa Legba, ouvrí barrière pour moins!
Papa Legba, coté petits ou?
Papa Legba, ou oué yo!
Papa Legba, ouvrí barrière pour li passer!

(Father Legba, open wide the gate!
Father Legba, where are thy children?
Father Legba, we are here.
Father Legba, open wide the gate that he may pass!)

The *papaloi*, a powerful clean-shaven black man of middle age with red turban and a bright-coloured embroidered stole over his shoulders, traced with cornmeal a cabalistic design on the bare earth before the altar. It measured perhaps twelve feet from end to end. Its circles, it was afterwards explained to me, represented, from left to right, earth sky, and sea. (Adepts of the esoteric will read here earth, air, and water, or if of a certain school will read earth, air, fire, and water, accepting a central sky-circle as a symbol also of the sun.) All these matters indeed entered into it, but the simpler interpretation was dominant. Forked marks, all connecting, with lines interjoining them with three circles, thence radiating towards the altar and reversely towards the worshippers, were symbols of the invisible paths through which the gods and mysteries would move.

Into the earth circle the *papaloi* poured oil, flour, and wine, while the people chanted, "*Wangol maît' la terre*" (Wangol is master of the earth). Into the sky circle he poured rum and ashes, while they chanted, "*Damballa Oueddo, ou maît' la ciel*" (Damballa Oueddo, thou art master of the sky). Into the sea circle he poured water, while they sang, "*Papa Agoué, li maît' la mer*" (Father Agoué, he is master of the sea).

A number of solos interspersed this general chanting. It was impossible to retain them all in memory. I could not make pencil notes there; not even Maman Célie was able afterwards to repeat them all for me, and the next day some of the singers were gone. There was one song to Papa Agoué, however, which I partly remembered because it had seemed to me beautiful, and later I rode to find the singer and transcribe it. It was:

Agoué, woyó! woyó!
Maîtr' Agoué reter lans la mer;
Li tirer canot.

Bassin blé
Reter toi zilet;
Nèg coqui' lans mer zorage;
Li tirer canot là.

Agoué, woyó! woyó!

(Hail to Father Agoué
Who dwells in the sea!
He is the Lord of ships.

In the blue gulf
There are three little islands.
The negro's boat is storm-tossed,
Father Agoué brings it safely in.
Hail to Father Agoué!)

When this singing and pouring of libations were ended, the *papaloi* sealed the open doorway by tracing across its earthen sill. Evil or unwelcome forces which sought to enter would become entangled in the lines and go wandering from circle to circle like lost souls among the stars.

This done, he began the real service, for which all thus far had been but a preparation. He stood with arms raised before the altar and said solemnly, "*Lans nom tout Loi et tout Mystère*" (In the name of all the Gods and all the Mysteries).

Maman Célie advanced at a sign from the *papaloi* and was invested by him, with the scarlet robe and headdress of ostrich feathers black and red, as *mamaloi* or priestess. This was accompanied by a shrill chant:

Ayida Oueddo, ou couleuvre moins!
Qui lé ou filer ou cou z'éclai!

(Ayida Oueddo, my serpent goddess,
When you come it is like the lightning flash!)

At the same time now I heard through the chanting a sharp long-drawn continuous hissing. It was Maman Célie, hissing like a snake, drawing and expelling the breath through her teeth.

I looked for Maman Célie's familiar sweet, gentle face, but beneath the black and scarlet plumes I saw now only what seemed a rigid mask. I felt that I was looking into the face of a strange, dreadful woman, or into the face of something which I had never seen before. As I watched, the cheeks of this black mask were deeply indrawn so that the face became skull-like, and then alternately puffed out as if the skull had been covered with flesh and come alive.

As the chanting died away, she whirled three times and flung herself prostrate before the altar with her lips pressed against the earth.

Emanuel, without donning sacerdotal garb, but now acting as a sort of altar servant, brought in the two red cocks. Each was handled gently, almost reverently, by the *papaloi*, as he knelt holding it and with white flour traced on its back a cross. One of the small sweet cakes was crumbled, and each cock must peck at it from the *mamaloi's* hand. This was awaited patiently. At the moment when each bird consented to receive the consecrated food, the priestess seized it and rose wildly dancing, whirling with the cock held by its head and feet in her upstretched hands, its wings violently fluttering. Round and round she whirled while the drums throbbed in a quick, tangled, yet steady rhythm. With a sudden twist the cock's head was torn off and as she whirled the blood flew out as if from a sprinkling-pot. The other birds, the black cocks and the dove, were dealt with similarly. As she danced with the white living doves, it was beautiful, and it seemed to me natural also that they should presently die. Blood of the doves was saved in a china cup.

A thing which had a different, a horror-beauty like a mad Goya etching, occurred when the black priestess did her death dance with the huge white turkey. Though far from feeble, possessed of great vitality, she was a slender woman, slightly formed, whose nervous strength lay not in muscular weight. When the turkey's wings spread wide and began to flap frantically above her head as she whirled, the great bird seemed larger and more powerful than she; it seemed that she would be dragged from her feet, hurled to the ground, or flown away with fabulously into the sky. And as she sought finally to tear off its head, sought to clutch its body between her knees, it attacked her savagely, beating her face and breasts, beating at her so that she was at moments enfolded by the great white wings, so that bird and woman seemed to mingle struggling in a monstrous, mythical embrace. But her fatal hands were still upon its throat, and in that swanlike simulacre of the deed which for the male is always like a little death, it died.

So savage had this scene been that it was almost like an anti-climax when the sacrificial goat was now led through the doorway to the altar, but new and stranger things, contrasting, were yet to happen before other blood was shed. He was a sturdy brown young goat, with big, blue, terrified, almost human eyes, eyes which seemed not only terrified but aware and wondering. At first he bleated and struggled, for the odour of death was in the air, but finally he stood quiet, though still wide-eyed, while red silken ribbons were twined in his little horns, his little hoofs anointed with wine and sweet-scented oils, and an old woman who had come from far over the mountain for this her one brief part in the long ceremony sat down before him and crooned to him alone a song which might have been a baby's lullaby.

When it was finished, the *papaloi* sat down before the little goat and addressed to it a discourse in earnest tones. He told the little goat that it would soon pass through the final gates before us all, instructed it in the mysteries, and pleaded with it concerning its conduct on the other side. But before it passed through the gate, he explained, certain magical changes, making its path easier, would occur on this side. Therefore it need have no fear. Upon its forehead he traced a cross and circle, first with flour and afterwards with blood of the doves. Then he presented to it a green, leafy branch to eat.

This goat had by now become inevitably personal to me. I had conceived an affectionate interest in him while the old woman was singing. I recalled what had happened to the other creatures at the moment they touched food, and I had an impulse to cry out to him, "Don't do that, little goat! Don't touch it!" But it was a fleeting, purely sentimental impulse. Not for anything, no matter what would happen, could I have seriously wished to stop that ceremony. I believe in such ceremonies. I hope that they will never die out or be abolished. I believe that in some form or another they answer a deep need of the universal human soul. I, who in a sense believe in no religion, believe yet in them all, asking only that they be alive—as religions. Codes of rational ethics and human brotherly love are useful, but they do not touch this thing underneath. Let religion have its bloody sacrifices, yes, even human sacrifices, if thus our souls may be kept alive. Better a black *papaloi* in Haiti with blood-stained hands who believes in his living gods than a frock-coated minister on Fifth Avenue reducing Christ to a solar myth and rationalizing the Immaculate Conception.

And so I did not cry out.

And the goat nibbled the green leaves.

But no knife flashed.

In the dim, bare anteroom with its windowless grey walls, the girl Catherine had remained all this time huddled in a corner, as if drugged or half asleep.

Emanuel had to clutch her tightly by the arm to prevent her from stumbling when they brought her to the altar. Maman Célie hugged her and moaned and shed tears as if they were saying goodby forever. The *papaloi* pulled them apart, and someone gave the girl a drink of rum from a bottle. She began to protest in a dull sort of angry, whining way when they forced her down on her knees before the lighted candles. The *papaloi* wound round her forehead red ribbons like those which had been fastened around the horns of the goat, and Maman Célie, no longer as a mourning mother but as an officiating priestess, with rigid face aided in pouring the oil and wine on the girl's head, feet, hands, and breast.

All this time the girl had been like a fretful, sleepy, annoyed child, but gradually she became docile, sombre, staring with quiet eyes, and presently began a weird song of lamentation. I think she was extemporizing both the words and the melody. She sang:

Cochon marron saché chemin caille;
Moins mandé ça li gagnin.
"Nans Léogane tout moon malade O!"

Béf marron saché chemin caille.
Moins mandé ça li gagnin.
"Nans gros morne tout moon malade O!"

Cabrit marron saché chemin caille.
Moins mandé ça li gagnin.
"Nans Guinea tout moon malade O!"

M'pas malade, m'a p'mourri!
(The wild pig came seeking me;
I said why have you come?
"Every one is sick in Léogane!"

The wild bull came seeking me;
I said why have you come?
"Every one is sick in the mountains!"

The wild goat came seeking me;
I said why have you come?
"Every one is sick in Africa!"

So I who am not sick must die!)

And as that black girl sang, and as the inner meaning of her song came to me, I seemed to hear the voice of Jephtha's daughter doomed to die by her own father as a sacrifice to Javeh, going up to bewail her virginity on Israel's lonely mountain. Her plight in actuality was rather that of Isaac bound by Abraham on Mount Moriah; a horned beast would presently be substituted in her stead; but the moment for that mystical substitution had not yet come, and as she sang she was a daughter doomed to die.

The ceremony of substitution, when it came, was pure effective magic of a potency which I have never seen equalled in Dervish monastery or anywhere. The goat and the girl, side by side before the altar, had been startled, restive, nervous. The smell of blood was in the air, but there was more than that hovering; it was the eternal, mysterious odour of death itself which both animals and human beings always sense, but not through the nostrils. Yet now the two who were about to die mysteriously merged, the girl symbolically and the beast with a knife in its throat, were docile and entranced, were like automatons. The *papaloi* monotonously chanting, endlessly repeating, "Damballa calls you, Damballa calls you," stood facing the altar with his arms outstretched above their two heads. The girl was now on her hands and knees in the attitude of a quadruped, directly facing the goat, so that their heads and eyes were on a level, less than ten inches apart, and thus they stared fixedly into each other's eyes, while the *papaloi's* hands weaved slowly, ceaselessly above their foreheads, the forehead of the girl and the forehead of the horned beast, each wound with red ribbons, each already marked with the blood of a white dove. By shifting slightly I could see the big, wide, pale-blue, staring eyes of the goat, and the big, black, staring eyes of the girl, and I could have almost sworn that the black eyes were gradually, mysteriously becoming those of a dumb beast, while a human soul was beginning to peer out through the blue. But dismiss that, and still I tell you that pure magic was here at work, that something very real and fearful was occurring. For as the priest wove his ceaseless incantations, the girl began a low, piteous bleating in which there was nothing, absolutely nothing, human; and soon a thing infinitely more unnatural occurred; the goat was moaning and crying like a human child. I believe that through my Druse and Yezidee accounts I have earned a deserved reputation for being not too credulous in the face of marvels. But I was in the presence now of a thing that could not be denied. Old magic was here at work, and it worked appallingly. What difference does it make whether we call it supernatural or merely supernormal? What difference does it make if we say that the girl was drugged—as I suspect she was—or that both were hypnotized? Of course they were, if you like. And what then? We live surrounded by mysteries and imagine that by inventing names we explain them.

Other signs and wonders became manifest. Into this little temple lost among the mountains came in answer to goat-cry girl-cry the Shaggy Immortal One of a thousand names whom the Greeks called Pan. The goat's lingam became erect and rigid, the points of the girl's breasts visibly hardened and were outlined sharply pressing against the coarse, thin, tight-drawn shift that was her only garment. Thus they faced each other motionless as two marble figures on the frieze of some ancient phallic temple. They were like inanimate twin lamps in which a sacred flame burned, steadily yet unconsuming.

While the *papaloi* still wove his spells, his hands moving ceaselessly like an old woman carding wool in a dream, the priestess held a twig green with tender leaves between the young girl and the animal. She held it on a level with their mouths, and neither saw it, for they were staring fixedly into each other's eyes as entranced mediums stare into crystal globes, and with their necks thrust forward so that their foreheads almost touched. Neither could therefore see the leafy branch, but as the old *mamaloi's* hand trembled, the leaves flicked lightly as if stirred by a little breeze against the hairy muzzle of the goat, against the chin and soft lips of the girl. And after moments of breathless watching, it was the girl's lips which pursed out and began to nibble at the leaves. Human beings, normally, when eating, open their mouths and take the food directly in between their teeth. Except for sipping liquids they do not use their lips. But the girl's lips now nibbling at the leaves were like those of a ruminating animal. Her hands, of course, were flat on the ground so that in a sense she perforce must have eaten without using them, somewhat in the manner of a quadruped; but in a castle near the edge of the Nefud desert I once watched closely a woman eating whose hands were tied behind her back, and that woman, opening her mouth and baring her teeth, took the fragments of food directly between her teeth, as any normal human being would. But this girl now pursed her lips and used them nibbling as horned cattle do. It sounds a slight thing, perhaps, in the describing, but it was weird, unnatural, unhuman.

As she nibbled thus, the *papaloi* said in a hushed but wholly matter-of-fact whisper like a man who had finished a hard, solemn task and was glad to rest, "*Ca y est*" (There it is).

The *papaloi* was now holding a machete, ground sharp and shining. Maman Célie, priestess, kneeling, held a *gamelle*, a wooden bowl. It was oblong. There was just space enough to thrust it narrowly between the mystically identified pair. Its rim touched the goat's hairy chest and the girl's body, both their heads thrust forward above it. Neither seemed conscious of anything that was occurring, nor did the goat flinch when the *papaloi* laid his hand upon its horns. Nor did the goat utter any sound as the knife was drawn quickly, deeply across its throat. But at this instant, as the blood gushed like a fountain into the wooden bowl, the girl, with a shrill, piercing, then strangled bleat of agony, leaped, shuddered, and fell senseless before the altar.

At the moment the knife flashed across the goat's throat, the company had begun to chant, not high or loud but with a sort of deep, hushed fervour, across which the girl's inhuman bleating had shrilled sharp as another invisible blade. Now they continued chanting while the celebrants performed their various offices. They chanted :

Damballa Oueddo odan q'icit
Mandé ça la! Oué!
Ayida Oueddo odan q'icit
Mandé ça la! Oué!

(Damballa and Ayida, behold the deed we have done as you commanded.)

The body of the goat was thrown as a ritually useless and no longer sacred thing through the door into the anteroom. The body of the unconscious girl, spattered with blood, was lifted carefully into Emanuel's arms and carried away, followed by two old women versed in magic who would attend her recovery. If Maman Célie, her face still like a terrible, inspired mask, bestowed one fleeting glance on either body, I did not see it. She was revolving slowly before the altar with the bowl in her outstretched arms and now held it to the *papaloi*, who received it, drank, then placed it on the altar, and with a little china cup poured libations within each of the three cabalistic circles on the earth. They also sang an invocation to Ybo, another of the ancient gods.

There was a pause, a lull, in which I who had been for hours too utterly absorbed to give myself a thought, recalled that all this ceremonial was leading up to an event which concerned me more deeply than any other present. The time had now come. A very old black man, deeply wrinkled, with a beard that was like Spanish moss turned snowy white, who had been sitting silent all the while, took from a bag at his feet a white cloth which he wound around his head, and a white embroidered garment like a cassock which he put over his shoulders. He invested himself without the aid of other hands as a black pope or emperor might have done.

He was not of our mountain. He had come riding upon a donkey from beyond the great Morne. Maman Célie had summoned him and had paid the expenses from her own purse. It was a thing for which she would never permit me to repay her. As he arose and beckoned me to kneel at last before the altar, there was absolute silence. He was Voodoo of the Voodoo, but as he laid his hand upon my head it was neither in Creole that he spoke, nor French, nor even the almost forgotten language of old Guinea. I heard as in a dream, low, clear, and deep as the voices of old men rarely are, "*In nomine Patris, et Filii, et Spiritus Sancti. Amen.*"

And when still kneeling there with my eyes closed, I heard as from a great distance and as an echo from years long past his sure voice intoning that most marvellous and mysterious of all Latin invocations, "Rosa Mystica . . . Tower of David . . . Tower of Ivory . . . House of Gold . . . Gate of Heaven," it seemed to me that I heard too the rolling of mighty organs beneath vaulted domes. . . .

Oil, wine, and water were poured upon my head, marks were traced upon my brow with white flour, and then I was given to eat ritually from the cakes upon the altar, to drink from the wine, rum, and syrups there. Parts of many cakes were crumbled together in a little cup and were put into my mouth with a spoon; likewise were mingled a few drops from each of the many bottles.

This, it seemed, had been a preliminary consecration rite in sincere inclusion of the Christian divinities, saints, and powers. Now the Voodoo chanting recommenced, and for the first time my own name was mingled with the Creole and African words. They were beseeching Legba to open wide the gates for me, Damballa and Ayida to receive me. A sort of mad fervour was again taking possession of them all. The old *hougan*, shouting now so that his voice could be heard above the singing, demanded once more silence, and placing both hands heavily upon my head, pronounced a long mixed African and Creole invocation, calling down to witness all the gods and goddesses of ancient Africa. Still commanding silence, he dipped his hand into the wooden bowl and traced on my forehead the bloody Voodoo cross.

Then he lifted the bowl, hesitated for a queer instant as if in courteous doubt—it was a strange, trivial thing to occur at such a moment—and then picked up a clean spoon. Maman Célie interfered angrily. So the bowl itself was held to my lips and three times I drank. The blood had a clean, warm, salty taste. In physical fact, I was drinking the blood of a recently slain goat, but by some mysterious transubstantiation not without its parallels in more than one religion other than Voodoo, I was drinking the blood of the girl Catherine who in the body of the goat had mystically died for me and for all miserable humanity from Léogane to Guinea.

One small thing yet remained to be done. I had been told that it would be done, and its meaning explained to me. I had been told also that for no white man alive or dead had it ever been done before. The *papaloi* took from the altar an egg which had surmounted a little pyramid of cornmeal, and holding it aloft in his cupped hands, pronounced incantation. As the blood had represented the mystery of death, sacrifice, and purification, likewise fertilization as it was poured upon the earth, the egg now represented rebirth, productivity, fertility, re-creation. Maman Célie, the priestess, took it from the hands of the *papaloi*, traced with it a new cross on my forehead, and dashed it to the earth. My knees were spattered. Then the priestess tore off her feathered headdress, and Maman Célie, the old woman, sank down beside me, put her arms around me, and cried, "Legba, Papa Legba, open wide the gates for this my little one."

GREEN JEWEL OF DEATH

by PRINCESS CATHERINE RADZIWILL

TO SAY that one emerald—no matter how huge—affected the history of a great nation for more than three hundred years is to create at once what lawyers call a reasonable doubt. And to suggest further that its influence was due to an ancient curse put upon the stone is not only a sure way to win ridicule, but also to be accused of an imagination lacking originality.

So let me say at the outset that I do not believe the legend about the Great Emerald being bewitched.

After one has come to America and has become a citizen of a nation with a rational history, and when one rides in subways and works in tall steel buildings, one forgets such things. Yet I must admit that when I first saw the green light of that big stone glittering from the bosom of the Empress Alexandra, and heard the indiscreet whisper of the story from a lady of the court as she counted off on her fingers the Great Emerald's victims, I was inclined to be credulous. For all of the story, except the part about the witch, is plain history that anyone may read.

There *was* such a man as Nikita Romanoff, and there *was* such a man as Boulouk Khan with a beautiful daughter. Nikita Romanoff *did* die a horrible death, and many Romanoffs thereafter, with the jewel always at hand to reflect tragedies in its cold green facets.

Remember, the last Czar and the Empress Alexandra were murdered in that cellar at Ekaterinburg *after* I had heard the story! So, you see, it is not an easy story to forget. Let me tell it as simply as possible.

First, a necessary bit of political history. When Ivan the Terrible died in 1584, he left the throne to his son, the feeble-minded Feodor. Then followed the "troubled years" of Russian history, when Tartars, Poles, and Swedes fought for possession of Russia's dreary and lonesome plains and for the conquest of the three hundred churches and shrines of stately Moscow, with the great treasures they contained.

Fortunately, perhaps, for Russia, Feodor was married to a beautiful woman, Irene Godounoff, who contrived that her famous brother, Boris, should rule the land in Feodor's name. This Boris Godounoff was a determined, relentless man, full of ambition, who made up his mind to become the next Czar. So when Feodor died, and Irene was hailed as Czarina by the assembled nobles, or boyars, as they were called, she refused the throne, and with her own hands placed on her brother's head the crown her husband had worn.

Boris triumphed, yet he knew himself to be a usurper. He knew that, even after Feodor's younger brother, Dmitry, had been assassinated at his command, there still existed lawful successors to the Russian throne in the persons of the Romanoffs, direct descendants of the great Rurik.

There were three of these Romanoffs—Feodor, Ivan, and Nikita—and to their destruction Boris set his hand.

The first was forced to enter holy orders after having been separated from his wife, Marfa, who was shut up in the solitude of the Ipatieff Convent in Kostroma. (What Boris never knew was that, thanks to the connivance of the Abbess of Ipatieff, Marfa continued to see her husband, and gave birth to a son who was one day to become the first of the Romanoff czars.)

The second brother, Ivan, died of a mysterious illness with which was mixed up a suspicion of poison. But the third, Nikita, was not so easy to dispose of. He had too many friends.

He was handsome and brave, beloved by women and popular with men. He was truly a hero of romance, and romantic adventures followed him throughout his career.

Nikita was the only one of the Romanoffs who did not care for politics, and who had no ambition to see the diadem of the Monomaques put upon his head. He cared only for a good time, to look into the dark eyes of a lovely maiden, or to enjoy a sumputuous banquet. He, the pious orthodox descendant of that Grand Duchess Olga who had brought Christianity to Russia, had become infatuated with an infidel, with a Moslem girl, the only daughter of a Tartar Prince, Boulouk Khan.

Boulouk—one of the few Tartars whose family had remained in Moscow after the khans had been driven back to Kazan—lived very quietly in a small house under the very ramparts of the Kremlin, and received few people. One of them, however, was Nikita Romanoff.

Nikita had met the beautiful Isma by chance, at a banquet given by the Czarina; and although Moslem women were not allowed to show their faces to men, he contrived to have an affair with her, and out of it a son was born.

Boulouk Khan asked Nikita to marry the girl. The younger boyar refused, saying that his religion forbade him to unite himself in wedlock with an infidel. The Tartar was furious, but kept silent.

So far, we have nothing but historical facts. Now comes the legend, which I will relate in the form that has come down to this day. It seems that Boulouk Khan, on the night following his interview with Nikita, went to seek the help of an old and famous witch.

The old woman received him in her den, a dark, underground cavern in a lonesome spot shunned by everybody. She listened to Boulouk's story and then asked him:

"You wish to be revenged on this man for the wrong he has done your daughter?"

"Yes, I do," replied the Tartar, "and not only on him but on all his race in the centuries to come."

The hag laughed, a harsh and cruel laugh.

"Your wish will be granted," she said, "and your revenge will perhaps be more terrible than you suspect. Wait a moment!"

She retired behind a curtain that divided her gruesome abode, and after a few minutes returned, holding in her hand an uncut emerald set in gold, fashioned as a clasp for a man's cloak.

The Tartar extended his hand towards it.

"Don't touch it!" exclaimed the old woman. "Don't touch it until I allow you to. The devil himself is in that stone."

She walked towards a cauldron and dipped the jewel in it, murmuring as she did so strange words in a strange language. Then she came back to where the terrified Boulouk Khan was standing.

"Here," she said, "take this jewel. Its beauty is unsurpassed, and its worth will go on increasing as the years pass by. But it is an accursed stone, and it will bring misfortune, sorrow, suffering, and death to all those who will possess it. Give it to Nikita Romanoff and you will see what havoc it will work. Now leave me the purse I see hanging from your waist, and go away from here, for this is no place for any but the Master of Evil to loiter in!"

That is the legend of the origin of the Great Emerald. Now we turn back to history, and find Boulouk Khan writing the following letter to Nikita Romanoff, the text of which has been preserved in the Russian archives:

> Boulouk Khan, the humble servant of the great and mighty Boyar Nikita Nikitich Romanoff, humbly craves his presence at a banquet at his house, and hopes he will honour his slave with his presence at it.

"The old dog evidently has forgotten all about his anger of the other day, and wants to make amends for it," the young man must have thought.

He went to the feast and enjoyed himself immensely.

Boulouk Khan had spared neither money nor trouble to make it sumptuous, and the day was already dawning before anyone thought of retiring. As Nikita was preparing to depart, his host stopped him.

"Great and mighty Boyar," he said, "grant me one last favour before you leave my house. Here is a stone that came to me from my ancestors, and which is supposed to have belonged to our great Genghis Khan himself. I have had it set as a clasp for your cloak. Honour me by accepting it, just to prove to me that you bear me no ill will for any differences we may have had in the past."

With these words he handed over to the astonished young man the Great Emerald.

Three nights later Nikita Romanoff was sound asleep in the arms of a woman to whom, it is said, he had been secretly married, when a great noise at the door of his room awakened him. The house was surrounded and invaded by a troop of armed men, the soldiers of Boris Godounoff.

Whether the usurper, who had spies everywhere, had heard the tale of the Great Emerald and fancied that the powers of darkness were now on his side, or whether he had simply become weary of waiting and decided to risk the anger of Nikita's friends, we shall never know. The fact remains that the young Boyar was seized and bound with heavy chains and thrown into a sledge waiting at his door.

He protested and cried out for help; but all his servants had been put out of the way, and, in spite of the entreaties of his wife, he was hurried away. For long weeks the prisoner and his guards travelled towards the Siberian wastes, Nikita lying on his back at the bottom of the sledge, so tightly chained he could move neither hand nor foot. All his money had been taken away; but, by design or coincidence, the emerald of Boulouk Khan had been left in his possession.

At last the sledge stopped in the midst of an apparently endless plain. Night was beginning to fall.

The officer in command of the escort gave a brisk order, and two men began digging a hole in the frozen ground. When the men climbed out of the deep pit they had made, the officer measured the depth of it and nodded his head.

He gave a signal, and the soldiers seized Nikita and flung him into the deep hole. The top was covered over with a rude roof and without further ado the escort rode away.

Nikita Romanoff lived on for three long years, sunk in the pit, without even the possibility of looking up at the sky. From time to time a piece of bread was thrown down and a pitcher of water lowered to him. At last, one day, the guard, hearing no sound from the living tomb, peered down and saw that Nikita Romanoff was dead at last.

They did not remove his body. Godounoff had given his orders, and all that was done was to fill up the pit with earth.

Time went on, and after Godounoff's death Nikita's nephew, Michael Romanoff, was hailed as Czar by the Muscovite boyars in the Ipatieff Convent at Kostroma. The new dynasty began its reign, which was to last exactly three hundred and four years.

Nikita Romanoff lay in his unconsecrated grave, forgotten by the world, until the day when, for a short period, Russia was ruled by a woman—the handsome, imperious Czarina Sophia, sister of the man who was to be known as Peter the Great.

She remembered the dark story of the victim of Godounoff's ambition and cruelty and sent men to Siberia with instructions to look for the mortal remains of her murdered kinsman. When they were found, she had them properly buried, and a chapel erected on the spot of his awful martyrdom.

Among the remnants of clothes dug from Nikita Romanoff's grave was found the Great Emerald of Boulouk Khan. Its gold setting had not tarnished, and the jewel itself had lost none of its weird beauty. The Czarina's messengers brought it back to her, and Sophia found it so fascinating that she immediately began to wear it on a chain around her neck. Her attendants and even her confessor warned her against it, for by this time the legend of the curse was being whispered around Moscow.

Sophia laughed at these warnings. She believed herself absolutely secure.

But the boy under whose name she was reigning was the great Peter. He also wanted to regin, and to reign alone.

One day Sophia was rudely dragged out of her Kremlin Palace and thrust into a convent. Only once did she ever emerge from her cell. This was on a fateful afternoon when, by order of her brother, she was taken to a window under which a scaffold had been erected and was forced to see each one of her faithful Stryeltsi officers led up in succession and beheaded. The miserable woman fainted at last, and, when she recovered her senses, found herself back in her religious prison, where she remained until her death.

But, before she had been led away from the Terem she was never to see again, the Czarina had contrived to squeeze into the hand of Eudoxia Lopoukhina, the wife of her brother Peter, the emerald of Nikita Romanoff. Not long afterwards, Eudoxia also fell into disgrace, and was banished by her merciless husband to make way for the Livonian peasant girl who was to become Empress of All the Russias.

When Eudoxia was bidding goodblye to her only son, Alexis, she gave him the emerald.

This unbalanced youth, who imagined himself strong enough to resist the will of his father, the Great White Czar, was tortured to death in the dark dungeons of the fortress of Saints Peter and Paul. Peter himself lashed him with the knout, and dealt the blow that killed him.

Alexis turned his eyes upon the Czar, and murmured, "Father, I forgive you!" then feebly put his hands to a little silk bag he wore around his neck, and clung to it until death mercifully released him. In the bag was Nikita Romanoff's emerald. It was brought to Peter after his son's body had been laid in his coffin. But the Emperor refused to touch it; instead he had it taken to the Treasury and put under lock and key.

There it remained until his niece, the Empress Anna Ivanovna, ascended the throne of Russia. The first time she looked through the imperial jewels, she took a fancy to the stone and presented it to her favourite, the famous Biren, who became Duke of Courland. The latter was disgraced and sent into exile by Anna's successor, the Empress Elizabeth Petrovna.

Remembering the evil reputation the stone possessed, Biren sent it back to his sovereign, in the hope, it was said, that it would work her evil. Elizabeth, however, did not care for it. She had it set in a ring, which she gave to her nephew—the man who later became Peter III.

Peter was celebrating his marriage to a young girl who later became known as Catherine the Great. Those who doubt the Great Emerald's evil influence point out that the sole gift of Catherine's hand would have been enough to bring tragedy into any man's life—even a nobler one than the coarse and brutal Peter.

The fact remains, though that not long after Peter succeeded his aunt to the throne, he was deposed by the Palace Guards and later strangled in the castle of Ropscha by Gregory Orloff, Catherine's favourite.

The emerald of Nikita Romanoff was removed from his finger with great difficulty after his death and brought back to the Imperial Treasury. The Empress Catherine refused at first to have anything to do with it.

The great sovereign was not a superstitious woman, yet somehow this stone inspired terror in her.

One day, after many years had passed and the murder that had taken place at Ropscha was beginning to be forgotten, curiosity overcame her. She had the Great Emerald brought to her, and was so captivated with its beauty that she decided to have it reset as an ornament for Marie Feodorovna, the wife of her son Paul. Two hours after she had sent for the court jeweller to discuss the matter with him, Catherine was struck down by an apoplectic fit and died that same evening.

After this, no one at court would touch without gloves the emerald of Nikita Romanoff, and friends urged Paul I to get rid of it. But the Emperor refused to entertain the idea of parting with this remarkable jewel. Instead, he had it set in the handle of a sword to wear on state occasions.

On the evening of the day when Paul had worn the sword for the first time, conspirators, acting under the direction of his son Alexander, broke into the Czar's bed-chamber, demanding his abdication.

Paul leaped up and seized the sword that bore the Great Emerald and attempted to defend himself. In the scuffle the stone was broken from its setting—and its owner mortally wounded.

Paul's son, Alexander I, would never even look at the jewel, and conceived the idea of presenting it to some church or shrine. But his confessor, the famous Abbot Photius, told him this could not be done, because the stone was supposed to have been cursed by Satan himself. This opinion the next sovereign, Nicholas I, seemed to share, and as long as he occupied the throne Nikita Romanoff's emerald remained hidden away in one of the strong-boxes of the Imperial Treasury.

There it lay until, many years later, the morganatic wife of Alexander II, the Princess Dolgorouky, having heard its sinister story, asked her husband to allow her to examine it. The Czar himself had never seen the fateful emerald, and when it was brought to him one morning at breakfast, he admired it immensely—so much, indeed, that, after having promised his consort to have it set for her in a pendant, he put it in his pocket to show to his favourite cousin, the Grand Duchess Catherine Michaelovna, with whom he was to dine that day.

On his way back to the Winter Palace, Alexander was blown to pieces by bombs thrown at him by nihilist conspirators.

The next day a police officer picked the emerald out of a snow bank on the spot where the Czar had fallen, and took it to the palace.

Once again Nikita Romanoff's jewel went into retirement. Alexander III and his consort, the Empress Marie, believed absolutely in its uncanny influence, and would not even allow it to be kept in any of the strong-boxes where their personal belongings were stored. The Empress, in particular, never wished it to be even mentioned in her presence, and is to this day persuaded that it caused all the calamities of the Romanoff dynasty.

Perhaps it was out of opposition to the Empress Marie that her daughter-in-law, the late Alexandra, refused to admit that a mere jewel could bring misfortune. She persuaded Czar Nicholas II to have the emerald set into a pendant, which she wore continually.

It was on Alexandra's neck that I saw this fatal jewel. She took it with her into exile when she went with her husband and her children to Siberia. Doubtless she was wearing it on that fatal and mysterious night in Ekaterinburg when the great Romanoff dynasty came to its tragic end.

Where is Nikita Romanoff's emerald now?

No one seems to know.

It has not appeared among the crown jewels that have been sold by the present rulers of Russia.

Superstitious people may be tempted to say that, having worked out its curse, it has been taken back by the devil to whom it belonged. But that, of course, is nonsense.

THE PHANTOM COACH

by ELMA B. EDWARDS

THE circumstances I am about to relate to you have truth to commend them. They happened to me, and my recollection of them is as vivid as if they had taken place only yesterday. Twenty years, however, have gone by since that night. During those twenty years I have told the story to but one other person. I tell it now with a reluctance which I find it difficult to overcome. All I ask, meanwhile, is that you will abstain from forcing your own conclusions upon me. I want nothing explained away. I desire no arguments. My mind on this subject is quite made up, and, having the testimony of my own senses to rely upon, I prefer to abide by it.

Well! It was just twenty years ago, and within a day or two of the end of the grouse season. I had been out all day with my gun, and had had no sport to speak of. The wind was due east; the month, December; the place, a bleak wide moor in the far north of England. And I had lost all sense of direction. It was not a pleasant place in which to lose one's way, with the first feathery flakes of a coming snowstorm just fluttering down upon the heather, and the leaden evening closing in all around. I shaded my eyes with my hand, and stared anxiously into the gathering darkness, where the purple moorland melted into a range of low hills, some ten or twelve miles distant. Not the faintest smoke-wreath, not the tiniest cultivated patch, or fence, or sheep-track, met my eyes in any direction. There was nothing for it but to walk on, and take my chance of finding what shelter I could, by the way. So I shouldered my gun again and pushed wearily forward, for I had been on foot since an hour after daybreak and had eaten nothing since breakfast.

Meanwhile, the snow began to come down with ominous persistence, and the wind fell. After this, the cold became more intense, and the night came rapidly on. As for me, my prospects worsened with the darkening sky, and my heart grew heavy as I thought how my young wife was already watching for me through the window of our little inn parlour, and thought of all the suffering in store for her throughout this weary night. We had been married four months, and, having spent our autumn in the Highlands, were now lodging in a remote little village situated just on the verge of the great English moorlands. We were very much in love, and, of course, very happy. This morning, when we parted, she had implored me to return before dusk, and I had promised her that I would. What would I not have given to have kept my word!

Even now, weary as I was, I felt that with a supper, an hour's rest, and a guide, I might still get back to her before midnight, if only some help could be found.

And all this time the snow fell and the night became darker. I stopped and shouted every now and then, but my cries seemed only to emphasize the silence that reigned everywhere. Then a vague sense of uneasiness came upon me, and I began to remember stories of travellers who had walked on and on in the falling snow until, exhausted, they sank down to embrace a sleep from which they never awoke. Would it be possible, I asked myself, to keep going all through the long, lonely night? Would there not come a time when my limbs must fail, and my resolution give way? When I, too, must sleep the sleep of death. Death! I shuddered. How hard to die just now, when life a few hours ago had seemed so full of promise! How hard for my darling, whose loving heart—but that thought was not to be borne! To banish it, I shouted again, louder and longer, and then listened eagerly. Was my shout answered, or did I only fancy that I heard a far-off cry? I halloed again, and again the echo followed. Then a wavering speck of light came suddenly out of the dark, shifting, disappearing, growing momentarily nearer and brighter. Running towards it as quickly as I could, I found myself, to my great joy, face to face with an old man and a lantern.

"Thank God!" was the exclamation that burst involuntarily from my lips.

Blinking and frowning, he lifted his lantern and peered into my face.

"What for?" growled he, sulkily.

"Well—for you. I began to fear I should be lost in the snow."

"Eh, then, folks do get cast away hereabouts fra' time to time, an' what's to hinder you from bein' cast away likewise, if the Lord's so minded?"

"If the Lord is so minded that you and I shall be lost together, friend, we must submit," I replied; "but I don't mean to be lost without you. How far am I now from Dwolding?"

"A gude twenty mile, more or less."

"And the nearest village?"

"The nearest village is Wyke, an' that's twelve mile 'other side."

"Where do you live, then?"

"Out yonder," said he, with a vague jerk of the lantern.

"You're going home, I presume?"

"Maybe I am."

"Then I'm going with you."

The old man shook his head, and rubbed his nose reflectively with the handle of the lantern.

"It ain't o' no use," growled he. "He w'ont let you in—not he."

"We'll see about that," I replied, briskly. "Who is He?"

"The master."

"Who is the master?"

"That's nowt to you," was the unceremonious reply.

"Well, well; you lead the way, and I'll see to it that the master shall give me shelter and a supper tonight."

"Eh, you can try him!" muttered my reluctant guide; and, still shaking his head, he hobbled, gnome-like, away through the falling snow. A large mass loomed up presently out of the darkness, and a huge dog rushed out, barking furiously.

"Is this the house?" I asked.

"Ay, it's the house. Down, Bey!" And he fumbled in his pocket for the key.

I drew up immediately behind him, determined to go in with him, and saw in the little circle of light shed by the lantern that the door was heavily studded with iron nails, like that of a prison. In another minute he had turned the key and I had pushed past him into the house.

Once inside, I looked round with curiosity, and found myself in a great raftered hall, which served, apparently, a variety of uses. One end was piled to the roof with corn, like a barn. The other was stored with flour-sacks, agricultural implements, casks, and all kinds of miscellaneous lumber; while from the beams overhead hung rows of hams, flitches, and bunches of dried herbs for winter use. In the centre of the floor stood a large object gauntly dressed in a dingy wrapping-cloth, and reaching half way to the rafters. Lifting a corner of this cloth, I saw, to my surprise, a telescope of considerable size, mounted on a rough movable platform, with four small wheels. The tube was made of painted wood, bound round with bands of metal; the speculum, so far as I could estimate its size in the dim light, measured at least fifteen inches in diameter. While I was yet examining the instrument, and asking myself whether it was not the work of some self-taught star-gazer, a bell rang sharply.

"That's for you," said my guide, with a malicious grin. "Yonder's his room."

He pointed to a low black door at the opposite side of the hall. I crossed over, rapped somewhat loudly, and went in, without waiting for an invitation. A huge, white-haired old man rose from a table covered with books and papers, and confronted me sternly.

"Who are you?" said he. "How came you here? What do you want?"

"James Murray, barrister-at-law. On foot across the moor. Meat, drink, and sleep."

He bent his bushy brows into a portentous frown.

"Mine is not a house of entertainment," he said, haughtily. "Jacob, how dare you admit this stranger?"

"I didn't admit him," grumbled the old man. "He followed me over the muir, and shouldered his way in before me. I'm no match for six foot two."

"Tell me, sir, by what right have you forced an entrance into my house?"

"The same by which I should have clung to your boat, if I were drowning. The right of self-preservation."

"Self-preservation?"

"There's an inch of snow on the ground already," I replied, briefly; "and it would be deep enough to cover my body before daybreak."

He strode to the window, pulled aside a heavy black curtain, and looked out.

"It is true," he said. "You can stay, if you choose, till morning. Jacob, serve the supper."

With this he waved me to a seat, resumed his own, and became at once absorbed in the studies from which I had disturbed him.

I placed my gun in a corner, drew a chair to the hearth, and examined my quarters at leisure. Smaller and less incongruous in its arrangements than the hall, this room contained, nevertheless, much to awaken my curiosity. The floor was carpetless. The whitewashed walls were in parts scrawled over with strange diagrams, and elsewhere covered with shelves crowded with instruments, the uses of many of which were unknown to me. On one side of the fireplace stood a bookcase filled with shabby folios; on the other, a small organ, fantastically decorated with painted carvings of mediaeval saints and devils. Through the half-opened door of a cupboard at the further end of the room I saw a long array of geological specimens, surgical preparations, crucibles, retorts, and jars of chemicals; while on the mantelshelf beside me, amid a number of small objects, stood a model of the solar system, a small galvanic battery, and a microscope. Every chair had its burden. Every corner was heaped high with books. The very floor was littered over with maps, casts, papers, tracings, and learned lumber of all conceivable kinds.

I stared about me with an amazement increased by every fresh object upon which my eyes chanced to rest. So strange a room I had never seen before; yet stranger still was its presence in a solitary farmhouse amid these wild and lonely moors! If what I saw aroused a keen curiosity, I was no lest intrigued as to the identity of my host and how he came to be living here. His head was singularly fine; but it was more the head of a poet than of a philosopher. Broad in the temple, prominent over the eyes, and clothed in an unruly shock of perfectly white hair, it had the appeal and much of the ruggedness that characterizes the head of Lüdwig van Beethoven. While I was yet observing him, the door opened, and Jacob brought in the supper. His master then closed his book, rose, and with more courtesy than he had yet shown, invited me to the table.

A dish of ham and eggs, a loaf of brown bread, and a bottle of admirable sherry, were placed before me.

"I have but the homeliest farmhouse fare to offer you, sir," said my host. "Your appetite, I trust, will make up for the deficiencies of our larder."

I had already fallen upon the viands, and now protested, with the enthusiasm of a starving sportsman, that I had never eaten anything so delicious.

He bowed stiffly, and sat down to his own supper, which consisted primitively, of a jug of milk and a basin of porridge. We ate in silence, and when we had done, Jacob removed the tray. I then drew my chair back to the fireside. My host, somewhat to my surprise, did the same, and, turning abruptly towards me, said:

"Sir, I have lived here in strict retirement for three-and-twenty years. During that time I have not seen many unknown faces and I have not read a single newspaper. You are the first stranger who has crossed my threshold for more than four years. Will you favour me with a little information respecting that outer world from which I have parted company so long?"

"Pray interrogate me," I replied. "I am willingly at your service."

He bent his head in acknowledgment; leaned forward, with his elbows resting on his knees and his chin supported in the palms of his hands; stared fixedly into the fire; and proceeded to question me.

His inquiries related chiefly to scientific matters, with the later progress of which, as applied to the practical purposes of life, he was almost wholly unacquainted. No student of science myself, I replied as well as my slight knowledge permitted; but the task was far from easy, and I was much relieved when, passing from interrogation to discussion, he began to formulate his own conclusions upon the facts which I had been attempting to place before him. He talked, and I listened spellbound. Later on I believe he almost forgot my presence, and only thought aloud. I had never heard anything like it then nor since. Familiar with most schools of philosophy, subtle in analysis, bold in generalization, his thoughts were expressed in an uninterrupted stream, and, still leaning forward in the same moody attitude with his eyes fixed upon the fire, wandered from topic to topic, from one speculation to another, like an inspired dreamer. From practical science to mental philosophy; from Watts to Mesmer, from Mesmer to Reichenbach, from Reichenbach to Swendenborg, Spinoza, Condillac, Descartes, Berkeley, Aristotle, Plato, and the Magi and mystics of the East, were transitions which, however bewildering in their variety and scope, seemed easy and harmonious upon his lips as sequences in music. By and by—I forget now by what link of conjecture or illustration—he passed on to that field which lies beyond the boundary of even conjectural philosophy, and reaches no man knows where. He spoke of the soul and its aspirations; of the spirit and its powers;

of second sight; of prophecy; of those phenomena which, under the names of ghosts, spectres, and supernatural appearances, have been denied by sceptics and attested by the credulous, of all ages.

"The world," he said, "grows hourly more and more sceptical of all that lies beyond its own narrow radius; and our men of science foster the fatal tendency. They condemn as fable all that resists experiment. They reject as false all that cannot be brought to the test of the laboratory or the dissecting-room. Against what superstition have they waged so long and obstinate a war, as against the belief in apparitions? And yet what superstition has maintained its hold upon the minds of men so long and so firmly? Show me any fact in physics, in history, in archaeology, which is supported by testimony so wide and so various. Attested by all races of men, in all ages, and in all climes, by the soberest sages of antiquity, by the rudest savage of today, by the Christian, the Pagan, the Pantheist, the Materialist, this phenomenon is treated as a nursery tale by the philosophers of our century. Circumstantial evidence weighs with them as a feather in the balance. The comparison of cause with effect, however valuable in physical science, is put aside as worthless and unreliable. The evidence of competent witnesses, however conclusive in a court of justice, counts for nothing. He who pauses before he pronounces, is condemned as a trifler. He who believes, is a dreamer or a fool."

He spoke with bitterness, and, having said thus, relapsed for some minutes into silence. Presently he raised his head from his hands, and added, with an altered voice and manner:

"I, sir, paused, investigated, believed, and was not ashamed to state my convictions to the world. I, too, was branded as a visionary, held up to ridicule by my contemporaries, and excluded from that field of science in which I had laboured with honour during all the best years of my life. These things happened just three-and-twenty years ago. Since then I have lived as you see me living now, and the world has forgotten me, as I have forgotten the world. You now know my history."

"It is a very sad one," I murmured, scarcely knowing what to answer.

"It is a very common one," he replied. "I have only suffered for the truth, as many a better and wiser man has done before me."

He rose, as if desirous of ending the conversation, and went over to the window.

"It has ceased snowing," he observed, as he dropped the curtain and came back to the fireside.

"Ceased!" I exclaimed, starting eagerly to my feet, "Oh, if it were only possible—but no! It is no use. Even if I could find my way across the moor, I could not walk twenty miles tonight."

"Walk twenty miles tonight!" repeated my host. "What are you thinking of?"

"Of my wife," I replied, impatiently. "Of my young wife, who does not know that I have lost my way, and who is at this moment, I am sure, in despair over my absence."

"Where is she?"

"At Dwolding, twenty miles away."

"At Dwolding," he echoed, thoughtfully. "Yes, the distance, it is true, is twenty miles; but—are you that anxious to make the journey before dawn?"

"So very, very anxious, that I would give ten guineas at this moment for a guide and a horse."

"Your wish can be gratified at less cost," he said, smiling. "The night mail from the north, which changes horses at Dwolding, passes within five miles of this spot, and will be due at a certain cross-road in about an hour and a quarter. If Jacob were to go with you across the moor and put you along the old coach-road, you could find your way, I suppose, to where it joins the new one?"

"Easily—gladly."

He smiled again, rang the bell, gave the old servant his directions, and, taking a bottle of whisky and a wineglass from the cupboard in which he kept his chemicals, said:

"The snow lies deep and it will be difficult walking tonight on the moor. A glass of usquebaugh before you start?"

I would have declined the spirit, but he pressed it on me, and I drank it. It went down my throat like liquid flame and almost took my breath away.

"It is strong," he said; "but it will help to keep out the cold. And now you have no time to spare. Good night!"

I thanked him for his hospitality and would have shaken hands with him but that he had turned away before I could make the gesture. In another minute I had traversed the hall, Jacob had locked the outer door behind me, and we were out on the wide white moor.

Although the wind had fallen, it was still bitterly cold. Not a star glimmered in the black vault overhead. Not a sound, save the crunch of snow beneath our feet, disturbed the heavy stillness of the night. Jacob, not too well pleased with his mission, ambled along in sullen silence, his lantern in his hand and his shadow at his feet. I followed, with my gun over my shoulder, as little inclined for conversation as himself. My thoughts were full of my late host. His voice still rang in my ears, his eloquence yet held my imagination captive. I remember to this day, with surprise, how my mind, greatly stimulated, retained so much of what he had said, troops of brilliant images, and fragments of splendid reasoning, in the very words he himself had used. Musing thus over what I had heard, and striving to recall a lost link here and there, I strode on at the heels of my guide, absorbed and unobservant. Presently—and it seemed only a few minutes since we had set off—Jacob came to a sudden halt, and said:

"Yon's your road. Keep the stone fence to your right hand and you can't fail to find your way."

"This, then, is the old coach-road?"

"Ay, 'tis the old coach-road."

"And how far do I go before I reach the cross-roads?"

"Nigh upon three mile."

I pulled out my purse, and he became more communicative.

"The road's a fair road enough," said he, "for foot passengers; but 'twas over-steep and narrow for the northern traffic. You'll mind where the parapet's broken away, close again' the sign-post. It's never been mended since the accident."

"What accident?"

"Eh, the night mail pitched right over into the valley below—a gude fifty feet an' more—just at the worst bit o' road in the whole county."

"Horrible! Were many lives lost?"

"All. Four were found dead, and t'other two died next morning."

"How long is it since this happened?"

"Just nine year."

"Near the sign-post, you say? I will bear it in mind. Good night."

"Gude night, sir, and thankee." Jacob pocketed his half-crown, made a faint pretence of touching his hat, and trudged back by the way he had come.

I watched the light of his lantern till it disappeared, and then turned to pursue my way alone. I had not now the slightest cause for concern, for, despite the darkness the line of stone fence showed distinctly enough against the pale gleam of the snow. How silent it seemed now, with only my footsteps to listen to; how solitary! A strange disagreeable sense of loneliness however soon stole over me. I walked faster. I hummed a fragment of a tune. I cast up enormous sums in my head, and accumulated them at compound interest. I did my best, in short, to forget the startling speculations to which I had but just been listening, and, to some extent, I succeeded.

Meanwhile, the night air seemed to become colder and colder, and though I walked fast I found it impossible to keep myself warm. My feet were like ice. I lost sensation in my hands, and grasped my gun mechanically. I even breathed with difficulty, as though, instead of traversing a quiet North-country highway, I were scaling the uppermost heights of some gigantic mountain. This last symptom became presently so distressing that I was forced to stop for a few minutes and lean against the stone fence. As I did so I chanced to look back up the road, and there, to my infinite relief, I saw a distant point of light, like the gleam of an approaching lantern. At first I thought that Jacob had retraced his steps and followed me; but even as the conjecture presented itself, a second light flashed into sight—a light evidently parallel with the first, and approaching at the same rate of motion. It needed no second thought to show me that these must be the carriage-lamps of some private vehicle, though it seemed strange that any such conveyance should take a road no longer used and regarded as dangerous.

There could be no doubt, however, of the fact, for the lamps grew larger and brighter every moment, and I even fancied I could already see the dark outline of the carriage between them. It was coming up very fast, and quite noiselessly, the snow being nearly a foot deep under the wheels.

And now the body of the vehicle became distinctly visible behind the lamps. It looked strangely lofty. A sudden suspicion flashed upon me. Was it possible that I had passed the cross-roads in the dark without observing the sign-post and could this be the very coach which I had come to meet?

No need to ask myself that question a second time, for here it came round the bend of the road, guard and driver, one outside passenger, and four steaming greys, all wrapped in a soft haze of light, through which the lamps blazed out, like a pair of glowing meteors.

I jumped forward, waved my hat, and shouted. The vehicle came down at full speed, and passed me. For a moment I feared that of the outer air and was pervaded by a singularly damp and The coachman pulled up; the guard, muffled to the eyes in capes and comforters, and apparently sound asleep in the rumble, neither answered my hail nor made the slightest effort to dismount; the outside passenger did not even turn his head. I opened the door for myself, and looked in. There were but three travellers inside, so I stepped in, shut the door, slipped into the vacant corner, and congratulated myself on my good fortune.

The atmosphere of the coach seemed, if possible, colder than that of the outer air and was pervaded by a singularly damp and disagreeable smell. I looked round at my fellow-passengers. They were three of them, men, and all silent. They did not seem to be asleep, but each leaned back in his corner of the vehicle, as if absorbed in his own reflections. I attempted to open a conversation.

"How intensely cold it is tonight," I said, addressing my opposite neighbour.

He lifted his head, looked at me, but made no reply.

"The winter," I added, "seems to have begun in earnest."

Although the corner in which he sat was so dim that I could distinguish none of his features very clearly, I saw that his eyes were still turned full upon me. And yet he spoke no word.

At any other time I should have felt, and perhaps expressed, some annoyance, but at the moment I felt too ill to do either. The icy coldness of the night air had struck a chill to my very marrow, and the strange smell inside the coach was so powerful that it gave me a feeling of intense nausea. I shivered from head to foot, and, turning to my neighbour on the left, I asked if he had any objection to an open window?

He neither spoke nor stirred.

I repeated the question rather more emphatically, but with the same result. Then I lost my patience and let the sash down. As I did so, the leather strap broke in my hand, and I noticed that the glass was covered with a thick coat of mildew, the accumulation, apparently, of years of neglect. My attention being thus drawn to the condition of the coach, I examined it more carefully, and saw by the uncertain light of the outer lamps that it was in the last stage of dilapidation. Every part of it was not only decrepit but in a condition of decay. The sashes splintered at a touch and the leather fittings were encrusted with mould, and literally rotting from the woodwork. The floor was I could see, in a dangerous condition. The vehicle, in fact, was foul with damp, and had evidently been dragged from some outhouse in which it had been mouldering away for years, to do another day or two of duty on the road.

I turned to the third passenger, whom I had not yet addressed, and hazarded one more remark.

"This coach," I said, "is in a deplorable condition. The regular mail, I suppose, is under repair?"

He moved his head slowly, and looked me in the face, without speaking a word. I shall never forget that look while I live. I turned cold at heart under it. I tremble even now when I recall it. His eyes glowed with a fiery unnatural lustre and his face was as livid as that of a corpse. His bloodless lips were drawn back as if in the agony of death, and showed the gleaming teeth between.

The words that I was about to utter died upon my lips, and a strange horror—an unspeakable dread—came upon me. My sight had by this time become used to the gloom of the coach, and I could see with tolerable distinctness. I turned to my opposite neighbour. He, too, was looking at me with the same startling pallor in his face and the same awful glitter in his eyes. I passed my hand across my brow. I turned to the passenger on the seat beside my own, and saw—oh, Heaven! how shall I describe what I saw? I saw that he was no living man—that none of them were living men, like myself! A pale phosphorescent light—the light of putrefaction—played upon their awful faces; upon their hair, dank with the dews of the grave; upon their clothes, earth stained and falling to pieces; upon their hands, which were as the hands of corpses long buried. Only their eyes, their terrible eyes, were living; and those eyes were all turned menacingly upon me!

A shriek of terror, a wild, unintelligible cry for help and mercy, burst from my lips as I flung myself against the door and strove in vain to open it.

In that single instant, brief and vivid as a landscape beheld in the flash of summer lightning, I saw the moon shining down through a rift of stormy cloud—the ghastly sign-post rearing its warning finger by the wayside—the broken parapet—the plunging horses—the black gulf below. The coach reeled like a ship in heavy seas. Then came a mighty crash—a sense of crushing pain—and then darkness.

It seemed as if years had passed when I awoke one morning from a deep sleep and found my wife watching at my bedside. I will not describe the scene that ensued and will tell you, in a few words, the tale she told me with tears of thanksgiving. I had fallen over a precipice, quite close to the junction of the old coach-road and the new, and had only been saved from certain death by lighting upon a deep snowdrift that had accumulated at the foot of the rock beneath. In this snowdrift I was discovered at daybreak by a couple of shepherds, who carried me to the nearest shelter and brought a surgeon to my aid. He found me in a state of delirium, with a broken arm and a compound fracture of the skull. The letters in my pocket-book showed my name and address; my wife was summoned to nurse me; and, thanks to my youth and robust constitution and to the care I received I survived the dangerous phases of my illness. The place of my fall, I need scarcely say, was precisely that at which a frightftul accident had happened to the north mail nine years before.

I never told my wife the fearful events which I have just related to you, but confided in the surgeon who attended me; but he treated the whole adventure as a mere dream born of the fever in my brain. We discussed the affair on several occasions until we found that our differing views provoked too sharp an argument and we never referred to it again. Others may form what conclusions they please—I *know* that twenty years ago I was the fourth passenger inside the Phantom Coach.

GHOSTS COME TO HELL

by PAT SCHOLER

PEOPLE who don't believe in ghosts are usually content to say so and pass on to other matters but not dapper, forty-year-old Welsh actor John Heel, now living in Sydney.

Early in his life Heel decided against the existence of ghosts. Since then he has devoted much of his time to proving he took the right line.

During his search for certainty, Heel became a member of England's Ghost Club, an association of people dedicated to coming to grips with Things.

He visited reputedly haunted buildings, confronted invisible barriers, pursued disembodied footsteps, fled from a voice urging him to kill himself, and explored the Great Pyramid of Egypt while leaving his body safe at home in his London flat.

Though these experiences might have shaken another man's disbelief in the supernatural, Heel has stuck to his theory that there's nothing about ghosts that science can't explain, given a little more time.

Ghosts, he insists, are not spirits returned from the grave, but a type of photograph. Everybody, so he reasons, leaves some impression or image in the atmosphere, and a person under stress leaves a very strong image which someone else may later see and call a ghost.

American scientists, he points out, claim they have developed a time camera, an infra-red device which looks back through time and takes pictures of what it sees. This camera, focused on an empty parade ground, is said to have taken a photograph of soldiers who were there some time previously.

Doesn't this, Heel asks, rather point up his theory that people leave an image in the atmosphere?

Heel would have appreciated having some such device as the time camera along with him on his ghost hunts. It might have come in handy, for instance, in that seventeenth century house in North Wales which was the scene of one of his first encounters with the Unexplained. Heel explored the house with a friend when he was only seventeen.

"The place was in excellent condition, yet it had been vacant for years because it was disturbed," Heel says in that richly dramatic voice which has interpreted so many roles in the English theatre.

"Ah yes, undoubtedly it was disturbed. Doors opened and shut. Across the staircase there was an invisible barrier so strong that when we tried to break through it we couldn't."

Would that be the work of a photograph? "Let's say of—a force," Heel replies, and his voice drops to a sibilant murmur which is quite unsettling. "Something had happened in that house. Something—rather horrible, I imagine, had left behind this supercharged atmosphere. Perhaps we disturbed it. Perhaps a sort of electricity caused the doors to open and shut."

One of Heel's lighter encounters with the supernatural (for lack of a more scientific word) occurred on Snowdon, the highest mountain in Wales.

"This is a story I cannot account for," Heel admits candidly. "All I can say is it happened." And the resonant voice takes up the tale of the Tylwydd Teg.

"The Welsh," he explains, "are a romantic and imaginative people. Through the centuries they have cherished the tradition of the Tylwydd Teg—the fairy music of Snowdon. I have heard this music.

"I was staying at the foot of Snowdon. One moonlight night it occurred to me that it was bright enough to climb a little way up the mountain and have a look at the view. I must confess that the thought also came into my mind—'I'll find out about the Tylwydd Teg business'."

By two o'clock in the morning, Heel had climbed some way up Snowdon. He was resting, admiring the moonlit view, when he saw, moving slowly down the mountain, a figure—a misty, wild-looking figure.

It was an old shepherd. "We greeted each other. And then I said to him, 'I've been wondering if there's anything to this Tylwydd Teg business'."

According to Heel, the shepherd told him there certainly was, and if he'd just keep quiet he'd probably hear for himself. "So we sat whispering for about a quarter of an hour," Heel relates, "and then suddenly I heard the music. Clearly, like dozens of tiny, tinkling bells—the fairy music of Snowdon."

He smiles as if he were still listening to that magical sound. "Well, after about a quarter of an hour the music died away. I said to the old boy, 'I'm privileged, I never thought I'd hear that. Astonishing'."

"The old boy," however, pointed out that there was little call for astonishment, because after all he had been sitting inside one of the enchanted circles of Snowdon—circles of bracken trodden down by the dancing feet of fairies.

"I looked around," Heel says, "and right enough, there was the ring of dead bracken, and I was inside it." In those circumstances, of course, he declares it was not remarkable that he'd heard the Tylwydd Teg.

Heel was in York, with Emlyn Williams' theatrical company, the next time he tangled with a Something which science has yet to explain. On this occasion the puzzle was set by the shade of a nun, known as the Grey Lady of the Theatre Royal.

According to talk around York, this stage-struck ghost often joined the actors during a performance or stood quietly watching them from the auditorium.

"The walls and foundations of this theatre, which was near York Minster, belonged to an ancient nunnery," Heel explains. "Below the stage was the nunnery well, where it was the custom of the artists to throw in a penny and make a wish—I did it myself.

"The stalls bar was one of the most perfect examples in all England of a Norman crypt.

"The backstage entrance was through a long, low, dark, stone tunnel. You felt there was something eerie there. The whole atmosphere was one of foreboding."

It being wartime when he was in York, Heel was often rostered on fire-watching duty after a show closed. It was on one of these occasions, when he was on duty with a member of the stage crew, that he heard the footsteps of the Grey Lady.

"Everything was quiet. We were having a cup of coffee together," Heel relates, "when I heard a sound like the pattering of footsteps in the tunnel. So I said to this chap, 'What was that sound?' He said, 'Don't worry. Happens all the time. Forget it'."

Heel, as a member of the Ghost Club, was simply not the man to accept advice of that sort. "The pattering sound crossed the wooden stage. I followed. I couldn't see anybody or anything.

"The footsteps led me up the spiral stairs to the dressing rooms. I knew the doors were locked, yet now they were opening as if at a touch. Lights were going on.

"I followed the steps from one dressing room to another. I followed them down the stairs again, I followed them down the stone passage and right out through the stage door. And there they just faded out on the roadway, in the direction of the Great West Door of York Minster."

In the following year in another theatre, the Royal in Leicester, he had another supernatural experience.

"The place was about one hundred and twenty-seven years old," he says. "I was managing it, as well as acting there. I had so much work to do I often stayed on in the theatre after everyone else had gone.

"I'd never had time to explore the place, so one night after the show finished I thought I'd take a look around. I'd heard there was a lot of furniture stored under the stage and I began with that.

"The furniture turned out to be simply covered with dust. Filthy I was in evening dress, so I decided to leave it for another time."

And then, he says, some impulse prompted him to make his way up through the gloom into the network of catwalks and galleries forty feet above the stage.

He explored the fly gallery, from which the scenery was manipulated, and the paint gallery, used by the scenic artists. He was halfway over the catwalk across the proscenium arch when he saw, in the wall next to him, a trapdoor.

He hesitated, then wrenched it open. There, stretching back across the roof of the auditorium, was a huge storeroom strewn with the debris of perhaps a century of super-colossal productions; papier mache columns, urns, tattered costumes, plaster statues mantled in the dust of the years.

Shutting the trapdoor, Heel proceeded along the catwalk, feeling his way through shadow pierced weakly by a small pilot light. "And now—" Heel's voice sinks, as he relates the story, "now came the first and only occasion in all this ghost business that I have been absolutely terrified.

"I began to get a feeling. A very curious feeling. Remember, I was forty feet above the stage. And I heard these words: 'Jerry wants you to do it—jump over. Jerry wants you to do it—jump over.' "

After a long pause—"Of course," Heel says in a normal voice, "I'm willing to admit I might not really have heard those words, that they might perhaps have existed merely in my subconscious—

"Anyway, I ran. I simply turned and ran. I got out of that theatre as fast as I could."

Next morning Heel called in the stage manager and the electrician who had worked for years at the Royal and asked them if there were any queer stories about the theatre.

Well, they said, there was the stagehand who went berserk. He'd rushed into the fly gallery, put a rope around his neck and thrown himself over. Now, what was his name again? Of course—Jerry.

They mentioned that there was the black shadow which sometimes appeared when they were working late. It had a habit of moving across the spotlight, blotting it out, they said. The shadow carried with it a clammy, chill feeling and a nasty smell.

"But although I stayed back with those men several times, hoping to see the shadow," Heel says, "I admit it never appeared when I was there. From which you might gather that I'm not the type to claim I see things when I don't."

Another case about which Heel gives a fairly detached report was that of St. Margaret's vicarage, Leicester. He remembers discussing this case with the Bishop of Leicester as they waited for their respective trains.

"When I first caught sight of the Bishop," Heel tells, "I noticed there was something odd about him. Then I realized what it was. He was not wearing his gaiters.

"Well. I greeted him in the usual way—'How d'you do, my lord, long time no see', and so on—and then I got around to the subject of St. Margaret's vicarage. I knew he'd arranged to visit the place and I asked him how he'd got on.

"Well, he was a broad-minded man, charming—so many bishops aren't, but he was. He said to me, 'Johnny, you'll have noticed I'm not wearing my gaiters'. So I said, 'Why yes, my lord'.

"He said, 'Johnny, between you and me, at that vicarage I was scared right out of them'."

One of the disturbing phenomena of St. Margaret's was a phosphorescent green light which would fill a closed room. Once the door was opened the light would fade, after which the air would be rent by a sound which might be described as a screaming laugh —or, perhaps, as a laughing scream.

Then of course there was the black-robed figure which walked up and down a flagged stone passageway—doing little harm, actually, by comparison with another figure in white which kept turning up in the staff quarters and frightening away the servants.

The vicar's harassed wife had to manage a household where cloths were pulled off tables by invisible hands (or something), sheets and blankets were whisked off beds and made to disappear in front of her, and cups and saucers took off from their shelves and sailed away into nothingness.

"Finally she'd lose her temper," Heel recalls, "and shout out, 'Oh, for heaven's sake give me back my things.' Then back they'd come, you know. Mysteriously, they'd all be returned to her, and the house would be quiet for a while."

Heel is certain that most of the phenomena at St. Margaret's were due to a poltergeist—defined in the dictionary as "a noisy ghost, a spirit assumed as the explanation of rappings and other unexplained noises."

"Poltergeists," Heel says, "are two a penny."

In his opinion, though, they are not spirits, but manifestations of something in the mind of an adolescent, usually a girl. The adolescent is seldom aware of the poltergeist's behaviour, which often suggests that of a disembodied bogie.

"Poltergeists can be horrible, evil," Heel insists. "But also they're silly. I mean, where's the point in picking up a chair, whirling it around and throwing it down again? Ridiculous.

"There was the case of the Battersea poltergeist. I saw the girl myself, just sitting there quietly watching television, unaware of this poltergeist thing operating all around her—hats flying, tapping on walls, a piece of chalk drawing a face on a blind.

"Oh yes. I watched that piece of chalk myself. Moving through the air, drawing, and nothing holding it."

Heel did not return to the vicarage to investigate the poltergeist of St. Margaret's. The Bishop asked him not to because he disliked the publicity which often attended an investigation by Ghost Club members.

Heel's relations with other churchmen in Leicester were not always so happy, especially after he produced James Bridie's "Mr

Bolfry," a play which brings the devil on to the stage to claim the soul of a parson.

Cast as the parson, Heel evolved what he feels was one of his most spectacular make-ups to turn himself into the crabbed old churchman. "I had to take the play off after three nights," Heel told us. "The church people said it was sacrilegious."

In 1951 Heel moved to London and because of an acute accommodation shortage, he and his wife and mother had to settle into shabby lodgings. It was then Heel read that the Dover Museum wished to sell an Egyptian mummy which had been in a room damaged in an air raid.

"I wrote," Heel recalls. "Purely for a joke, of course. I was invited down to Dover, however, and found that the mummy had lost some of its bandages—it seemed that workmen had searched it for ornaments—but I was impressed by the fine preservation of the body.

"I made an offer for it. An absurd offer, really—£3. And the museum jumped at it.

"When I recovered from the shock it seemed to me extremely peculiar that the museum should be glad to dispose of the mummy for such a small sum. However, I arranged with a road cartage firm to pick up the mummy and deliver it to my digs. Their charge was 25s.

"That made £4 5s. altogether for a mummy—a twenty-one-year-old boy, according to the museum, a priest of Isis of 2,500 years ago.

"Later I received a letter from the museum saying that a chap living in south London had been interested in the mummy, and would like to meet its new owner. So I wrote to this man—Stanley Forsythe—and he invited me to go to see him."

Forsythe explained to Heel that, as a child, he'd spent many happy hours in the Dover Museum looking at the mummies and so he had a particular interest in the specimen Heel had acquired.

"I'm going to make you an offer," Forsythe told Heel. "At the top of this house there's a furnished flat, five rooms, self-contained. I'll let you have it for 35s. a week if you will bring your mummy with you, store it in the basement, and allow me to help with the restoration."

That was the way Heel acquired a comfortable flat and a famous address—34 Lancaster Road, South Norwood. It was at No. 34

that such celebrities as Sir Oliver Lodge and Sir Arthur Conan Doyle had attended seances. "That hóuse," Heel says, "was literally saturated with psychic emanations."

Forsythe, the landlord, turned out to be a writer with a side interest in Egyptology and anatomy. After sessions in the basement cleaning up the coffin and re-winding the outer bandages of the mummy, Forsythe became convinced that the body was not that of a twenty-one-year-old boy but of a girl of about sixteen. In the hope that spirits would confirm his theory, he arranged a seance.

For the occasion, the mummy was carried upstairs to the dining-room. There, under the bright light of an electric chandelier, the seance proceeded in the presence of reporters from the London papers, three spiritualists, Forsythe and Heel, and two friends.

The medium who conducted the seance over the Egyptian mummy was, in Heel's words, "a young woman who kept a confectionery shop and couldn't even tell you who Tutankhamen was.

"Yet after she'd gone into a trance," Heel relates, "she came straight over to me and in a strange voice, the voice of an old, old man, described a temple. It seemed to be a cross between a Greek and Roman building, and I couldn't make much sense out of it.

"The voice said a girl had died and had paid a terrible price for a crime committed. Then the voice changed into that of a young girl. And this is the message I received (I make no comment on it):

" 'My name is Katrina. I was accounted fair in the eyes of the Pharaoh and all the land of Egypt. I died and was buried. I sinned against my Pharaoh and I paid the price.

" 'I was a priestess in the temple of Orkon. You have saved my body from destruction and so long as you shall keep me safe within these walls I will do harm to all those who would hurt the dwellers within these walls. Protect me, preserve me. In life I suffered acutely from a painful disease.'

"A few weeks later a young doctor said he'd like to examine the mummy and I gave him permission.

"Somehow the newspapers got hold of the story. My word, you know, it's a good job I've got a sense of humour, otherwise I might easily have lost my temper. The heading the *Sunday Dispatch* gave the story was, 'He is sending his mummy to see a doctor.'

"Ah well. Three days later I received the doctor's report. It said that the mummy was the remains of a girl of sixteen, that there were not sufficient internal organs to give a definite cause of death, and that she had suffered from spondylitis.

"In other words, the medium's Katrina voice had been right in claiming the body as a girl's, and right about her suffering from a painful disease."

Confirmation of statements made in the medium's old-man voice came, Heel adds, from Egyptologist Sir Alan Gardiner. He wrote that the mummy dated from the Graeco-Roman period of Egyptian history and probably from the reign of Osorkon II or III.

Later, despite her promises to be nice to her hosts, Katrina began to misbehave. Heel's mother insisted she had seen queer shadows moving about in the basement.

"I suspected something was disturbing the dust so as a test I spread powdered cement over the floor. I locked the door so that nobody could go in. Later, I inspected the place. The dust had been disturbed. Then, lights began to go on and off in our flat. We began to hear footsteps. One afternoon they crossed the room behind the settee where my wife and I were sitting."

All this indicated to Heel that Katrina must be dissatisfied with life in a basement, so he brought her upstairs and gave her a room of her own in his flat. Sure enough, the disturbances ceased.

"But then a very curious thing happened," he says. "I spent all one night wandering, so it seemed, inside the Great Pyramid of Egypt.

"Everything was clear, as real as anything I'm looking at now. I seemed to be searching for somebody. I felt I wanted to tell them something.

"I said to my wife in the morning, "I've had a wonderful time—I've spent the entire night in the Great Pyramid. I seemed to be looking for somebody.' Of course she laughed—'Looking for your mummy, were you?'

"Now, nobody else heard what I said. Yet when I came home that evening I received a note left by my landlord's wife.

"She had written, 'I have a strange story to tell you. Last night I dreamed I was in the Great Pyramid of Egypt. I was looking for you and couldn't find you. It seemed I had something to tell you about your mummy.'

"Well, that shocked my wife pretty badly."

It was rather a relief to Mrs. Heel to leave the mummy behind when, in February, 1958, she and her husband emigrated to Australia.

In his new country, Heel has maintained his interest in the disturbed images usually referred to as ghosts. His investigations have led him to a suspected poltergeist or two, but there's really been nothing to come up to his experiences in Britain.

"There are simply no very ancient buildings here," he points out. "No crumbling arches. None of those marvellous ruins.

"Though, of course," he adds thoughtfully, "It isn't strictly necessary for a house to be old to be haunted.

"Why, in Croydon, England, it happened in a new pair of semi-detached red brick council houses. The tenants had been in them only a few weeks when the trouble started. They were haunted by a crying baby.

"This baby just cried and cried. You could hear it from the roadway. You could even pinpoint the spot in the room where the noise came from. But you just couldn't see any baby.

"In the end, the tenants of both the houses moved out.

"Mind you," Heel adds, "that's not to say there was a ghost. No doubt there is some perfectly rational explanation. I'm sure there is. And one of these days, science will find it."

WAGES OF ENVY

by MARK BARTHOLOMEUSZ

JUSE APPUHAMY, Sinhalese, never liked those who talked too much. Unnecessary speech, he felt, was a sign that the speaker was a man of words, rather than deeds. So as a golden rule, more or less, he minded his own business, kept himself to himself, worked like a galley slave at his job of selling vegetables at the neighbouring fairs, and looked after his family with commendable zeal.

As a result of his labours over the years, he slowly but surely began to thrive. One day he found that he was able to afford the money to buy a new cart and even more important, a fine, sturdy bull, to take his produce to market.

Most of Juse Appuhamy's neighbours in the Ceylon village, where he lived, hated to see him perched on top of his fully laden new cart, driving his bull to market with the arrogance of a king. It irked them to think that Juse Appuhamy who had started life as a labourer, like many of them, working in the rice fields for others, had over the years become successful. There was a time, they recalled, when he could hardly afford a rag to his back. But now he always wore a well laundered shirt and a new sarong.

They regarded with envy his neat little tiled cottage with its even neater compound, swept regularly every day by Ran Menika, Juse's wife. Every bit as industrious as her husband, she, too, was careful of her appearance even when she was busy in the kitchen. The couple's detractors preferred to ignore the fact that it was their own indolence that had kept them poor. Neither would they admit that Juse Appuhamy and his wife had thrived because of their own efforts. Rarely did their day begin later than cocks-crow and the couple's three healthy children were a credit to their parents.

While the rest of the village slept, Juse would be feeding his bull and preparing for his daily round to the outlying districts.

Meanwhile Ran Menika—so named because of her ran or

golden complexion—would start baking the hoppers which Juse relished as though they were the rarest delicacies. She always felt that her toil was well worthwhile, when she saw with what relish her husband ate the meal she had prepared for him. On rare occasions he would even tell her, quietly but with a tenderness she was quick to recognize:

"There is not a woman in this village, Menika, who can bake a better hopper or make a finer coconut sambol."

Ran Menika would pause in her work for a moment, glance at her husband, as if to remind herself of how handsome he was, and say:

"It's your belly talking again."

Juse would answer with a smile, "No, that's not quite true. I am sure you know it isn't."

So while Juse Appuhamy and his wife prospered, there grew between them and the villagers a veritable wall of resentment. Among the most hostile was Juse's immediate neighbour, Marthelis, a thin, characterless man who lived with his wife and family on three acres of land which had been given to him many years ago by the government. Now, Marthelis had allowed more than half of his acreage to be reclaimed by the jungle and his attempts to grow coconuts and vegetables on the remainder were only half-hearted. He preferred to spend too much of his time earning easy money by selling an illicit brew to the villagers and using most of this income to challenge all-comers to a game of cards called "Buruwa".

He was not a very good card player though, and lost more often than he won. His wife, Prema, an unkempt creature with hard eyes and sunken cheeks, had truly little to be happy about. She shared a broken-down hut with her husband and children the roof of which leaked badly whenever it rained.

Every time Marthelis or his wife looked towards the opposite compound and saw the neat reliable red tiles on their neighbours' roof, their envy increased.

Prema especially, by that queer logic peculiar to villagers, began to feel that their poverty was due, in some inexplicable way to their neighbours. Never for a moment did she ascribe it to her husband's feckless ways; for strangely enough, she cared for him despite the scant attention he gave her or the children. One night it rained so heavily that in no time at all, the hut was full of little pools of water. Prema's two small daughters had hardly a place that was dry to sleep in and began to cry and whimper. In desperation Prema drugged them to sleep with a herbal concoction well known to the villagers and placed them on a mat in the one dry place in the room. When they finally dozed off to sleep she joined her husband, who sat quietly smoking a beedi (a rolled leaf like tobacco).

For a long time neither spoke. They were both deep in their own thoughts. The rain continued its steady murmur for a while and then slowly dwindled to a drizzle. Prema at length unburdened herself of her thoughts.

"I know who has brought us all this bad luck over the years," she said dolefully.

"Who?" asked Marthelis innocently, though half suspecting the answer.

"Who else but that filthy woman in the next plot," said Prema viciously. "It isn't natural for our family to go on having this bad luck for so long. Yes, for fifteen years I have been your wife and I haven't even a tiled roof to show for it. I live in the same mud hut as you brought me to when I first got married. Only now it leaks a lot more."

"So how could that woman cause our ill-luck?" asked Marthelis.

"Aiyo," said Prema. "As though you don't know."

"Do you think they have done something?"

"I don't think they have done something. I know it."

Marthelis' latent hatred towards his neighbours allured his interest in what his wife was saying.

"How do you know for certain?" he asked quietly.

"I went to the Pusari (priest) this morning at the shrine in the forest."

"You went to see the Pusari?"

"Yes."

"Alone?"

"Yes."

"You shouldn't have done it," said Marthelis. "Not when you have a husband to go with you."

"When a woman has a husband who plays cards for most of the day," said Prema, with a trace of annoyance, "she must learn to do things for herself."

Marthelis merely took a long pull at his beedi. For a few moments there was silence. But his curiosity got the better of him.

"What did the Pusari say?" he asked nonchalently.

"He went into a trance first before the shrine to his God and then the God spoke through him."

"I know. I know all that," said Marthelis impatiently, wondering why his wife had to waste his time with all these very familiar details. "What I want to know is what did the God say?"

Prema came to the point at last.

"In a deep voice which seemed to come from his belly, he said that a tall, fair, well dressed woman with a mole on her right cheek, living almost next to our property, had buried a charm in our garden."

"Charm!" Marthelis could not conceal the fear he felt when he heard the dreaded word.

"Yes," said Prema. "And who else but Ran Menika. Is she not as the God described her, even to the mole on her right cheek."

Marthelis paused for a moment deep in thought. "The God cannot be wrong," he said at length, "if he described our neighbour so exactly. Where did he say the charm was buried?"

"It is the kind of charm which no one can ever find and was buried many years ago."

"No one can ever find?" Marthelis really was alarmed.

"Yes. But don't be frightened. The Pusari also said that the power of this charm could be cut."

"By whom?"

"By him, of course."

Marthelis sighed with relief. He felt as though a great load had been lifted from his chest. "I suppose," he said, finally, "we will have to take him an offering of some kind when next we go to see him."

"Yes," said Prema. "When I went for water this morning at the wewa (lake) I asked Aunt Marthina what I would have to take, apart from the nine limes and the husked coconut that the Pusari asked me to bring for the cutting ceremony and she said that all we needed was a two rupee note."

About a week after this conversation Marthelis and Prema both found that they were constantly thinking of what had been done to them by their neighbours, to bring them under the spell of an evil demon, and their consequent misfortunes and poverty. It rankled so much within them that they could not help but speak about it to others in the village. Very soon, the revelation of the Pusari concerning Juse and his wife became known to everybody.

Villagers nodded their heads wisely and said, "We always knew that those two were not people to be trusted. The Forest God is never wrong. This explains why they have far more money than the rest of us. They are people who dabble in charms and are able to secure the aid of the demons to help them prosper. Prema and her husband agreed whole-heartedly. Even the handful of acquaintances, who had no grudge against Juse and his wife, began to regard them as something of a threat. They didn't want too many dabblers in black magic in their midst.

The couple had no inkling of the evil rumours that daily were whispered behind their backs. Juse, of course, was aware of the part played by gossip in village life, but he would hardly have believed it even if he had been warned of the dangerous situation that was developing.

Perhaps the last straw was when Juse acquired a handsome transistor set and Prema and her husband heard the sound of music from their neighbour's compound. They were furious as they huddled together in their miserable hovel and, there and then, decided they would no longer delay their visit to the Pusari so that the evil spell which had bound them to poverty for so long should be destroyed for ever.

A visit to the Pusari was not an easy undertaking but Prema and Marthelis were determined to bring about a change in their fortunes or ensure, at least, the ruin of Juse Appuhamy and his wife. So, one morning, they packed a loaf of bread and some bananas into a cloth bag and also took with them a husked coconut, nine limes and a note worth two rupees as offerings.

Shortly after starting their journey they left the road that led out of the village and took to a path through the thick forest. They had five miles to trudge before they came to the shrine. Marthelis thought the journey would never end. He was afraid of the great forest and the silence and gloom. The sun overhead could not penetrate the barrier created by the height of the enormous trees and every shadow filled Marthelis with foreboding. He wondered what he would do if a leopard crossed their path and could hardly repress a shudder on remembering that his wife not long ago had come here alone. The only sign of wild life was that of an occasional jungle fowl which darted into the undergrowth as they approached.

After about two hours they finally came to a clearing at the end of which stood a great tree under which was a crude little structure built of stone and cement and consisting of two rooms. In one of them the Pusari slept, ate and lived, in the other he communicated his revelations from the deity.

As Marthelis and Prema approached the Pusari was intoning a litany before the God he worshipped, symbolized by a massive black image only vaguely suggesting a human outline. On each side of the idol, which stood upon an altar or stone shelf, stood jars containing smouldering joss sticks. Streamers of smoke coiled and uncoiled as they burned, radiating a sickly sweet perfume. At the foot of the image a large flame burned steadily in a clay receptacle filled with oil. Behind the flame was a mirror which appeared to glow eerily as it reflected the rays from the flame.

The Pusari appeared to sense that Prema and Marthelis were watching him from the entrance. Unhurriedly he concluded his devotions and came out to meet his visitors.

"So you've come," he said quietly addressing Prema rather than her husband.

"Yes," said Prema, shifting uneasily.

"I'm glad you have brought your husband with you. It will be easier for me to cut the power of the charm."

Marthelis glanced at the Pusari but was too awed to speak to a man said to have power over spirits and demons. The priest had a strong, bony face and a commanding presence.

"Have you brought the limes?" he asked.

"Yes," said Prema.

"Give them to me," he said.

Prema rummaged within the cloth bag which still hung from her husband's neck, brought out the limes and gave them to him.

"Have you brought the husked coconut?" asked the Pusari again.

This time it was Marthelis who answered. "Yes," he said, and extracted the coconut from his bag. The Pusari took the coconut without a word and re-entered the shrine room.

Prema and Marthelis followed quietly behind him. The Pusari placed the limes and the coconut on a side of the altar and then he took a red sash which lay there and tied it round his waist. All he wore below the sash was a white cloth which extended up to his knees. His hairy chest was bare of clothing and was streaked horizontally with markings of ash.

"I shall start praying to the God," he said quietly.

Prema thought the whiteness of his eyes was startling and so was the blackness of his face, which was also streaked with ash. His reddish brown beard like the hair on his head was matted. For a moment she felt frightened in his presence.

The ascetic seemed to sense her fear. "Now," he said, "I want you to calm yourself and to be silent. Your husband too. The great god of the forest will come only if you deserve his aid." With these words he clasped his palms together, bowed his head and began to mumble something in a slow monotone.

Neither Prema nor Marthelis could understand what he said. Gradually the priest's voice rose from a whisper to a full-throated call while, at the same time, the upper part of his body began to sway from side to side.

Marthelis and Prema watched intently the weird movement of the Pusari's body. Quite suddenly he became convulsed and his body began vibrating at tremendous speed. His words became a meaningless babel and with each vibration there was a report like a pistol shot; so that ultimately Prema and Marthelis both felt as though the room was filled with the staccato rattle of some curious machine. The noise ceased as suddenly as it had begun and with it all movement by the Pusari himself. A deathly silence filled the room. The ascetic turned slowly away from the image to face Prema and Marthelis.

Prema couldn't repress a shudder when she saw the ascetic's eyes. They were gazing at her and yet through her. Then he slowly raised his hand and placed it on her forehead. He spoke now in a deep voice, so deep thought Prema that it couldn't possibly belong to a human being.

"You and your husband have suffered greatly," he said in clear intelligible Sinhalese. "But the God of the Forest will bring your sufferings to an end."

Prema felt as though a strange force was radiating from his fingers and coursing through her whole body. She was quite convinced that the God himself was talking. The ascetic touched Marthelis' forehead too in a similar manner. He turned slowly towards the altar and took one of the limes and then a knife. Resting the lime on Prema's head he cut it gently. For a moment he gazed at the two halves of the lime and then threw them on the floor.

Once again Prema and Marthelis heard the priest speak strangely as if the words of another were being transmitted through him.

"Not till a seed within the lime is cut exactly in half is the spell that binds you to poverty destroyed," it said.

With this pronouncement the ascetic took another lime from his altar and this time cut it over the head of Marthelis. Once again the seeds were whole and intact. He continued the ceremony using the remaining limes over the heads of Prema and her husband in turn. But every time the seeds remained intact. Prema and Marthelis had almost given up hope when he came to the eighth lime. This time he severed the lime in two over Marthelis' head.

"Ah," intoned the ascetic. "The seed has been cut exactly in half. The God of the Forest has destroyed the spell. Go back to your hut. You will no more be under its evil influence."

Both Prema and Marthelis felt at that moment as though a tremendous burden had been lifted from their spirits. They were overjoyed at their reprieve but there was hatred in their hearts for the people who had kept them poor.

The ascetic turned again towards the image and with head bowed low start to pray. Once more his body began to vibrate violently, but this time there were no staccato sounds. Gradually the rapid movement of the body ceased and he seemed to become his usual self again.

His chest was bathed with sweat as he came up to Prema and Marthelis and spoke to them in his normal voice. They could hardly believe that this was the same Pusari who had spoken to them earlier.

"You have a long way to go now, haven't you?" he asked casually.

"Not too far," said Prema making light of the situation.

"Do not worry about the future," he said.

But Prema had made up her mind that she would do something much more positive than await the arrival of better times. She would take her revenge for all that had been done to them. Yes, she was going to visit Malhamy the famous sorcerer who lived in the village next to their own. She would seek his aid to bring misfortune upon Ran Menika and her husband. When she whispered her thoughts to her husband he fully agreed. So with a final nod to the ascetic they left the shrine in the forest. But before they did so they dropped a two rupee note into the bowl kept at the entrance for the offerings of those who came for assistance.

For a few days after the visit to the forest shrine, Prema was aware of a great sense of relief; that oppressive burden of continued poverty which weighed down the spirits of both her and her husband seemed to become lighter. Even Marthelis no longer felt as despondent as he once did about his domestic affairs. Both he and Prema decided that it was the power of the Forest God, wielded through the agency of the Pusari, that had brought them this change in spirit; this feeling that all would be well in the future.

But after about a week, doubts began to nag them. As long as Ran Menila was alive and capable of doing something to them again she was a threat to their security. It was not that they doubted the Pusari's assurances but it seemed like folly not to see Malhamy the Kattadiya (sorcerer) at once. They could tell him what the God had revealed to them through the ascetic and ask for a charm with which to take their revenge.

No sooner they had decided on this trip than they made the journey to the village in which Malhamy lived. It wasn't more than ten miles away and it cost very little by bus from their own home.

Malhamy, contrary to what Prema expected of him, was not the thin, diabolic sorcerer with deep set penetrating eyes that she had imagined. He was a fat, hairy chested man with a great round belly and a face as full as a ripe melon. His eyes twinkled good-naturedly as he stood barefoot on the veranda of his home, clad only in a sarong.

What was even more surprising was that his home was quite different from the majority of mud huts in their village. It was built of brick, neatly white-washed, and had a roof of red tiles. A radio set stood ornamentally in the principal room and there was even a carpet on the veranda floor. A large Ford Prefect stood outside the porch and Malhamy had obviously climbed from humble origins to become one of the more prosperous people in the village.

At first, despite the twinkle in his eye, Prema and Marthelis were awed by the signs of opulence they saw. But Malhamy soon put them at their ease.

"Sit down," he said in hearty manner, rubbing his naked paunch with two fat palms.

The feeling of awe soon thawed and Marthelis even succeeded in smiling as he took a seat on one of the upright chairs placed along the veranda. Prema followed suit.

Malhamy sat down on another easy chair opposite his clients and began to talk.

"Now," he said, smiling broadly, "what is your trouble?"

As usual Prema did most of the talking. "Our neighbours buried a kodivinia (charm) in our garden many years ago," she said.

"Kodivinia!" Malhamy had ceased to smile.

"Yes," said Prema.

"How do you know they did this?"

"The God of the Forest told us. We've had bad luck for fifteen years."

Malhamy nodded his head as she spoke. These were not the first clients to come to him with revelations from the famous Pusari.

"The God of the Forest is rarely wrong," he said. "Well, what do you want me to do?"

"We want you to help us to take our revenge," said Prema.

"Do you want your neighbours to die?"

"No," said Marthelis promptly. "We do not desire their death."

"Do you want them to be harassed by spirits or demons so that they can never prosper again?"

"Yes," said Prema. "If you can do that, specially to Ran Menika the woman mainly responsible for our misery, we will be amply revenged. It is time her pride was humbled."

"It is not a difficult matter,' 'said Malhamy. "But you will have to assist me."

"We will do anything you ask," said Prema.

"Very well," said Malhamy. "Bring me a three by four inch sheet of copper leaf tomorrow and leave it with me. I shall require also the names of your neighbours, both wife and husband, and their birth dates if you happen to know them. If you don't it won't matter. A charm is generally more effective however, when used on significant occasions such as birthdays. I will charm the copper leaf and then return it so that all you've got to do is bury it somewhere near your neighbours dwelling. If Ran Menika walks over the buried charm at any time it will take effect.

"Within two weeks she will be so completely in the grip of the power invoked by the charm that she will become the victim of terrifying nightmares. Illness will overcome her and, for as long as the demon continues to haunt their home, your neighbours will experience nothing but despair and misfortune."

Malhamy ceased talking and looked intently at his clients, trying to fathom the impact of his words. Marthelis was plainly a little scared, now that he began to see the implications of his mission. But Prema smiled as she asked, "Are you sure all this will come to pass?"

Malhamy laughed. "I haven't been known as the most powerful Kattadiya in these parts for nothing," he said. "People come all the way from the big city of Colombo to this remote village to see me."

Prema remained thoughtful. Malhamy, she reflected, lived in great comfort and he could hardly have succeeded in doing so all these years on a false reputation.

"I will bring you the copper leaf tomorrow," she said, "and also the information you require. But how much will we have to pay you?"

"I will accept payment only if my charm is successful," said Malhamy, smiling broadly again. "Of course rich people from the big towns sometimes pay me as much as five hundred rupees for a successful kodivinia."

Prema started. Five hundred rupees was a fortune. But the sorcerer soon allayed her fears.

"Don't be dismayed," he said, benignly. "From people who are villagers like myself I very rarely accept more than fifty rupees."

Marthelis shifted uneasily in his seat while Prema was silent. Even fifty rupees was a large sum to people as poor as themselves.

Malhamy seemed to read their thoughts. "I can see that even fifty rupees would be too much for you," he said. "Very well, I shall do this for you as a special favour for thirty rupees. Only I don't want you to mention this to anyone in your village."

"Hondhemai," (we agree) said Prema and Marthelis, together. "For that price we are willing to bind ourselves to pay you."

Malhamy's face creased into a happy smile. "Now you must remember," he said, "that this is a special favour. For those who really cannot afford I don't believe in charging sinful prices."

Prema and Marthelis returned to their village after their

audience with the sorcerer. It wasn't easy for them to secure the necessary information about the exact date of birth of their neighbour Menika. But after some delicate enquiries, made so skilfully that nobody suspected her motives, Prema finally managed to learn the details. The next day, armed with this information she bought the necessary copper leaf from the village goldsmith and took the bus to Malhamy's place, accompanied by her husband.

A week later Malhamy returned the copper leaf to his clients. The plain surface of the leaf was now etched on either side with two charts consisting of squares. Within each square were strange symbols, like birds or reptiles numbers and occasional letters from the Sinhala alphabet. What these meant neither Prema nor Marthelis could fathom.

Prema took the copper leaf from the sorcerer and handled it gently as though it was some precious metal.

"We are very grateful to you," she said.

"We will let you know if it is successful," said Marthelis.

"It should succeed," said Malhamy, in a sinister tone. "It is now invested with the power of the Yaksa Lokey."

Prema almost dropped the charm when she heard the words which meant "Demon World".

"Don't worry," said Malhamy reassuringly. "You can safely hold it in your palm. It only works against those whom it is intended to harm."

There was nothing more for Prema and Marthelis to do but return to their hut and wait for nightfall. They were both determined to put their plan into action at the earliest moment. Fortunately it was a moonless night and after nine o'clock, while the whole village slept, they could bury the charm unobserved.

Marthelis was the first to suggest a suitable place. "Let's bury it at the entrance to their veranda," he said, as he and Prema stood in their own doorway, about to set out on their mission.

"No," said Prema, after a little thought. "It's too close to their rooms. Somebody might hear us digging. I think it would be better if we buried it right opposite their main gate. Ran Menika goes to market daily and she is bound to walk over the charm."

Marthelis thought there was sense in what she suggested. So taking a little torch, a garden fork, and of course, the charm, he and his wife walked quietly through their own front garden till they came to the main road. A few yards walk down this road brought them to the gateway of their neighbours' home.

Marthelis soon got down to digging a hole. It wasn't a difficult task as the soil was soft and sandy. When he reached a depth of a foot or so he buried the charm and then filling up the hole with earth he covered the traces of his deed with the fine grained sand that formed the outer surface of the soil.

"Nobody will suspect that a charm has been buried here," said Prema, approvingly, as she flashed the torchlight and examined the surface of the earth. Marthelis rose with a grunt. He too, was well pleased. It was time to return to their own hut and await developments.

They were about to do so when they heard a sudden, furtive rustle. It came from the bushes which stood on either side of the main gate. Prema and Marthelis were both startled. Had they been observed? For a few seconds they stood quite still but nothing happened. Prema switched on the torch and played the light around and then sighed with relief. All they saw was the rear of a rabbit darting away into the darkness.

Juse Appuhamy and his wife meanwhlie remained entirely unaware of the sinister scheme of their neighbours. Juse drove his vegetable cart to the market, as was his custom, while his wife, Ran Menika, fulfilled her daily chores with her usual thoroughness.

In the evenings at above five o'clock, when she'd finished washing the two younger of her children at the well, she would take her shopping bag and go to the village store to buy her provisions for the next day. Her eldest daughter, now close upon thirteen years in age, looked after the two younger children, until she returned.

Now this was a routine that Prema was well aware of and, ever since the night the charm was buried, she began to keep watch at her window waiting for something dramatic to happen.

But for about two weeks nothing unusual took place. Prema, whose desire to harm her neighbours had long become a mania with her, felt her hatred of Ran Menika more unbearable than ever with every day that passed without event.

"May lightning strike the bitch," she'd swear, to herself, as she saw Ran Menika return daily from shopping, her bag laden with provisions and none the worse for the charm. She seemed to walk proudly, like a queen, through the gateway as if to announce to the whole village that nothing in the world would ever break her spirit or that lovely slender body of hers so neatly encased in its close fitting jacket. When Prema compared her own shabby and dirty dress with that of Ran Menika the contrast was so great that she spat through the window in spite.

One night Ran Menika went to bed as usual after tucking her three children to sleep. As she sank on to her comfortable mattress she snuggled up to her husband, Juse, who was already snoring and let her thoughts drift. It was good to be sleeping on a mattress, she thought. How many villagers could boast of a nice solid bed and a mattress. She remembered the first years of her marriage when she had nothing more than a mat to sleep on. Ah, it was good to have a husband like Juse, a hard-working honest man who had provided her and the children with all their needs. It was worth loving and being loved by him. She didn't regret the many sacrifices she had made in the way of clothes and even food just to see him happy, with more money to improve his business and now they were about the most flourishing couple in the village.

The flame from the kerosene lamp on the table by their bed cast its rays over Juse's face. His hair was beginning to turn grey she noticed. Poor man; He worked very hard and now time was beginning to show its marks. But his body was still bronzed and sinewy and tough. His face, though ever so slightly wrinkled beneath the eyes, exuded confidence. Yes. He was still handsome. He was her man.

As these thoughts passed through her mind, Ran Menika felt a strange sense of warmth, security and above all tenderness. Slowly she sank into sleep.

After about an hour of dreamless sleep she began to enter a strange world. She was in a dark and dismal forest with long overhanging creepers and she was walking alone through an animal track which seemed to stretch endlessly into the distance. She passed a shrine under a huge tree and she espied an aged asectic mumbling before a little effigy. She kept on walking. Elephants and leopards began to pad behind her, following, following all the time. She tried to run but couldn't. The track ahead of her became gloomier and gloomier. She was filled with panic as the animals kept up their pursuit and she made a final despairing effort to run, when she saw a little hut standing isolated on a side of the track. With a tremendous effort she got to the door of the hut and pulled at its handle with every ounce of strength in her body. The door burst open and she saw . . . the dead, staring eyes of her husband, whose body was sprawled on the floor, with a serpent sliding over him. She screamed as she reached despairingly for the body of her husband. . . .

Juse Appuhamy woke up with a start when he heard his wife's cries and he found her writhing on the bed clutching desperately at him. He caught her firmly by the arm and jolted her into awareness. Her body was trembling and hot with perspiration. She took one look at her husband's face, heaved a huge sigh of relief and rested her head upon his chest.

"What was it Sudha?" (darling) he asked, tenderly as he took her in his arms.

"I had an awful dream that you were dead," she whispered, as a fresh tremor passed through her whole body. "It was terrible."

The next day Ran Menkia was much too busy to worry about her dream of the previous night. There were so many things to be done in the house for her husband and children that she hardly noticed the passing of time as one chore followed another.

When the evening was far gone she went to the store once again for provisions. About half an hour later dusk began to settle over the village and Ran Menika finished her marketing as quickly as she could in order to be with her family before it got dark. It didn't take her more than fifteen minutes to get to her little home but in that short space of time the whole atmosphere of the village seemed to change. In the half light which preceded darkness it was hushed. It was the time when villagers believed that spirits and phantoms begin their nocturnal prowling.

Ran Menika felt a little uneasy that she happened to be returning home so late that day. She recalled the dream of the previous night and a little shudder passed through her body. She wondered for a moment whether it meant bad luck. Was it a warning of things to come? It was in this sombre frame of mind that she turned through the entrance to her home when suddenly a rabbit darted out of the undergrowth, crept swiftly between her feet and disappeared. As the animal brushed past her she felt a sudden charge of fear and a rush of blood through her heart, so much so that she nearly dropped her bag of provisions. She was still trembling when she walked through the gate to her home, trembling so much that the blood seemed to drain out of her face and Juse, who had also returned home, couldn't help but notice the paleness of her features under the rays from the veranda lamp. He reached for the lamp which hung suspended from a beam and turned the flame a little higher, to have a closer look at her. She looked ghastly under the flame.

"What happened?" he asked, trying to conceal his alarm.

"A rabbit . . . a rabbit . . . a . . . a . . ." stuttered Menika finding it difficult to explain what she felt.

"Well. What's wrong about a rabbit?" asked Juse slightly mystified.

"It . . . it . . . darted between my feet and . . . and . . . disappeared," said Menika still feeling her body tremble with a fear that she couldn't explain.

"Where did it happen?" asked Juse quietly.

"At the gate, just when I was walking through it."

"But surely, you don't have to fear a rabbit that darts between your feet?"

"I know. I know. But, but, I was still very frightened," said Menika, her words trailing to a whisper. "I don't know, I don't know why I should have been so frightened."

"Come Sudha" (darling), said Juse, slowly, as he relieved his wife of the provisions. "Let's go to the kitchen and have our meal."

He sensed at that moment that what his wife needed was solace and a chance to forget, not questions.

Before he went to bed that night Juse was a little perturbed and he could read the look of worry on his wife's face, although she didn't say anything. She seemed to carry out her duties of seeing that the children ate their rice and curry early, in a listless, half hearted manner. She hardly said a word as she gave him, too, his meal and stood by him till he finished. Finally, she ate herself, following the custom, by which she had her meal only after the rest of the household had eaten.

The unusual silence on the part of Ran Menika seemed to depress even the spirits of the children who hardly said a word between them as they ate. On any other occasion there'd generally be a babble of sound from the rickety table at which they sat opposite their father, mildly disputing with each other over something or other.

Juse felt the onset of a sudden uneasiness because of the unaccustomed silence. He was used to laughter and chatter from the children and the bright cheerful voice of his wife who had always something to tell him at dinner time about the village gossip or the antics of the children.

He tried to appear nonchalant. So rising from his seat he closed a window and then switched on the little transistor set which lay on another table. As the cheerful Sinhala music of Sarala Gee (light songs) filled the room with its rhythms, the oppressive atmosphere seemed to lift.

But the music of the radio brought only temporary relief. At eleven o'clock the announcer closed station for the night and the children had long since gone to sleep on their mats. The silence was disturbing. Apart from a "Yes" or "No" Ran Menika had hardly spoken a word. When she got to bed with her husband she moved close to him as if she needed all the protection he could give her.

It didn't take her long to fall asleep but for Juse, to whom sleep usually came quickly, it was different for once. He was worried about his wife's behaviour over the last two days. First she has a terrible dream about his death and then she allowed herself to become scared out of her wits by a rabbit. Try as he might he couldn't fall asleep.

He heard the wall clock in the room strike twelve midnight and with some pride realized that he was one of the few people in the village who could afford such a luxury. The heat in the room was almost unbearable. Not a breath of air stirred, though the window was open. At about half past one Juse found his lids getting heavier and then finally he dozed off

Suddenly, though, he was jolted awake by a fearsome scream. It was his wife. She had leapt out of the bed and was staring at her husband with a look of terror.

"The doll, the doll," she shouted wildly. "It came into my body. It came into my body."

Those were the last sensible words that Juse heard from her. Even as he watched her, all his senses alert, yet too shocked to do anything, she began to dance, oblivious of the fact that the cloth she wore round her body was falling to her feet.

It was the wild meaningless dance of a half naked woman who was and yet wasn't his wife. In the light of the moon which filtered through the open window she seemed like a marionette motivated by something other than her own self. She seemed in short, possessed.

For a few moments Juse was just rooted to his bed, watching the weird dance by his wife. No, a thing like this just couldn't happen to his Ran Menika of all people, who hadn't harmed a soul in all her life. But it was happening before his eyes in his very own bedroom. There was no mistaking her stupid, inane, disjointed movements, a hideous parody of a dance. He had seen something similar before when a relative of his had seemingly become possessed by a demon.

Something told Juse that the only remedy was a terrific shock to her system. So raising his hand he slapped her violently across her face. She ceased dancing, gazed at him with just an inkling of recognition and then realizing she was almost naked she bent down, retrieved her cloth and wrapped it round her body. Juse took hold of her hand and gently drew her to the bed. There was a vacant look in her eyes as she gazed towards the window and tears began to trickle down her cheeks. But she was once again, despite the vacant look, more or less, herself.

"What happened to you Menika?" asked Juse gently as the trembling of her body ceased.

"I had a bad dream."

"Again?"

"Yes. . . ."

"What did you dream?"

But Menika was silent as though reluctant to recall her experience.

"What did you dream?" asked Juse again.

Menika spoke at last with difficulty. "I dreamt that I was walking alone through our village. In the distance . . . I saw, I saw a cloth doll. It was made of cloth but yet, but yet, it was alive, and it was hideous to look at. It came walking fast, fast, right towards me and then it entered into my body and I screamed. I don't know what happened after that."

Juse was silent for a few moments, as though collecting his thoughts. Finally he said very quietly.

"Don't you know that you danced before me just a few minutes ago, half naked?"

"No," said Ran Menika, listlessly. "I don't know."

From that moment Juse wondered whether he would have to consult a Kattadiya or sorcerer, one of those who had mastered the art of exorcism, apart from many other accomplishments such as producing charms and talismans. But before he made a final decision he decided to wait another day and see whether the phenomenon happened again.

Juse's worst fears were to be confirmed and, unfortunately, the children were witnesses on the second occasion when their mother rose from her bed possessed by a demon power and began her strange and tortured performance. Very soon everybody in the village knew of what was taking place in the house of Juse. Many were secretly glad and hoped that it would not be easy to find a cure for the stricken woman. Prema and Marthelis, in particular, gloated over the fact that Ran Menika was ill.

"I hope she dances for the rest of her life," said Prema to her husband when she received the good news.

Marthelis chuckled. "Our Juse will have to spend a lot of money if he wants to cure his Menika," he said, "there are not many Kattadiyas as good as Malhamy."

Prema agreed. "I think we had better go tomorrow and pay him," she said.

Marthelis didn't reply immediately. Money was always a problem. "Do you think we can afford the thirty rupees?" he said at last.

"Don't worry," said Prema. "I've sold my old pair of earrings."

Marthelis was shocked. "What!" he exclaimed. "Your only pair of earrings?"

"Yes," said Prema. "It was worth the sacrifice."

As Marthelis looked at the large bony features of his wife's face, embittered and hardened by suffering, he knew better than to argue the point.

Meanwhile Juse Appuhamy acted quickly. He journeyed by bus to a village about sixty miles away from his own where he knew of a famous sorcerer called Siyadoris who was said to be even better than Malhamy, though not quite so affluent.

Now Siyadoris, unlike Malhamy was a thin, fair complexioned man with sunken cheeks and deep set thoughtful eyes. He was well known as a sorcerer who never used his knowledge of the occult to do evil. He lived in a humble little mud hut with a cadjan roof, bordering the main road, and the only other occupant was a youth about twenty-three years in age, who he called his Golea (pupil). This Golea assisted him in all his exorcism ceremonies. When Siyadoris heard Juse's story he was deeply concerned.

"Your wife does seem possessed by a demon," he said, as he squatted on his veranda, listening to the details. "But first let us chew on the beetle leaf. It will help us to think clearly."

Juse accepted the beetle leaf that he was offered and Siyadoris continued. "I can come to your house in about three days time," he said, "but meanwhile I want you to set up two altars made of tender coconut palms. In one of them you must put, on the night of the ceremony, offerings of rice and fruit and flowers. This will be the offering to the Deviyos (deities) who will help me in my efforts to drive the demon out. On the other altar you must have the offerings to the demon, that is, rice, cakes, and meat. Also buy a cock-bird for the occasion just in case the demon expects a live offering."

When Juse returned home that day he felt much easier in his mind. He had done all he could think of and it now remained for Siyadoris to drive out the demon who had brought misfortune on Menika. On the night of the ceremony, well illuminated by a petromax lamp, Ran Menika was laid on a mat in the garden, her head resting on a pillow, while Siyadoris commenced the overture to the ceremony.

Clad in a simple white banyan and a white sarong with a cylindrical drum slung from his shoulders he walked up to the altar dedicated to the benevolent spirits or deities, joined his palms together and intoned with bowed head, "May the blessings of the Deviyos (deities) attend this ceremony. May the demons be driven from the body of this sick woman."

With these opening words he intoned a few more verses in praise to the benevolent deities and then only began the ceremony proper. Returning to the centre of the clearing in which Ran Menika lay he beat the first clear rhythm on his drum. The rhythm was taken up on a much smaller drum by a local assistant whom he had hired for the occasion. Thus base and treble drums combined to produce the first weird rhythms of the Yak Natum (Devil Dance).

As the weird, yet deeply melodious, throb of the drums was

heard someone burst through the crowd of villagers, who had gathered to watch the ceremony, and with a great leap commenced to dance. This was the sorcerer's Golea or pupil who wore on his head a hideous wooden mask. Huge black eye-balls jutted out of the mask, painted garishly in red. From a gaping cavern of a mouth flanked by fierce looking tusks, white teeth projected. The nose was curved like the beak of a hawk. Above the head of the mask slender cobras, beautifully carved, wound their way upwards till their puffed hoods met in the centre. A white banyan, flouncing red skirt and white stockings from thighs to ankles completed the ensemble of the dancer.

Ran Menika meanwhile, lay on the mat, a sheet covering her up to the shoulders. Her lips seemed bloodless in the bluish light from the lamp and damp wisps of hair straggled over her face. Her eyes had sunk deep in their sockets and were gazing blankly at the dancer. A few solicitous relatives sat by her side fanning her with folded newspapers. These were the women, who, fortunately for Juse, had taken things over when they realized that Ran Menika was in no condition to attend to her daily work.

The dancer continued leaping to the rhythm of the drums. In one hand he held a glowing faggot which he waved about his body creating intricate lines of light as he danced. At intervals he threw some inflammable powder on the torch and great tongues of flame leapt skywards, flushing the darkness of the trees for an instant with amber.

At about two o'clock in the morning Ran Menika, who hitherto had been on her mat, gazing fixedly at the dancer, as though mesmerized by his movements, suddenly came alive. She leapt up from her mat, flung the sheet that covered her, aside, and stared with bloodshot eyes at the dancer.

Siyadoris, who as master of ceremonies had been watching everything, increased the tempo of his rhythm. Easter and faster he beat the drum until the tempo became a frenzy. The dancer became a whirling mass of movement, so fast that one could barely distinguish the outlines of his body.

Ran Menika, meanwhile began to tremble. She looked terror stricken at the crowd around her and tried to escape but immediately her relatives held her arms. Suddenly her body heaved. She struggled violently before collapsing in a swoon.

The dancer, too, at this moment was galvanized into a final

burst of movement which he kept up for almost ten minutes. Then spent he too heeled over. While he was still on the floor in his hideous mask, Siyador advanced towards him.

"Who are you," he asked the fallen dancer in a tone of authority.

"I am Kalu Kumara," said the dancer, in a voice which seemed peculiarly high-pitched.

"Kalu Kumara himself?"

"Yes. Kalu Kumara, the Black Prince, himself."

The onlookers gasped as they heard the reply, Kalu Kumara, they knew, was a demon of great power who generally tormented women. But Siyadoris was by no means awed. He was truly master of the situation.

"Have you left the woman?"

"Yes," said the high pitched voice, "but only for a moment."

"And now you possess the body of my golea?"

"Yes."

"Leave him, too. Leave the vicinity of the woman for good."

"No. I will not leave."

"Leave him immediately," shouted Siyadoris.

"No, no," said the voice, its high-pitched tone becoming almost a shriek. "I will not leave till you have given me an offering."

"What offering do you want? We have laid out rice, cakes and flesh for you on your altar. What more do you want.

"I want a live offering."

"Will a cock-bird suffice?"

For a moment there was silence, as dancer and sorcerer gazed at each other, one on the ground and the other standing menacingly above him. Finally the high-pitched voice said, "A young cock-bird will suffice."

"If we offer you a cock-bird," said the sorcerer, "what sign will you give us that you've left the vicinity of the woman for good.

"I will tear a branch off the Jak Tree in this garden."

The sorcerer gave a sign to Juse who had bought a young cock-bird for this eventuality. The bird was given to the dancer who with both hands held it aloft by the neck. The crowd surged closer. There was a moment of silence and then a collective gasp of horror as the dancer tore the bird's neck apart with his powerful hands, and dropped it on the ground. Someone picked up the bouncing cock-bird with the severed spinal column and took it to the altar of the demon.

A few minutes later there was an ear splitting sound and a huge branch of a Jak Tree in the garden crashed down to earth. The villagers scurried to avoid it. Meanwhile, the dancer too had fallen into a swoon and lay limply, limbs stretched out on the sand. The sorcerer sprinkled some water on his face and body and recovering, he rose slowly and pulled off the mask that he wore.

Ran Menika, too, had risen from her mat and from that moment onwards she began talking to Juse Appuhamy and all those who surrounded her as though nothing had happened. Among the many onlookers there were two people who were bitterly disappointed and furious at the successful outcome of the ceremony—Prema and her husband Marthelis.

Neither Juse nor his wife suspected the evil role that their neighbours had played in this grim affair. But when a week later Prema was found dead on her mat one morning by her husband, with a look of terror in her staring eyes, they began to wonder. It is a common belief in villages that when a person harnesses the aid of a demon, he or she runs the risk of death at the hands of this same demon, should their sinister purpose fail.

I AM A PSYCHIC DETECTIVE

by HORACE LEAF

IF you don't believe in ghosts—and of course you don't—I cannot expect you to believe in ghost laying, and I can hardly expect you to believe the amazing things I am about to tell you.

I shall not try to convert you. There was a time when I didn't accept such things, either.

All I ask you to believe is that I, Horace Leaf, Fellow of the Royal Geographic Society, earn my living by ghost laying, and that, in the process, I have actually had the experiences set down here.

If you will go that far with me, I think you will not regret it.

First, lest you think me utterly crazy, I should explain that this ghost-laying business was not my idea—that it was, as a matter of fact, forced upon me.

My friend the late Sir Arthur Conan Doyle was the one who first introduced me to the subject, although I had read, as you undoubtedly have, of the so-called occultists of the Middle Ages who claimed to be able to banish troublesome spirits by tracing circles or interlacing triangles on the floor of the "haunted" room.

Sir Arthur's ghost laying was of a more scientific nature, and was undertaken by him simply as part of his long experimentation with psychic phenomena. He had come to believe that what we call spirits were actually departed spirits who, for some reason, were chained to this earth, and that, once this spiritual chain was broken, they could cease to trouble either themselves or others.

It was not difficult for me to accept this theory. I had had the common experience of feeling that certain friends who had died under unusual or violent circumstances were frequently close to me. More difficult to believe was that a living person could get through to these restless spirits, talk to them, and free them from their bonds. Well, I did not have to wait long for a demonstration on this point.

You may have read in the papers of Conan Doyle's attempts to lay the ghost of Lenin. Some people living in a house in London where the Marxist dictator had once lived, found themselves—or, as you would say, *thought* they found themselves—haunted by his ghost.

Sir Arthur visited the house, and took with him the Rev. Vale Owen, a well known clergyman, and myself, both of whom he had found useful as instrumentalities in his psychical experiments.

No one was more surprised than I was when—quite contrary to my own intentions at the time—*I* laid the ghost of Lenin. At least I got the credit for doing so—and that credit, vouched for by Sir Arthur Conan Doyle, changed the whole course of my life.

I had never known there were so many people who were troubled with ghosts—beg pardon, who thought they were. Requests came in from all over the world, asking me to perform a service similar to that which I had apparently performed for those harassed Londoners.

At first I laughed at these epistles, and at myself. A ghost layer! That was good. But the number of them and the sincerity of them finally wore me down. I began experimenting with this alleged power of mine, and found that I could voluntarily give myself up to some other self whose gifts were quite different from my own.

I cannot explain what happens to me as clearly as I could wish, because I do not know much about it myself. But I am told by those who have listened to me under these conditions that I speak without a trace of the British accent normally mine, and in a mellow voice of distinctly Oriental quality, and that I use the terms "sahib" and "memsahib" instead of "sir" and "madam".

Make what you will of that!

The point is that year after year my reputation as a ghost layer has steadily increased, and that it has taken me all over the world.

I was not surprised, therefore, to find myself, in the late summer of 1931, in New Orleans, a guest in an eighteenth-century house which boasted, among other attractions, the loveliest ghost I have ever known.

The house itself was almost as beautiful as the beautiful girl who haunted it. It was situated in the picturesque Old French Quarter of the city. Its exterior was enriched by semicircular verandas with elaborate iron railings wrought by slaves. Its interior featured a noble marble staircase.

"I have dismissed my servants for the night," said my white-haired host, as he led me to a door which gave on a courtyard. "We shall not be interrupted."

"At least, not by living things," I said.

He laughed uneasily and switched off the electric lights. The great house was apparently in total darkness except for a flickering candle. Holding this high above his head, he bade me precede him into the courtyard.

It was a moonless, starless night. I was vaguely aware of vegetation, of leaves shimmering in the candlelight. Then all was still again, and black.

"I think," said my host, "that I owe you an explanation of the happenings which preceded the manifestations you are to observe tonight. My ancestors on my father's side came to what is now Louisiana with Ferrier. My mother's people arrived with Don Antonio de Ulloa in 1764. Some years later the man who built this house, a great-great-uncle of mine named Simon de Rouvroy, came over from Santo Domingo, and brought slaves.

"Among the slaves were a half-caste mother with two sons and a daughter. The father had been half Negro and half Spaniard; the mother was a mixture of Negro and French. The daughter, however, showed no signs of her African blood. Judging by her ghost, she was very beautiful. At sixteen she bore my uncle a child which he afterwards brutally murdered.

"The crime deranged the young mother and she soon died insane. There is every reason to believe that Simon had her strangled by a big slave called Julius in the room to which I am leading you."

"Is that where the manifestations occur?"

"You shall see. Come!"

I followed gropingly to a long row of former slave quarters. A door yielded to the turn of old Mr. de Rouvroy's key and disclosed an inner row of small rooms like cells, which had no windows—or, so far as I could see, any other ventilation.

"This little room," said my host, standing aside and bidding me enter the narrowest and darkest of them, "is where Juanita met her death."

"Juanita was the beautiful slave girl?"

"Yes. Her two brothers died here too."

"Of strangulation?"

"No. Simon didn't bother. He just chained them up and left them to suffocate. They haunt the place too. And so does Julius. We'll meet them all tonight. We'll see The Hand, too, or its work."

"The Hand?"

"Yes. One of Uncle Simon's favourite forms of torture was gradual mutilation of his victims."

By the faint light of the candle I observed that two chairs had been placed side by side in the centre of the narrow room, and that a handsome Japanese screen had been set up in one corner, with a gap between it and the wall wide enough for one person to pass through.

Now, frankly, I didn't like that screen. It savoured too much of magic and sleight of hand. My host must have sensed that I was a bit disturbed by it, for he told me that I would soon see the reason for it. Further to avoid suspicion, he handed me an ordinary writing pad and pencil, and asked me to place them behind the screen.

"The Hand," he said, "may wish to write."

Of course I used this opportunity to make a thorough examination of the wall. It was, you may take my word for it, unpleasantly solid. I was satisfied that the door through which we had come—and which, by the way, Mr. de Rouvroy had shut and locked after us—was the only entrance to the room.

Motioning me to one of the chairs, and seating himself in the other, he blew out his candle.

I do not know how long we waited in the darkness, but after what seemed like an interminable time, there was a noise as of people moving.

"They are here," my host remarked laconically.

He had barely uttered the words when from behind the screen there stepped one of the most beautiful women I have ever seen—slender, graceful, with a mass of lovely black hair which contrasted with her ivory skin. She was as white as the White Lady of Avenel. Her body had the allure of Aphrodite. If it is possible for a man of flesh and blood to fall in love with a ghost—and I am not at all sure that it isn't!—he might perhaps have lost his heart that night in Simon de Rouvroy's death cell.

I had a feeling the old Creole gentleman beside me was watching closely to see the effect on me.

"This is Juanita," he said pleasantly. "Juanita, let Mr. Leaf feel the texture of your hair."

To my amazement, the phantom form walked slowly up to me and, lifting a few strands of her hair, let them fall on my hand. Then, raising her long slender fingers, she threw me a kiss and receded behind the screen.

"Is that all we get of Juanita?" I asked.

I again had the feeling that my host was watching me closely and with a not too friendly eye. Could it be possible that he, old man though he was, had already fallen in love with the beautiful half-caste? But when he answered my question, it was with the usual disarming casualness.

"Don't worry, my dear sir. We shall see quite enough of her before the night is over. This is the anniversary of my uncle's crime—and there is always the devil to pay here on anniversaries. Perhaps—"

He stopped abruptly. Emerging from behind the screen was a giant Negro with the arms and hands of an ape. In a stride he had crossed the cell to where I sat, and was glowering threateningly down at me.

"This is Julius, the strangler," explained my host; and as he spoke, the figure—to my great relief—sank out of sight through the floor.

My attention was now attracted by a faint scraping behind the screen, as if someone was scribbling, not with a pencil but with a bad pen. My thoughts went at once to The Hand. A sheet of paper came fluttering over the screen and fell close to my feet. Mr. de Rouvroy relit his candle. I picked up the paper and tried to read the ill-formed Spanish words written on it. I could not, and my host again snuffed his candle.

As he did so, the cathedral clock struck eleven; and as the last throb died away, I heard weeping and moaning. Every now and then I also caught the faint jangle of chains, accompanied by sighs and groans.

"The brothers," he whispered. "It doesn't look as if they are going to get through tonight."

The more attentively I listened, the more distinct these sounds became. They seemed distant, or to come through a wall, but with a persistency that was most horrible, inured though I was to ghostly phenomena.

Whether this unearthly experience caused my imagination to run riot, I cannot be sure, but I could have sworn that I saw walking about the room a stoutish Spaniard with a fine-cut beard and fierce moustaches. In one hand he carried a whip and in the other a small knife. His eyes were preternaturally bright. The whole expression of his face was terribly malignant.

Mr. de Rouvroy said he did not see this apparition at all. When, however, I described it to him, he assured me that it coincided with his great-great-uncle.

For professional reasons, I should have liked to stay longer in the death cell. It was probable, I thought, that if I succeeded in laying the old butcher's ghost first, I should have no trouble laying the others.

His great-great-nephew, however, was now as impatient as if he had an appointment he must keep. Perhaps he had! Anyhow, he insisted almost crossly that it was time to go to bed. And indeed it was, for as we groped our way back across the courtyard, the clock in the cathedral tolled out midnight.

Once again in the main house, Mr. de Rouvroy offered me a Scotch-and-soda, which I declined. I had thinking to do, and I needed a clear head. The old gentleman did not press me. He seemed tired.

But as we approached the beautiful marble staircase, all his casualness dropped from him. His body became tense, rigid. With his free hand he clutched me to save himself from falling. Then, pulling himself together, he turned once again to the staircase. It was no use. He could not bring himself to set foot on those marble steps.

Finally I drew from him the reason. It was on this staircase, a hundred years ago that very night, that Simon de Rouvroy had snatched from the arms of his favourite slave girl their newborn son, dashed out its brains, and tossed its body to the floor below.

The telling of the story seemed to give him strength. Without further ado, he started to ascend the staircase. A little more than halfway up, he stopped and pointed to the broad rail. "It was here," he said in a hoarse voice, "that my uncle brained the baby."

As he bade me a rather stiff good night at the head of the stairs, he remarked with a quizzical smile:

"We shall see what we shall see."

I was in no mood for sleep. Several things had puzzled me. Mr. de Rouvroy had been at great trouble and some expense to bring me from London to Louisiana to rid his home of these restless spirits. Yet he seemed unmistakably to enjoy their presence and to be on the friendliest terms with them. Juanita had obeyed him implicitly. Even Julius, the strangler, had melted away at his first word. . . .

Suddenly there were terrific noises in the room adjoining mine. For a moment I wondered if my host, who seemed to have lost his taste for my company, was taking this odd way of unnerving me and driving me from his house. I did him an injustice. When I opened the door and ran out on the landing, he was already there, obviously as alarmed as I was.

"Even on anniversary nights there never—" He didn't finish that sentence.

Juanita—her face distorted with grief and fright her arms holding the bleeding body of her child—was ascending the stairs.

Her body was so transparent that we could see through it the stairs and balustrade. She passed so close to me that I could have touched her—but my arms hung helpless at my sides.

Unseeing, she glided across the landing and disappeared into the room whence the sounds had been issuing.

"My uncle's bedroom," the old gentleman managed to say, then tottered towards the stairs.

I think he would have fallen their length if I had not caught him firmly by the shoulders. He was very limp. His whole body seemed to have been drained of every bit of energy it possessed. Suddenly I knew what I should have known the moment that first spectre had appeared from behind the death-cell screen.

The nephew of Simon de Rouvroy was—without knowing it—a materializing medium!

Of course, if you don't believe in ghosts, you don't in mediums; but at least you know that there are people in this world who have the gift of making spectres *seem* to appear before the eyes of sensible people like yourself. You may rest assured that Mr. de Rouvroy was one of these people, and that—if you insist—he "fooled" me and "fooled" himself as I have described.

Personally, I believe, too, that this elderly aristocrat used his mediumistic powers—unconsciously of course—to bring these spirits out of their hiding places to make for him a ghostly holiday.

But that is neither here nor there.

If he had a sufficiently good reason for wishing to rid his

property of these phantoms, he would be quite willing to stay away and give me a free chance to labour with them.

Fortunately, he did have a very good reason for desiring to render his estate ghostless. He wished to sell his property, so that he might go to France to live in the land of his ancestors—a goal which, I am happy to say, I was able to help him achieve.

I'll wager, though, that he sometimes thinks fondly, perhaps regretfully, of the beautiful Juanita!

THE OLD LADY OF BATTERSEA

I suppose it will surprise you that one supernaturally gifted as a ghost layer—I can hear you laughing!—should need to go to a dentist.

But it happens that I cut two quite normal sets of teeth before I discovered that, under certain circumstances, I could "see things" that most other people could not see, and found myself—much to my surprise—earning my living by doing so.

It was while Basil Trencher, my dentist of many years' standing, was giving the second of those sets their semi-annual going over that he told me of the "haunted" house he owned in the Battersea section of London.

"You know, Leaf," he said, "that I am not a fussy man."

He had two hands, a mirror, and a pair of pliers in my mouth at the moment, so I said nothing.

"I shouldn't have minded a couple of well behaved ghosts in the old house," he continued, in a tone which showed that he didn't believe in ghosts any more than you do. "It was to be expected, I suppose, that a building so old, so sombre, and so sparsely occupied should be a prey to its past."

He laughed gaily.

"But, you see," he said, "I had a sort of branch office there, and what I objected to was having my patients continually falling downstairs—and then claiming that someone had pushed them!"

It was bad enough, he explained, when two angry females maintained that he himself had done the pushing. But the crisis arrived when a testy old gentleman, who had suffered a dislocated thigh, threatened to sue on the ground that he had been shoved by "an unseen hand."

At this point, Basil Trencher, who was a man of peace, decided to abandon the old three-story house on Queen's Road, and confine his practice to his principal office, in the fashionable region near Hyde Park.

Financially, the closing of the Queen's Road establishment meant little to the distinguished dental surgeon. Professionally, however, he had valued the wider experience it afforded him. Sentimentally, too, the place had a claim on him. The Trenchers had lived in the old house for generations, and a beloved uncle had left it to him.

There was also the practical problem of what to do with the property. It wouldn't have been readily leasable, anyhow, because of the Queen's Road traffic and the proximity of the railroad. But now, with the reputation it had acquired for accidents and bad luck generally, there was nothing that could be done with it in an income-producing way.

In fact, no one could be persuaded to live in it on any terms, except a faithful caretaker, who occupied the top floor.

"There is an atmosphere about the place," continued Trencher, "an eerie something which seems to hang like a cloud around it. I can't describe that exactly. It is something that is felt rather than seen."

This detail interested me more than anything else he had told me—"clouds" being among the most dependable signs of ghosts. "You feel this cloud yourself?"

"I do. In fact, now that I have cut my daily ties with the place, I have become increasingly unwilling to enter the house. Perhaps you had better go out yourself, Leaf, and try your spells on it."

Spells! I am no more of a spell caster than you are, my doubting reader. Perhaps not so much, for you may be a salesman or a musician or a writer for the cinema or an actor or a poet, whereas I am just a plain student of psychical research, who couldn't cast a spell if he wished to—and wouldn't if he could.

The only difference between my relations with so-called ghosts and some other people's is that I get along better with them. Ghosts behave very well for me! The reason, I have always thought, is that I do not think of them as hideous creatures stalking around in sheets, but as restless spirits prevented, for some unknown reason from getting away from this earth.

Far from casting spells over these poor distracted creatures, I try to reach them and talk to them and comfort them just as if they were living beings in distress, and help them, if I can, to break the unnatural bonds which tie them to a life in which they no longer have a place.

It was in this spirit that I continued my inquiry into the weird doings in the house in Battersea.

"And your old caretaker?" I asked. "Has she had any unfortunate experiences?"

"More than anyone else. This evening, if it is convenient for you, I will run you out to Queen's Road, and you can question her."

Shortly after ten he called for me at my rooms in a rakish high-powered sports roadster which he drove through the traffic with an abandon which was much more frightening to me than a hundred ghosts. Yet, when we pulled up at the old Queen's Road house, this man, who had just risked death a dozen times, was obviously afraid to enter the door of his own property.

"Mrs. Toms," he said to the stoutish middle-aged caretaker who answered the bell, "this is my friend Mr. Leaf, and he is to do anything he wishes."

With this wholesale certification, he was gone. And I must say that for a few moments after the door swung to, leaving the silent woman and myself in the darkness of the lower hall, the "cloud" to which Trencher had referred seemed thick enough to cut. I could see nothing. All I could hear was the caretaker groping in the shadows behind me.

At length she struck a match. The flame made little headway against the almost impenetrable gloom, but it apparently enabled Mrs. Toms' more accustomed eyes to locate two candles on a small table. She lit both of these, handed me one and took one herself.

"Have you no electricity or gas?" I managed to say.

"Only candles and lamps," she replied.

She seemed so taciturn that I thought it wise to break the ice with a thorough inspection of the premises before embarking on any campaign of inquiry.

The house was high-ceilinged, marble-floored, heavy-moulded, like many another in south London. The basement was given over to dining room and kitchen, now unused. The first-floor front had been the dentist's waiting room. Everything was as he had left it.

The first-floor rear was empty. Trencher had not used it. He preferred, so Mrs. Toms said, the better light of the second-floor rear, which was reached by the stairway that had caused so much trouble.

This staircase was somewhat more twisted than is customary today, but in no sense treacherous in itself. I examined it carefully by the light of my candle—creeping up slowly from one step to another. The treads were worn by many footsteps into an unevenness that should have retarded rather than accelerated a fall.

The second-floor front was a bedroom, now, of course, unused. Mrs. Toms made no move to show it to me.

The second-floor back was where Trencher had done his dentistry. It was from this room that his patients had emerged on to the landing whence, according to their testimony, they had been given the shoves which had sent then hurtling down the twisting staircase.

"It won't be necessary for me to intrude on your privacy right now, Mrs. Toms, so if you care to leave me alone for a while—"

The good lady needed no further hint, but bolted upstairs to her own quarters. I could hear a door slam and a key turn. Except for the flickering flame of my candle, I was alone in the darkness.

Now it was inevitable that my curiosity should centre on the one room which Mrs. Toms had not offered to show me—the second-floor front.

Here was the very s[illegible]t where Basil Trencher's patients claimed to have been pushed.

There was a closed door.

Was it possible that the person who did the pushing, whether living or dead, was hidden behind that door?

I groped my way along the wall by my candle's uncertain light. As I opened that door, it failed me altogether.

I didn't bother to relight it. There was enough light from the street to show me the room's contents—a high wooden bed stripped to the mattress, two straight chairs, an overstuffed chair, a worn carpet, and a huge dark-coloured tallboy, either walnut or mahogany, which stood like a gloomy sentinel opposite the windows.

On the tallboy, supported by a twisted metal holder, was a large unframed photograph of a very disagreeable-looking old woman—

without doubt, a former occupant of the room. In spite of the malignant expression, there was a distinct structural resemblance to the features of my friend Trencher.

Having satisfied myself on this point, I replaced the photograph, drew the blinds tight, pulled a chair to the centre of the room, and sat down to wait.

I may have waited half an hour. It seemed much longer. I tried to keep my mind on trivial things unrelated to the night's experience. It was natural, though, that my eyes should wander in the direction of that photograph, and that I should be acutely conscious that those sinister features were staring down upon me.

It was not natural, however—and I was quite unprepared for it—that the portrait, whose outlines I could just make out in the semidarkness, should suddenly rise in the air and fall with a thud on the top of the tallboy.

I had scarcely recovered from the shock of this bewildering occurrence when I perceived a cloud revolving slowly around the prostrate portrait, which forthwith rose to a vertical position and—well, of course, you won't believe me, but I must tell this as I saw it—and *seemed* to come to life.

I rubbed my eyes, to see if I was dreaming; then covered and uncovered them to make sure that the vision I saw was objective. I shall never forget the sneer on that old woman's face, the curl of the lips when they moved as if trying to speak.

"What is it you wish to say?" I asked.

Then clearly came these words:

"Get out of my house!"

Next moment the portrait fell at my feet.

Taking due account of the possibility of some illusion, I considered the strictly physical factors. My chair was a good ten feet away from the tallboy. It was hardly conceivable that the photograph, supposing that it had been simply shaken from its perch by a tremor caused by passing traffic, could have traversed that distance. When I again replaced it, I noticed that the top of the tallboy was covered with a thick coat of dust. The picture itself, and the arms of the chair in which I sat, had been in the same condition. The rest of the house, on the other hand, even to the steps of the stairs, had been scrupulously clean.

Mrs. Toms, I thought, does not open this door for herself any more than she does for me.

So I went up to her quarters.

"Have you a family living with you, Mrs. Toms?"

"I did have," she answered reluctantly.

It took time, but cautious inquiry elicited from her the information that she had spent eighteen years in this house as Trencher's caretaker. The first thirteen years were uneventful, even happy. Her husband remained healthy and steadily employed. Her two children, a boy and a girl, completed their schooling and became self-supporting. She herself waxed comfortably buxom. Then, suddenly, everything began to go wrong.

Her husband, who had never known a sick day in his life, contracted an incurable lung trouble of which he was even now dying in a near-by nursing home. Although this misfortune was in no way attributable to the ghost on the staircase or to the talking photograph, it was while the husband and father was being removed from the house on a stretcher the ghostly manifestations began. The boy, George, fell down the twisting staircase and broke his thigh. He still walks with a pronounced limp. The daughter, Gracie, fell down it just six months later, and has never since had the proper use of her left arm.

Both young people refused to live there any longer. For their mother's sake, however, they refrained for some time from suggesting that the house was haunted. It was only after a visiting friend of the family had tumbled down the same flight of stairs, and swore that she had been ruthlessly pushed by an invisible presence, that the daughter broke down and admitted that she, too, had been pushed.

Since then, Mrs. Toms said, no less than sixteen people had fallen down these stairs, and she herself had been saved by the narrowest of margins.

"Did you, too, feel that you were pushed?" I asked.

"I did."

"Why didn't you move away?"

"It was a good job here."

"Do you know of any tragedy that occurred in this house *before* all these mishaps began?"

"No, sir. The Trenchers were very quiet people—not only Mr. Basil, sir, but his aunt—"

We had come down now, and were again on the fateful second-floor landing. Although I could not see her face, I distinctly felt that Mrs. Toms had just caught herself up sharply, as if she regretted her mention of Basil Trencher's relative.

"This aunt you speak of—was she a Miss Trencher?"

"Yes."

"Does she live here?"

"She doesn't live anywhere. She's dead. About five years ago, she *was* run over, crossing the road outside the house."

"Five years, you say? Was that before or after your husband's first illness?"

"Before—but why do you ask all these questions? Miss Trencher was a nice old lady. She couldn't have anything to do with the hauntings. She *couldn't!*"

I ignored her protest. "In which room did she sleep?"

I could feel rather than see her eyes turn involuntarily towards the closed door to the second-floor front.

"Shall we go in?" I said, just to test her.

She made no reply, and no move. Holding my candle well above my head, I advanced alone towards the door. As I was about to take hold of the knob she shrieked:

"Don't do it! Don't go into that room! You don't know what might happen! She's a fiend, that old woman!"

Fiend? Old woman?

Not a "nice old lady" after all!

Good Mrs. Toms had evidently been restrained by a combination of household loyalty to her Mr. Basil and desire not to stir up the ghostly occupant of the second-floor front. Now, however, the dam was down. Hate, fear, and candour flowed from her like a torrent.

Old Miss Trenchard, in whose room I had had my extraordinary experience, had been an evil termagant, hated by all, especially by those who knew her best. Her habits were intolerably dirty, her behaviour indicative of heavy secret drinking. At her worst, her temper waxed so violent that no one dared approach her.

Chief anathema to her hate-distorted mind was nephew Basil. Up to the time of her death she had held her hatred somewhat in check, presumably because she was totally dependent on his charity. After death, she had seemed still to be somehow in awe of him, for she had made no direct attack on him.

Apparently, though, she had made up her mind to drive him

and all other occupants from the building—and was jolly well succeeding in doing so.

By now I was thoroughly convinced that I had found the ghost that must be laid. All that remained for me to do was to win the confidence of that malevolent old woman in the talking photograph.

The task proved far simpler than I had hoped.

From the old lady's own lips I learned that she was unable to find peace because she had died with a grievance. Slightly mad, she had felt that the Queen's Road house, law or no law, belonged to her and not to her nephew, and she was determined that he should never live in it or otherwise enjoy it.

When I convinced her that he thought so little of it that he had no intention of ever crossing its threshold again, she threw me a look of intense relief and straightway disintegrated.

I know you will not believe that I actually talked with this evil ghost, or that such a ghost ever existed. But the fact remains that all those people did fall downstairs, and that all of them claimed they were shoved by a hand they could not see—and that after I had finished with the occupant of the second-floor front no further falls occurred!

A FULL HOUSE

My acquaintance with Mr. Godfrey Kent went back over many years, but always, until he walked into my office in London to consult me, we had met only between the pages of his delightful books, which are as well known on your side of the Atlantic as on mine.

"Just how do you go about laying a ghost?" he asked as he settled himself in one of my office chairs.

"My work," I said, "doesn't describe very well. I would much rather demonstrate it."

"I appreciate the difficulty," he replied. "But do you work as a magician or as a normal human being?"

I did my best to keep back a smile.

"Not a magician, surely—and not always, I suppose, as what you would call a normal human being. Sometimes the normal senses are enough. Many gentle apparitions, for instance, I can talk to—"

"You talk to them?"

"Why, yes. That's all there is to ghost laying, really: talking to these poor souls, finding out from them just what is binding them against their wills to this earth."

"You talk to them as you are talking to me?"

"That's the point. Sometimes, as I was saying, I can make myself understood in my own personality. Sometimes I have to have the help of a second personality working through me. You believe, don't you, that we all have two personalities, the one we normally use and the one which we could use if we had the power —as I seem to have—to summon it?"

"I know something of that theory," he said. "My old friend Conan Doyle used to talk to me about it."

"You had a good teacher. He was my friend, too."

"I know. That's why I am here. That's why I am asking you to come down to Hertfordshire with me."

In a quarter of an hour we were weaving our way in his big car through the streets of Greater London.

It was as I had thought. Life was being made intolerable for the author and his entire household by noises which they had tried in vain to account for.

As is usual in such cases, the servants were at first suspected. In fact, the most persistent of the disturbances had been traced from the room in which they habitually originated along a passageway and up to the servants' quarters on the next floor. Several people had heard footsteps ascend the stairs to the door of the butler's room, and had distinctly heard the latch rattle.

Far from denying the testimony of these persons, the butler acknowledged that he too had heard the footsteps, seen the latch move, and on one occasion actually observed the door swing open. He hadn't mentioned the matter at the time, for fear of losing his position. Now, however, the poor man had begged and received permission to sleep in the village. But during his absence the disturbance had continued.

That was as much as my host had told me when we rolled up to the Elizabethan mansion which the Kents had recently purchased.

"Please take me at once to the room," I said.

"Mrs. Kent's sewing room and study," he informed me, throwing open a door at the end of the main hall.

Both that night and the next I spent alone in that room. During neither was there anything to see or hear. But I have learned to be patient.

With me on the third evening was my friend the Reverend Mr. Vale Owen, who accompanied Sir Arthur Conan Doyle and me when he laid the ghost of Lenin, and who is himself possessed of recognized psychic powers.

We had no sooner drawn the blinds, put out the lights, and settled ourselves in easy chairs than we began to have "goose flesh". A damp chilliness gradually pervaded the room. Owen felt only the lowering of the temperature and the eeriness which naturally accompanies strange supernormal phenomena; but my limbs slowly stiffened until I had to take care not to pass into a state of complete catalepsy.

Presently we heard a number of faint taps, which seemed to come from a bookcase standing opposite the window. The taps became distinct knockings. I went to the door. There was no one there. So I went back to my chair, and tried to visualize the sort of person who was making these weird noises.

What followed was a complete surprise to me. As we sat there silently in the darkness, we were soon aware of a dim phosphorescent light shining halfway between us, which grew gradually brighter until it illumined the whole room. Out of this light there stepped a charming old lady of seventy or seventy-five, dressed in the ultra-feminine costume of the first half of the eighteenth century. Her snow-white hair was partially covered by a cap of the most delicate lace. From her eyes and lips came the gentlest of smiles.

"Who are you, madam?" my companion asked.

"A former inhabitant of this house."

"What brings you here?"

"Oh, I always visit here when I wish to."

"It must be you, then," I interjected, "who walk along the passage outside and up the stairs to the corner room on the next floor."

"I always go that way," she said. "This room was my bedroom, and the room upstairs was the nursery."

With that, she vanished. Soon, however, we again heard her

voice. This time she mentioned her name, Lady Matilda Dudley, and reiterated that she had during her lifetime tenanted the house —a statement which we subsequently found to be true.

I asked her to promise never to visit Mr. Kent's house again. If ever there was an indignant ghost, it was that old lady!

"I shall do nothing of the sort," she retorted. "I owned this house before he did, and I shall come here when I like. If any one is to get out, it must be he."

"I am sure," I said, "that he would have no objection to your coming here whenever you wished, Lady Matilda, if it makes you happy to do so. What he wishes to be spared is the noise of your nightly progress from this room along the passage and up the stairs."

Her manner changed instantly from anger to concern. As I had suspected, she had not been aware she was causing any uneasiness. She promised that her future visits would be noiseless.

I made no further effort to lay this gentle ghost. Somehow, I felt—and my feeling, I am glad to say, was justified by subsequent events—that Matilda Dudley was the kind of ghost that would keep her word.

We sought our host to receive his congratulations.

He looked sceptical. "A woman, you say?"

"Yes; and she has promised not to—"

I never finished that sentence.

A shriek like that of a dying man rent the atmosphere. More shrieks followed, and groans; they came apparently from a cellar under the main stairway.

"That must be Curtayne!" exclaimed Mr. Kent.

"Curtayne? Have you more than one ghost here?"

"I didn't think so. But, frankly, the ghost I was expecting you to find was a man."

These cries we had just heard, he said, did not occur so frequently as the sound of steps in the corridor, and had been accepted as simply another manifestation of the same troubled spirit. The story he now told us will doubtless seem to you unbelievable. When finally convinced against his will that the disturbances which were driving him and his household to desperation were supernormal, he had sought out the well known medium Mr. Vout Peters. He had told Peters nothing. He had even concealed the whereabouts of the estate by a night motor ride from London. Then, still basically sceptical, he had awaited results.

The famous psychic did not succeed in laying the ghosts. That isn't his business. But he did tell Kent that his fine old mansion had played an important part in the Civil War of the seventeenth century which resulted in the beheading of Charles I. On one occasion, Petérs insisted, a young Cavalier of King Charles' army had been tracked to the cellar under the main stairway and brutally slaughtered by the Roundheads.

Furthermore, the medium declared that the body of the murdered man had been buried close to an old wall bordering the estate, but that this wall had since been knocked down and all trace of the grave lost.

The last statement impressed Kent, as he already knew from old plans of the property that there had been such a wall. Further research disclosed that the medium had also been right about the murder of the young Cavalier, Rupert Curtayne by name.

"Is there an entrance to that cellar from this floor?" I asked.

"Yes. Under the stairs."

He led me to it, and I descended, with my candle, through a trap door into the dungeonlike hole from which the shrieks were again issuing. From the odour that assailed my nostrils, I could well believe that the dead man's remains were still rotting there. However, I encountered nothing more terrifying than his astral body—which appeared almost immediately, garbed in the torn but still gay costume of the Cavaliers.

There was nothing vindictive about this spiritual manifestation, either. The owners of the mansion in Curtayne's time had given him sanctuary. He bore no grudge against the present occupants of the house. He was simply chained, presumably by the brutal circumstances of his death, to the scene of it. In short, Rubert Curtayne's gentle ghost was as desirous of getting away as I was to have him. Therefore I had no difficulty at all in laying it to the satisfaction of Kent—whose relief and that of his household was touching.

"Thanks to you," he said, "my family and I are to have our first good night's sleep in months."

The words had scarcely passed his lips when there came from the drawing room on the right of the main hall a sharp explosion, like the report of a pistol.

Still another ghost in this historic country house?

"Have you heard that before?" I asked.

"Many times—but never in the same evening that I heard the cries from the cellar. Naturally, I thought it was the same ghoulish creature manifesting himself in different ways. Is it possible, Mr. Leaf, that the laying of one ghost might—what shall we say?—automatically release another?"

I told him that, according to psychical research, it was distinctly possible.

"What are you going to do about it?" Mr. Owen asked.

"I am going to interview the one in the drawing room."

Whereupon I persuaded my companions to go to bed as they had planned, and disposed myself to await developments. None came that night. But on the next night I was rewarded by a most startling experience.

Without warning, there stepped straight out of the table in the centre of that stately room a handsome young dandy dressed in frilled habiliments. My candle had long since gone out. There was, however, enough moonlight in the room to illumine his eyes, which gleamed maliciously at some unseen foe.

The young man was very angry. His lips moved rapidly but gave forth no words. He was evidently defending himself against the accusations of invisible accusers. I got the impression that he had been cheating at some game and had been caught at it.

For several moments I could not make out any of the persons with whom he was arguing. Then two of them came into view. One, a big florid man who bore a strong resemblance to the young dandy, was talking as fast as he. The other was a small timid-looking old fellow who seemed to be trying to reconcile the two.

The peacemaker might have succeeded if the dandy hadn't raised his hand to his sword's hilt. The big man thereupon whipped out a long pistol and shot him dead.

On the sound of the shot, the scene faded out.

Later inquiry disclosed that the death of the young dandy had actually occurred in that room in precisely that manner. He had quarrelled over a game of cards with his own father, William John Ransome, and the older man had shot him in self-defence.

Meanwhile I had a feeling that the ghost would reappear. It

did—but not in objective form. The young gambler did not stand before my eyes. Believe it or not—and you probably won't—his spirit entered my body. It spoke through my lips. Foul blasphemy, oaths that I had never heard poured through them as I vowed vengeance on him who had shot me. Through no will of my own, I was participating in an incident which must have happened in the last half of the seventeenth century.

Then, as suddenly and inexplicably as it had come, the spirit which possessed me took its departure. I was once more plain, unfrilly, unprofane Horace Leaf of the twentieth century, engaged —albeit, at the moment, none too successfully—in my business of ghost laying.

What had happened was nothing unusual. Students of the psychical are convinced that ghosts frequently take possession of the body and mind of the person who is trying to master them.

In this instance, as soon as I had dispossessed myself of the spirit, I was able to rid the drawing room of hauntings as completely as I had the cellar.

It was a more difficult job, however, because this young gambler was a very difficult ghost!

THE INCUBUS

Of all a professional ghost layer's critics, none is so severe as the average doctor.

Imagine my surprise, therefore, when a note came to me from my old schoolfellow, Dr. Stanley Thwaites, the famous Harley Street nerve specialist:

> With this I am sending you my patient, Major C. Eversleigh Calthrop, V.C., O.B.E., late of the 7th Fusiliers. I have been treating him for delusions, but the incisions in his flesh are—well, I do not know what to think they are. Perhaps he is more in your line than he is in mine. Anyhow, better have a look at him.
>
> Yours sceptically,
>
> Stanley Thwaites.

"Show the Major in," I said.

I confess I was surprised. For Eversleigh Calthrop was not the type one would suspect of thinking he saw ghosts. Tall, erect, broad-shouldered, India-tanned, he was the picture of all that a retired military man of fifty-five should look and be.

"Thwaites is the one who is having delusions," I thought to myself.

On closer inspection, however, the Major betrayed unmistakable signs of severe nervous strain. There was no doubt about it: this once doughty soldier, who had acquitted himself with distinction in the guerrilla warfare of the Far East and who had won his Victoria Cross in the dark days on the western front, was badly frightened.

He had lived since his retirement at Richmond on Thames, in a quiet respectable inn. Life had moved serenely for him and for its other occupants, gentlefolk like himself, until the previous year, when they had been joined by a new lodger, very rich, very ignorant, very old, and so dirty and malodorous that they finally served notice on the proprietor that the newcomer must go.

The old man went, but not without vowing vengeance on Major Calthrop, whom he had singled out, probably with justice, as the ringleader of the movement against him. A few days later, the angry old man committed suicide. That was seven months before this visit.

Of those months, the Major now told me his story. He would no sooner turn out the light, he said, and get into bed than he would be aware of a great staring evil eye peering insolently down at him out of the darkness. Each night it grew bigger, more malicious; yet always it was the eye of the dirty old man. At first, if he closed his eyes, he shut it out. Later on he seemed to see it whether he closed his eyes or not. He could not escape.

One night, lying there in a cold sweat with his evil eye upon him, he thought he observed an eerie white mist revolving rapidly close to his chest. At the same moment he felt a curious drawing sensation about his heart, as if energy were being sucked out of him.

"Every night after that," he whispered, "the cloud appeared. Then suddenly, one night, the cloud burst, and out of it peered the head of a human ape."

He covered his eyes with his hands.

"Was there any resemblance," I prompted, "to the former lodger?"

"That's it, Mr. Leaf, that's it!" he almost shouted. "It was an ape—but it was the old man!"

One night he woke to find, to his horror, that the creature was in bed with him. With the strength of desperation, he pummelled and kicked it until it seemed to fade away into nothingness. But night after night it returned. Finally it brought along a sickly white animal resembling a small bear, which seemed to have no body, only a head and a large mouth.

In my professional experience I had heard many weird tales, but none which so taxed credulity as this. The man's obvious sincerity, however, as well as his reputation as an officer and a gentleman, precluded the possibility that he was trying to hoax the doctor and me. There seemed, therefore, to be only one plausible explanation: Major Calthrop was insane.

He must have read my thoughts, for he hastily bared his neck and chest and revealed the small red marks which had so puzzled Thwaites. There was no doubt that they had been caused by sharp teeth.

Was it possible that I had to deal, not with a mere ghost, but with some ghostly vampire?

"Any other evidence of this character?" I asked.

"Yes, but not here. I should be glad to show you footprints, if you care to come to the inn."

"At what hour do these apparitions appear?"

"About eleven o'clock."

"I will come tonight before eleven," I assured him.

The situation was alarmingly complicated by my doubt as to the Major's sanity. To be sure, he had not dreamed those marks on his neck and shoulders; but he might have acquired them in some way not at all connected with such apparitions as he described. I did not fear ghosts, even human apes with hair all over their faces and bodiless white bears, half so much as I did a crazy man who might leap at me in the dark and destroy me in his mad frenzy.

Altogether, my ride to Richmond in a taxicab was attended with forebodings. Major Calthrop was waiting for me on the steps of the inn. In the dim light of the porch lamps, the ravages of fear and despair were deeply written on his twitching face.

The house itself, however, was unexpectedly reassuring, entirely matter-of-fact. There was nothing unusual, either, about the stairway up which the Major led me. His room was not exactly cheerful, but its stiff spick-and-spanness was no setting for horrendous doings.

My doubt of the man's sanity was growing at every step. Then my eyes caught the ghostly imprints of which he had spoken. They were very faint. A casual glance would not have distinguished them from the pattern of the wallpaper. But there were literally hundreds of these pawlike marks, with dinstinct five-toe impressions. They were especially numerous on the wall at the head of his bed. Several of them, apparently the most recently made, were covered with a dark red substance which I was able to scratch off with my fingers.

"My blood," the Major said simply.

"Do these creatures attack you only in bed?" I asked.

"At first that was so. Now they follow me all over the room."

"That being the case, Major, I will ask you to sit here."

I drew a straight-backed chair to the centre of the floor. Then I drew from my briefcase several ordinary Chinese joss sticks. Two of these I lighted and handed to my host, who had silently taken his position as instructed.

"You will please hold one in each hand," I said.

Without question he obeyed. Whereupon I pulled the heavy window drapes and plunged the room into darkness. Then I groped my way to a seat against the wall near the electric-light switch.

The joss sticks were for defence against the Major, not against ghosts. If he was indeed a madman, he might attack me in the dark. So long as he held the lighted sticks in his hands, I would be sure of his whereabouts. If he dropped them, I could turn on the light.

For a long time we sat thus. Then he whispered:

"Do you see anything?"

"No," I said.

"You will. I feel that sensation I told you about."

You will have to take my word for it that everything else I tell from now on is exactly as I saw and heard and experienced it. A dim phosphorescent cloud seemed to form between us. At first it was small and swirling and near the Major's breast, but it rapidly grew larger.

"You see that?"

I did not have time to answer. Even as he spoke, the cloud swung suddenly around and I saw distinctly the dark hairy head he had described to me.

The joss sticks in the Major's hands were trembling now. Suddenly he dropped them and sprang to his feet with a blood-chilling shriek.

Next moment he was upon me. I thought he had lost his reason and was attacking me. Then I saw all too clearly the cause of his distress. Towering over us was the figure of a stout man. One coarse dirty hand was clenched in a gesture of hatred. The other brandished a thick walking stick. The face—and this was the most terrifying thing of all—was the face of the giant ape that had sprung from the cloud.

"Save me! Save me! This time he will kill me!"

As the Major spoke, the horrific creature deliberately raised its cudgel and brought it down in the direction of his head. I turned on the light.

The threat seemed so real, the peril so imminent, that I expected to hear the crash of the club on the Major's skull, but I heard nothing; and if he felt anything, he gave no sign. He made no effort to move from the position into which he had flung himself. His arms were rigid around my neck, his body a dead weight. He was whimpering like a frightened baby.

Finally I roused him. The apparition had disappeared with the turning on of the electric light, but it was evidently still in the room. We both heard dull thuds like the thumping of a heavy stick on the floor.

In spite of these portentous sounds, however, the soldier in Eversleigh Calthrop soon reasserted himself. We picked up our joss sticks and prepared for our second vigil.

This was to be brief. I had no sooner switched off the light than I felt something soft brush against my left leg, and heard what seemed like a small soft body squirming slowly across the room in the direction of the hapless Major, who seemed to have lost consciousness. Leaning forward to rouse him again, I was startled to hear a low growl. In the glow from the fallen joss sticks

I distinctly saw the shadowy form of a small shapeless slimy white animal, about to spring.

I don't mind saying I was at my wits' end. What should I do? The Major settled the question by leaping to his feet with a scream of pain. I could hear him staggering around the room like a drunken man. Then he lurched heavily against me—and we fell together to the floor.

Freeing my right arm, I ran my hand over his body until I felt the slimy pelt of a small hairy animal with its face buried in his neck. There was no question now about the ghost's having materialized in the loathsome form of a deadly vampire.

It was out of the question for me to rise and find the electric switch. The heavy body of the Major had fallen on my left arm and pinned my whole left side to the floor. But I was prepared for just such an emergency.

From my pocket I pulled a small electric torch. Pressing the button, I turned its light full strength on the head of the incubus. The creature let go its hold on the Major's neck and swung around on me. But the bright light proved too much for it. With one growl, it fell to the floor, where it disintegrated and left no sign of its visible existence.

At this point there came a loud and peremptory knocking on the bedroom door. The effect on the Major was immediate. Once more he won my admiration by getting up manfully and walking resolutely to the door.

Outside, backed by a half dozen badly frightened guests, stood an angry—and also frightened—proprietor. To his demands for an explanation of the uproar, my good Major replied with dignity and poise, and not a little ingenuity, that we had been "rehearsing a play".

It took me six weeks to lay the ghost. During all of that time I spent part of every night in the room where first he and then he and I together had had the encounters with his strange and terrifying guests. The reason for the long delay was a simple one. I couldn't persuade the spirit of the vindictive old man to go away until I could show him that his victim no longer feared him, and that vengeance was no longer his.

THE MAN THEY COULDN'T HANG

by JUDGE MARCUS KAVANAGH

THE events hereafter narrated I consider more remarkable than any other in the world's record of criminal prosecutions. They will leave etched into the reader's mind an ineradicable wonder.

Of what does a condemned man think when he is standing on the trap, his arms pinioned behind him, and his knees belted together? And when the black cap is drawn down over his face so that all the old world in which he has dwelt those many years—that gruff, rough old world which has so buffeted him, but which upon his leave-taking he finds he loves so terribly—at that last instant what does he wonder about and what questions sweep through his groping, bewildered soul?

So far as I can find out only one man in history has ever been able truthfully to inform us of this, and that man was John Lee of the village of Babbacombe, which place lies over two miles from Torquay and under the high rocky shores of Devon.

The events suggested in the foregoing suppositions actually happened to Lee on February 24, 1885. After that he never ceased talking about them until a natural death ended all his recollections in the autumn of 1929.

Through these forty-four years there ensued not one night that, in a cold sweat, he did not start from his sleep trembling and out of some vivid dream in which he endured again that awful hour. He lived its agony again and again in his waking thoughts.

John Lee was born in Glamoray, Devon. His parents were very poor people. His father died when he was young. He seemed a little "queer" to many. A homeless person with a bit of mental twist lives separated by a high wall from the rest of the world.

Always Lee was slight of build, dark-faced, restless-eyed, morose, and world-hating. Were he hailed today before an American court for any offence, the judge probably would at once send him to a psychiatrist. Somewhat shrinking and cowardly, too. Maybe that was the reason why he never dared but once to stray far from the rocky shores about Devon.

Nevertheless at the age of sixteen the lad went into the navy, but was disqualified for illness after a short service. He turned rapacious. It is no wonder that before long he ran into the police.

Mrs. Keyes, a wealthy elderly woman, lived at Babbacombe. This woman occupied a pretty cottage nestling against the hills, within call of the beach. She employed as a cook Elizabeth Harris, a step-sister of Lee and, except their mother, his only living relative.

Notwithstanding the two had never been over-friendly, the step-sister took pity on his wretchedness and prevailed upon her mistress to take him in as a butler. This she did in January, 1883. Not many months went by before Lee's predatory tendencies floated to the surface. He stole a guitar from his employer's house and sold it. His mistress set out to discharge the ungrateful fellow and started to tell him so, but he cried and pleaded, seemed so wretched and helpless, that she relented and kept him in her service, punishing him, though, by deducting from his wages until the instrument was paid for.

It is curious, when one comes to think about it, how often fate picks on some out-of-the-way spot for a stage upon which to exhibit world-stirring criminal phenomena. In the events about to be related it will prove inexplicable how an insignificant, unworthy, friendless individual like John Lee could invoke an invisible, mysterious, impalpable force against which all the power of British law and British authority should fall helpless.

But this happened, beyond all question. On the night of November 14, in the year 1884, fate settled on the lovely hidden village of Babbacombe for a crime of such unexcelled cruelty and ferocity that next day every newspaper in Britain vibrated its horror.

It appeared that this Mrs. Emma Ann Keyes, a lady of high connection, admired and respected for her goodness and charity, had been found by her servants at daylight, fully dressed, lying upon the floor, hacked to death. The assassin also had attempted to burn the dwelling.

There appeared no attempt at robbery and no discernible motive for the crime. Besides its mistress, the family consisted of Jane and Eliza Neck, two sisters who had been servants in the cottage forty-one years; Elizabeth Harris, the cook, step-sister of John Lee; and John Lee himself. Not one of these claimed to have heard any sound during the murder. The police at once proclaimed the crime an inside job. In a few days John was arrested.

The evidence of his guilt, when accumulated, seemed absolutely conclusive. The recital of the incriminating facts would be outside the purpose of this story.

Sufficient to say that no one who read the newspaper accounts or who was at all conversant with the widely known circumstances believed Lee innocent. The evidence of his half sister helped put the noose around his neck. He stood without a friend on earth, deeply execrated and actively hated through the length and breadth of south England.

He was brought before a magistrate at Torquay, and, after a hearing before the magistrate, was remanded to Exeter for trial. He was then twenty years old.

The next assize was held at Exeter on February 2, 1885. The trial took place on the 16th of that month. During the hearing Lee sat, one knee crossed over the other, curious and impassive as any spectator. He was vigorously defended, but paid small attention to his lawyer. As one damning fact piled on top of the other, as witness after witness pointed deadly fingers to the dock, he sometimes smiled. Occasionally he turned to his guards to say, "I didn't do it. They can't hang me."

When his own turn came, Lee made a bad witness for himself, although stoutly maintaining his innocence. The jury was out only forty minutes and returned a verdict which meant death. Even when the judge put on the black cap and bade Lee arise for sentence, the condemned stood up stiffly, quietly, and unmoved, and faced the judge.

"Prisoner at the bar," said the court, "you have been convicted of one of the most cruel and barbarous murders in all the annals of crime. You have three weeks of life left to you. No power on earth can save you. I adjure you to spend these few days in preparation for meeting your God and your Maker, to whom you must make answer. You will be taken hence to the prison from whence you came, you will be there safely detained till the twenty-fourth day of this month, and you will then be taken by the sheriff of this county to some safe and convenient place and hanged by the neck until you are dead. And may God have mercy on your soul!"

A deathly hush in the courtroom followed. To the surprise of everyone, Lee broke the silence. His clear voice, unmoved, unafraid, answered the judge:

"My lord, you have wondered at my calm demeanour through the trial. It is only right that your lordship and all the people should understand why I am so unmoved. I will tell you why. I am innocent. The Lord on high knows I am innocent. He will never permit me to be executed. He has told me not to be afraid, and I trust Him."

Ordinarily, to look any certain misfortune steadily in the face as it approaches for an appreciable period dims to a great degree its terror. Soldiers realize how, after a time, the fear of bullets diminishes. To lie in one's bed with the knowledge that one's end is a certain coming event, and to wait, fumbling the sheets and staring at the ceiling through long days and pain-ridden nights, often creates a wish for a more sudden consummation. Time drags terribly. That is an experience many of us will have to go through, however.

It is different with the doomed assassin. To realize, as the convicted felon does, that inevitably in a certain spot, at a fixed hour of the clock, on an arranged day near at hand, he shall face an ignominious destruction, makes the sudden days gallop with incredible velocity. The dread of the rope about their necks is why so many murderers attempt suicide.

However, John Lee evidenced not the slightest apprehension. No visitor came to the cell except the prison chaplain. These visits came to their end always in an argument, the clergyman striving to make the prisoner realize the certainty of his doom and the convict refusing to accept that realization. The execution was set for eight o'clock on the morning of the 24th.

Two or three days before that the executioner and his staff came down from London and erected the scaffold in an old coach house which stood in the prison yard.

On the very night before the time of Lee's proposed execution, the chaplain said to him:

"Have reason, John. There isn't the slightest chance for the Home Secretary to commute your sentence. No one is asking him to. You haven't a single friend in the universe except God. Let's you and me get on our knees and prepare for you to meet Him."

The confidence of Lee towered serene and immovable as Mont

Blanc. "I never in all my life saw anyone as stubborn as you are, parson," he retorted. "Haven't I told you He has promised that I would not be hanged? Do you think He's going to break His promise? What does the Home Secretary amount to alongside of Him?"

It had rained heavily for several days and yet the morning of the execution saw the narrow streets of the ancient city of Exeter thronged with visitors. There was nothing an outsider could see. The scaffold stood in the coach house in the prison yard, altogether invisible from the street. And yet, impelled by that inexplicable, morbid feeling so common to humanity, hundreds waited for hours, only to catch a glimpse of the black flag which is hoisted over the prison as a sign that the judgment of the law is satisfied.

There was an added attraction on this occasion. Berry, the famous—or, if you like, the infamous—executioner, had come down from London a few days before and had slept in the jail. There might ensue a glimpse of him.

Berry, unobserved by Lee, had watched the convict in his cell and made a mental note of his height and weight. Then the hangman, as was his custom, constructed a dummy of about the same proportions. He experimented with this lay figure that evening. Now there is no doubt of this. Witnesses still live who can testify to it. The trapdoor and all the ghastly apparatus worked perfectly.

The next morning, after breakfast, Lee, his pipe still in hand, rose startled when the officials in charge of the awful ceremony appeared suddenly at his cell door. Berry on these occasions was all for haste. He boasted that two minutes of preparation sufficed.

Before the culprit realized, he was thrust into the midst of a little procession in the hall, his arms strapped to his sides. The governor of the jail, with two warders, stood at the head. Lee with the chaplain came next, the latter chanting the litany for the dying. Close behind them Berry and two assistant hangmen followed.

The procession moved slowly down the corridor towards the exit, across the cobbled yard into the coach house, where the gallows stood and where a small party of invited spectators waited at its foot. As they came in, the officials responded to the litany, Berry answering loudest.

And now let Lee himself tell what followed, as he often afterwards related over the bar at his public house or from his improvised pulpit in the latter days when he turned evangelist.

"Well, sirs," he would say, "as we stumbled along down the corridor past the other prisoners in their cells, the words of the litany kept knocking inside my heart; but I wouldn't join answering them, for, you see, I knew I wasn't going to die and it was inappropriate.

"Then, too, the noise from the street outside the walls dazed me a bit. It was like the rise and fall of waves in a storm breaking up against the rocks at Babbacombe. Every second or so a laugh or a shout darted up like a sea-gull above the roar. When I was up on the gallows I could hear the mob outside screeching at me. It was awful!

"I kept going on kind of dazed like, Berry pushing me forward to make me go faster, till all at once we came to the barn where the scaffold stood with two or three men waiting on it and a score of others loitering at its foot. When I climbed up and faced them I said: 'Lord, you're keeping me in unnatural suspense. Why don't you hurry with my saving?'

"They pushed me on to the trapdoor and strapped my knees together. I looked at the people below me in the yard. There were a dozen I had known all my life. Not one of them looked sorry for me or even friendly. Some of them looked sober, some sneered up at me, and one or two grinned.

"That gave me an awful, desolate, sick feeling in my heart. Still I wasn't afraid. But I must admit that when Berry fastened the knot of the rope under my ear my teeth began knocking together in spite of myself and my heart barely fluttered. For one moment I lost hope. God forgive me that insult! That minute was when they pulled the black cap down over my face. 'Lord,' I says, 'have you gone back on your word?'

"In the next second what was going to happen? I wondered, terribly scared. Would I be tossing in the roaring flames of hell, as my sins deserved, or listening to the music of heaven, as we are promised? I stood suffocating for air because of the cap.

"Suddenly I realized something had gone wrong with the gallows. Berry and the others were kicking and twisting at the trapdoor I was standing on. They kept muttering excited orders to each other. Presently the crowd down below began talking and shouting. I was pushed off the trapdoor while someone worked on it.

"I shouted: 'I'm smothering! Take off this cap!' Then I heard the sheriff say: 'Take off the cap and send him back to his cell. We have a right to take his life by hanging, not by smothering.' So they unstrapped my legs and I stumbled back into the prison. My ears were throbbing and my brain was twisting around and around. My, but I was glad! The Lord had kept His promise. When I got back in my cell I lay down all of a tremble, my face white like snow and all covered with icy sweat."

This is what actually happened: When the lever which held up the trapdoor was pushed, the door refused to move. Again and again the officers pushed and twisted and stamped, but the trap remained obdurate. Berry, angry and humiliated, began work to find out what was the matter. After the prisoner was removed, a warder foolishly stepped on to the door, another pushed the bolt, and lo! the drop slipped down and the deputy fell through to the ground, injuring himself badly and nearly breaking his leg.

John Lee had been lying on his cell cot a half hour when the official procession again appeared. "What!" he cried, astounded. "You're not going to try that foolishness again, are you? Haven't you heard Providence speak?"

But again he was led, indignant and protesting, down the corridor, over the yard, up to the gibbet. No word was uttered by any of the grim-faced men who marched around him, except the chaplain, who began once more, though in a rather apologetic strain, the litany for the dying. But as they crossed outside, the mutterings and cries of the crowd were plainly audible.

Once more the fastened legs and the noose—again the black cap—again the pushing of bolts and levers. Wonder of wonders! No force or power could make the hinged door of death fall out of its place. The condemned stood as solidly and safely on the scaffold as if he trod the paved highway. After they removed him for the second time to his cell, the trapdoor worked again without a second's difficulty or hesitation. The dummy fell through and swung below at the first pressure of the bolt.

Remember, this is no unvouched story nor merely imagined occurrence. The facts as above related were seen by still living witnesses, were published in all the European papers, and were established as the basis for official government action.

At his wit's end, the sheriff telegraphed all particulars to the Home Secretary.

Whatever punishment the death penalty includes is all suffered by the culprit before the fatal stroke which ends his life. The cold agony of fear which to the last instant tortures the victim constitutes most of his punishment. For a condemned person to go up on the gallows twice means little short of his being punished twice. Nevertheless the Home Secretary wired back at once: "Proceed with the execution." So the murderer of poor Mrs. Keyes for a third time had to go through all the agony of the penalty for murder. Perhaps the suffering became actually intensified by the suspense of the undefined hope which to a certain degree held his fear in abeyance.

When the executioners appeared for a third time at Lee's cell door, the man sprang from his cot, angry and frantic. "What!" he shouted. "You here again? Haven't you any sense at all? Don't you know you can't do it? I'm surprised at you!"

Even as he spoke Berry had again fastened his elbows to his sides and before he could protest again the procession was hurrying Lee down the hall to the place of execution. The news of the two previous failures had spread out into the city; shops were closed and half the population surged with the others up against the prison gates. Though now the public rage was a little modified. Already murmurs against the sentence sprang up here and there in the crowd. Men shouted hoarse, angry contradictions at each other over the heads of their neighbours.

Their voices reached the scaffold. At two or three places in the crowd on the streets fights started.

Inside the jail yard most of the spectators gazed in half pity at the white, sagging figure which was being partly supported on the trapdoor while the noose for the third time clutched his bowed neck. "I'm not afraid—I know you can't hurt me—but my knees are kind of shuddering, so I can't stand straight." These were stout words though they ended with a sob.

Two of the assistants took hold, one on either side, being careful not to lean a foot on the trapdoor. The black cap again shut the world from the faded gaze of the culprit. No one had any doubt but that the trapdoor would work this time. Since the second attempt they had tested it four times with the dummy. At each trial the dummy had shot down through the opened door and swung freely in the presence of all.

In this third effort Berry himself pressed the bolt. There could be no trick. The excitement in the jail yard grew intense. The crowd below surged up under the scaffold, the victim hung limp in the arms of two deputies. The prisoners in their cells began an unearthly screeching. Through five awful minutes this contest of the law against the invisible and omnipotent force which opposed the law continued. The invisible champion won, and they carried Lee back to his cell.

The prison throbbed with perturbed mystery. What could be done? Further attempts must amount to mere torture. All this ended about eleven o'clock in the forenoon.

The under sheriff, Mr. H. M. James, caught a train, at the moment fortunately waiting, and hurried up to London. In the meantime Berry found out the reason for the difficulty. The recent heavy rains had swelled the planks on the scaffold. By sawing away the edge of the trapdoor he had repaired the machine so that now it would work quick, certain, and without a flaw.

The authorities were preparing to lead the condemned out once more when a telegram arrived from the London Home Office: "The death sentence of John Lee is commuted. He must instead go into penal servitude during His Majesty's pleasure."

There is little interest in what happened to the assassin after. Sufficient to say that his imprisonment continued till December 12, 1907, when he was released. Some speculators set him up in a public house in the expectation that the notoriety of his case might prove attractive to trade. This for a short time happened, but he proved an erratic and irresponsible business man, so the speculation failed. Then he turned evangelist, and used his experience on the scaffold as a text, preaching whenever he could find any sort of congregation.

So far as breaking the laws was concerned, his life continued a model one. He never failed to assert his innocence of the murder. He married, left his wife, wandered to America, and died in 1929.

Sir William Harcourt, the Home Secretary, was called severely to account by the press and in the House of Commons for letting off a cold-blooded murderer. So hard was the censure pressed that the statesman sought to sidestep his responsibility and lay the blame on a subordinate.

As to the affair at Exeter, a great deal of discussion ensued, one party contending that the mere swelling of the boards was quite a natural accident. The blundering on the scaffold resulted, they said, from the excitement of the event, that there was nothing providential about it. Others argued that Providence always uses natural causes for its results. The miraculous event was providential in its time and method. And they concluded that the result established the innocence of John Lee. "What about the success with the dummy?" they demanded.

However, if the event was providential, may it not rather be understood as proving his guilt? Do we not place too much terror on the idea of dissolution? Is it nearly so great a misfortune as we imagine and is not all of its agony composed in its apprehension? May it not be, in short, that the crime of John Lee was so ungrateful, so cruel, so atrocious, that Providence made him suffer the death penalty not once but three times?

WHITE LADY OF THE HOHENZOLLERNS

by CLYDE CLARKE

THE Royal Palace in Berlin was ablaze with light. Before the dressing-table in her boudoir the Queen smiled at her reflection in the mirror. She was wearing a gown of ivory brocade embroidered in silver that she had secretly ordered from her native Hanover. Opening a silver-bound casket, she lifted glittering jewels and let them slip through her fingers, joyously, as a child might play with running water. To her they represented buried hopes and vanished dreams, and tonight she was to wear them again after many years. There was the diadem she had worn as the bride of Frederick William I, the diamond necklace her brother had sent at the birth of her first child, and the bracelet her husband had clasped upon her arm when at last, after fervent prayers and long waiting, their son, the future Frederick the Great, was born.

She rose and surveyed herself in the long Venetian mirror and was almost happy. Then Princess Ulrica came in.

"Gracious, mama," she exclaimed, "you look as if Heaven and all its stars had fallen upon you. You are beautiful! Did our most Royal King and father command you to appear tonight in those lovely jewels?"

"Hush, child! You know how the King despises ornaments and luxuries. If he could see me he would die with rage."

"No, sweet mamma, he would calculate how many giant soldiers he could hire for his personal Guard for the price of this necklace, or how many miles of military roads he could build with this diadem."

"Don't speak of the King, child! Think of other things, of whom you will command to dance with you at the ball this evening. Your father will soon be thinking of a prince for you, for he intends you to be a Queen."

"I will marry whom I please," the little Princess said haughtily, "and I shall wear diamonds every day if I wish to. I will not be miserable as poor brother Frederick is."

"If your father commands, you must obey—as we all do," Sophia sighed, kissing her daughter lightly on the cheek.

They went into the ante-room, and at that moment Poellnitz, the Grand Chamberlain at the Court of King Frederick the First, threw open the doors and announced that the guests were assembled.

As they followed the Grand Chamberlain through the crowd of richly dressed women and men covered with stars and orders, Sophia managed to whisper to Ulrica: "The King has commanded us to be merry tonight. And take care, child, Frederick has spies everywhere. When you speak to Poellnitz, remember that he repeats every word to the King."

After making the grand tour of the *salons* the Queen seated herself at a card-table with the Margrafin Maria Dorothea and the English and French Ambassadors. Never had she been more gracious, more queenly. Behind her chair stood two maids of honour. She turned to them now and then to give some order or to send them to look after the young princesses, who were dancing in the next *salon*.

Suddenly the music ceased. The May evening seemed very still. An ominous silence oppressed the room. Then, from the other wing of the palace came the sound of loud knocking—hammer blows resounding in slow, solemn rhythm.

The Duke of Holstein spoke to General Schwerin, so that the Queen might hear: "Is the King at work in his carpentry shop? I thought he could not leave his chair."

"They say he has worked all day at his carpentering," the General replied. "He thinks his gout will be better and his arms and legs will be less stiff if he uses them."

The Queen tried to smile and go on with the game. She turned to Poellnitz who was standing near: "Why does the music stop? Do have them play on. It is so much more cheerful."

She played her cards absently, as the music started again. Then she turned to one of her maids of honour: "Have the princesses come to me as soon as the dance is over," she commanded, her face grave.

But before the command could be obeyed, the Princess Amelia, pale and horrified, rushed to her mother, greatly agitated.

"My dear child, what is wrong?" the Queen cried.

"The Lady in White!" Amelia whispered, her voice trembling. "I saw her as I looked out the window. She was moving among the lilac bushes!"

The Queen turned pale. She rose instantly and in another moment all were standing. In the tomb-like stillness that fell over the rooms they could hear the rhythmic beat of the hammer in the other wing of the palace. A faint perfume of lilacs was in the air.

The Grand Chamberlain came very softly to the Queen's side. He bowed. "Your Majesty, command me!" he said, his voice a trifle unsteady.

"Has anyone else seen 'The Lady in White'?" she asked, anxiously.

"Yes, Your Majesty. Several of the sentries have seen the spectre, but not in this part of the palace. The figure was seen floating—"

"Where?" she whispered. "Floating where? Tell me."

"In the gardens and around the corridors of the other wing of the palace."

The Queen recovered herself quickly: "I command that the dance proceed!" She was still very pale, but she turned to soothe Princess Amelia. "It is nothing, child, it is but a myth. Go back to your dancing and be gay. Remember, we are commanded by the King to be happy tonight."

Amelia went away reluctantly with a young margrave who had accompanied her, and the Queen talked in whispers to General Schwerin.

The English Ambassador was curious, and he asked the French Ambassador, in a low voice: "The Lady in White? Who is she? I do not understand."

"It is the legendary spectre that has haunted the ruling family of Prussia for centuries," the French Ambassador whispered. "It always portends the death of a member of the Imperial family. If it wears white gloves, it means a woman is to die; if black gloves, it means the death of a man. It is said always to appear before the death of a Royal personage."

As the music started again the Queen resumed her seat at the card-table and calmly arranged her cards. "Let us play," she said.

In the wing of the palace occupied by the King, there was

silence. Frederick William sat alone in his bare room. Slowly he raised himself from his chair and extended his arms.

"They think I am suffering, chained to my chair!" he cried. "But I have no pain tonight. The work has cured the pain!" He stretched his arms and moved his fingers gleefully.

"They think that the doors of the Royal vault will soon open to receive my corpse. But Frederick William will not die! My son shall not reign! This weak, riotous youth, this dreamer! Prussia has no need of this sentimental boy, who finds the tones of his flute sweeter than the sounds of trumpets and drums! Never shall Prussia be ruled by a dreaming poet!"

His breath came fast. He was trembling with rage. "Bah! the fool has said that Voltaire was as great as a king—yes, greater than the kings anointed by the Pope! A fool shall not govern Prussia. The King will live!"

Worn out by this outburst, he sank into his chair again, murmuring: "They think I shall die, but I shall be well. I have commanded Sophia to give a ball that the world could see that the Queen and my daughters are gay and happy!"

He called the servant who awaited his pleasure in the adjoining room and commanded him: "Call together the gentlemen who compose my Tobacco Club, and arrange everything for a meeting of that august body!"

"But those gentlemen, Your Majesty, are at the Queen's ball," the servant said, astonished.

"Then go for them. Bring them quickly. Poellnitz must come, and Eckert, and Baron von Goltz and Hacke, Duke of Holstein, and General Schwerin. Quick! In ten minutes they must all be here, but," he cautioned, raising a shaking finger, "let no one know why he is sent for. Only whisper to each one that he is commanded to come to me. Tell him he must tell no one where he is going. I will not have the Queen's ball disturbed. She must be happy tonight! Go!"

In ten minutes six gentlemen, their faces very pale, stood in the King's ante-chamber.

"What does this sudden summons mean?" they asked each other anxiously. No one knew.

The servant entered the King's room. His Majesty, dressed in the full uniform of his Guard, sat at a round table, on which the pipes and the mugs filled with foaming beer were already placed.

He had condescended to fill a pipe with his own hands, and was on the point of lighting it at a nearby candle.

"Sire," the servant said, "the gentlemen are waiting in the anteroom."

"Do they know why I have sent for them?" the King asked, blowing a cloud of smoke from his mouth.

"Your Majesty forbade me to tell them."

"Well, go now and tell them I am more furiously angry today than you have ever seen me, that I am standing by the door with my crutch, and that I command them to come singly into my presence."

"What is the matter? Why is the King so angry? What orders do you bring from His Majesty?" the men questioned the servant in anxious whispers.

The servant assumed a terrified expression as he replied:—"His Majesty has never been so outrageously angry. Woe unto him over whom the cloud bursts. He commands that each you enter the room alone. Go now! For heaven's sake do not keep your King waiting. I fear for what may happen to you!"

The men looked at each other in consternation. No one wished to be first to encounter the King's rage.

The Grand Chamberlain, bowing to the Duke of Holstein, said: "Your Grace has precedence."

The Duke winced. "No," he said, "you are well aware that His Majesty does not regard Court etiquette on these occasions, and would be most indignant if we paid any attention to it. Let us not displease him. Go first yourself, my dear friend."

"Not I, Your Grace. I would not dare to take precedence in this group. The King would be angry with me. If you decline the honour, it is due to General Schwerin."

"Gentlemen," interrupted the servant, "His Majesty will become impatient and then more angry."

"But, my God, who will dare go first?" Count von Goltz cried.

"I will," said Councillor Eckert. "I owe everything to His Majesty, I will place my life at his service." He braced himself, and with firm steps went to the door and opened it.

His companions saw the King's eyes flash as he raised his crutch over the head of his favourite, and then the door closed. Though they heard no sound, they waited anxiously.

Poellnitz spoke to the servant in faltering tones: "Against which of us is the anger of the King directed? Is it I?"

"Alas, I do not know," the servant replied. "Let the next one enter. His Majesty must not be kept waiting."

Poellnitz stepped boldly to the door, and as he entered they saw the King standing in threatening attitude inside the door. Each time this scene was repeated, and then General Schwerin, the last of the six, went in to the King's presence.

This time the King was not standing at the door. He lay in his arm-chair, laughing until the tears rolled down his withered cheeks.

"The joke succeeded to perfection," he said, exultantly. "Even you, Schwerin, who never knew fear on the battlefield, are trembling with fear."

The General tried to smile: "Yes, Sire, a shot is a trifling thing compared with a flash from your eyes. I have no fear of death, I only fear the displeasure of my sovereign."

"Give me your hand, Schwerin," the old monarch said. "You are a brave fellow. And now, gentlemen, away with all constraint and etiquette. We will suppose the King to be at the ball. I am only your companion, Frederick William. I will now proceed to the opening of the Tobacco Club. Tell your very best guardroom jokes. Make me laugh!"

The big empty room was lighted by but four tallow candles, for the King would tolerate nothing beyond bare necessities, and the four streaks of light seemed pale and sickly in the blue smoke that filled the air.

"Light more candles," the King commanded his man-in-waiting. "Our Tobacco Club must present a festive appearance tonight so that the contrast between it and the ball be not too great." Then he spoke to the Grand Chamberlain: "Tell me, Poellnitz, is the Queen's ball a brilliant one? The Queen—is she gay, and are the princesses dancing merrily?"

"I have never witnessed a more magnificent spectacle, Sire, nor has Her Majesty ever been more beautiful. I had no idea she possessed such priceless jewels."

The King's face set in its accustomed hard lines. "Fill the glasses, Jochen," he said to the valet. Then a harsh laugh escaped his lips. "So she has put on her jewels, has she? They are taking advantage of my absence. They think I am writhing on a bed of pain."

Poellnitz put down his mug and smiled. "The Queen has good

reason for being happy tonight, for Your Majesty is not ill. You have worked all day in your carpentering shop. In the ballroom above the music we could hear the blows of your hammer."

Frederick took a long draught of beer, and the lid snapped loudly as he banged the mug on the table. "I should not be surprised if Frederick had clandestinely come over to this ball," he said. "He thinks to govern Prussia with his book-learning and his poems. A dreaming scholar can never be a good king. He who wields pen and fiddle-bow instead of a sword and sceptre, will never be a good general."

Poellnitz set down his mug quietly and said quickly, in soothing tones: "Your Majesty forgets that this is a sitting of the Tobacco Club and not of the State Council. Let us be gay as the others are gay tonight. Your pipe is out and your mug is empty, Sire!"

"True," said Frederick. "Fill my mug, Jochen, I shall drink to the health of him who first overcame fear and dared to enter this room. Who was it? I have forgotten. You are all cowards in my presence. Raise your glasses! Drink!"

"The toast is to the Privy Councillor von Eckert, Sire," said Count Hacke with an ironical smile.

"He entered the chamber as he goes into battle," Poellnitz laughed, "in the spirit in which he took leave of all the fine breweries and artfully constructed non-smoke chimneys which he built. He marched courageously into the Royal presence." The King's favourite was far from popular with the other officers.

Eckert's face was pale in the flickering light, and he scowled at Poellnitz, as the other men laughed heartily.

"Really, your wit this evening is dazzling, Poellnitz," he said. "I am charmed with your pleasantries."

"Silence!" Frederick commanded. "No more of this raillery."

Suddenly the door opened and the King's valet appeared.

"Your Majesty," he said, "your orders have been obeyed. The White Salon is ready. The last work of your hands has been placed there for your inspection. The paint is quite dry."

"Illumine the White Salon!" Frederick cried, struggling to his feet and throwing his mug on the table. "Jochen, give me your arm!"

In the grand ball-room the music went on without pause at the

Queen's demand. The May air was soft and the scent of lilacs drifted through the open windows. The face of the Queen was pale but very sweet under the glittering diadem, and she tried to smile as she played her cards.

Suddenly the Princess Sophia Dorothea, who stood nearby, gave a low cry of terror and fell back into the arms of a maid of honour. "The King!" she whispered. "My God, the King!"

In the corridor, approaching the doorway, they saw Frederick, his eyes flashing, his limbs trembling. Supported by his valets, he came slowly towards the room.

The Queen whispered to the attendant behind her: "Remove my long ear-rings and the necklace quickly!" Then she calmly played a queen on the table before her. The French Ambassador played a king.

"Lost!" she said, trying to smile. "So must the Queen ever be lost when the King comes."

Frederick fixed his blazing eyes upon her and called her name. A hush fell over the room. She rose instantly and went to him, a faint smile on her pale face.

"Ah, my husband," she said, "what a pleasant surprise you have prepared for us! It is most amiable of Your Majesty to honour this feast with your presence."

The King grasped her arm savagely and his voice was harsh: "It is necessary in the midst of earthly pleasures to be reminded of the fleeing vanity of earthly things. I am come to administer this medicine to your vain and sin-sick soul. Come with me! All of you. Follow me! Let none remain behind!"

In vain the Queen pleaded with Frederick to tell her his plan. She could only walk tremblingly at his side and go with him. She knew not where.

The King kept his eyes steadily before him. His face was set and hard. He did not speak. The bejewelled ladies and gentlemen of his Court followed the Royal pair in a long, glittering procession. No one dared to disobey the King's orders. Though it looked like a wedding procession, the courtiers and their ladies felt as if they were marching towards their doom.

The Queen looked anxiously from side to side, anticipating some new terror as the long parade passed through the flower-decked dressing-rooms, through the brilliantly lighted ante-chamber, on through the endless corridors and up the long staircase, until at last they reached the door of the White Salon, which Frederick had built and adorned.

At the King's command the doors were thrown open and he led Sophia into the room.

She gave a cry of horror: *"Two coffins! Your Majesty—what does this mean?"*

"Yes, two coffins, mine and yours. I have made them with my own hands. I finished them tonight—while you revelled. In these coffins we will soon rest and all earthly vanity and glory will be at an end. No one will then fear my glances or my crutch. No one will admire the glittering jewels of the Queen. Dust will return to dust and the King and Queen will be nothing more than food for worms."

Under the crystal chandeliers the lights glared in the marble whiteness of the room. For a moment no one moved or breathed.

Then Sophia summoned her courage and spoke softly: "Not so, my King! The dust of common mortals will be scattered in every direction by the hand of Time. But from our dust history will build enduring monuments!"

As she spoke the Queen seemed endowed with fresh beauty. She needed no royal diadem, no gleaming jewels to enhance her queenly bearing. She was the wife of the King of Prussia, the sister of the King of England, the mother of the future King of the Prussian Empire.

Her composure angered Frederick. With a trembling hand he pointed to the statues of his ancestors that adorned the room. His tone was imperious, terrifying: "So, then, let my ancestors see how well we will look in our coffins! The world knows that jewels become you and that I am a fine fellow in my uniform, but let us try our coffins!"

The Queen faltered: "Oh, my King—"

"Do not waste precious time—you have wasted enough at the card-table this evening. See if you can take your place with grace and dignity in this coffin I have made for you with my own hands. Lay yourself in your coffin, Sophia, that I may see a picture of you that you can never behold. I have brought you here that we may try our coffins."

"This is a cruel jest, Frederick!" There was a tremor in her voice, but she turned to one of her maids of honour and said:

"Duchess, give me your hand. I am very weary, and for a time I shall rest in peace upon this bed."

As the Duchess took her trembling hand, the Queen lifted the skirt of her royal robe slightly and stepped over the edge of the coffin. Proudly erect she stood for a moment and then, with dainty grace, she stooped and stretched her body until with closed eyes she lay still and calm in the white coffin.

The rudely made coffin creaked and groaned. A murmur of horror came from the richly attired company.

The King stood looking on, his features set in cruel lines. After a few moments Sophia opened her eyes and looked up at him. His eyes avoided hers and he stared at the floor.

Slowly the Queen arose, very pale, but with her imperial dignity unbent. The Duchess held out a hand to assist her, but she declined it, saying: "Kings and queens must leave their coffins by their own strength and greatness, sustained by their deeds alone."

With these words she stepped over the edge of the coffin and, bowing profoundly to the King, said: "Your Majesty, it is your turn now."

The King looked at her darkly and stepped awkwardly into his coffin. He called some of his courtiers to assist him in lying down. "Here I will soon sleep," he said.

Sophia reached her hand to him. "May that time be far removed, my King," she said.

At that moment the awed silence of the room was broken by loud piercing cries and the sound of hastening feet in the antechamber.

Frederick sat bolt upright in his coffin, a look of terror in his drawn face: "What is it? What has happened? I demand to know!"

The major-domo stepped forward with shaking limbs: "Your Majesty, the sentries in the corridor have seen the figure of a tall woman clad in white—she passed the whole length of the corridor and entered this room!"

"The Lady in White!" cried Frederick, falling as if broken to pieces in his coffin. The courtiers recoiled and the ladies stood paralyzed with amazed horror. Only the Queen was calm.

Frederick suddenly sat up in his coffin and asked in a creaking voice: "Did she wear white gloves or black?"

For a moment no one spoke. A deep silence pervaded the room. The scent of lilacs drifted in from the palace gardens.

At last the major-domo dared to break the silence: "She wore black gloves, Your Majesty."

"Black! That means I am to die," Frederick cried. "Help me from this coffin! You will put me back soon enough!"

As morning dawned, Her Majesty, the Queen, stood at the window of her apartment and looked out into the mist of the new May day. White lilacs hung in pallid clusters from bending boughs. Birds twittered softly among the leaves. Ghostly swans swam placidly, skirting the water-lilies on the border of the lake.

Beyond all that she could see with her eyes was the castle at Rheinsberg, where the Prince Royal was sleeping peacefully, his flute on the table at his bedside.

In his bare room across the misty garden the King lay dying. She knew that the time was at hand when Frederick William II, afterwards known as Frederick the Great, was to ascend the throne of Prussia.

THE SHADOW AND THE FLASH

by JACK LONDON

WHEN I look back, I realize what a peculiar friendship it was. First, there was Lloyd Inwood, tall, slender, and finely knit, nervous and dark. And then Paul Tichlorne, tall, slender, and finely knit, nervous and blond. Each was the replica of the other in everything except colour. Lloyd's eyes were black; Paul's were blue. Under stress of excitement, the blood coursed olive in the face of Lloyd, crimson in the face of Paul. But outside this matter of colouring they were as like as two peas. Both were highstrung, prone to excessive tension and endurance, and they lived at concert pitch.

But there was a trio involved in this remarkable friendship, and the third was short, and fat, and chunky, and lazy, and, loath to say, it was I. Paul and Lloyd seemed born to rivalry with each other, and I to be peacemaker between them. We grew up together, the three of us, and full often have I received the angry blows each intended for the other. They were always competing, striving to outdo each other, and when entered upon some such struggle there was no limit either to their endeavours or passions.

This intense spirit of rivalry obtained in their studies and their games. If Paul memorized one canto of "Marmion", Lloyd memorized two cantos, Paul came back with three, and Lloyd again with four, till each knew the whole poem by heart. I remember an incident that occurred at the swimimng hole—an incident tragically significant of the life-struggle between them. The boys had a game of diving to the bottom of a ten-foot pool and holding on by submerged roots to see who could stay under the longest. Paul and Lloyd allowed themselves to be bantered into making the descent together. When I saw their faces, set and determined, disappear in the water as they sank swiftly down, I felt a foreboding of something dreadful. The moments sped, the ripples died away, the face of the pool grew placid and untroubled, and neither black nor golden head broke surface in quest of air. We above grew anxious. The longest record of the longest-winded boy had been exceeded, and still there was no sign. Air bubbles trickled slowly upwards, showing that the breath had been expelled from their lungs, and after that the bubbles ceased to trickle upwards. Each second became interminable, and, unable longer to endure the suspense, I plunged into the water.

I found them down at the bottom, clutching tight to the roots, their heads not a foot apart, their eyes wide open, each glaring fixedly at the other. They were suffering frightful torment, writhing and twisting in the pangs of voluntary suffocation; for neither would let go and acknowledge himself beaten. I tried to break Paul's hold on the root, but he resisted me fiercely. Then I lost my breath and came to the surface, badly scared. I quickly explained the situation, and half a dozen of us went down and by main strength tore them loose. By the time we got them out, both were unconscious, and it was only after much barrel-rolling and rubbing and pounding that they finally came to their senses. They would have drowned there, had no one rescued them.

When Paul Tichlorne entered college, he let it be generally understood that he was going in for the social sciences. Lloyd Inwood, entering at the same time, elected to take the same course. But Paul had had it secretly in mind all the time to study the natural sciences, specializing on chemistry, and at the last moment he switched over. Though Lloyd had already arranged his year's work and attended the first lectures, he at once followed Paul's lead and went in for the natural sciences and especially for chemistry. Their rivalry soon became a noted thing throughout the university. Each was a spur to the other, and they went into chemistry deeper than did ever students before—so deep, in fact, that ere they took their sheepskins they could have stumped any chemistry or "cow college" professor in the institution, save "old" Moss, head of the department, and even him they puzzled and edified more than once. Lloyd's discovery of the "death bacillus" of the sea toad, and his experiments on it with potassium cyanide, sent his name and that of his university ringing round the world; nor was Paul a whit behind when he succeeded in producing laboratory colloids exhibiting amœba-like activities, and when he cast new light upon the processes of fertilization through his startling experiments with simple sodium chlorides and magnesium solutions on low forms of marine life.

It was in their undergraduate days, however, in the midst of their profoundest plunges into the mysteries of organic chemistry, that Doris Van Benschoten entered into their lives. Lloyd met her first, but within twenty-four hours Paul saw to it that he also made her acquaintance. Of course, they fell in love with her, and she became the only thing in life worth living for. They wooed her with equal ardour and fire, and so intense became their struggle for her that half the student-body took to wagering wildly on the result. Even "old" Moss, one day, after an astounding demonstration in his private laboratory by Paul, was guilty to the extent of a month's salary of backing him to become the bridegroom of Doris Van Benschoten.

In the end she solved the problem in her own way, to everybody's satisfaction except Paul's and Lloyd's. Getting them together, she said that she really could not choose between them because she loved them both equally well; and that, unfortunately, since polyandry was not permitted in the United States she would be compelled to forego the honour and happiness of marrying either of them. Each blamed the other for this lamentable outcome, and the bitterness between them grew more bitter.

But things came to a head soon enough. It was at my home, after they had taken their degrees and dropped out of the world's sight, that the beginning of the end came to pass. Both were men of means, with little inclination and no necessity for professional life. My friendship and their mutual animosity were the two things that linked them in any way together. While they were very often at my place, they made it a fastidious point to avoid each other on such visits, though it was inevitable, under the circumstances, that they should come upon each other occasionally.

On the day I have in recollection, Paul Tichlorne had been mooning all morning in my study over a current scientific review. This left me free to my own affairs, and I was out among my roses when Lloyd Inwood arrived. Clipping and pruning and tacking the climbers on the porch, with my mouth full of nails, and Lloyd following me about and lending a hand now and again, we fell to discussing the mythical race of invisible people, that strange and vagrant people the traditions of which have come down to us. Lloyd warmed to the talk in his nervous, jerky fashion, and was soon interrogating the physical properties and possibilities of invisibility. A perfectly black object, he contended, would elude and defy the acutest vision.

"Colour is a sensation," he was saying. "It has no objective reality. Without light, we can see neither colours nor objects themselves. All objects are black in the dark, and in the dark it is impossible to see them. If no light strikes upon them, then no light is flung back from them to the eye, and so we have no vision-evidence of their being."

"But we see black objects in daylight," I objected.

"Very true," he went on warmly. "And that is because they are not perfectly black. Were they perfectly black, absolutely black, as it were, we could not see them—ay, not in the blaze of a thousand suns could we see them! And so I say, with the right pigments, properly compounded, an absolutely black paint could be produced which would render invisible whatever it was applied to."

"It would be a remarkable discovery," I said non-committally, for the whole thing seemed too fantastic for aught but speculative purposes.

"Remarkable!" Lloyd slapped me on the shoulder. "I should say so. Why, old chap, to coat myself with such a paint would be to put the world at my feet. The secrets of kings and courts would be mine, the machinations of diplomats and politicians, the play of stock-gamblers, the plans of trusts and corporations. I could keep my hand on the inner pulse of things and become the greatest power in the world. And I—" He broke off shortly, then added, "Well, I have begun my experiments, and I don't mind telling you that I'm right in line for it."

A laugh from the doorway startled us. Paul Tichlorne was standing there, a smile of mockery on his lips.

"You forget, my dear Lloyd," he said.

"Forget what?"

"You forget," Paul went on—"ah, you forget the shadow."

I saw Lloyd's face drop, but he answered sneeringly, "I can carry a sunshade, you know." Then he turned suddenly and fiercely upon him. "Look here, Paul, you'll keep out of this if you know what's good for you."

A rupture seemed imminent, but Paul laughed good-naturedly. "I wouldn't lay fingers on your dirty pigments. Succeed beyond your most sanguine expectations, yet you will always fetch up against the shadow. You can't get away from it. Now I shall go on the very opposite tack. In the very nature of my proposition the shadow will be eliminated—"

"Transparency!" ejaculated Lloyd, instantly. "But it can't be achieved."

"Oh, no; of course not." And Paul shrugged his shoulders and strolled off down the brier-rose path.

This was the beginning of it. Both men attacked the problem with all the tremendous energy for which they were noted, and with a rancour and bitterness that made me tremble for the success of either. Each trusted me to the utmost, and in the long weeks of experimentation that followed I was made a party to both sides, listening to their theorizings and witnessing their demonstrations. Never, by word or sign, did I convey to either the slightest hint of the other's progress, and they respected me for the seal I put upon my lips.

Lloyd Inwood, after prolonged and unintermittent application, when the tension upon his mind and body became too great to bear, had a strange way of obtaining relief. He attended prize fights. It was at one of these brutal exhibitions, whither he had dragged me in order to tell his latest results, that his theory received striking confirmation.

"Do you see that red-whiskered man?" he asked, pointing across the ring to the fifth tier of seats on the opposite side. "And do you see the next man to him, the one in the white hat? Well, there is quite a gap between them, is there not?"

"Certainly," I answered. "They are a seat apart. The gap is the unoccupied seat."

He leaned over to me and spoke seriously. "Between the red-whiskered man and the white-hatted man sits Ben Wasson. You have heard me speak of him. He is the cleverest pugilist of his weight in the country. He is also a Caribbean Negro, full-blooded, and the blackest in the United States. He has on a black overcoat buttoned up. I saw him when he came in and took that seat. As soon as he sat down he disappeared. Watch closely; he may smile."

I was for crossing over to verify Lloyd's statement, but he restrained me. "Wait," he said.

I waited and watched, till the red-whiskered man turned his head as though addressing the unoccupied seat; and then, in that empty space, I saw the rolling whites of a pair of eyes and the white double-crescent of two rows of teeth, and for the instant I could make out a Negro's face. But with the passing of the smile his visibility passed, and the chair seemed vacant as before.

"Were he perfectly black, you could sit alongside him and not see him," Lloyd said; and I confess the illustration was apt enough to make me well-nigh convinced.

I visited Lloyd's laboratory a number of times after that, and found him always deep in his search after the absolute black. His experiments covered all sorts of pigments, such as lamp-blacks, tars, carbonized vegetable matters, soots of oils and fats, and the various carbonized animal substances.

"White light is composed of the seven primary colours," he argued to me. "But it is itself, of itself, invisible. Only by being reflected from objects do it and the objects become visible. But only that portion of it that is reflected becomes visible. For instance, here is a blue tobacco-box. The white light strikes against it, and, with one exception, all its component colours—violet, indigo, green, yellow, orange, and red—are absorbed. The one exception is *blue*. It is not absorbed, but reflected. Wherefore the tobacco-box gives us a sensation of blueness. We do not see the other colours because they are absorbed. We see only the blue. For the same reason grass is *green*. The green waves of white light are thrown upon our eyes."

"When we paint our houses, we do not apply colour to them," he said at another time. "What we do is to apply certain substances that have the property of absorbing from white light all the colours except those that we would have our houses appear. When a substance reflects all the colours to the eye, it seems to us white. When it absorbs all the colours, it is black. But, as I said before, we have as yet no perfect black. *All* the colours are not absorbed. The perfect black, guarding against highlights, will be utterly and absolutely invisible. Look at that, for example."

He pointed to the palette lying on his work-table. Different shades of black pigments were brushed on it. One, in particular, I could hardly see. It gave my eyes a blurring sensation, and I rubbed them and looked again.

"That," he said impressively, "is the blackest black you or any mortal man ever looked upon. But just you wait, and I'll have a black so black that no mortal man will be able to look upon it—*and see it!*"

On the other hand, I used to find Paul Tichlorne plunged as

deeply into the study of light polarization, diffraction, and interference, single and double refraction, and all manner of strange organic compounds.

"Transparency: a state or quality of body which permits all rays of light to pass through," he defined for me. "That is what I am seeking. Lloyd blunders up against the shadow with his perfect opaqueness. But I escape it. A transparent body casts no shadow; neither does it reflect light-waves—that is, the perfectly transparent does not. So, avoiding highlights, not only will such a body cast no shadow, but, since it reflects no light, it will also be invisible."

We were standing by the window at another time. Paul was engaged in polishing a number of lenses, which were ranged along the sill. Suddenly, after a pause in the conversation, he said, "Oh! I've dropped a lens. Stick your head out, old man, and see where it went to."

Out I started to thrust my head, but a sharp blow on the forehead caused me to recoil. I rubbed my bruised brow and gazed with reproachful inquiry at Paul, who was laughing in gleeful, boyish fashion.

"Well?" he said.

"Well?" I echoed.

"Why don't you investigate?" he demanded. And investigate I did. Before thrusting out my head, my senses, automatically active, had told me there was nothing there, that nothing intervened between me and out-of-doors, that the aperture of the window opening was utterly empty. I stretched forth my hand and felt a hard object, smooth and cool and flat, which my touch, out of its experience, told me to be glass. I looked again, but could see positively nothing.

"White quartzose sand," Paul rattled off, "sordic carbonate, slaked lime, cullet, manganese peroxide—there you have it, the finest French plate glass, made by the great St. Gobain Company, who make the finest plate glass in the world, and this is the finest piece they ever made. It cost a king's ransom. But look at it! You can't see it. You don't know it's there till you run your head against it.

"Eh, old boy! That's merely an object-lesson—certain elements, in themselves opaque, yet so compounded as to give a resultant body which is transparent. But that is a matter of inorganic chemistry, you say. Very true. But I dare to assert, standing here on my two feet, that in the organic I can duplicate whatever occurs in the inorganic.

"Here!" He held a test-tube between me and the light, and I noted the cloudy or muddy liquid it contained. He emptied the contents of another test-tube into it, and almost instantly it became clear and sparkling.

"Or here!" With quick, nervous movements among his array of test-tubes, he turned a white solution to a wine colour, and a light yellow solution to a dark brown. He dropped a piece of litmus paper into an acid, when it changed instantly to red, and on floating it in an alkali it turned as quickly to blue.

"The litmus paper is still the litmus paper," he enunciated in the formal manner of the lecturer. "I have not changed it into something else. Then what did I do? I merely changed the arrangement of its molecules. Where, at first, it absorbed all colours from the light but red, its molecular structure was so changed that it absorbed red and all colours except blue. And so it goes, *ad infinitum*. Now, what I purpose to do is this." He paused for a space. "I purpose to seek—ay, and to find—the proper reagents, which, acting upon the living organism, will bring about molecular changes analogous to those you have just witnessed. But these reagents, which I shall find, and for that matter, upon which I already have my hands, will not turn the living body to blue or red or black, but they will turn it to transparency. All light will pass through it. It will be invisible. It will cast no shadow."

A few weeks later I went hunting with Paul. He had been promising me for some time that I should have the pleasure of shooting over a wonderful dog—the most wonderful dog, in fact, that ever man shot over, so he averred, and continued to aver till my curiosity was aroused. But on the morning in question I was disappointed, for there was no dog in evidence.

"Don't see him about," Paul remarked unconcernedly, and we set off across the fields.

I could not imagine, at the time, what was ailing me, but I had a feeling of some impending and deadly illness. My nerves were all awry, and, from the astounding tricks they played me, my senses seemed to have run riot. Strange sounds disturbed me. At times I heard the swish-swish of grass being shoved aside, and once the patter of feet across a patch of stony ground.

"Did you hear anything, Paul?" I asked once.

But he shook his head, and thrust his feet steadily forward.

While climbing a fence, I heard the low, eager whine of a dog, apparently from within a couple of feet of me; but on looking about me I saw nothing.

I dropped to the ground, limp and trembling.

"Paul," I said, "we had better return to the house. I am afraid I am going to be sick."

"Nonsense, old man," he answered. "The sunshine has gone to your head like wine. You'll be all right. It's famous weather."

But, passing along a narrow path through a clump of cottonwoods, some object brushed against my legs and I stumbled and nearly fell. I looked with sudden anxiety at Paul?

"What's the matter?" he asked. "Tripping over your own feet."

I kept my tongue between my teeth and plodded on, though sore perplexed and thoroughly satisfied that some acute and mysterious malady had attacked my nerves. So far my eyes had escaped; but, when we got to the open fields again, even my vision went back on me. Strange flashes of vari-coloured, rainbow light began to appear and disappear on the path before me. Still, I managed to keep myself in hand, till the vari-coloured lights persisted for a space of fully twenty seconds, dancing and flashing in continuous play. Then I sat down, weak and shaky.

"It's all up with me," I gasped, covering my eyes with my hands. "It has attacked my eyes. Paul, take me home."

But Paul laughed long and loud. "What did I tell you?—the most wonderful dog, eh? Well, what do you think?"

He turned partly from me and began to whistle. I heard the patter of feet, the panting of a heated animal, and the unmistakable yelp of a dog. Then Paul stooped down and apparently fondled the empty air.

"Here! Give me your fist."

And he rubbed my hand over the cold nose and jowls of a dog. A dog it certainly was, with the shape and the smooth, short coat of a pointer.

Suffice to say, I speedily recovered my spirits and control. Paul put a collar about the animal's neck and tied his handkerchief to its tail. And then was vouchsafed us the remarkable sight of an empty collar and a waving handkerchief cavorting over the fields. It was something to see that collar and handkerchief pin a bevy of quail in a clump of locusts and remain rigid and immovable till we had flushed the bird.

Now and again the dog emitted the vari-coloured light-flashes I have mentioned. The one thing, Paul explained, which he had not anticipated and which he doubted could be overcome.

"They're a large family," he said, "these sun dogs, wind dogs, rainbows, halos, and parhelia. They are produced by refraction of light from mineral and ice crystals, from mist, rain, spray, and no end of things; and I am afraid they are the penalty I must pay for transparency. I escaped Lloyd's shadow only to fetch up against the rainbow flash."

A couple of days later, before the entrance to Paul's laboratory, I encountered a terrible stench. So overpowering was it that it was easy to discover the source—a mass of putrescent matter on the doorstep which in general outlines resembled a dog.

Paul was startled when he investigated my find. It was his invisible dog, or rather, what had been his invisible dog, for it was now plainly visible. It had been playing about but a few minutes before in all health and strength. Closer examination revealed that the skull had been crushed by some heavy blow. While it was strange that the animal should have been killed, the inexplicable thing was that it should so quickly decay.

"The reagents I injected into its system were harmless," Paul explained. "Yet they were powerful, and it appears that when death comes they force practically instantaneous disintegration. Remarkable! Most remarkable! Well, the only thing is not to die. They do not harm so long as one lives. But I do wonder who smashed in that dog's head."

Light, however, was thrown upon this when a frightened housemaid brought the news that Gaffer Bedshaw had that very morning, not more than an hour back, gone violently insane, and was strapped down at home, in the huntsman's lodge, where he raved of a battle with a ferocious and gigantic beast that he had encountered in the Tichlorne pasture. He claimed that the thing, whatever it was, was invisible, that with his own eyes he had seen that it was invisible; wherefore his tearful wife and daughters shook their heads, and wherefore he but waxed the more violent, and the gardener and the coachman tightened the straps by another hole.

Nor, while Paul Tichlorne was thus successfully mastering the problem of invisibility, was Lloyd Inwood a whit behind. I went over in answer to a message of his to come and see how he was getting on. Now his laboratory occupied an isolated situation in the midst of his vast grounds. It was built in a pleasant little glade, surrounded on all sides by a dense forest growth, and was to be gained by way of a winding and erratic path. But I had travelled that path so often as to know every foot of it, and conceive my surprise when I came upon the glade and found no laboratory. The quaint shed structure with its red sandstone chimney was not. Nor did it look as if it ever had been. There were no signs of ruin, no débris, nothing.

I started to walk across what had once been its site. "This," I said to myself, "should be where the step went up to the door." Barely were the words out of my mouth when I stubbed my toe on some obstacle, pitched forward, and butted my head into something that *felt* very much like a door. I reached out my hand. It *was* a door. I found the knob and turned it. And at once, as the door swung inwards on its hinges, the whole interior of the laboratory impinged upon my vision. Greeting Lloyd, I closed the door and backed up the path a few paces. I could see nothing of the building. Returning and opening the door, at once all the furniture and every detail of the interior were visible. It was indeed startling, the sudden transition from void to light and form and colour.

"What do you think of it, eh?" Lloyd asked, wringing my hand. "I slapped a couple of coats of absolute black on the outside yesterday afternoon to see how it worked. How's your head? You bumped it pretty solidly, I imagine.

"Never mind that," he interrupted my congratulations. "I've something better for you to do."

While he talked he began to strip, and when he stood naked before me he thrust a pot and brush into my hand and said, "Here, give me a coat of this."

It was an oily, shellac-like stuff, which spread quickly and easily over the skin and dried immediately.

"Merely preliminary and precautionary," he explained when I had finished; "but now for the real stuff."

I picked up another pot he indicated, and glanced inside, but could see nothing.

"It's empty," I said.

"Stick your finger in it."

I obeyed, and was aware of a sensation of cool moistness. On withdrawing my hand I glanced at the forefinger, the one I had immersed, but it had disappeared. I moved it, and knew from the alternate tension and relaxation of the muscles that I moved it, but it defied my sense of sight. To all appearances I had been shorn of a finger; nor could I get any visual impression of it till I extended it under the skylight and saw its shadow plainly blotted on the floor.

Lloyd chuckled. "Now spread it on and keep your eyes open."

I dipped the brush into the seemingly empty pot, and gave him a long stroke across his chest. With the passage of the brush the living flesh disappeared from beneath. I covered his right leg, and he was a one-legged man defying all laws of gravitation. And so, stroke by stroke, member by member, I painted Lloyd Inwood into nothingness. It was a creepy experience, and I was glad when naught remained in sight but his burning black eyes, poised apparently unsupported in mid-air.

"I have a refined and harmless solution for them," he said. "A fine spray with an air-brush, and presto! I am not."

This deftly accomplished, he said, "Now I shall move about, and do you tell me what sensations you experience."

"In the first place, I cannot see you," I said, and I could hear his gleeful laugh from the midst of the emptiness. "Of course," I continued, "you cannot escape your shadow, but that was to be expected. When you pass between my eye and an object, the object disappears, but so unusual and incomprehensible is its disappearance that it seems to me as though my eyes had blurred. When you move rapidly, I experience a bewildering succession of blurs. The blurring sensation makes my eyes ache and my brain tired."

"Have you any other warnings of my presence?" he asked.

"No, and yes," I answered. "When you are near me I have feelings similar to those produced by dank warehouses, gloomy crypts, and deep mines. And as sailors feel the loom of the land on dark nights, so I think I feel the loom of your body. But it is all very vague and intangible."

Long we talked that last morning in his laboratory; and when I turned to go, he put his unseen hand in mine with nervous grip, and said, "Now I shall conquer the world!" And I could not dare to tell him of Paul Tichlorne's equal success.

At home I found a note from Paul, asking me to come up immediately, and it was high noon when I came spinning up the driveway on my wheel. Paul called me from the tennis court, and I dismounted and went over. But the court was empty. As I stood there, gaping open-mouthed, a tennis ball struck me on the arm, and as I turned about, another whizzed past my ear. For aught I could see of my assailant, they came whirling at me from out of space, and right well was I peppered with them. But when the balls already flung at me began to come back for a second whack, I realized the situation. Seizing a racquet and keeping my eyes open, I quickly saw a rainbow flash appearing and disappearing and darting over the ground. I took out after it, and when I laid the racquet upon it for a half-dozen stout blows, Paul's voice rang out:

"Enough! Enough! Oh! Ouch! Stop! You're landing on my naked skin, you know! Ow! O-w-w! I'll be good! I'll be good! I only wanted you to see my metamorphosis," he said ruefully, and I imagined he was rubbing his hurts.

A few minutes later we were playing tennis—a handicap on my part, for I could have no knowledge of his position save when all the angles between himself, the sun, and me, were in proper conjunction. Then he flashed, and only then. But the flashes were more brilliant than the rainbow—purest blue, most delicate violet, brightest yellow, and all the intermediary shades, with the scintillant brilliancy of the diamond, dazzling, blinding, iridescent.

But in the midst of our play I felt a sudden cold chill, reminding me of deep mines and gloomy crypts, such a chill as I had experienced that very morning. The next moment, close to the net, I saw a ball rebound in mid-air and empty space, and at the same instant, a score of feet away, Paul Tichlorne emitted a rainbow flash. It could not be he from whom the ball had rebounded, and with sickening dread I realized that Lloyd Inwood had come upon the scene. To make sure, I looked for his shadow, and there it was, a shapeless blotch the girth of his body (the sun was overhead), moving along the ground. I remembered his threat, and felt sure that all the long years of rivalry were about to culminate in uncanny battle.

I cried a warning to Paul, and heard a snarl as of a wild beast, and an answering snarl. I saw the dark blotch move swiftly across the court, and a brilliant burst of vari-coloured light moving with equal swiftness to meet it; and then shadow and flash came together and there was the sound of unseen blows. The net went down before my frightened eyes. I sprang towards the fighters, crying:

"For God's sake!"

But their locked bodies smote against my knees, and I was overthrown.

"You keep out of this, old man!" I heard the voice of Lloyd Inwood from out of the emptiness. And then Paul's voice crying, "Yes, we've had enough of peacemaking!"

From the sound of their voices I knew they had separated. I could not locate Paul, and so approached the shadow that represented Lloyd. But from the other side came a stunning blow on the point of my jaw, and I heard Paul scream angrily, "Now will you keep away?"

Then they came together again, the impact of their blows, their groans and gasps, and the swift flashings and shadow-movings telling plainly of the deadliness of the struggle.

I shouted for help, and Gaffer Bedshaw came running into the court. I could see, as he approached, that he was looking at me strangely, but he collided with the combatants and was hurled headlong to the ground. With despairing shriek and a cry of "O Lord, I've got 'em!" he sprang to his feet and tore madly out of the court.

I could do nothing, so I sat up, fascinated and powerless, and watched the struggle. The noonday sun beat down with dazzling brightness on the naked tennis court. And it *was* naked. All I could see was the blotch of shadow and the rainbow flashes, the dust rising from the invisible feet, the earth tearing up from beneath the straining foot-grips, and the wire screen bulge once or twice as their bodies hurled against it. That was all, and after a time even that ceased. There were no more flashes, and the shadow had become long and stationary; and I remembered their set boyish faces when they clung to the roots in the deep coolness of the pool.

They found me an hour afterwards. Some inkling of what had happened got to the servants and they quitted the Tichlorne service in a body. Gaffer Bedshaw never recovered from the second shock he received, and is confined in a madhouse, hopelessly incurable. The secrets of their marvellous discoveries died with Paul and Lloyd, both laboratories being destroyed by grief-stricken relatives. As for myself, I no longer care for chemical research, and science is a tabooed topic in my household. I have returned to my roses. Nature's colours are good enough for me.

IN THE FOOTSTEPS OF SVENGALI

by a GERMAN POLICE COLONEL AS TOLD TO KURT SINGER

DAME FATE can play some amazing tricks, once she pinions her victim with treacherous claws. In my lifetime as a police officer, serving forty years in the C.I.D. of various branches of the German police organization, I had never come across a case like this, the story of a misused and violated woman trapped into depths so dark that it was hard to believe they could possibly exist. When I met her, she was a confused remnant of a human being with little real knowledge or will of her own. She had indeed faced the unendurable.

It took us over a year to crack this case, one of the vilest crimes ever committed in the history of hypnotic criminology. Now, during my retirement, I am trying to recollect and reconstruct the events of those fateful months. I have my notes, some files, and my own unhappy memories to help me.

I remember a bleak winter day in 1934. Rain beat down in an endless stream. Through my windows I saw trees, wind-whipped and bare. This was the third day of the storm, and a break was not in sight. I particularly recall the occasion because my assistant brought a rain-drenched man into my small office. Rivulets cascaded from his black umbrella; his green Loden cape was soaked, and his face red with cold.

He was an irate man, and made no effort to conceal his anger. "Heil Hitler," he screamed, a salutation which neither I nor many of my Heidelberg Catholic associates appreciated. He demanded attention, and I could see how greatly he needed to be helped.

"Do take off your coat," I urged in an effort to calm him.

He complied nervously and accepted a chair in front of my desk. He was small and slim and looked hungry and unhappy. My first thought was that he might be unemployed as were so many in those days, but as we talked I found that E.B. (let's call him Ernst Baumann) was a civil servant who had worked for the old regime, was retained by the Hitler government, and now held a small, unimportant position. Under his impoverished guise there showed good manners and a fair amount of education. His attitude was servile. Obviously, I was a police chief whom he wished to impress, and to this end he vacillated between indignation and flattery, patriotism and entreaty. But it was plain he was in trouble and wanted my help.

His problem gradually came to the surface. Ernst Baumann was worried about his wife. She had been good to him, but now she was in some undefined danger. What danger? Baumann was reluctant to reveal specific facts. He spoke rapidly, and often shuddered as if he were still chilled from the rain. His increasing nervousness impeded his ability to organize a coherent story so that I could understand his problem.

I listened quietly to Baumann for twenty minutes, making a few random notes, until I felt it was time to interrupt his monologue.

"Now, if I understand your complaint correctly, you want the Heidelberg police to arrest a man whose name you do not know. You say your wife has given this mysterious, unknown man three thousand marks."

"Ja, ja, Herr Polizei Oberst," he agreed, wagging his head violently. I waved him to be quiet and continued:

"You claim the man who received the three thousand marks is a medical doctor who used a false name. Further, you say you do not know his address and you are unable to give a description of him?"

"Jawohl, sehr richtig."

"And you tell me your wife does not know the whereabouts of this doctor either, but that she has been under treatment from him for at least a year, and probably longer. You further state that this person has misused your wife under hypnosis, and as a result of hypnotic suggestion."

"Ja, meine Frau hatte hypnotische Behandlung."

The man before me was horrified by his own story. It was painful to watch his nervousness. He either drummed on my desk top with his thin fingers or he wriggled his feet like a small child in school who is unable to reach the floor.

There were many questions that needed an answer, but I felt certain that Baumann would be of little help. Why, I mused, had he not brought his wife along with him to tell the story? If such a person as he had described really existed, a monster who used hypnotism to conquer and enslave women, who then was he? Baumann was obviously not able to identify him and I could not be sure that my visitor was trustworthy. He could be a lunatic challenging windmills of imagined wrongs or trying to revenge himself against a wife whom he had discovered looked elsewhere for her pleasures.

Baumann must have sensed some of my doubts; perhaps my face mirrored my puzzled thoughts.

"I know my story seems unbelievable, but *bitte, Herr Polizeioberst*, do believe in me. God knows I have tried to find the doctor at many addresses but could never locate him. He gave these hypnotic treatments to my wife merely by putting his hand on her head. He told her she would become calmer, feel drowsy and fall into sleep immediately. My wife comes from peasant stock. She is a hard worker. She has never suffered from nervous ailments before. I tell you, this man is a devil who has made her suffer, and the most diabolical thing of all is that Paula cannot remember anything that happens while she is under the doctor's influence. He orders her during the hypnotic sleep to forget everything . . . everything . . . everything . . ." His voice trailed off in a moan.

This had to be enough for the time being. I told Ernst Baumann that he would hear from us. I wanted to talk to his wife and to discuss the case with psychiatrists at the University of Heidelberg and with some other experts on the subject of hypnosis.

Baumann appeared to be somewhat relieved when he left, although I am sure he knew I was still dubious about his story. First of all, I wanted to determine Baumann's reliability, as well as learn something about his character.

In 1934, I knew practically nothing about hypnosis beyond a few facts gleaned from popular books and magazines, and exposure to the antics and showmanship of stage hypnotists. I had superficial knowledge of some mysterious cases of hypnotic crimes, but I had tended to write them off as weird events having little to do with my own work in Germany. I was aware, though, of a prime factor in hypnotism about which there could be no dispute: no crime can be induced by hypnosis if the subject is morally opposed to such an act. Ergo, a person trained not to kill will not murder under hypnosis. He will awaken from his trance. A person trained to believe stealing is wrong will not steal, nor will anyone violate his precepts of right and wrong through hypnotic suggestion.

Thus, on that blustery day in 1934, I had little reason to believe that Ernst Baumann, the frail little man who had just left my office, would send me out on a journey to reach frontiers heretofore unknown to me.

I dictated a resume of the case and sent it on to Dr. Ludwig Mayer at the Heidelberg University, asking for his opinion and help. I also requested an interview with Mrs. Baumann, but not before Dr. Mayer, one of Germany's outstanding specialists in the field of psychiatry and psychological criminology had examined her.

A subsequent medical report from the University stated that after thorough examination, Mrs. Paula Baumann showed no symptoms of illness, or abnormal signs of forgetfulness, or mental disturbances. However, the report went on to say, many questions concerning the accused doctor appeared to produce in the patient a total lack of memory.

Dr. Mayer suggested to our department and to Mrs. Baumann that she be subjected to a hypnotic experiment during which certain questions would be directed to her. Paula was co-operative. She was helpful and humble to abjectness itself.

The initial results were limited. I am now quoting from our old and closed police files. The woman while under Dr. Mayer's hypnotic sleep declared:

"He always put his hand on my forehead. Then I lost my mind. I became tired and then I knew nothing about myself any more."

Paula was an excellent hypnotic subject. Dr. Mayer experienced no difficulties in inducing sleep. As I watched her, I saw before me only a shadow of what must once have been a pretty, vibrant woman. Obviously she had lost weight. Her face was haggard, worried, and her expression relaxed only when she was in the limbo of some world of her own, unknown to us.

Dr. Mayer confirmed one simple fact. By claiming she had been hypnotized by an unidentified person, Paula endorsed her husband's story and complaint.

The next step was obvious. Dr. Mayer had to use several additional sessions to produce a hypnotic sleep deep enough to reach Paula's subconscious.

Again I quote from the bulky police files which record Paula's testimony during hypnosis.

"It was before my marriage. One day I left home and took a train to Heidelberg. I had pains in my stomach and wanted to see a doctor. At one of the stops along the line, a man entered my compartment and sat opposite me. He began the conversation which led to my mentioning I was ill. He said he knew as soon as he saw me that I was sick. He told me he was a homoeopath and nature-healer. He introduced himself as Dr. Bergen from Karlsruhe-Daxlanden. He said he recognised my ailment and could treat it. When the train stopped at Graben, he invited me to take a cup of coffee with him but I declined. I felt uncertain about him. Later he helped me when I left the train. He carried my bag.

"Suddenly he took hold of my hand, and I had the strange feeling that I no longer possessed any will-power of my own. I felt strange . . . hazy and confused.

"Later on, he ordered me, personally or by letter, to come to the railway station at Karlsruhe and also to Heidelberg. He always met me at the station.

"But I cannot remember where he gave me treatment."

These were trying days for Mr. and Mrs. Baumann. The innumerable tests and endless questions were hardly conducive to the one thing Paula needed more than anything else just then—a time to recover in conditions of peace and quiet. Instead, she was being constantly bombarded by interrogators, an army of medical students and police officers, psychologists and psychiatrists. We set up devious mazes of questions with traps, baits, lures and penalties. In retrospect, perhaps I was wrong to insist that Paula had a moral obligation to co-operate in helping us to solve the mystery in which she, as well as ourselves, were engulfed. There were days, after hypnotic sessions with Dr. Mayer, when I feared she would collapse, thus ending everything. On the other hand, I reasoned, she had the assistance of the best doctors to be found anywhere, and her case was certainly unique in the annals of criminology and psychiatry. As is generally done in obdurate cases, hypnotism was repeated several times. Each session cut deeper and produced new evidence for the police, but no further details about our elusive Svengali.

One day, Paula Baumann, in a hypnotic state, said :

"Sometimes I was in a room in Heidelberg . . . but I can no

longer remember where. He picked me up at the foothill of the castle, took my hand and said everything would be totally dark around me. We walked for some time. Then we came to some stairs. We went up two flights. He opened the door. I entered, and he closed it. For the first time, it was light. The room was simple and small. There was a couch and a wooden table. He put his hand on my forehead. 'You will be calmer and calmer,' he said, 'calmer and calmer. Sleep . . .' I don't know what happened after that. I don't know what he did with me, or to me. I can't remember anything."

Our meetings with the psychiatrists were rapidly evolving into a college course. Inspired, aggravated, taunted and curious, I began studying Freud, Mesmer and the other pioneers in the field of hypnosis, with something that resembled fury. Bernheim and Liebault became old friends and I could reel off their theories with an ease that surprised even myself. Each page I read helped me to understand this case a bit more. At last I was even able to suggest a few leading questions which I felt might help Dr. Mayer in his effort to unearth some small detail about the unknown man which would betray his identity.

While Dr. Mayer probed for the solution of his problem with Paula's mind, we had our own more specific problems. We had no inkling of the man's appearance, the colour of his hair, his height, weight or marks of identification.

It was rapidly becoming painfully clear that the criminal had instilled post-hypnotic suggestions and such powerful taboos in the mind of the victim that Paula's amnesia was complete in certain areas. And those were the segments we wanted.

Like a skilful surgeon cutting through human tissue, Dr. Mayer cautiously sliced through the gauze that shrouded Paula's subconscious, the vault of all her past experiences.

Dr. Mayer had one ally alone . . . time. Not only does time heal, but it can also unlock artificially introduced memory blocks. With endless patience the eminent psychiatrist was slowly forging the key to fit those locks. I often sat and listened with admiration, for Dr. Mayer was cunningly beginning to hoodwink the criminal we were after, to fool and outwit the doctor-hypnotist.

I was present when the door of Paula's memory first began to swing open. Dr. Mayer had induced a deep hypnotic sleep. He then suggested to her that he was the original doctor, the hypnotist who treated her and held her spirit and her mind. Paula responded. She agreed that Dr. Mayer was the man she had met on the train. When questioned she gave a personal description of the man we wanted.

We were delighted by the progress. I searched police files and located all possible suspects who answered her description.

The next session was discouraging. In her deep trance, Paula refused to identify any of our pictures from the files. Furthermore, she retreated again into her amnesia. We knew we had failed. The post-hypnotic block was still in effect and, it appeared, more deeply entrenched than before.

But in our gloom, there sprang a ray of light from the outside. We surmised that Paula had outlived her mission in the life of the man we wanted. Eventually, we reasoned, he would find a new victim.

He did. We received an official complaint from a citizen in Speyer concerning a man who had swindled a credulous patient under his care.

Frau Ursula Bunzel filed the complaint. Her description of the swindler coincided with that given by Mrs. Baumann while under hypnosis. Slim as were the facts, the police in Speyer arrested the suspect and booked him as Franz Walter. We asked that he be transferred to us in Heidelberg.

Herr Walter was a good-looking man in his early forties, although he appeared to be younger. He was well-groomed and spoke easily and confidently. When questioned, Walter looked surprised and declared emphatically that he had never seen Paula Baumann. When we brought her in to confront him, neither showed the slightest sign of recognition.

In an inept attempt to spring a trap, I asked Walter to hypnotize Paula.

"How can I," he said, "I know nothing about hypnotism."

In another vain attempt to incriminate him I asked him to put his hand on Frau Baumann's head. He readily complied. Nothing happened. Paula did not resist.

Later, when Paula spoke of the incident, she said, "I felt nothing. Walter evoked no emotion such as I felt when I was hypnotized by my doctor. My doctor gave me a hypnotic sleep through a different emotion and I felt far more . . ."

Another police staff meeting was called. Dr. Mayer was not surprised that we had failed to establish any link between Paula and Franz Walter. Hypnotic results, he explained to us laymen, are not produced by mirrors or commands. The important element on the part of the hypnotist lies in his absolute appearance of confidence and authority. In the meeting of Walter and Paula, there was no faith-prestige relationship established. Any weakness, uncertainty, or disbelief makes the completion of a trance impossible. The hypnotist can, at will, destroy such an aura which results in reluctance and resistance against hypnosis on the part of his subject. If Walter did not want to hypnotize Frau Baumann, we could not force him to do so.

Obviously this had been the case. Walter had touched Paula as impersonally as if he were touching an inanimate object. His mind was not behind his well-manicured fingertips.

Our job, then, was to break through Paula's walled-in memory which we had approached, but never yet entered.

Dr. Mayer's continuous probing was an agonizing experience for this woman. I could not resist admiring her, fearing for her, and even hating her at times for her failure to respond. The frustrations set up by our questions, our relentless questions that ricochetted off her locked door, took their toll. She developed severe speech impediments. These periods of stuttering and stammering became a part of both her waking and her trance life.

As a team, we tried everything known to psychiatric medicine.

One of our first steps was to play what seemed to be a childish game with Paula. "Can you remember your name? Can you remember your father's name? Can you remember the name of the street you live on? Can you remember the first letter of your name? Can you remember the first letter of your doctor's first name?" This seemed to lead nowhere.

We moved on to word association tests. One word in memory or experience leads to another and another. Perhaps through such devious routes, we might gain an insight.

But the post-hypnotic command of silence was still a gag in Paula's mouth.

At this impasse, we counted the passing of six fruitless months. Was there a word the criminal had used which would automatically reintroduce the command of silence, even when in an awakened state?

Hundreds, yes thousands, of painful questions were directed

at this poor woman, but nothing of importance emerged. Evidently Walter was not the man we wanted, for no tell-tale evidence against him could be found.

Nine months later Dr. Mayer was still concentrating on a series of word association tests. Under hypnosis Frau Baumann was asked to visualize anything she wished when certain words were spoken.

"A room . . . a bed . . . a dinner . . . drinking wine . . . romance . . ."

Again Frau Baumann was co-operative, but her answers showed her to be an earthy woman with little imagination and no romance. Her associations were realistic and concerned with her husband, old age, money, illnesses. In short, the many hours produced nothing that helped us explore the one segment of her past that we so vitally needed.

Almost a year to the day that Herr Baumann had come into my office, rain-drenched, we made our first positive progress.

The experiment this day was no different from any other. Dr. Mayer was still searching for a lead word that would produce some glimpse into Paula's memory. Again Paula was in a deep hypnotic sleep when Dr. Mayer asked her to tell what she visualized in connection with the word "bath".

"Bath," he said softly. "What do you remember about a bath? Think hard. Bath . . . bath."

Paula frowned. It was apparent that she was straining to help, to dig out some fragment that was tantalizing her. "Oh ja, ich sehe vor meinen Augen . . . I see a towel." The woman on the couch spoke slowly. Suddenly she seemed pleased and spoke quite freely. "The towel was made of white frotté."

"Is there anything else you remember about the towel . . . any details such as the pattern, a second colour perhaps?"

Paula was manifestly struggling again. After a moment she answered again, "Ah ja. The towel had a light-blue stripe. There was also a smaller towel in the bathroom. We took a bath together. I took the smaller towel to dry myself. It was also made of white frotté, but it had lavender stripes."

I must confess I was unimpressed with Paula's description of towels. Had she described the man we wanted, I would have leapt with excitement, but the size, type and colour of bathroom toiletries interested me not.

By this time we had amassed many folders of reports on Paula and her reactions to the association tests. "Lavender" was no more, even less of a clue than some others we had arrived at before. For instance, the word "shoes" had lead Mrs. Baumann to say: "Shoemaker . . . five marks."

Others were:

Leichtbinó (trademark).
Automobile: "6071"
Combarus
Laxative
17: "Write doctor . . . don't come . . . dark . . . 19 . . . 8."

Dr. Mayer hung on to the clue of the shoes. "You speak of shoes, shoemaker and five marks. What does that mean in your life? Think hard."

Suddenly Paula broke through another protective layer of her amnesia lock.

"The doctor bought his ten shoes in Speyer at the store XYZ. He gave them his old shoes and paid five marks in addition."

Paula had barely completed her sentence when I sent one of my men to Speyer to investigate her lead. He returned with the word I expected: the transaction had occurred several years before. No one could remember the incident. Again we were forced to wait for a new clue to spring from the miasmal swamp of Paula's mind.

"Leichtbino," said the psychiatrist. "What do you think about when I say this word? What do you see? What do you think about?"

In her sleep, Paula showed anxiety. "Leichtbino . . . leichtbino . . . The doctor said if I were ever to go to court, the word 'leichtbino' would come into my mind. I would fall ill. I would be unable to say a word against him. Instead I would testify in his favour."

"Automobile . . . 6071. What does that mean to you?" persisted Dr. Mayer.

Paula, still under hypnosis, answered, "We went swimming one day, I think . . . I think I saw a car with the number 6071."

I gave a gasp of relief. Here was a tangible fact, something we could really follow. But again we failed. 6071 was the licence plate of a rental car which had changed owners three times in the intervening years. It was impossible to trace the person who rented the automobile on a vague date to go on a vague trip somewhere.

From my report of the case thus far, it would appear as if I spent all my time in Dr. Mayer's office, sitting beside Paula

Baumann and watching her struggle through the maze of her amnesia. This, however, is far from the truth. In addition to our usual routines as police officers, we were also following every lead she had suggested. We tried to analyze every movement she made, every word she uttered and every flight of fancy we could conjure from our sessions with her. In addition, we combed the files of Europe for every hypnotic faker listed in the rogues' galleries. We interviewed many women who claimed, rightly or wrongly, to have been raped during hypnosis, swindled by men with strong personalities, or led astray by charmers.

For a long period, I kept a wary eye on Paula's husband. It was quite feasible that he was behind this caper in order to extort their savings of three thousand marks. Later I was forced to toss this hypothesis overboard. The weak-willed, puny, high-strung little man possessed none of the qualifications necessary to be a hypnotist.

During the year of concentrated study in the field of hypnosis and the extraordinary opportuntiy to watch a master psychiatrist at work, I had learned one operational fact. A skilled hypnotist *can* overcome the moral resistance of his victim just as a lion tamer finally handles his beast. A human being, for instance, can be lured to kill if given the proper training, just as a lion which has a basic instinct to kill, can be taught to open its jaws around his trainer's head. This then was the answer to a case I had handled several years before. In this crime a hypnotist had plotted a murder by the simple means of convincing his subject that a loaded Browning was merely a child's toy revolver. The hypnotist collected the dead man's insurance money. It was a crime with no fingerprints of the killer on the gun. The murderer was hundreds of kilometers away when the Browning was fired by his victim under hypnosis.

Again we returned to the endless, repetitious, boring word "games". "Combarus" was one of the first words Paula had uttered under hypnosis. It meant nothing to us, but Dr. Mayer continued to pursue her background association with the term. At last she gave a lengthy dissertation which opened another segment of her memory:

"The doctor and I often went to Speyer. Once we ate at the Zähringer Hof. Another man came to our table. He was called Dietzen and was the branch manager of some company. The two men talked together. I remember the doctor said proudly, "Today

I will accomplish it. She will go with you, Dietzen, and do what you want her to do.' Dietzen gave the doctor a twenty mark bill and left. We remained at the table a little longer. Later we walked along the main street. On a corner we met a maid. She had red hair and said I should go with her to Herr Dietzen. . . ."

Paula had stopped, and we all sat as if we were on the edge of a precipice.

Then she continued in her same slow drawl such as a child who is just learning to speak: "Before I met the maid, the doctor had put his hand on my forehead. He said, 'You will be without any will of your own. You will follow every command Herr Dietzen gives you. You will do everything he wants you to do. Afterwards you will remember nothing. You will think of the word "combarus" and slide into a deeper sleep than you have ever known. You will never, never remember what happened to you, or where you were.'

"This happened several times. At each meeting I received such commands and the word 'combarus' was used. I fell into a state of lethargy, lack of will and lack of energy."

Paula rolled in agony on the couch. She turned her head right and left as if wishing to whip all thoughts from her brain.

"Until today I did not remember a thing about this. What am I? I'm not a prostitute! I'm not a bad woman! I will jump into the Neckar. I cannot live with this memory. I am so ashamed!"

For a split second it appeared that Paula was about to leap, to run, to jump into the Neckar river which skirts old Heidelberg.

Dr. Mayer was ready to calm her. "It is all right," he said. "You are going to wake now. When you do, you will not know what you have said, but you will feel relaxed because you have said it. You will be glad that you can remember. You have nothing to be ashamed of, and you will be glad of that. You will be more cheerful and relaxed than you have been in a long time . . ."

Paula left the office smiling as we had never known her to smile before. She stood erect, the picture of relaxed poise.

For the rest of us, it was not so easy. Our worst fears were rapidly being confirmed. Had the doctor organized his own white slave traffic? The shackles of hypnosis were certainly more difficult to remove than those of iron.

We sent out a search for a Herr Dietzen, knowing full-well the name was false. The charlatan-doctor would have been much too clever to introduce his flesh-buyer by his correct name.

Our department collected a file on every known hypnotist in Germany. From the bulk, we had three men whom we viewed with suspicion and kept an eye on. The criminal misuse of knowledge in the field of hypnotism was a never-ending shock to me.

There was, for instance, a laboratory technician, Richard Karlbach, who had hypnotized his fiancée in his apartment. During her trance, he used her as suited his fancy. This was diabolical enough in itself, but Karlbach's perverted sense of humour had inspired him to plant a recording machine under his bed. When he had awakened the girl, she knew nothing of the events that had transpired. Karlbach was only too pleased to use the tape to enlighten his betrothed as to her behaviour.

Karlbach's ex-fianceé was willing to help us find Richard, but he had apparently vanished. A month later we scratched the scoundrel off our list. Karlbach had been put for a year in a concentration camp for making an obscene remark about Hitler. After six months, however, he escaped and as far as we could tell, was in Czechoslovakia. At any rate, we had details that he was not in Germany during the period of Paula's frightful experiences.

Again we returned to Dr. Mayer's office. What had Paula meant when she said "17 ... write ... doctor ... don't come ... dark ... 19 ... 8 ...?"

It was a relief to know that each session with Dr. Mayer seemed to help Paula. Since the first rays of light began to creep through the crevices, Paula looked better, was more calm, and appeared to be gaining weight.

Dr. Mayer again posed the question of the strange combination of words and numbers.

Paula stumbled in her speech as she told her story: "The doctor said that whenever I could not come and see him because my husband might suspect something, I should write to Karlsruhe F. Street 17. When I wrote him, there would be darkness all around me. I would not be able to remember what I had written ... or that I had written ... ever."

More facts saw the daylight. The numbers 19 ... 8 were used by the hypnotist to lock her memory. The moment these were mentioned, Paula could not remember any incident. In case she was ever brought to court, she had been instructed to think of 19 ... 8, at which moment she could volunteer no information.

As double insurance, the hypnotic devil also instilled the idea that if she ever broke the 19...8 command for silence and forgetfulness, Paula would fall on her face and die.

The sinister hypnotist cultivated an intricate tangled cable of techniques in Frau Baumann's mind. Even the illustrious Dr. Mayer was often hard pressed to know which wire to snip next. Our hypnotist had worked with his own rhythm and chose to toss his victim from one extreme to another with the precision of a regulated pendulum.

In the meantime, we were making history... at least medical history. Psychiatrists, psycho-analysts and doctors came to Heidelberg from all over the world. Everyone was armed with some theory or other to help this poor woman who, in the final analysis, stood alone.

Throughout the days and months that went by so quickly, Dr. Mayer plodded steadily along. By now we had developed a long list of lead words which automatically clicked Frau Baumann into a hypnotic trance. Strangely enough, the word "laxative" was one which brought about hypnotic sleep in which Paula responded readily to suggestions.

Almost by accident we discovered that if we counted in sequence: 1, 2, 3, 4, to 8, there was no effect. But the moment the number 10 was uttered, our patient went into deep sleep.

These "fantasy" words had almost ruled and ruined Paula's life. Now it was up to us to remove any other post-hypnotic suggestion which still controlled her memory. This objective became almost as important to me as finding the ruthless criminal hypnotist.

Nor had the incredible "doctor" overlooked the powers of religion. We learned Paula had been threatened repeatedly that if she ever broke through the post-hypnotic spell and betrayed her hypnotizer-lover, her father would die the next morning and Paula would find herself in the fiery pit of hell after death, doomed to roast in agony throughout eternity.

This discovery brought new problems. The fear of hell had evidently been so effective that the poor woman was willing to pay any amount to undo her "sins", irrational as they were to a normal mind. Faces leered at Paula and the Devil was hot on her heels. The hypnotist painted a hideous mirage.

Theomania is not new, nor is it an unknown phenomenon. We recognized all the hallucinations planted into this simple woman's mind, but so far we had failed to give her real and constructive help.

We held hope that time would help to wear away her memory block. We learned to our horror of still greater and more imaginative crimes committed by Paula's mental master.

The "doctor" had sold Paula to men for money, sometimes to more than one in a single night. He prefaced each venture of this kind with his typical pattern which brought on fear of reprisal if Paula refused to obey his commands. With voodoo-like threats he said that if she ever attempted to open the door to her memory, if she ever tried to recollect her past actions, Paula's fingers would immediately become stiff and finally rot away.

In one hypnotic session, Dr. Mayer tossed out a bombshell and we felt the repercussions. "Paula," he said, "I don't want to know any secrets, but when did the doctor tell you these things?"

Paula answered quickly, "In 1930". We were stunned. The two had been operating as a team for four years—four years with a great, gaping vacuum of memory for the poor victim.

Perhaps it was the shock of the monstrosity of the crime that made me think in a different direction. Or perhaps it was the old police adage that ivory doesn't grow from a rat's mouth that inspired me to take a week's vacation. Or perhaps it was my personal superstition that every crime case gets worse before it gets better . . . if it is to be solved at all.

I wanted a respite from Mrs. Baumann and her world of frightful fantasy. I needed to think and the opportunity to organize my mind which was beginning to whirl between fact and illusion, between reality and dreams. The files would go with me. In some quiet, peaceful place I would read and reread every report, every piece of evidence and would try to find a pattern from the crazy mixed-up pieces. I was at a dead end, but I had company there. So was Paula.

Deep in the heart of the Black Forest, perhaps I would find the bliss of knowledge, the light of insight. I was proving to be no Sherlock Holmes who could deduce by clever logic, and Dr. Mayer was no Watson with the medical answers. We were a similar pair, with the painful exception that the Holmes-Watson combination invariably came up with the solution to the crimes they investigated.

Spare me the details. I didn't sleep well despite the long hikes

I took in the woods. I read with great interest the biography of Hanussen, Hitler's sinister astrologer and hypnotist who was murdered by the same Nazis whom he had helped.

Then the truth hit me with the directness of a bolt from the blue!

If you will excuse the personal reference, I was taking a bath. Paula's lead word came to me—"bath". Hadn't Paula spoken of a bath she had taken with the "doctor" and described the towels, the one with a blue border and the other with lavender?

I leaped from the old-fashioned tub which had once held the royal bodies of some of the Württemberg dukes, and dashed, dripping, to my files. It was a sort of sixth sense that told me I had the answer. The case was not wrapped up yet, but I felt I possessed a lead that would take me to that answer. I left for Heidelberg the next day.

Franz Walter, the suspect, we still held behind bars as a swindler, but we had discarded him as a possibility in our search for the "doctor". But a search of his room had disclosed towels such as Paula described. Some were bordered in lavender, others in blue, all were frotté. There was no other kind in his living quarters. We felt Walter was our man, but we still had to prove involvement.

I take no credit for solving this case. Anyone could have thought of the towels as the vital clue, but the reference had been made so fleetingly and seemed so inconsequential, stupid and non-sensical that we all forgot about it as the case moved along.

Herr Franz Walter, in the meantime, had enveloped himself in a false sense of security. The hours of his hell still awaited him. Little did he realize that he was caught in the vortex of his own mad ambitions and that the law was now ready to execute a just but belated retribution. When our suave Svengali was confronted by Frau Baumann for a second time he exuded self-confidence as a barrel oozes lard.

I expected him to deny everything. I also made certain he did not know the police held a trump card against him. The man who sat in our police office had driven Paula close to insanity. To analyze him was not easy.

Walter was a man of contradictions: an evil genius on the one hand—plain, ordinary, shy, stupid and cruel on the other. But whatever components made up his total personality, it was evident he was a successful criminal hypnotist. His words held a certain fascination even for me.

He wore a large diamond and was prone to flash it, almost unconsciously, in the face of the person whom he was addressing.

A review of his case history told us that Franz Walter came from one of Germany's better families. He was apparently very ambitious, had gone to college, was involved in a fire which had burned most of the hair from his body, had never seen his mother again, and ignored his old friends. For a few years he studied at Heidelberg but did not complete his medical training, there or anywhere else. Being a man who preferred the security of shadows, he made an effort to remain in the backwaters of life. Although no books turned up in our search of his rooms, we found that Walter was a student of the philosophies of Tibet, India and well educated in the field of mysticism, hypnosis, yoga, Zen and theosophy.

There were always women in his life, and his taste leaned towards young girls who were impressionable, inexperienced . . . and easily hypnotized. He generally stayed away from University students, women who travelled extensively, and the intellectual crowd. Obviously, their backgrounds made them unlikely and more difficult prey for his tactics.

Walter was capable of conjuring all kinds of hallucinations in the minds of his feminine victims. Hallucinations are one of the real unexplained miracles of the mind. In this type of trance, a clever hypnotist can lure his subject to behave as commanded.

We finally succeeded in proving that Walter's pawns had stolen money and jewels for him, prostituted themselves and, in short, answered to his beck and call.

His evaluation of women was excellent. Walter chose only those who were free of inhibitions, prejudice, those who lived on faith and trust, those who wanted to be loved and loved a master. He carefully avoided sceptics.

Franz Walter denied everything. Even after I had broadly hinted that I had amassed a great deal of evidence against him, and that his confession would perhaps lighten his sentence, he maintained his innocence.

"I have never seen Frau Baumann before. Furthermore, I know nothing about hypnosis. I'm the innocent victim in a case of mistaken identity . . . either that or some *halunke* has framed me!" It is undeniable that he wore a cloak of dignity at all times.

Walter countered our questioning by attempting to assemble some character witnesses. He declared he was no swindler and the money he had received from Frau Bunzel was a legitimate loan which he needed to tide him over, since Germany was then caught in the grip of unemployment. Yes, he agreed, he had held many jobs before. He worked as a salesman, a technician and a motor repairman. For a time he taught in a girl's finishing school until the idea of managing a small hotel caught his fancy. We knew witnesses existed who could confirm the various jobs Walter had held, but other than to mention time and place, they knew little about him.

Walter was indeed a dreamer. At one time during our conversations, he became so carried away with the things he hoped to do that he even asked me to help him. I stared at him in amazement, at the suggestion. But be that as it may, the scoundrel was a smooth talker, a man with a golden tongue.

And there was Paula, poor, confused Paula, who was still fighting her way out of the cobwebs of a waking sleep. I advised Walter to prepare for a confrontation with Paula Baumann. It was my hope that a solemn admonition might strike some sort of terror, fear or remorse in this strange man-demon.

As the next session between Paula and Franz began, the air was tense. Walter was apparently unmoved, but neither was he relaxed. Paula avoided his eyes, and she spoke more softly than ever.

"Is this the man who hypnotized you for four years?"

"I think so."

"What makes you think so?"

Paula hesitated before she said: "I know."

At this point neither Frau Baumann nor Herr Walter had been given any indication of the clue of the towels. We were riding it out with this fact which we hoped would smash the case if we came to an impasse.

Herr Walter seemed more confident as the clock ticked on. It was evident he felt he could talk himself out of any incrimination. He was probably at that moment complimenting himself on his skill with post-hypnotic suggestions which were keeping Paula from screaming his guilt.

There was something noticeable, however, going on. Both Dr. Mayer and I were acutely aware of it, and we exchanged glances several times. When Walter spoke to Frau Baumann, his voice lowered and became monotonous, slow, lacking in variation of pitch. It could have been just such a drowsy bedroom voice that he used to make the first verbal suggestions to his subject. Even I sensed the feeling of relaxation, tiredness in the eyes, a need for rest.

His technique was obvious, but this sort of evidence would never stand up in court.

I discussed my problems with Dr. Mayer who immediately suggested another hypnotic experiment during which he would ask Mrs. Baumann how she felt about Walter now. I thought it was a good idea.

This session produced a new development. Paula no longer referred to her tormentor as "doctor" or "Dr. Bergen" but called him Walter or Herr Walter and admitted she was upset meeting Franz again at the hearing.

"I know now," she continued, "that he no longer has any influence over me. My fingers will not get stiff and rot away. I will not die and go to hell . . . yet . . . when I think of Walter I feel that my fingers are a little furry . . . yes, like fur . . ."

Paula looked haggard after our session and was damp with perspiration. The maniacal spell was lifting but was not yet completely dissipated. A furry feeling. Her memory was not yet free, even now.

In fairy tales some subjects never completely awaken, resting in eternal sleep until Prince Charming comes to awaken his princess. And not every hypnotist is a Prince Charming. We knew that hypnotized subjects awaken sooner or later, but the hypnotist alone has the power to arouse his medium on his own terms and at any time he desires. How long would Paula's post-hypnotic suggestion last. No one knew. Evidently we can explain the physical mechanism of the brain but we cannot explain how its operation makes us feel and act.

We had now worked on this case for well over a year. Even though I did not have conclusive proof, I had to prepare our findings to hand to my superiors. From that point on, the legal machinery would have to roll on by itself with the precision we were accustomed to. The final decision would be left to the courts for their objective judgment. The indictment was contained in a huge dossier. Witnesses were lined up by the dozen; the state assembled the best available medical experts, but before the case reached the courts there was still a lapse of another few months. During this time Dr. Mayer continued his tests with his patient, Paula Baumann, our prime witness.

The famous psychiatrist and his staff of assistants were obsessed by the idea that it was possible, under hypnosis, to produce a hallucination in which Paula would believe she was confronted with the original hypnotist, Bergen, alias Walter. Dr. Mayer used a university student in the role of Bergen for the experiment, in the hope to have our make-believe "Doctor Bergen" cut through the memory lock with new counter suggestions. Our faked Doctor Bergen would try to give new suggestions which might remove the real Bergen's previous post-hypnotic commands. The experiment worked. Under hypnosis Dr. Mayer finally reached her. He asked Paula to recount some of the old conversations and the letters she and Bergen had exchanged. Paula began to talk:

"It was during the autumn of 1930. It was a Tuesday and about 6:30 in the evening. There was still the glow of twilight in the sky. Dr. Bergen took my hand and said, 'Come now. We will leave the hospital. Otherwise people might see us.'

"We went to an exit on the left. He continued to lead me. He said, 'It will be darker and darker around you. Soon you will no longer see anything. Just walk on. I'm leading you.'

"I walked with open eyes but couldn't see a thing, not a single person. I was blank. I thought of nothing. We went on and on through the night."

Dr. Mayer interrupted her gently. "Paula, think hard. You can remember the names of the streets. Tell me about the street-car tracks, the houses, stores, trees. The order to forget is moving away from you more and more. You can remember details now, can't you? You know where you were..."

Paula struggled, but unsuccessfully.

"I don't remember the street. He told me to walk on and on. 'You do not know where you are,' he said. He told me nothing would happen to me. He still held my hand. It was absolutely dark, and he whispered to me, 'All is dark... absolutely dark. You do not know where you are. Now step with me. We will go up... up... up...'"

Paula paused for a moment. "He opened the door to his room.

Suddenly I could see again. It was all light. This happened many times."

Old flashes of memory were hurting Frau Baumann. The reconstructed scene was too vivid. She hesitated to continue. Dr. Mayer had triggered the clash between old post-hypnotic commands and new suggestions.

Dr. Mayer insisted that she tell more. Old commands she had previously obeyed, he said, could not now be imposed on her. Paula covered her face with her hands, shook her head in rejection of the new order and cringed like a child who is about to be slapped.

A minute later she continued: "The Doctor—Walter—he said I should lie on the couch. I was his patient and would receive his treatment. He put his hand on my forehead and said I would sleep. I received the treatment, I received the calm sleep, and I could hear him saying, 'You know nothing. You remember nothing of what happened here and you will not remember it later . . . or ever.' "

Paula began to cry. Dr. Mayer was unmoved. Instead he seemed to feel he was reaching a crisis and urged Paula to continue talking.

"Later on," Frau Baumann whispered, "he asked me if I knew what he had done to me. I don't know, but later I remembered he gave me a very long kiss while I was lying on the couch. I pushed him away. I wanted to call for help . . . but I couldn't. It was like a nightmare. He stroked my body and kept saying, 'Sleep, sleep . . . sleep. You cannot do anything. You cannot even call out.'

"Then he took my hands and tucked them under my waist. He pressed my elbows against the couch. 'Now you cannot move,' he said, 'and when you awaken you will remember nothing.'

"But now, for the first time, I do remember. I had forgotten for such a long time. He used me sexually. That whole horrible thing is alive for me now."

Paula's voice had risen. She was approaching a state of hysteria. Dr. Mayer ceased his challenges. He released the pressures, and Paula became more calm. In all, it had been a horrible session to witness. I suffered for this woman who had lived through an inferno of bestiality and terror.

But Dr. Mayer was methodically cutting his way to her sanity. Inch by inch he severed the strands in the cables.

The following day Dr. Mayer again worked with Frau Baumann.

Under hypnosis, the scientist presented her with a blank sheet of paper.

"This is one of Walter's letters. Read it to us."

During previous sessions, Paula had been unable to recall any letters she had received from Walter, but during this trance, she again delved into her own slowly opening memory. She read slowly. There were some words she could not pronounce. These she spelled for us.

"Your appointment is on the 13th of this month at the Heidelberg railway station. I will be waiting for you at the exit at 6:00. Dr. Bergen. Destroy this letter."

An eerie feeling permeated the room when we watched Paula read from the blank piece of stationery. She read line for line, pointing her finger at every word she saw in her mind, but which was not actually there.

From the sessions we learned many new things. Walter, or Dr. Bergen, had suggested to Paula that her old stomach ailment was cured but she now suffered from new illnesses. We were able to list at least six different suggested afflictions Paula suffered in four years. The "doctor" suggested internal operations which cost the unwitting woman stiff fees. These were performed. Afterwards Paula felt severe pains in her imaginery wounds but never questioned the fact that Dr. Bergen allowed her to walk home alone.

After the abdominal "surgery" and subsequent successful healing, the charlatan dreamed up additional and surprising physical problems for his subject. Paula could not use her fingers or arms. The bent fingers, as commanded by post-hypnotic commands, curled into the palms of her hands and, as the nails grew longer, bit into the flesh. "Dr." Bergen then performed another operation, bandaged her hand . . . and charged another exorbitant fee.

By this time my small office was bulging with piles of reports on this *case celebre*. We had the testimony of Herr Baumann. We also had sworn affidavits from two other women who claimed to have been hypnotized by Walter. One was a woman librarian who had loaned numerous books on hypnosis to a man who resembled our photographs of Walter. She also inferred he had made advances towards her.

Ernst Baumann was a mere shadow. He was a broken man,

desperately in debt and in constant fear of new and incomprehensible surprises. He was a husband who had seen the delicate structure of their marriage shattered by some unseen force, just as glass can be broken by a sound of high frequency beyond the wavelengths of human perception.

Baumann described Paula's sicknesses and their domestic quarrels. He had, as he could prove, insisted she see a local doctor. Paula pretended she had gone and afterwards blamed her ensuing ills on the local physician.

Ernst had found himself in a whirlpool of disaster, confusion and accumulating debts. He spent all his savings, then turned to her parents, his friends, and finally the pawnbrokers. Walter received it all.

As the controls over her mind ebbed away, Paula spoke more and more freely "Today I know where all the pains came from. I know it for the first time. Dr. Bergen, Walter, was dissatisfied with me. When I did not deliver money, he told me I should commit suicide. He said, 'You have no money for me. You will be sorry for that. You will suffer more than ever, have greater pains than ever. You have no idea of the kinds of agonies I will inflict upon you. You will suffer so much, you will beg to pay me to help you.' I would wretch with new pains until he put his hand on my head . . . and the pains left me.

"I was so afraid of the suffering that I did everything for him—and with him."

If we had thought these were Walter's only crimes, we would have been naive indeed. Walter had successfully deceived the world for a long time. His past accomplishments made him self-assured. We let him believe that the evidence against him in our files was concerned solely with Frau Bunzel's complaint that he had swindled money from her. Our prisoner thought that, if proven guilty, he would be sentenced to a year or less. However, I made sure the Bunzel case would be incorporated as only a part of a greater trial.

Walter had no way of knowing the many other specific charges we were amassing against him.

We had every reason to believe that he had plotted the murder of Paula's husband.

Having tired of Paula, at least physically, the doctor had teamed up with a young, easy-going, vivacious widow who owned an elaborate home overlooking the Neckar. Since she was expensive in her tastes, her lover was required to earn more money than ever before. Her rapacity hatched Walter's plans to kill Herr Baumann and through Paula, obtain the insurance money.

Walter's mistress of the moment harboured no compunctions about co-operating with us. Franz Walter was not a great love of hers, merely a pleasant means to live gaily. She helped us reconstruct his daily pattern of his life during the previous eighteen months.

Walter was apprehensive during this time, for Herr Baumann was asking too many questions about a Dr. Bergen who was not listed in any telephone book, and who was not named in the rosters of the medical profession. If Baumann were to become more inquisitive, Walter's prosperous existence was at stake. The solution, however, was relatively easy. He would kill Herr Baumann, but no blood would be on his own hands. Paula would be the instrument of murder.

She helped fill in the details about this period. The weekly and daily treatments with Dr. Mayer continued. Each session loosened Walter's hold over Paula's mind. She talked more clearly, with less fear, less falteringly. She remembered many facts tucked in the recesses of her mind. We were startled and greatly pleased when the patient began to relate facts in her waking state, without the aid of hypnotic release and freedom.

"It was during the years of 1933 and 1934. There were many irritations, quarrels, and troubles between Franz and me. Most of them sprang from my medical treatments, Dr. Bergen, and the great costs involved. He said it would be best if my husband were to disappear. He pointed out that I would be rid of him for ever and would not have to put up with his chicaneries. In addition, he said I would be better off financially because of Franz's insurance and my widow's pension. 'Go to the pharmacy,' he said, 'and buy *Kleesaltz*. It will serve your purpose. Put it in his food. No one will know if something happens.'

"At first I refused with all my power, but I grew weaker and weaker. I had no control over myself and could not think at all. When I arrived home, my husband saw I was nervous and upset. He gave me strictest orders not to leave the house. Therefore, I had no chance to buy the poisonous salt, although I had a desperate desire to leave as directed. By the next day the power had lessened and I no longer had such a strong urge.

"The next time I met Dr. Bergen, he was angry. 'When you go home,' he said, 'you will take the gun out of the desk and hide it so that it will be near you. When your husband is asleep, remove the safety catch. Place the gun against his temple and fire. Then put the gun in his hand. It will look as if he killed himself.'

"I said I could not do such a thing, but the doctor threatened me with more pains. He put his hands over my eyes and commanded me to do as he said. He murmured something. I do not know what it was.

"The next day I took the gun out of the desk and hid it behind the picture that hung over our bed. That night I arose several times and tried to do his bidding. I was drawn to the gun. Finally I removed the safety catch, and approached my sleeping husband. I placed the gun near his temple and pulled the trigger. But the gun only clicked. It had been unloaded. Ernst suspected me. He leaped from bed and berated me unmercifully, even threatened to go to the police.

"I reported all this to Dr. Bergen when I saw him again. He was angry with me too. Again he put me to sleep. This time he said, 'You know your mushrooms well. Go into the woods and pick both good and poisonous varieties. Cook two pots. Serve the edible ones to yourself but give the red-topped ones to your husband.'

"This I did. But Ernst ate only two bites of them. They didn't taste right, he said. Three hours later Ernst fell dreadfully ill with stomach pains. I brewed some peppermint tea for him. I couldn't understand what had happened. When I hear the word mushroom even now, I have the sensation of ice cold water running down my back.

"Next Dr. Bergen gave me some white powder to put in Ernst's coffee. He said it would make bubbles and I must watch that my husband did not notice them. God must have been with me because on my way home the little box spilled and most of the powder was scattered in my handbag. Even the little that was left gave Ernst such severe cramps that he went to see a local physician."

Our detectives had found the bag. There were still traces of the poisonous white powder to corroborate her story.

Poor long-suffering Ernst Baumann! It was the first time he heard the story. Its magnitude and intricacy were beyond his comprehension.

Walter never gave up. He was persistent. Next he ordered Paula to cut the cable of Herr Baumann's motor-cycle brakes. This she did, and Ernst ran against a railroad gate. He and the woman with him were only slightly injured.

Walter, with more desperation than ingenuity, gave the same command again, and again Ernst was involved in an accident, this time with minor arm and knee injuries.

The "nine lives" of Ernst Baumann were aggravating to Walter. He reasoned that if the husband could so neatly slip from death, Paula might be easier to eliminate. Why not lure his subject to commit suicide? This would absolve him of all suspicion, rid him of a woman who was proving to be a tiresome nuisance and perhaps Ernst and the woman with him on the motor-cycle might even welcome her passing.

Had Walter's scheme worked, his worries would have been over. But when a criminal, like a dictator, becomes angry, he is likely to make errors.

Walter no longer found Paula a challenge. He shortened each session with her because his widow-mistress was waiting in her villa. "Do as I tell you," he said. "You have many worries, you ache with unbearable pains, you are upset about money problems and the accidents your husband has been having. Go to your local physician and tell him you want some Pantopon tablets to help you sleep. Do not eat anything for one day. Drink a little hot wine and take five tablets. Set your alarm clock for midnight. When you awaken, take five more tablets. Set your clock again for 2:00 and take the rest. Be sure to destroy the paper in which the pills are wrapped. Flush it down the toilet. Destroy the paper!"

In telling this event, Paula continued: "But our doctor refused to give me the tablets. He must have saved my life."

Dr. Mayer maintained Paula never had a clear idea what she was doing while she operated in her somnolent state of slavery. But it was interesting to note the malicious motivation given to her under hypnosis. Walter suggested that her attacks against Baumann were not intended to end in her husband's death, but were merely to frighten him.

In promoting Paula's suicide, Walter stressed her illness from which death would be a pleasant escape. Her blood, he said, was in the process of turning into a stream of pus. It was far better to end all pains than to face the future of slow, agonizing, cancerous destruction.

Among the witnesses many had seen Walter and Frau Baumann together at the railroad station or near his apartment. One, a dainty little eighty-year-old lady, sat with Paula on the train, after Frau Baumann came from the doctor. In her confusion, she told the old lady her suicidal plans. The newly-found companion launched a lecture. Life was, she pointed out, a gift from Heaven itself. The Lord had presented it, and He alone had the right to take it away. There were, she continued, limitless cases of miraculous healing through faith as well as medicine, and Paula must have strength and belief, in spite of her doctor's diagnosis. Paula was relieved by this conversation.

But Walter's persistency was almost pathological. In another session, he told Paula that even if she were not to die suffering, she had still better commit suicide because her husband was in love with another woman. Had he not been with a female friend at the time of the accident? Surely it would be better for everyone if Paula would swim out into the deep, rapid current of the Neckar river.

Again Paula was saved by her loose tongue. A neighbour, overhearing some chance prating about suicide, followed her to the river's edge and stopped the hypnotized woman before she could leap into the murky water.

This period in her life was best summed up by Frau Baumann's testimony in court:

"I was under constant pressure. At home Ernst constantly harangued at me and wanted to know what was going on. How could I tell him when I didn't know myself? I was in constant pain which was only relieved when I saw Dr. Bergen, but he made my life miserable too, because he threatened to kill me if I betrayed him. And how could I be certain I would not? I was living in a painful darkness. I endured the unendurable."

Ernst Baumann's first visit to my office dated back to 1934. Our investigation lasted two years and the case finally came to trial in June, 1936. Any time-schedule I had set for us in this case certainly proved to be erroneous. Whenever I thought we had covered the entire ground, we were faced with new surprises.

Walter steadfastly denied his guilt . . . until we unearthed his accomplice. This was an unexpected turn of events for me. Such a diabolical scheme appeared to be a lone-wolf operation. It was impossible there could be two such loathsome human beings. Furthermore, Frau Baumann had never alluded to anyone else, and we were certain from her co-operative spirit that Walter's paramour was only interested in helping him spend the money he brought in.

It was almost a chance remark that opened up this new lead. Paula mentioned that a police officer had once stopped her on the street and asked a number of personal questions. From our files we knew this was unlikely, and our men maintained they had not seen her until the case came up. The idea of a decoy arose immediately. But who was this "police officer?" Was the camouflage to frighten her?

Again Dr. Mayer resorted to hypnotism. Paula then remembered the man was a friend of Walter, known to her as Alfred. Alfred also held power over Frau Baumann. Walter instructed Paula that when Alfred used the word "Filofi" she was to sink into a trance and obey his orders. Further prying proved that the hypnotist had set up still another safeguard for himself. When Alfred used the cue word, Paula would accept his confusing instructions to make sure the police never obtained the details of their operation.

The accomplice in the plot was a plumber whom we shall call Peter Fahrig. His task was to find men who were willing to pay for the entertainment Paula could give while hypnotized. He was also a convenient delivery man for stolen jewels which had to be disposed of. We arrested Peter with no difficulty. During the two years we knew of practically all Walter's swindles, his women, his contacts, and the few friends he had.

Fahrig was as easy to break as Walter had been stubborn. He readily admitted his part in the many deals and when we brought the two men face to face, Franz Walter, for the first time, lost his self-assurance.

And, for the first time, the cunning hypnotist admitted his guilt. Between anger and docility, arrogance and subservience, he told his life-story of crimes. Most of them we knew... petty thievery, misuse of women, general skulduggery. His family background was traced for us once again: an unloved childhood and early youth in a family which teemed with alcoholics, divorce, insanity and violence.

The case that took two years to investigate was wound up in

three weeks of court hearings. Our humble chairs and benches were filled with important people from all over the world—medical men, psychiatrists, psychologists, newspaper reporters, writers.

The defence underlined some of the expert findings that Paula Baumann had never been the most stable or intelligent personality. She had had extra-marital contacts, thus proving her lack of moral fibre. She was, they pointed out, a weak woman who suffered from a pathological need for attention, influence and leadership, which her husband was unable to provide.

Walter did not deny his indirect attempts to murder both Herr and Frau Baumann. He claimed temporary insanity because of his panic.

The court was puzzled, as we had been, by the fact that Herr Baumann had shown such enormous and unfailing patience, and so little suspicion during the years. It seemed unlikely, to the point of disbelief, that the marital partners did not discuss and evaluate their perilous posititon and perplexing problems.

The reign of Franz Walter over his reluctant subject, Paula Baumann had lasted almost six years. To this, Paula stated in court: "I am no longer the person I was. If I were ever obsessed by the need to be ruled by someone else, I have been cured of this fallacy. I am stronger now and ready to start a new life with my husband who suffered so much on my account."

At the end of the third week of trial, the judge pronounced the sentence: ten years imprisonment and hard-labour for Franz Walter. Peter Fahrig received a four-year term in prison.

The judge summed up his reason for his sentence and, in so doing, reminded everyone in court that they had entered a psychological region which is the labyrinth of man himself. He warned everyone to tread lightly on their journeys into the mind—into man, the Unknown.

GHOSTLY STEPPES

by PRINCESS MARINA CHAVCHAVADZE

IN Russia, ghosts and stories about them are not the traditions of centuries, as is the case in Western Europe. With us, the belief in the supernatural is usually based on natural phenomena and the emotions which they inspire, and this condition, besides representing a survival of paganism, creates friendly and inimical beings who take part in the daily life of the Russian peasant.

Any close communion with Nature is bound to result in a belief which necessitates giving a supernatural explanation of those forces which especially stimulate the imagination, in fact all over the world the worship of Nature Spirits persists in one form or another.

The best known Russian Nature Spirit, associated solely with woods and forests, is known as the Lieschy, whose whole-time occupation is either to make travellers lose their way, or else to frighten them out of their wits. In this respect he somewhat resembles the Fata Morgana of Italy, the Feu Follet of France, the Erle King of Germany, and the English Will o' the Wisp and Jack o' Lantern. Another spirit, the Domovoy, who frequents all inhabited places, is more or less the companion of the Russian peasant. The Domovoy is a frivolous, irresponsible creature, who indulges in all kinds of practical jokes in the farms and cottages, but, unlike the Pixies, the Brownies, and the Leprechaun, the Domovoy does not believe in work, so he never helps, but only hinders. He specializes in hiding things when they are most needed, he loves to bang doors, and startle harmless old people dozing by the fireside, although, to do him credit, he thoroughly succeeds in putting fear into the hearts of incorrigibly naughty children!

The Domovoy touches the heights of his semi-malicious activities when he appears in the kitchen and meddles with the cooking, spoiling the cakes and bread by making the "batch" as flat as the proverbial pancake or else as heavy as lead.

All domestic worries, great and small, are put down to the

Domovoy, but as this joyous scapegoat possesses a back sufficiently broad to bear the multitudinous charges laid to his door, he continues, even in modern Russia, to pursue the uneven tenor of his way.

The reason for the dearth of ghosts in Russia may be due to the changeable conditions of life throughout her history, and, more prosaic still, to the comparatively recent use of stone in building, which not only has prevented the creation of ancient houses and castles, but has deprived new ones of the traditions inseparable from antiquity. But wherever the boundaries of Russia touch on the older civilizations of the Caucasus, or Baltic Provinces, ghosts and their stories immediately enter into local legends.

I do not wish to give the impression that ghosts do not walk in Russia. In most important houses dating from the seventeenth and eighteenth centuries you find the usual family ghosts, omens and warnings, and some of our well-known authors—Gogol in particular—have made ample use of the supernatural element in their midst.

No doubt the atrocities and poignant dramas of the revolution accounts for many present-day "returns", some of which haunt the scenes of their violent exits from life. Hauntings in the prisons are a foregone conclusion, and the wraiths of the murdered Imperial Family must be inseparable from Ekaterinburg. Even in 1924 the place was enveloped in an aura of tragedy, and when Isadora Duncan visited it she described in sombre terms. "You have no idea what a living nightmare is, until you see this town," she wrote. "Perhaps the killing of a certain family has cast a sort of Edgar Allan Poe gloom over it. The melancholy church bells ring every hour, fearful to hear.... We saw the house and the cellar where they shot a certain family. *Its psychosis seems to pervade the atmosphere. You can't imagine anything more fearful.*"

And there are many other tragedies of those days which have left their imperishable record on souls, and on environment.

My first ghost story, which provided one of the greatest sensations of pre-war Petersburg, concerns a haunted house situated on the Vassilevsky Island opposite the Nicolaevsky Bridge.

The house had been unoccupied for many years, and eternally it lived up to its sinister reputation as "a house under some prodigious ban of excommunication". However, two students, who disbelieved in any kind of superstition, and scoffed at supernatural manifestations, planned to destroy the legend, by passing the night there, holding themselves in readiness to tackle any ghost bold enough to appear.

The owner of the property, anxious to reinstate the house as a selling or letting proposition, gladly gave permission to the ghost seers to stay as long as they liked, and he made arrangements to have a good fire lighted in what was known as the "haunted" room, besides supplying two chairs and a table, as the friends proposed having supper before commencing their "watch". Everything was soon in readiness. Provisions and wine were sent in, and a goodly supply of candles to lighten the darkness, completed the equipment for the night.

C. (for it is better to describe him by an initial) arrived punctually at the time fixed for the meeting. Apart from his mulish obstinacy where the supernatural was concerned, he was a nice young fellow, who entered into the spirit of the adventure on this cold rainy autumn evening, and, as he liked his "comforts", he was cheered by the thought that the vigil would not take place in a fireless room. He therefore unlocked the front door with pleasurable anticipation, not only of being "thrilled", but also of being warmed.

The hall was in darkness, and when C.'s electric torch flashed here and there, he understood how different "empty" houses *feel* at night. During the day they are just *empty*: at night they become alive, and belong to the unseen—or to the shadows of those who have lived and died within their walls. At night, the complainings of any old house are *pathetic*, especially when its creaking old bones resent the burden of the years and the dry rot which gradually eats into its heart. To suffer like this a house *must* be old, and few modern buildings possess the capacity either for suffering or for endurance.

Upstairs, someone was singing, and C. recognized his friend's voice in company with a curiously distorted echo.

"Keeping up his spirits," said C. to himself; but suddenly the echo set in movement something definitely malignant; the house became a receptacle for an immense resistless power, and C. sensed an imperishable record of incarnate evil.

Reproaching himself for possessing too great an imagination, C. went upstairs, and opened the door of the room from whence the voice, and the echo, proceeded.

A fire of ships' timber blazed on the open hearth, and flames of red, blue, green, and faint lilac danced and pursued each other upwards in a cheerful riot of colour. The table was set for supper, and lighted candles in heavy candlesticks stood on a marble side buffet—a relic of the house's former state. In this respect, the room had nothing approaching the supernatural about it.

Taking off his heavy overcoat, C. greeted P., and asked him how long he had been waiting.

"I didn't know you meant to steal a march on me," he said.

"Merely my fancy," answered P. "I wanted to get in touch with the Unseen."

"And—did you?"

"Yes—and no." And he began to sing in a voice lacking all youth and clearness, the sound cleaving the warm wood-scented air like a meteor. C., hitherto only accustomed to hearing P. sing students' songs, with an occasional excerpt from some musical comedy, was, by turns, attracted and repelled; he even experienced a vague feeling of panic; for a moment it seemed as if a devil were making music. With something of an effort he said:

"Well, let's have supper. By the way, in what language were you singing? I couldn't understand a word of it."

"Naturally *not*," said P. smiled at him across the table, a wicked, cynical smile, which perplexed the already puzzled C. This might be P. who sang and smiled, but it certainly was *not* the familiar light-hearted P. of the daily round. He said nothing, and tried to think, and act, normally, but from time to time he looked at his friend, who was enjoying his supper with a healthy appetite, whilst C. ate sparingly, and only drank a couple of glasses of wine.

At last P. began to talk about the house. "I wonder what we shall see," he said. "Don't you think it is a little presumptuous to disturb well-buried evil by reason of senseless curiosity? Perhaps this house belongs to one who is adored through fear, whose strength lies in destruction, and who might *resent* our intrusion."

"But you were the first to propose to investigate the hauntings," said C. "Have *you* by any chance become a convert to the religion whose god is adored through fear?"

P. threw him a dark look. "We won't discuss religion. Better by far to toast midnight in a libation to evil." He tossed off the contents of his glass, refilled it, and flung the red wine on to the merry flames. "A libation to evil!" he cried. Suddenly his whole personality changed, and with a leer he turned to C. "You poor fool," he cried, "to attempt to measure your strength against those whose strength is invincible. You thought to destroy the indestructible, to uproot, as easily as weeds, forces whose roots are older than time. Do you not think that you deserve punishment?" As he spoke, P. rose from his chair, still smiling his cruel, mocking smile, and C. stared at him, incapable of thought or movement, conscious only that he was a helpless prisoner of the powers of darkness.

The last thing C. remembered was P.'s tiger-like spring. His throat was seized by fingers which burnt like acid into his flesh, then darkness fell.

Next morning C. and P. were absent from the University, and, as they had missed a special noonday lecture important to both, some fellow-students, who knew about the experiment at the haunted house, decided to go and see what had become of the ghost hunters.

To their disappointment, there was nothing "frightening" about the place—the silken curtains spun by successive generations of spiders waved across the windows, and when the door opened to admit the autumn air, an inquisitive ray of watery sunlight darted across the floor and up the broad staircase, followed by the little group.

When they went into the room on the first floor, cold grey ash and burnt-out candles met their eyes; afterwards they noticed an overturned table, and broken plates, and particles of food strewn on the floor, where the spilt wine looked like a stream of congealed blood.

Something lay under the debris. This was C.—evidently in a dead faint—or worse. There was no sign of P., so while two of the young men busied themselves in bringing C. round, the others hurried upstairs to see if P. was anywhere in hiding.

The rooms were empty, save for gigantic bloated spiders scuttling away in the gloom. The dust of years rose like musty incense from cracks in the boards as the searchers walked over them, and, in the garrets, battalions of bats clung to the worm-eaten beams.

The students concluded that P. had gone suddenly mad and attacked C. in a moment of frenzy. There was nothing else to do but to take C. back to his home (he was now somewhat restored, but incapable of saying anything), make inquiries at P.'s lodgings, and, if necessary, report the affair to the police.

A closed carriage was ordered, and C., looking as if he had passed the night in Hell, and not in an empty house, was restored to his family, who, although alarmed at his condition, could not resist the chance it gave them to repeat the familiar formula, "I told you so", on every possible occasion.

The next halt was at P.'s lodgings a few streets away. The inquiry as to whether he was at home instantly produced a running commentary from the landlady. "*Was* he at home? Yes, he *was*, and judging from his appearance, likely to remain at home for the next few days." She didn't know whether too much learning, or too much seeing life, made anyone sleep like the dead. "He came in at two o'clock yesterday afternoon, went straight to bed, and has not got up since. Sleeping all the time." It would be a good thing to rouse him—so far she hadn't been able to do anything with him.

More than ever amazed, the young men went to P.'s room. Sure enough, there he was, sleeping, and snoring heavily.

"And yet she says he went to bed at *two o'clock* yesterday afternoon," said the leader, and, with another willing helper, he shook the sleeper as one shakes an apple on the topmost bough; P. reluctantly opened his eyes.

"What on earth are you fellows doing in my room?" he grumbled.

They explained the reason, and, awakened to some purpose, P. sat up, and stared at them uncomprehendingly; at last the gravity of their story gradually dawned on him.

"Then it *was* yesterday that we planned to go to the house on the island?" He was assured that it was so. "And you come and tell me some cock-and-bull story about finding C. half murdered, and that there were evidences of two people having eaten together. . . . Are we all mad? *I've never stirred out of this place*—my landlady can prove it. I forgot the appointment, but I remember I felt curiously tired, and had a sort of drugged sensation, when I came back to lunch; in fact I became so drowsy that I went to bed. I never gave a thought to C., or to any haunted house, so if there *were* two people at supper *the second one wasn't me*."

There for the moment the matter ended. P.'s twenty-eight hour alibi was verified by his landlady and her servant, as well as by a friend who had called later in the evening.

On the other hand, C.'s incredible story was confirmed by the condition of the room, his own pitiable state, and the statements of eye-witnesses; but, strangest of all, the imprints on his throat could never have been made by the spatulated fingers of P.'s rather pudgy little hand.

The mystery of this authentic story of the supernatural has remained unsolved. It created an immense amount of talk and speculation in Petersburg, but no clue was ever found as to the identity of C.'s supper companion. It was a clear case of like and unlike, with something deeper still, something that made even unimaginative people *afraid*, and when shortly afterwards the owner of the house on the island decided to pull it down, not one stone was left upon another of the ill-omened place with its evil entities and unsolved mysteries.

The following account is wholly concerned with death warnings peculiar to certain families in one form or another, and involved friends of mine, Baron and Baroness R., who owned a beautiful estate in the country, where the ruins of an ancient tower stood in the gardens surrounding the house. The tower had only one window, and, as the stairs had long since been destroyed, it was merely a picturesque inaccessible "shell", covered with ivy, and a few windsown wild flowers.

According to tradition, whenever a member of the R. family died a light gleamed through the tower window although nobody could give a practical reason to account for it.

One summer evening, Baron R.'s two daughters and a friend went for an after-dinner stroll, and, not noticing how far they had walked, found themselves to all intents and purposes lost in the soft darkness of a moonless night. Fortunately, the woodland paths on their father's estate were well kept and clearly defined, so it was not difficult to "feel" their way back to the gardens, and as they walked up the avenue dominated by the stairless tower, the girls stopped, and a little shiver passed from one to the other. They had both seen *a light shining in the tower window*, with a curious searchlight effect, partly phosphorescent, and partly flame, which streamed like a white ribbon on the night. The sisters looked at each other. . . .

"Do you see anything?" whispered the elder girl.

"Yes," faltered her sister, "there's a light in the tower."

To their friend, who did not know the story of the death warning, she said, trying to speak naturally, "Surely there's a light somewhere?"

"Of course there is," he laughed; "why, it's in the tower—however has anyone managed to get up there? Perhaps they've flown in," he added.

The light was still shining in the barred window when they returned to the house, and it continued to shine until an hour later, when a telephone call came through, informing the Baron of the sudden death of his eldest son.

Afterwards the stairless tower became part of the darkness.

On Saturday, February 28, 1881, another and more ghostly kind of warning occurred in our family, the recipient being the young Countess S., and it is necessary, in the interest of truth, to say that on this particular evening no discussion of any kind had taken place about ghosts or psychic phenomena, and the Countess had gone to bed in a perfectly normal frame of mind.

The first hour or so she slept soundly, then she awoke with a start, to see by the dim light of the vielleuse someone leaning over the low bed-rail.

The figure was that of a pale-faced old man with a long white beard, wearing some kind of a flowing dark robe. His expression was gentle, mingled with a sense of tragedy, and the Countess heard him say, very solemnly:

"Tomorrow, at noon, the Emperor Alexander II will be assassinated."

He then disappeared, and the terrified Countess awakened her husband, and told him of her vision and the old man's ominous words.

The Count, however, was nothing if not a sceptic and considered dreams and their interpretation, and indeed anything appertaining to the supernatural as old wives' tales and unworthy of serious consideration. He listened patiently to the story of the old man's warning, laughed a little, comforted his wife, and told her to go to sleep.

The young wife, though, was not imaginative, she really wanted to go to sleep, but the old man appeared twice more during that nerve-shattering night, and each time he warned her of the approaching assassination of the Emperor. After the third visitation, she lay weeping silently, with frayed nerves, by this time absolutely convinced that it was the Emperor's last day on earth.

That morning Count S. was on duty with his regiment for the trooping of the colours at the Mikhailovski Manege. This ceremony was to take place in the presence of the Emperor, and, knowing what time it would be over, the Countess hurried along the Embankment to meet her husband as he came back. She was more than ever impressed with the drama of the night, and she felt the only way to combat her fears was to face up to her problem, and not wait for someone to tell her the best, or the worst.

Directly she saw her husband riding towards her she knew from his expression that the old man of her vision had spoken the truth, and although Count S. was a soldier, with a soldier's self-control, a little of his composure failed him when he saw his wife's pale face, and read the unspoken question in her frightened eyes. So he said, very quietly:

"You were right. The Emperor has been murdered."

I wish I could finish this true family record with some more interesting details, but none are available. It is a fact that Countess S. saw the apparition on three occasions during the night, and her husband corroborated her statement. In any case, the Count could not have prevented the assassination of the Emperor, and it is doubtful whether anyone in his entourage would have listened or paid any attention to the story of a waking dream. But those who query the validity of the supernatural in daily life may justifiably argue that the ghostly warning ought to have been given direct to the Emperor, or to one of the officials responsible for the arrangements on that fatal morning.

However, in many cases of supernatural manifestations the real explanation often remains a mystery.

MURDEROUS NIGHT ON PINAKI ATOLL

by WILMON MENARD*

WILLIAM SOMERSET MAUGHAM's intense interest in occultism, ancient civilizations and primitive superstitions and taboos is plainly incorporated into his countless short stories, essays, plays and novels. The main theme in many of his tales is dire retribution or nemesis, for example, his stories *Of Human Bondage*, *The Letter*, *Rain*, *The Pool* and *The Painted Veil.*

His personal life too was greatly influenced by the occult sciences. He was not a Christian and died, as he had lived, a fierce infidel. He told me, "The only god that is of use is one who is personal, supreme and good. I remain an agnostic and the practical outcome of agnosticism is that you act as though god did not exist. The day will come when Christianity will be as archaic as Mayan sun worship."

Before his death on December 16, 1965, Maugham gave strict orders that there was to be no funeral oration, no religious ceremony performed over his urn of ashes, which was to be buried in the precincts of King's School in Canterbury—and his wishes were respected.

But in his personal life, in his literary creativity, he was a devout believer in the occult sciences. His translations of ancient Greek history, Indian philosophy, Spanish essays and papers on mysticisms of the Dark Ages illustrate his in-depth studies and beliefs in practices pertaining to alchemy, astrology, divination, incantation and magical formulae.

Admirers of Maugham are familiar with the cabalistic design which is a trademark on the dust jackets and the title pages of all his books. I found this strange symbol over the entrance to his

* Wilmon Menard holds doctorates in anthropology and sociology and is considered an authority on the Pacific Ocean. He is the author of the biography-odyssey, *The Two Worlds of Somerset Maugham.* However, Maugham's encounter with the treasure hunter was not included in the book and is related here for the first time.

elegant Villa Mauresque on Cap Ferrat on the French Riviera. Inside the villa on the entrance wall, on ashtrays, stationery, cigarette cases, matchbooks, fireplaces and radiator grille-work, this unique symbol was a constant reminder of his affinity with the occult sciences. He explained to me that it was a talisman to ward off evil. His father, a legal adviser with the British Embassy in Paris, had brought it back from one of his trips to French Morocco, having discovered it in the Blue Atlas mountains beyond Marrakesh. I understood it to be a Moorish representation of the human hand, meant to protect, as might the Christian crucifix, its possessor from harm of all kinds. Leonard Lyons, the American columnist who visited Maugham a number of times, described it as "a TV aerial capped by a pronged nose cone but it has no relation to the century's twin threats, television and missiles."

Willie Maugham counted among his close friends Sir Arthur Conan Doyle, creator of the Sherlock Holmes tales and an avid exponent of occultism, and they exchanged numerous letters on the occult sciences. Maugham once joined in a seance to communicate with Conan Doyle after his death.

Rudyard Kipling, another close friend of Maugham, knowing his interest in Indian philosophy and occultism, encouraged him to go to India for a new setting for future short stories and novels. Maugham went but he told me, "It was too late in the day for me. I was at that time, you must know, an 'old party'; I had lost much of my youthful zeal for exploration and adventure and India was too vast, too strange, too challenging. Nevertheless, India fascinated me, altered some of my precepts of Indian occultism."

The Razor's Edge, which has a strong occult theme, was the result of his India trip. The character of Larry Darrell in the novel, enacted by the late Tyrone Power in the movie, was a seeker of truth in the mystery of life and Maugham admitted to me privately Darrell represented his own searching spirit.

When I started my research and interviews with Maugham, which led to the publication of my book, *The Two Worlds of Somerset Maugham* (1965), a puzzling incident recurred frequently as we sat together in his study or on the terrace. He would abruptly terminate the conversation. The first time this happened I glanced at him in surprise. He was leaning slightly forward, his head inclined towards the closed door, his hooded eyes cynical, his lips smiling. It was an expression one might wear when anticipating the entrance of a tedious friend. In a few minutes he settled back in his chair; his breath escaped in a loud sigh as no knock sounded on the closed door.

The second time it happened he said to me casually, "He comes when I least expect him. But I can tell when he's outside listening, waiting, ticking off the seconds."

At first I imagined he spoke of an inquisitive servant but after the incident was repeated several times I asked one afternoon, "Who's outside, Willie?"

Calmly he replied, "Death. A truly relentless brute who won't be kept waiting much longer. When one is young neither the sun nor death can be looked at with a steady eye. But when you are old, as I am, you become conditioned to listening with amusement to his furtive stalking of you. I have looked out across the world from many sea-coasts and valleys and from the summits of our highest mountains. When one considers the vastness of the universe with its innumerable stars and its spaces measured by thousands upon thousands of light-years I am overwhelmed. I realize we are inhabitants for a little while of a small planet revolving around a minor star which in its turn is a member of one of unnumbered galaxies. I experience then my most profound belief in infinity, in the occult sciences."

One afternoon, several months after we had started our interviews he suddenly broke off the dialogue to tell me of a persistent dream he had had as a young man in London and of his growing fear that he would die of strangulation in mid-life.

He said, "The original dream, which was repeated at intervals, was of being choked to death by huge hands, a true garroter's fingers gripping my throat. I always awoke gasping and wheezing as if in an asthma attack and for days afterwards my throat would be sore and constricted and there would be marks on my neck. I surmise that in my subconscious struggles I clutched my throat causing the discolorations.

"In Bombay I was never at rest, knowing of the cult of thuggee who garroted victims. It got so I couldn't wear a tight collar or necktie without being reminded of my disturbing dream. And for anyone to touch my throat, even my wife Syrie or my daughter Liza, caused me almost to panic. Such was the power of my dream of being choked to death! I suppose many people have their own special form of death-visitation in a dream."

"Do you have those dreams now?" I asked.

He smiled and shook his head, then massaged his neck with fingers agitated by palsy. "The dream came to an end and at last no longer haunted my conscious hours. It didn't recede from the consciousness back into the subconscious. Nothing quite as casual as that! You see, I was, in my late forties, almost choked to death by a madman. It was quite identical to my dream. And so, as I escaped with my life, that was the end of the dream. The fulfilment of the dream rid me of my curse. The obsession was cast off."

I urged him to tell me about the violent climax of the dream which he never had written for publication.

It is told here for the first time, his close encounter with death on a lonely atoll of the Tuamotu Archipelago of French Oceania.

While Maugham was in Tahiti in 1917 researching the life of the French painter Paul Gauguin for his novel, *The Moon and Sixpence,* Gerald Haxton, Maugham's secretary-companion, introduced him to Captain Viggo Rasmussen, the famous Danish trader and skipper of French Oceania and the Cook Islands. It was Captain Viggo who told Maugham about a strange white man who was living on the atoll of Pinaki of the Tuamotus where he was searching desperately for pirate gold believed cached there.

When Louvaina Chapman, the part-Tahitian owner of the Tiare Hotel where Maugham was staying who became "Tiare Johnson" in his *Moon and Sixpence,* heard he intended to visit the treasure hunter on Pinaki she became intensely agitated.

"Vairee no-good you go there, Mawg-ham! Bad *pifao* (curse) on Pinaki long time now. Plenty bad white men hide gold there, gold belong *mitinare* (missionary). God punish that *popaa maamaa* (crazy white man) who hunt that gold, you wait see! More better you stay Tahiti, forget Pinaki!"

But Maugham, sensing a possible story, sailed with Captain Viggo and Haxton on a trading voyage through the maze of coral isles north-east of Tahiti.

Before they arrived at Pinaki Atoll Captain Viggo told Maugham and Haxton a brief history of the reputed pirate trove.

In December of 1859 four adventurers roaming South America as mercenaries in sporadic revolutions there, Luke Barrett, an American, Archer Brown, a Britisher, a Spaniard named Alvarez and an Irishman, Killorain, slaughtered the crew of a schooner off the coast of Peru. They also killed the Jesuit priests who were accompanying a shipment of church-owned gold bars, large golden jewelled candlesticks, a chest of priceless rings, bracelets, crucifixes, images and a small chest of Spanish gold coins. The small vessel had left Pisco, Peru, for a northerly port where the treasure, valued at an estimated 7,000,000 dollars, was to be hidden.

After this mutiny the pirates sailed across the South Pacific into the waters of the Tuamotu Archipelago and on one of the more than 80 coral atolls of this group presumably buried the treasure.

The ultimate fate of the pirates and the vessel was told years later by one Charles Edward Howe, a Scotsman living in Australia, who claimed to have come into possession of a map and papers found in the effects of an eighty-five-year-old Irishman, allegedly Killorain, who had died as a charity patient in a public ward of a Sydney hospital.

Killorain, according to Howe's account, had told him of the Tuamotuan atoll where the treasure had been buried, of the subsequent voyage across the South Pacific to Australia where the schooner was scuttled some miles offshore at Cooktown. The pirates had rowed ashore in the longboat, gasping out a story of shipwreck at sea.

Later, while trying to earn sufficient money to organize an expedition to retrieve their treasure, Barrett and Alvarez were killed by aborigines while working in the Palmer goldfields. Archer Brown had died in prison while serving a term for manslaughter. Killorain served out a similar prison term to become, in May, 1912, at the advanced age of 87, a watchman at Rushcutters Bay, Sydney. Howe previously had met Killorain at a Sydney boarding-house and had befriended him so, Howe explained, to repay him when he died the Irishman had given him a map of Pinaki Atoll which he had kept hidden those many years. Charlie Howe had checked the Irishman's story partly substantiating Killorain's wild tale and in February, 1913, Howe had arrived on Pinaki.

James Norman Hall and Charles Bernard Nordhoff, authors of *Mutiny on the Bounty*, in one of their earlier books of travel in French Oceania, *Faery Islands of the South Seas*, made separate explorations through the Tuamotus. Nordhoff met Charlie Howe on Pinaki Atoll in 1920 and described him as "this strange Scot on his island criss-crossed with trenches."

Howe eventually was deported from French Oceania following a complaint by the natives of nearby Nukutavake Atoll that he was selling copra and pearl shell which rightfully belonged to them to passing trading schooners.

In the mid-1930's Howe was heard of again when a British journalist named William Edwards showed up in Papeete, Tahiti, with a party of treasure hunters, saying Howe had given him valuable papers and a map establishing the Peruvian treasure as being on an atoll near Makemo Island in the Tuamotus. I was in Tahiti at this time and met Edwards. This expedition ended ignobly when drink, arguments and pursuit of Tahitian strumpets dissipated their enthusiasm and money.

It is rumoured that Charlie Howe was killed in a car accident either in Sydney or Auckland.

Maugham described to me, during a visit at his Villa on the French Riviera, his arrival at Pinaki. It was a true coral atoll, formed of a number of reef-islets covered with coconut palms, pandanus and scrub. The southern ocean breaking over the protective reefs created a silvery surf which marked her position in the turquoise sea.

"It was like a green garland cast down by a Polynesian god upon the ocean," said Maugham. "I secretly envied the treasure hunter an isle all to himself."

Off the north-western reef of Pinaki Captain Viggo jerked the rope of the bell and the pure tones carried inshore on the trades.

"I hope we're not ringing for a dead man," Captain Viggo grunted. "This American, or Australian, or whatever he is, lives alone here; anything could happen."

But from inshore came a low, far-reaching note blown upon a conch shell.

A half hour later, while Maugham watched through binoculars, a tall man in ragged shorts, his nearly naked body burned a deep mahogany hue by the equatorial sun, paddled cautiously in an outrigger canoe through a narrow breach between two small reefs. Once beyond the line of breakers he approached swiftly.

Maugham saw that the man was sinewy, with broad shoulders and thin hips and a hard flat stomach. "There wasn't a pound of excess weight on him; I judged him to be in his early fifties. But there was something odd about the way he was paddling, slightly off-balance, as if he had a physical infirmity. Then I saw his right hand was missing and the stump of his canvas-wrapped wrist was lashed by fish cord to the staff of the paddle."

Captain Viggo explained, "He lost his hand two years ago. He vas svimming back from the reef viz a string of fish he had speared and a small shark came up under him for a free meal and took avay his hand, too."

He added, "He's been hunting for the gold for three years."

The man brought his *piroque* smartly amidships to the Jacob's ladder and climbed up nimbly.

"Thank you for stoppin', matey," he said in a hoarse voice. "I'm just about out of everythin'."

Captain Viggo stared at him. "My God!" he finally gasped. "Vat happened to you?"

Then Maugham saw that Barker's right eye socket was fitted with a false eye carved out of pearl shell! A convex piece of white pearl shell had been affixed there like a monocle and superimposed on it, in the centre, was an iris of bluish nacre, with a small pupil formed of a miniscule peg of darker pearl shell that held the false eye together.

"Just another accident, worse luck!" Barker grunted. "I was out fishin' by torch on the reef and one of those damned needlefish buried its bloody bill clear to the back of my eye socket."* He removed the pearly orb and handed it to Captain Viggo. "Not a bad job, eh? I wear it all the time, even sleepin', to keep dirt, insects and saltwater from foulin' up the bloody hole."

"Barker told us, 'In this blinkin' climate it went rotten quick and the socket finally popped it out. A stinkin' mess of corruption it was too. I kept washin' it out with gin. Not long afterwards the French gunboat, *Zelée*, making a run through the Tuamotus, stopped offshore here and I came aboard and let the Doc have a look at the blinkin' hole. He did a quick bit of surgery and scraped it all out nice and proper and gave me some bandages and ointment. It doesn't give me any trouble now.'

* The needlefish or houndfish (*tylosurus crocodilus*) ranging in size from one to six feet, is known and feared in Tahitian and Tuamotuan waters under the native name *aavere.* With its long slender body and long bone bill, it can generate sufficient propulsion to whiz through the air with incredible speed, its target at night customarily a flashing light. Overshooting, needlefish have pierced the necks and stomachs of natives and some whites, causing grave wounds and even deaths. They are found also in the Gulf of Mexico and in other tropical and sub-tropical seas.

"I tried to get Barker to talk about the Peruvian treasure but he suddenly became hostile and uncommunicative. He said sharply to Captain Viggo, 'Have your Chinee supercargo figger what I have comin' for my copra and pearl shell and I'll load my supplies and get ashore. I have work to do.'

"Before he left he did tell Captain Viggo the French Colonial Administration in Pepeete, Tahiti, had notified him his visa would not be renewed, that he would have to leave French Oceania within seven months."

"I was anxious to see him in his primitive environment," Maugham told me. "So in the late afternoon I insisted I would visit the atoll alone and Captain Viggo reluctantly ordered a Tahitian seaman to row me ashore."

"In a cluster of pandanus and small coconut palms, up from a stark white beach of coral rubble, I found Barker's hut. He was not at home. The simple structure of driftwood and palm leaves was snug. All his possessions were neatly stowed. He had made a crude table out of a packing case; a Bible, its leather cover mottled by mildew, was the only object on the top. In a corner, carefully stacked were shovels and other tools. It was apparent Barker was a meticulous person."

In the palm grove behind, Maugham found a number of square excavations the size and shape of graves. Down the beach he saw evidence that Barker had penetrated the coral with pick and crowbar. Even out in the water there were large exploratory holes.

Maugham sat down with his back against a palm to await Barker's return. "I remember thinking if Barker had come here to live apart from his fellowmen, at peace, he could perhaps have survived indefinitely. Driven, as he was, by his mania for pirate gold, there could be only one destiny for him."

The blinding reflection from the sunlit lagoon and the tropical heat were soporific and Maugham dozed off.

He had no idea how long he had slept when a sudden noise awakened him and he jerked to a sitting position.

"I found myself staring up into the sunlight at a shadowy figure looming over me. It was Barker glaring down at me. The total sinister effect was enhanced by that ghastly pearl shell eye and its fixed stare."

Barker dropped the lobster trap he was carrying and moved

closer, legs spread apart, straddling Maugham's extended limbs. "What in hell are you doin' ashore here?" he demanded.

"W-w-why, I just thought I'd come ashore and have a c-c-closer look at Pinaki," Maugham replied nervously. "And, of course, I hoped to have a chat with you."

"I think I made it clear to you that I didn't want any bloody company here—at any time! I don't have anythin' to say to you!"

Maugham started to rise to his feet. "I'm truly sorry if I've upset you. I didn't mean to intrude. I just thought..."

"Aye, you *just thought!* You just thought you'd sneak ashore here when my back was turned and spy on me! And now you got it all figgered out how you'll sail off nice and proper and write all about me, and then this island will be crawlin' with crooks tryin' to do me out of my treasure. You bloody, interferin' Limey!"

And Barker hurled himself savagely upon Maugham, knocking the wind out of him. With his handless arm, he encircled his neck, and the fingers of his left hand found Maugham's throat and dug in deeply.

"I remember that all the time he was attacking me he was cursing obscenely. A bolt of lightning had struck his brain. He had become a raving madman with homicidal purpose. My breath was quickly cut off and the effect of the strangulation was almost instantaneous. There were flashing lights in front of my eyes and a tight sensation in my head. Before passing out, my last sensory impression was his distorted face, hideously engorged with blood, and the palms and sky, whirling in my fading sight. I felt it was the end for me. My horrible dream had become a reality."

When Maugham regained consciousness he was sprawled in the bottom of the dinghy. Pulling himself up to the gunwales he saw the Tahaitian seaman, standing ankle-deep in the sea-wash across the outer reef, fending off with an oar the crazed white man of Pinaki.

"You go a-hella-you back!" The crewman was yelling, brandishing the oar. "If no do, I bust yo' gawd-damn head off!"

Barker was howling, "I've got a shotgun... and the next crook who comes ashore here... You get him to hell off this island!"

Maugham felt the boat move, felt the grating sound of its keel across the edge of the coral reef, then a rocking motion as the strong backwash carried it into deeper water.

Slumped amidships, coughing and choking, Maugham could hear Barker's ranting across the widening stretch of sea.

"As God is my witness, I have endured hell here and I will not be denied my just rewards! Even God has tried to punish me for searchin' for holy gold stained with the blood of sacred men. I know my Bible and the exhortation in St. Matthew's gospel: *And if thy right eye offend thee, pluck it out and cast it from thee. And if they right hand offend thee cut it off and cast it from thee.'* "

Then the sound of the breakers on the seaward side of the coral rampart drowned out his voice.

When Maugham came aboard the schooner Captain Viggo nodded grimly. "He's a dangerous man and I must report this to the police in Papeete."

Later, when Maugham stood at the rail and night covered the sea and the atoll he could see a faint winking light in Barker's hut on Pinaki. "My conviction was firm that Barker's days on his atoll were very short. He was physically handicapped and now, bereft of reason, the end could only be a tragic one."

Maugham did not learn of Barker's ultimate fate until several years later.

"News at that time didn't travel very fast out of the South Pacific. However, Captain Viggo's letter finally did catch up with me. Barker had died wretchedly and alone on Pinaki without, of course, having found any trace of the Peruvian treasure. Perhaps you'd like to see Captain Viggo's letter."

Written in a bold hand the letter stated the facts as these: A hurricane had slashed through the Tuamotus and Pinaki had been athwart its destructive course. Captain Winny Brander, sea-captain son of John Brander, one of the first pioneer Scots traders in Tahiti and a friend of Captain Viggo, had sailed past Pinaki to see how Barker had fared. Shorn palms, coral-strewn beaches fouled by dead stinking sea creatures, were eloquent testimony to the tempest's fury. Floating bottom-up in the frond-and-coconut-choked lagoon was Barker's splintered outrigger canoe. His hut had been completely demolished; just a few scattered sheets of rusty corrugated iron remained.

Farther inland, at the base of the aerial roots of pandanus growths, they had found Barker's skeleton, picked clean by crabs, rats and sea birds.

Captain Viggo ended his letter, "There was no doubt that it was Barker, because one hand was missing. Winny put the bones in a copra sack and buried them in one of the 'graves' Barker had dug on the atoll. I asked Winny if he had seen anything of an artificial eye made out of pearl shell but he said he hadn't. Perhaps a crab plucked it out of the socket of the skull and carried it down into his hole on the beach. Had Winny brought back that false eye I surely would have sent it on to you as a souvenir of your unforgettable visit to Pinaki."

Maugham picked up his triple martini in the champagne goblet and took a full swallow. His hand was trembling, either from advanced years or from the memory. He muttered, "I don't think I would have cared too much to have such a curio to remind me how close I came to having my neck wrung! Anyway, it was the end of a bad dream."

Just recently I sailed past Pinaki on a voyage from Manga Reva (in the Gambier group) to Tahiti. It was just after dawn and seeing the low coral atoll with its tracery of palms etched against an opalescent sky was a moving experience because of Maugham's encounter with the crazed treasure hunter there. The green wreath of reef islets is more picturesque than the mind can imagine.

The Tahitian skipper was of no disposition to permit me to go ashore while he waited, hove to. So I stood in the stern watching Pinaki Atoll merge its low silhouette with the morning sea-haze and I remembered what James Michener, of *South Pacific* and *Hawaii* fame, once said to me concerning the Tuamotus:

"To say that men have died in such lonely places, engulfed in disillusion and despair, is merely to point out that on a lonely atoll, as in most cities, good men find loveliness, weak men find evil . . ."

A PUBLISHER'S STRANGE EXPERIENCE

by KURT SINGER

SCHOLARLY men have given great attention to the inexplicable facts in life. The strange phenomenon of unknown influences has puzzled all ages, all cultures and all people.

The following account of an amazing coincidence opens up an enormous area for investigation. The event might be described as a comparatively trivial circumstance, but the facts can speak for themselves. The gentleman who told me the story said : "I can do no more than state them and vouch for their truth."

I have known Jeffrey Simmons, the publisher, for twenty years. I dare to call him my friend. He has been one of my severest critics as well as one of my best associates in many a publishing venture.

I remember Jeffrey Simmons as a young man. He came fresh from Oxford University with great dreams of publishing the world's best books, the classics, the immortal pioneers in literature among the courageous writers who were willing to risk their lives for their beliefs.

He, as all of us, has mellowed with the years and has accepted the realistic facts of life and of men.

Jeffrey Simmons comes from an old and fine family with great traditions in Britain. His is one of the oldest publishing houses in England, and this is the story he told me :

"In my career as a publisher (which, as you know, extends over twenty-two years), I have only once had to pulp a book. (This is done more frequently in America, where traditionally unsold books are returned to the publisher, but it occurs rarely in England.) It happens that a paperback novel, published by my company, was bound with a cover intended for another book. The printer decided that his easiest course was to reprint and bind the entire work; hence the need to pulp the faulty stock.

"I went into our Production Manager's office and asked him

whether he knew anyone who would pulp a book. He said not, adding that in a long experience at his job he had never needed to do so.

"By chance, there was in his room at the time a young boy employed by us who had occasion to visit that particular office very rarely. This boy said that he knew a firm near where he lived —Phillips Mills of Battersea (who I have since ascertained are very well known in their field, but of whom at the time I had never heard).

"I at once called our switchboard operator and told her to look up the number of these people and to telephone them. She said: 'Their representative is here.'

"I thought at first she was joking, but no—at that very moment when I chanced to go upstairs to our production office, and when by chance there was in that office a young boy who would not normally have been there and who knew about Phillips Mills, their representative chanced to pass our building, and actually called in!

"He told me that Essex Street, where our offices are situated, was on his beat, and that he had walked by us literally hundreds of times in years past, but that he had never called in before. He could not explain what impelled him to do so now.

"This event occurred several years ago, and I may add that, to the best of my knowledge, he has never called in since."

Those scientists who have tried to reach across the frontiers of the mind in our time have testified that similar events have happened to many a person, many a time.

Dr. Carl Jung, perhaps the greatest psychiatrist since Dr. Sigmund Freud, has written extensively about such phenomena, and he spoke of synchronisity. Dr. J. J. Rhine, who decided to research in the field of thought transference at Duke University, has his scientific explanations for such happenings and has proven to the world that there is thought transference where the rays of one brain might reach the receiver of another brain that is ready to receive.

I think there are established reasons to believe that these telepathic powers are natural attributes of all minds. In most human beings they are dormant or have been lost owing to the fact that as civilization became more and more complex they were less and less necessary.

Many animals retain these telepathic powers to a far greater degree than most humans. I have lectured on this subject many times, usually at universities and schools.

I tell my audiences that anybody who has ever watched a flock of birds maneouvre simultaneously in the sky knows that some strange communication makes the feat possible. What about the strict rule in a bee state? What about intercommunication among fish? What about the swallows leaving England in autumn, flying to Africa and returning to the very same place next spring? How can this be explained if not through thought waves?

Everyone of us has felt these thought waves. The phone rings and you know who is calling you. Telepathy must have been man's earliest form of intercommunication. We have lost it now, just as our physical structure has changed during the ages. Our eyes are weaker, our smelling capacity inferior, our taste degenerated. It is not too much to believe that some of our brain senses have also deteriorated.

While we have lost some of our sensitive powers, we still face a group of mental phenomena which we call intuition, instincts, hunches, premonition, coincidence, or foreboding. In primitive man, science finds that many of the powers we have lost in our civilization still exist.

Many of us think we have good hearing, but the savage will hear for many more miles. Lost cats and dogs will smell their way home over hundreds of miles. Our sense of smell has deteriorated in comparison. We know how to read maps, but the natives have their own sense of orientation far superior to ours. Our sense of direction is very questionable. Blindfold a man and he cannot walk straight; he is lost in a fog.

Primitive peoples and creatures in the animal world have maintained their telepathic communicative power. They can hear, sense, and understand mental vibrations beyond our comprehension. Elephants in a herd can communicate with each other through telepathy. Insects have the same ability: There is nothing supernatural about the dog who had travelled with his master, a fisherman, for twelve years and one day refused to enter the fishing boat. Neither harsh words nor beating helped. He refused to go out on the sea. He knew more than his master. His sixth sense was better developed. He knew that a few hours later a dangerous hurricane would begin to blow. This dog saved his master's life. He could sense the imminent danger just as animals in South America know, hours ahead, when an earthquake will strike and run fearfully from the danger.

I believe that telepathic communication reaches the subconscious mind of man and there is not always a bridge between the two minds, conscious and subconscious. Any animal or any native tribe can anticipate changes of weather—without occultism, but through wave vibrations—which otherwise only a seismograph can do for us who have lost this sixth sense.

Any Eskimo or Masai can sense imminent danger. The Tibetan Lamas can communicate with each other without writing or speaking. The shepherds in the mountains of Yugoslavia can communicate with each other in the same silent way, as Louis Adamic has observed.

Stage and vaudeville "telepathists" have fooled the public often by the use of tricks and accomplices, but the thousands of experiments made by Dr. Rhine at Duke University and in Britain, Sweden, Germany and the Soviet Union, have convinced more and more scientists that there is a full scientific explanation for telepathy.

THE MOUNTAIN OF DEVIL WORSHIPPERS

by W. B. SEABROOK

I HAD hoped that our first sight of Bagdad would be its famous golden domes and minarets. Instead it was smoke from the ice factory, but as we got nearer, the domes and minarets appeared, mysterious and beautiful amid palm trees, lighted by the slanting rays of the sun and rich with the glamour of old Haroun Al-Raschid's court and the *Tales of a Thousand and One Nights.*

Our first closer impression of Bagdad enhanced the romantic spell, for we drove towards the southern bridge, through the purely native quarter of the city on the west bank of the Tigris—along a wide avenue, magnificently shaded by palm trees, lined on both sides by coffee shops with hundreds of divans before them, on which sat and reclined throngs of Arabs in long, sashed robes, some shaven-pated and bareheaded, others in turbans. Here might the ghosts of Sinbad and the hunchback tailor wander and feel themselves in the Bagdad of other days.

But when we crossed the wide, muddy river and turned into the new street which the British had cut through the centre of the city, romantic dreaming gave way to real surprise. Crude frame buildings were everywhere, some with second-story false fronts, garish American motion-picture billboards, last year's films—a tattooing establishment with signs in English and French, garage yards with high board fences and big English signs in box-car letters, motor cars honking everywhere, mostly flivvers. It was like a new western oil town at its worst. And this was Bagdad! Of course, it wasn't; but it was a part of our first impression.

We went to the Maude Hotel and were given a comfortable room with a balcony overlooking the river and another window directly over the hotel terrace, on which white-uniformed waiters were already laying the tables for dinner. While baths were being prepared, we got into pyjamas and turned on the electric fan. It's all very well to talk of plain cool water as the best thirst-quencher, but we consumed two quarts of bubbling Apollinaris, liberally dosed with Holland gin and lime-juice, and it tasted better than the purest spring-water that ever flowed.

By the time we had had our baths, the terrace had been lighted in the dusk, and an orchestra was playing *Tosca.* We put on our dinner-clothes and went down to dine. The service and food were excellent, almost as elaborate as the Ritz.

The air was pleasant, like a moderately hot summer night in New York. It gave no hint of the deadly heat from which Bagdad suffers during the middle hours of the day. We dined and slept well and awoke refreshed.

My interest, at that time, was not in Bagdad. I was concerned only in seeing Mrs. Seabrook comfortably established, having her meet some of the Arabian families to whom we had letters—for she was more interested in that than in official circles—and in getting on to Mosul and the Yezidees.

The first part of this programme was settled most completely on the late afternoon of that day, when, after riding in an open carriage through a winding maze of covered bazaars and streets in one of the oldest quarters, we lifted the enormous iron knocker upon the gates of Howeja Mirzi Yacoub, Persian by birth, but lifetime inhabitant of Bagdad, and one of the ablest doctors in Irak.

Our letter was from his son, who was studying at the Turkish medical school in Constantinople, and with whom we had formed an intimate friendship.

How to describe Oriental hospitality—particularly when one comes recommended by a beloved son from whom there has been no recent news?

Dr. Yacoub, it seemed, was out, but the turbaned manservant, as soon as he gathered that our coming concerned, in some way, the son of the house, ran with the letter and our cards to "*El Sitt*" —the lady.

She could not have stopped even to open the letter, for the servant came rushing and beckoning down the stone steps into the courtyard where we stood waiting, and conducted us to a terraced roof-top—where stood the lady, who took us both literally to her bosom.

She was very large, motherly, swathed in folds of finest white muslin, hair hanging over her shoulders in two thick braids, gold anklets, bare feet in sandals of wood inset with silver—and two beautiful diamonds in her ears—but these were outshone by her fine, big face, which beamed with joy. We both loved her at first sight. She patted our hands.

"You are friends of my son—ah, happy welcome." She called down into the courtyard and sent a servant scurrying to meet her husband and bid him hasten. And, all the time, a thousand questions about her son. When had we seen him last? Was he happy? Was his colour good? Had he been doing well with his studies? Had he been ill?

Katie assured her that the son was blooming with health, prospering in his studies, and that all was well with him.

This good news so overcame the dear old lady that she threw both arms around Katie's neck and cried so that tears ran in streams down her cheeks. And in no time at all Katie was crying with her. They hugged and sobbed as if their hearts were breaking. Here were two women who had never laid eyes on one another until five minutes before, now crying their eyes out in each other's arms—because the son of one of them was well and happy! Women are weird creatures—but I well understood that Katie would be safely looked after in Bagdad whether I went journeying on to the mountain of the Yezidees—or to the Mountain of the Moon.

We sat and talked more calmly. Dr. Yacoub arrived, a man of great charm and dignity. His welcome was less emotional on the surface, but he, too, was very glad to see us. Servants made coffee over a charcoal fire, on a lower roof in the courtyard.

Would we not come immediately and live with them? No? Well, then, we must come back many times. But even so, we could not leave the house on their first visit without taking with us a gift, for the sake of their son. We protested while they discussed what it should be. They led us into a big drawing-room, walls covered with huge Persian tapestries, gilded Louis Seize furniture on a hard earthen floor. The dear lady was for immediately tearing down and bundling up one of the finest hangings. Katie restrained her by physical force. Not to offend her, we accepted a small inlaid brass tray. But next day, the tapestry was sent to us at the hotel. And the Yacoubs were as a second mother and father to Katie when I left her a few days later for the country of the Yezidees.

I had counted on a certain Suleiman Pashati to help me in

whatever arrangements were necessary about getting into the Yezidee mountains. I sent my letters to him, and next evening he called at the hotel. When he came in I thought there must be some mistake. He had been described to me as the elder son of one of the oldest and most old-fashioned princely families of the pure Bagdad strain. I had vaguely expected a turbaned prince with flowing robes and jewelled dagger, for there are many such in Arabia who hold to the old traditions of dress. Instead he looked like a rising young Wall Street broker, tailored by Fifth Avenue's best, and I found he had come in a swanky little Stutz roadster. He was affable and charming. His English, on the whole, was better than mine. He knew very little about the Yezidees, but he knew his Bagdad, and after reflecting a bit, his advice was shrewd and practical.

"You dont' want to go to Gertrude Bell—you don't want to go to the British at all. They'd either stop you or send somebody in uniform along, which would be just as bad. It's in the Mosul region—Nineveh. The excavations. I know the man who ought to help you."

We went out and got into his roadster, drove north up Bagdad's main street, around a corner, and entered a little hand laundry which, with its counters and piled-up ticketted bundles, was not very much unlike laundries in that other Bagdad-on-the-subway. The proprietor was a spectacled, elderly man in his shirt-sleeves, who turned out to be an antiquarian. The laundry was his "side-line". He took us to a back room where there were a roll-top desk and a little iron safe. He dealt in Asyrian cylinders and other antiquities, in a small way, with most of the world's big museums. Before I left he showed me letters from the University of Pennsylvania and the British Archaeological Society. He had been many times to Mosul, in connection with the Nineveh excavations. He knew, if the man could be found, just the right person to help me, a certain Mechmed Hamdi—also once employed in connection with the work at Nineveh, who had been several times among the Yezidees, made a study of the cult, and written a pamphlet about it, he believed, in Arabic.

Luckily this Mechmed Hamdi was easily found next day—a grey little badger of a man he proved to be, in a red fez and shabby frock-coat, with keen, likeable eyes—a real fund of scholarship—eager to be of service as soon as he discovered the matter concerned one of his pet subjects—in a word, an amiable, down-at-heel professor.

Ten minutes' conversation convinced me that he knew more about the Yezidees than any man I had yet met. Also he knew personally their ruler Said Beg, and exactly how to get from Mosul to Sheik-Adi. We liked each other, and in less than ten more minutes he had agreed—for a very modest consideration—to make the trip with me.

For a professor, he handled the arrangements very well. Some mornings later—after a wholly uneventful journey by third-class carriage to the rail head a half-day north of Bagdad, and then by easy stages in an old Pugeot, cheaply hired, to Mosul—we found ourselves on mule-back, with a pack mule and guide in front of us, ambling north-east among green foothills and valleys gay with flowers, towards higher and more rugged hills, in the shadow of the Kurdish mountains.

During the previous days, Mechmed Hamdi had supplied me from the rich store of his sound knowledge such facts as he thought I should know in advance concerning the strange sect we were going to visit. And he continued his discourse as we ambled along on our mules. It was practical rather than academic. I would find the Yezidees trustworthy, he said, and hospitable, but there were certain things always to be remembered when among them which, if forgotten, could lead to serious trouble.

One must take care never to pronounce the name of Shaitan (Satan) and must avoid the use of any words or syllables, whether in English, French or Arabic, which could, by any chance, be mistaken for that word—such Arabic words, for instance, as *khaitan* (thread) and *shait* (arrow).

One must neither wear nor exhibit any article of clothing that was blue—no necktie of blue, for instance, no ring with a blue stone in it—for blue is taboo and anathema among the Yezidees, because it is supposed to have magical properties inimical to Satan. Blue amulets and charms, particularly blue beads, are worn universally among Moslems as a protection against devils and to ward off the evil eye. All babies and almost every domestic animal in certain parts of Arabia have a necklace or collar of blue beads, and I have even seen a woman, in the bazaar at Bagdad, with a string of blue beads on her Singer sewing-machine, to prevent demons from breaking or tangling the thread. Blue, therefore, was a colour accursed among the Yezidees, who worshipped the Arch-Demon.

A third prohibition was that one must take care never to spit in a fire or to put out a dropped match by stepping on it with the foot, for to them all fire is sacred.

Since they were confessedly worshippers of Satan, I asked Mechmed Hamdi why was it forbidden to pronounce his name.

It was prohibited in their scripture, their Khitab al Aswad (Black Book), he said, of which he himself had studied the copy of a partial translation made from Kurdish into Arabic more than a hundred years before by one of their own priests in the Sinjar. In the Black Book, Shaitan says:

> *Speak not my name nor mention my attributes, lest ye be guilty, for ye have no true knowledge thereof; but honour my symbol and image.*

The basis of the Yezidee belief, as Mechmed Hamdi outlined it to me, was briefly this:

God created seven spirits "as a man lighteth one lamp after another", and the first of these spirits was Satan, whom God made supreme ruler of the earth for a period of ten thousand years. And because Satan was supreme master of the earth, those who dwelt on it could prosper only by doing him homage and worshipping him.

Since the true name was forbidden, Mechmed Hamdi told me, they referred to Shaitan as Melek Taos (Angel Peacock) and worshipped him in the form of a brass bird.

I asked Mechmed whether he had ever seen this bird, and he said absolutely no, and that he knew of no man not a Yezidee who had ever seen it, but that it was supposed to be rudely carved, more like a rooster than a peacock, mounted on a brass pole, of such size as one man might easily carry.

While the name of Shaitan was forbidden, he said—so much so that if a Yezidee hears it spoken, their law commands him either to kill the man who uttered it or kill himself—yet we could talk freely with them about Melek Taos "as we could to a Christian about Jesus."

Pushing steadily forward and upward, by winding stony paths, we were gradually leaving the valleys below us, rising to more rugged, jagged, rocky hills; but still there were mulberry and olive trees, so that the route, while wild, was not desolate. In early afternoon we halted by a spring, had lunch, and allowed the mules to rest. We planned to reach Baadri, the stronghold of Said Beg, easily an hour or so before sunset.

In the late afternoon, we passed one or two stone villages along the slopes, which Mechmed said were Yezidee. I saw, at a distance, women cultivating the fields. They were unveiled, some in black, others in tucked-up robes of bright red or yellow. A man leading three pack donkeys tried to avoid saluting us, but mumbled *Marhaba* (a rough "hello") as he passed. He also was Yezidee, in baggy white trousers, black tunic which reached to his knees, a wide, red sash, and a red cotton turban wound round his rusty felt cap.

Now and again, but rarely, we passed others afoot, usually carrying a sack or some rude farm implement. These first worshippers of Satan were evidently a habitually peaceful people engaged in tilling their soil, but if they showed no open hostility towards us, neither were they friendly.

Towards five o'clock, on a mountainside several miles ahead of us, we had our first view of the castle of Said Beg, ruler and "Black Pope" of the Yezidees. It was a boxlike, flat-roofed structure, apparently unornamented, like a blockhouse or fortress, and so indeed it seemed as we gradually drew closer. It stood isolated on a slope, and the little village of Baadri with clustering low stone houses lay several hundred yards below it.

The castle gate stood open, unattended. We dismounted and entered a big, bare rectangular courtyard, where servants came, greeted us civilly, and went out to look after our mules, while one went to announce our arrival.

A few moments later, Said Beg himself appeared. He was a man of perhaps fifty, in black tunic and big red turban, with a large nose and a long, sparse dark beard. Immediately he recognized Mechmed Hamdi, shook hands with him, and bade us both a hospitable welcome.

It was hard to convince myself that I was actually in the presence of the ruler of the Devil-Worshippers—the man whose name was surrounded, among superstitious Moslems, by tales as terrifying as those told in Saladin's day of the Old Man of the Mountain, King of the Assassins—the monster who devoured young silver-girdled virgins nightly, and who, as I had been told in Aleppo, had murdered his own father to become Mir—for he seemed no different from any other grave and courteous Oriental host, and in the most matter-of-fact way set about making us feel at home and comfortable.

He evidently made no distinction between English and American, and told me that I was welcome because my countrymen had stopped the murder and persecution of his people and that now a Yezidee could journey safely even to Bagdad and could walk openly in Bagdad's streets without fear of being set upon by Christians or Moslems and slain.

We would please excuse him that night, because, not forewarned of our coming, he had other necessary occupations, but his home was ours, and on the morrow he would accompany us to Sheik-Adi, to visit the temple and shrines of his people.

Our luggage was taken into a big rectangular hall. We washed ourselves in water poured from earthen jugs by a servant in the courtyard. Pallets and cushions were brought into the hall and arranged for us, and a little later a brass tray laden with dishes was brought in and deposited on the floor—grilled mutton, a sort of pilaff, quantities of ripe olives, a big bowl of clabbered milk—and presently we lay down to sleep as safely and soundly in Satan's castle as I had ever slept in the houses of the godly.

I was awakened at dawn, after a sound sleep in the castle stronghold of Mir Said Beg, by a servant who announced that the mules were already saddled for our journey further up the mountain to the temple of Satan and the sacred shrine at Sheik-Adi.

It was for this "unholy" pilgrimage that I had ventured, with some misgivings, to the slope of Mount Lalesh.

Fortune had favoured me, and now the Mir himself, supreme ruler of the Devil-Worshippers in all Asia, black-bearded, in scarlet turban, with a great black cloak swathed round him against the morning mists, was condescending to be my guide. At his side rode his adolescent son, who, if he followed historical precedents, might in later years slay the Mir and rule as Black Pope in his stead. Behind them I rode with my friend the learned Mechmed Hamdi of Bagdad, and in our rear, on a donkey, one of Mir Said Beg's servants followed.

We were approaching a sanctuary which few Arab Moslems or Christians have ever seen, but which they all discourse about with voluble superstition as a nest of diabolical mysteries from which one might not return alive. Now that I was actually among the Yezidees, as guest of their own prince, I knew that there was nothing to fear, and wondered as we rode how many of the other wild tales would turn out to be untrue—the Courtyard of the Black Serpent—the Tower of Satan from which occult vibrations of evil were broadcast to sway the destinies of the world—the temple hewn from the solid rock, leading down to vast subterranean caverns stained with the blood of human sacrifice.

Phantasm and embroidery, doubtless; but experience had already taught me that often, in Arabia, the seemingly wildest fictions prove on closer examination to be based on distorted fact. So now, as we ascended towards the shrine of Satan, I had high hopes of seeing "some strange thing"—perhaps many.

The ride from Baadri to Sheik-Adi, the Mir had told us, would take only an hour. A stony bridle path, winding upward among ravines and rocks, had left the castle out of sight behind, and still mounted, twisting, through wild, barren scenery—but when we crossed a ridge and finally had our first glimpse of sacred Sheik-Adi, clinging to the terraced slope of a mountain, it was not wild and desolate—for among the walls and rocks were foliage and grass, many mulberry trees and olive trees in full leaf.

The entire hillside was dotted with hundreds of uninhabited stone huts—shelters, the Mir told us, for Yezidee pilgrims who visited the shrine. The temple itself, in their midst, appeared as a collection of rambling walls, surrounding terraced courtyards and flat-roofed buildings, above which there was a glimpse of two small white-washed, cone-shaped domes.

Behind it and above, surmounting a higher ridge, was a white fluted tower shaped like a sharpened pencil-point—and from its top brilliant, dazzling rays of light, as if from a heliograph, actually flashed towards us! The sight of it thrilled me, for this, whatever its exact purpose, I knew was undoubtedly one of the "Towers of Shaitan", the fabulous "power houses" which figure in the tales and myths of Arabia, Persia, and Turkestan. I hoped we would be permitted to see what was inside it.

Meanwhile the path, which we now followed on foot, leading our mules, took us between old crumbling walls and under arches to a larger archway which gave into a wide courtyard, around which was built a flat-roofed monastery in which the priest in charge of the temple and his associates lived. He came out, an old greybeard, in white robes and red sash and turban, kissed the Mir Said Beg's hand, and then saluted us.

Like any sacristan of a Christian cathedral, the old priest of Satan offered his services to conduct us through the temple. Mir Said Beg and his son left us. Mechmed Hamdi and I followed our new guide down a flight of stone steps, through a gateway which he unlocked for us, into a little rectangular walled yard whose northern wall was the face of the actual temple, built against and into the living rock of the mountainside. This was the "Courtyard of the Serpent". And the serpent's actual dominating presence was there—though it was not alive. It was a stone serpent standing on its tail, carved in high relief, and glistening black in the sunlight on the grey wall, at the right of the temple door. Many other symbols were carved in the façade of the temple—a two-edged beheading axe, a harrow, a pair of scissors, and square Kurdish symbols. The façade of the temple faced south. In the south-east corner of the courtyard, sunk into the pavement, was a small rectangular pool. But most of all I was interested in the black serpent on the wall. The priest observed this and signed for me to inspect it as closely as I liked. He did not seem to regard it with exaggerated reverence. He told me that it was *alamt el akl* (symbol of wisdom), and I was sure it must be the lineal descendant, mythologically, of that same serpent which tempted Eve. The priest had touched it casually as he spoke, and he was not annoyed when I ventured repectfully to stroke its tail. I wanted to see what its glistening black substance was—whether it had been carved, as I had at first supposed, in relief from the rock, or was perhaps of some inset metal. It was the same stone as the rest, cut in relief, and some of the black came off on my finger. Whereupon this amiable priest of Satan explained to me—with the astounding matter-of-factness which I think has no parallel in western psychology—that in the old days the serpent had been kept polished with black lead, but that now they did it with harness-blacking made by the *Engleysi* and bought in Mosul. The black lead was more durable, but the harness-blacking gave the snake a finer appearance. I duly admired it. And then he conducted us into the temple.

It was a gloomy rectangular stone chamber, perhaps fifty feet long, shaped like a shoe-box, its length lying east and west. The first thing I noticed was dozens of little flickering points of light at irregular spots in the wall. These came from small iron dishes, set in niches, in which lighted wicks floated in olive oil. These, he told us, were kept continually burning. The arrangement of the temple was curious and difficult to describe. Down its middle, from end to end, ran a row of stone pillars, and between these pillars from base to base of each ran a low wall, which one could almost step over.

It divided the chamber longitudinally into two separate parts with floors on a different level—that nearer the door being a few feet lower. In a corner, on the lower level, another rectangular pool was sunk.

There was no altar of any sort, but midway in the northern wall was an iron grating and behind it a dark inner chamber, hewn, I think, from the rock. There was no entrance directly into it, but farther along the north wall was a door, giving inward against the mountain, to which the priest led us. Through this door we entered a small square chamber, over which was the smaller of two cone-shaped domes we had seen from outside, and under the dome was a sarcophagus-like tomb. At the right was a small closed door which led apparently into the bowels of the mountain, while at the left was an open door leading to the dark chamber which I had peered into through the iron grating. We entered this chamber and found, beneath the larger of the two domes, another tomb, covered with a black pall, which, the priest told us, contained the remains of Sheik Adi, the founder of their sect. Beyond it another door led to a third inner chamber, where were stored many earthen jars of oil for the lamps.

Mechmed Hamdi began telling me in French, which the priest could not understand, of the supposed cavern or crypt, hidden in the bowels of the mountain, beneath our feet, which he had wanted to see on former occasions. He said he had been refused on the ground that strangers could be permitted to enter it only by special order of the Mir Said Beg himself. The closed door from the adjacent chamber was supposed to lead to it.

Now that Said Beg was here and seemed friendly disposed, we decided that it could do no harm at least to make the request. This Mechmed Hamdi did, in politest Arabic, suggesting that if the priest were not too greatly inconvenienced, and if Said Beg graciously permitted it, we would like to see the lower chambers.

The priest seemed uncertain, but was willing that we should

consult the Mir himself. And so we did when we went back and found him awaiting us in the upper courtyard.

He told us we might descend the steps and look in, but that there was nothing to see—"it was just a cave." The priest procured a torch, and we re-entered the temple, went through the little door, down a very old flight of damp stone steps, through a dungeon-like passage. At the foot of the steps where we stopped and stood, we found ourselves in a vaulted cavern, partly natural, it seemed, and partly hewn from the rock, and around a corner the sound of rushing water—a sound which we had heard as a murmur in the upper temple, but had supposed to come from some near-by stream flowing down the mountainside. We could not see the whole of the cavern, or guess how far it extended. Its floor at the foot of the steps was covered with water, which I guessed from the slope to be not more than ankle-deep. But the priest made it an excuse to deter us from going farther, declaring that there was no use getting our feet wet, since there was nothing more to see. I peered about by the light of the torch to see whether I could observe any inscriptions on the wall, any signs of an altar, niches, or other indications that the place was used for ritual purposes—and though the light was flickering and bad, I was pretty surely convinced that there was nothing of the kind within our range of vision. It was a place admirably suited to the weird and dreadful rites which Arab Moslems assured me were conducted there in the worship of Satan—including, they insisted, human sacrifice—but I must admit that there was nothing to offer the slightest intimation that it was currently used for such purpose. Except for stimulating the imagination and making one wonder what secret scenes, in recent or earlier times, that mysterious cavern of Satan had witnessed, our partial penetration of it was interesting chiefly as establishing the fact that the whole temple edifice was constructed over subterranean caverns and streams and springs, some of the water of which was led into the pools we had seen in the temple and courtyard above. I learned later that the Yezidees believed these waters flowed by a subterranean river across all Arabia, underneath the desert, from the miraculous spring of Zem-Zem in Mecca. The fountain of Zem-Zem, like the Kaaba, with its black stone, was holy to the ancient idolatrous Arabs many centuries before Mecca became the sacred city of Islam. I found that the Yezidees regarded both fire and water as sacred elements.

I would have given a month of my life to explore those caverns completely, and shall always wonder what I might have found around the angles of the rocks—what other chambers, what altars, what relics of ancient or modern sacrifice. I have since had nightmare dreams of wading ankle-deep through the water at the foot of the stairs, of turning a corner and, beneath a great vault like a cathedral, coming upon a dreadful red, fiery altar—but actually there and wide awake, the only thing which made me believe there might possibly be an altar of some sort in the cavern was the fact that there was no sign of one, or even an emplacement for an altar, in the temple above.

Hamdi was of the firm opinion that rites of some sort were still practised there—but it was only an opinion. We saw nothing actually to confirm it.

Another mystery was the fluted cone-shaped tower, with its light-flashing pinnacle, on the mountain above, which we went to see after we had climbed up from the crypt and emerged from the temple.

It rose from the flat roof of a big vault of whitewashed masonry, so that the roof made a wide platform around the tower's base. The tower itself was likewise of whitewashed stone, and the glistening peak which cast fiery rays of light in all directions was a highly polished ball of burnished gold or brass. When the sun was overhead, a man looking across the valleys from any direction, east, west, north, or south, would be bound to see its darting heliographic rays. Here was a most practical explanation of the belief in the "power house" from which occult emanations or vibrations were sent out to cast a Satanic spell upon the world.

We entered the vault beneath the tower and there found the *turbah* of another of the old devil-worshipping saints, placed immediately beneath the tower's hollow, dome-like shaft. But otherwise it was empty. I looked about for the sinister figure who was supposed to sit in the tower day and night, weaving his potent incantations. I asked outright the innocently worded question whether any priest ever came there to pray, and I was thrilled when our guide answered that the regular priests did not, but that the *kolchaks*, who I learned later were the *fakirs* or miracle workers of the Yezidees, often came to this *turbah* and remained in it making magic for many days! So that part of the fabulous tale was literally true—though it scarcely followed that, whatever the *kolchaks*' belief in their own diabolical powers, their incantations had been directly responsible for the World War, the Russian Revolution, or the Wall Street explosion, which were among the events a certain captain of the British secret service—since dismissed and shut up in a sanatorium, I am told, because he had become cracked on occult mysticism and magic—had assured me were directly attributable to the "controlling emanations sent out by the priests of this infernal cult". He had assured me as well that, to his personal knowledge, a man had been murdered—at long distance—in the Savoy Hotel in London, by similar Yezidee priestcraft. I am so constituted as not to be able to believe these things—but there are thousands of highly educated people, not in sanatoriums, either, who do believe them; and I suppose that if they had seen what I saw in the Mountain of the Yezidees, their worst suspicions would have been confirmed.

More interestingly definite than the reputed magical influence of the tower was a ceremony which the priest described to us as having taken place less than a month previously, and which he said was repeated every spring. I wish indeed that I could say I had witnessed it. It concerned a bull, of which I had heard in Aleppo; but it seemed that it was a white bull, instead of black as I had been told. This bull, the priest now told me, was decorated with garlands of red flowers, a vein in its throat was opened, and it was led or dragged in procession round and round the tower, on the wide stone platform, until the tower's white base was bathed in the crimson circle of its spurting blood. It was *zain k'tir*, he said—"very beautiful"—nor did he seem a bloodthirsty wretch in saying it, but rather was like some benevolent Italian village padre describing to sympathetic travellers the beauties of a procession of the Madonna which they had missed by arriving after Easter. I began to have a fondness for the old man such as I had not felt towards the more exalted Mir Said Beg, whom, though he had been a most courteous host, I did not find sympathetic or lovable as an individual. The story, by the way, that he had murdered his father for the succession, I was reliably informed in Bagdad later, was not true, though it is generally believed by the natives of Irak. The former Mir, Ali Beg, died peacefully some ten years ago in his bed. But Ali Beg's father and grandfather before him had both been murdered when their sons or nephews became old enough to rule—in one case through the connivance of son and mother—and it seems that there was some ancient law by which the son of a Mir was exculpated by his people if he thus slew his father, and automatically became Mir in his father's stead.

During the three days we remained on Mount Lalesh among the Yezidees, I was not fortunate enough to gain the intimate friendship of Mir Said Beg, though we returned to his castle that afternoon and remained his guests. But something like a friendship sprang up between me and the old priest, whose name was Nadir-Lugh. He invited us to come again when we took leave that afternoon, and the following day, with the Mir's permission, accompanied this time only by a servant, Mechmed Hamdi and I rode up to see him. We made no further exploration of the temple or its environs—I think we had already been shown everything it is permitted any unbeliever to see—but sat and "visited" with him, on a stone bench in the upper courtyard, in the shade of a mulberry tree, with our backs comfortably against the wall.

Mechmed Hamdi had told me that while it was forbidden, at least theoretically, on pain of death to pronounce the name of Shaitan, we might freely mention their Satanic god by his other name, Melek Taos (Angel Peacock); and Nadir-Lugh, when he found me eager to hear whatever he might be free to tell concerning the cult he served, was amiable and loquacious. I discovered that not only was a part, at least, of their doctrine no secret, but that they taught it willingly and had made native converts from other religions.

I had begun by asking Nadir-Lugh to tell us of their great "saint" and founder, Sheik Adi, who lay buried in the temple—but there was a preliminary point that he was first determined to make clear to us.

"Do you believe in God?" he asked me with startling directness—and it seemed to me the strangest of questions, coming from a priest of Satan. I did not know whether he wanted me to answer yes or no, so I replied truthfully, that I supposed I did, but that I was not quite sure what I meant by God.

"Well, we, of course, also believe in God," he told me; "but our difference from all other religions is this—that we know God is so far away that we can have no contact with Him—and He, on his part, has no knowledge or interest of any sort concerning human affairs. It is useless to pray to Him or worship Him. He cares nothing about us.

"He has given the entire control of this world for ten thousand years to the bright spirit, Melek Taos, and Him, therefore, we worship. Moslems and Christians are wrongly taught that he whom we call Melek Taos is the spirit of evil. We know that this is not true. He is the spirit of power and the ruler of this world. At the end of the ten thousand years of his reign—of which we are now in the third thousand—he will re-enter paradise as the chief of the Seven Bright Spirits, and all his true worshippers will enter paradise with him."

I liked his casual and simple explanation. Whatever its merits or demerits as a doctrine, it was logically and admirably stated.

Having established this point of Satanic theology to his satisfaction and ours, he went on to tell us about Sheik Adi. He reckoned, as nearly all Arabs do, whatever their sect, by the Islamic calendar, and told us that Sheik Adi, founder of the Yezidees, had been born near Baalbek—ancient City of the Sun whose colossal ruins lie on the western skirt of the desert near Damascus—in the fifth century, which would make it the twelfth by Christian reckoning.

Sheik Adi had travelled in Persia, where a revelation had come to him through fire (possibly contact with the Zoroastrian fire worshippers) and had founded the Yezidee cult here where we sat, on Mount Lalesh.

For many years Sheik Adi had ruled, and the cult had grown—and then he had decided to make another pilgrimage. In his absence, Melek Taos himself had taken a human form exactly resembling that of the absent Sheik Adi and had appeared among the Yezidees, who believed that he was indeed their Sheik who had returned among them. For three years Melek Taos was the ruler—and when the real Sheik Adi returned from his pilgrimage, the Yezidees, believing him to be an impostor, fell upon him with their swords and slew him; whereat Melek Taos resumed his own true form, told them that Sheik Adi, whose sacrifice at their hands completed the founding of the religion, would be with them on the Day of Judgment, and that he should always be revered as their greatest saint.

The old priest then told us how Sheik Adi would appear and save them on that last day.

"The souls of all true Yezidees will be carried into paradise in a wicker basket on the head of Sheik Adi, and will submit to no reckoning or trial in the last judgment."

I ventured to ask if it were proper for him to explain why their Bright Spirit was worshipped in the form of a peacock, and this is the extraordinary tale he told me:

Jesus was a spirit who came to earth and took the form of a man, to wage war on Melek and wrest the earth from his dominion. When Jesus hung on the cross, being crucified, the magic was such that if he had been able to carry out his purpose and die in the form of a man, it would have given him power and dominion. Melek thwarted this with his greater magic by taking Jesus from the cross alive, expelling him from earth, and hung on the cross in his stead a figure without substance which seemed to the watchers to be Jesus.

When this figure without substance seemed to die and was laid in a tomb, it dissolved and disappeared. The two Marys came to the tomb, found it empty, and were astonished.

Melek then appeared to them as an angel and told them to have no fear for their friend Jesus, who had been taken from the cross and sent safely away to other worlds.

They refused to believe Melek, and in order to convince them of his power, he slew a peacock which was in the garden, took out its entrails, cut it into pieces, and then brought them all together again to make a living bird more glorious and beautiful than the one which he had slain.

Then he himself entered the body of this bright bird and flew away. Therefore he is called Angel Peacock, and the bird is his symbol.

"Was it ever permitted," I asked, "for profane eyes to look upon this symbol?"

This he did not answer directly, but said that the image was kept in a secret place in the mountains of the Sinjar, many days' journey to the west, and only brought to the temple on Mount Lalesh at certain times. I did not question him any further on this score. He was so very amiable in answering other questions that for courtesy's sake I did not want to press him on any that he chose to avoid. In fact I begged that if, in my ignorance, I asked questions about things which were secret or forbidden he would forgive me.

When I questioned him about the origin of the Yezidees as a

people—who seemed to me mixed Arab and Kurdish—he declared that they were the children of Adam, but not of Eve!

"How could that be?" I eagerly inquired—and supposed that I was going to hear some new tale of that amazing Lilith, whom mediaeval monkish legend describes as a beautiful fiend in the form of woman, who was Adam's first wife before Eve was created, and who left him to become the paramour of the Serpent. But the old priest's tale ran otherwise.

It seems that Adam and Eve had a quarrel about their children—the same sort of quarrel that many husbands and wives still engage in, a sort of clash between paternal and maternal jealousy. Adam said: "These children are entirely mine. I am their real parent. From me comes their life. You are nothing but the vessel in which they were carried until they were big and strong enough to come out of it."

Eve retorted: "You are all wrong. The children are entirely mine. They grew as a part of my body, and you had nothing whatever to do with it."

So Adam and Eve, unable to agree, decided to put their difference to a practical test.

Adam made an *oya* (a sort of rude pottery jug) and put into it earth and water, mixed to make a thick mud, to which he added some of the "vital juices" from his body, and sealed it up.

Eve also made an *oya*, filled it with mud, put some of her "vital blood" into it, and likewise sealed it up. And the two jars were buried "like ostrich eggs" in the warm sand and left there for the period of thrice three months.

At the end of that time Adam dug up his jug, and was about to break it open, when something began kicking and crying inside, the jug cracked and broke open "like an egg", and a baby boy appeared—the son of Adam alone.

But when Eve dug up her jug, there was no sound or movement, and when she took a stone and broke it, there was nothing inside but dry, dead dust.

Eve was then humbled and Adam took her again to wife, and together they had many children, who became idolaters, Jews, Moslems, and Christians—the progeny of Adam and Eve.

But from the son who had been born to Adam alone, without Eve's co-operation, came the race of the Yezidees.

Nadir-Lugh's old wrinkled face beamed when I told him how

one of the greatest *Engleysi* scientists, Professor Haldane of Oxford, had predicted that, in another hundred years, babies might actually be grown in laboratory jars—an experiment strikingly similar to that which he had recounted as having taken place in the Garden of Eden—except that Professor Haldane was of the opinion that it would require the vital fluids of both male and female, merged, to make the experiment successful.

The old man gave due consideration and replied that now this might be true, as human beings were at the present day constructed —but that since Adam was originally created complete, containing within himself both the male and female principle, as the nipples on man's breasts still show, it was quite likely that the original experiment took place just as it had been related.

He added that in paradise all difference of sex would again be wiped out, and that each soul would inhabit an angelic body which would be neither male nor female, but the perfect union of both in one.

While we were so frankly on the subject of sex, I asked him to tell me, if he would, of the marriage customs and ceremonials of his people.

He told me that each Yezidee who could afford it was permitted to have four wives, but that many of them had only one—that on the occasion of a marriage there was a great dance which lasted all day long, in which both men and women "leaped", but that during this wild rejoicing the bride was shut up all alone, in a dark room which no single ray of light was permitted to penetrate, and that the first light she saw was the torch carried by the bridegroom when he entered to release her.

In the religious part of the ceremony, he said, earth and water were mixed into a loaf of bread and broken over the bride.

I was wondering meanwhile about the stories that among the Yezidees the Mir had the same right as mediaeval feudal lords in Christendom to lie with the bride on the first night, before the husband. I supposed that if there was such a custom, the Yezidees themselves must regard it as proper, and that, therefore, there could be no harm in asking.

The priest replied that there was indeed such a law, but that it was an ancient law and that, so far as he knew, in his own lifetime it had never been put into actual practice.

As for the silver bridal girdle or "corset" in which I expressed an interest, I might see one of them for the asking, he said, at Baadri, or in any of the villages.

As we rode returning to the castle of Said Beg that afternoon, I told Mechmed Hamdi that I would very much like to go down into Baadri, or to some other village, and see not only the girdles, but something of the common everyday life of the Yezidees. He advised me against it and doubted that the Mir would permit it, even though he himself was friendly to English-speaking people. He said that the Yezidees had been persecuted and murdered, and reviled and hated so long by all other Arabs, that while they would certainly offer us no hurt or insult—knowing that we were among them with the permission of the Mir and stopping under the Mir's roof—yet we would not be really welcome, and that it would be uncomfortable.

I felt that he was right. Already I had seen much more than I had dared to hope, and assented willingly to his suggestion that we return the following day to Mosul.

When the Mir Said Beg learned that we were preparing to depart on the next morning, he came at once to the reception hall which had been converted into our guest-room and asked if we had been shown everything I wished to see.

He was under a great debt of gratitude, he said, to the English, with whom he insisted on identifying me, because they had stopped the persecution which his people had endured for centuries, and he was happy that I had come to visit Mount Lalesh. Was I certain that I had seen everything I wished?

I told him there was one thing more which I had heard about in Aleppo and wanted very much indeed to see, if it was proper and possible, and not inconvenient. I knew perfectly well that he would think I meant the image of Melek Taos, the brazen Angel Peacock, and after a slight, embarrassing pause, I quickly explained that I had heard of the unique beauty and design of the girdle worn by Yezidee brides, and that since I was a great admirer of Oriental craftsmanship, I should like very much to examine one.

He was surprised but well enough pleased, I think, that just after he had been expressing such friendship for the English, he would not be forced to refuse a last request. It was quite easy, he said. He called a servant, and then went out himself. And I think he sent down into the village. At any rate he came back in about half an hour with a really beautiful piece of crude, barbaric jewellery in his hand, which jangled as he walked—quite the widest belt I have ever seen or expect to see—two broad, curved silver bands, fastened together at the back with a broad piece of black leather, and joined at the front with a long silver pin which went through like a loose rivet, with a little ball at the top, fastened by a chain. The silver part of the belt was not like a double buckle, lying flat in front, but was curved so as to encircle the waist like a corset when locked in place by the pin. It was heavily bossed and crudely set with a number of big red and yellow stones. Closer examination showed that it was of no great intrinsic value. The silver was backed with lead alloy, and the stones, of course, were of the kind described as semi-precious—but it was savagely, barbarically magnificent.

When I handed it back to Said Beg and thanked him, he put his hands behind him and said : "No, no ! You will take it with you as a souvenir of Mount Lalesh." And so, after much protestation and thanks, I did. And I still keep it as one of the strangest of my Arabian mementoes.

I wish that I might write of having actually witnessed some secret, mysterious Yezidee ceremonial or ritual—but I did not, nor do I believe any stranger among them ever has; so I confine myself to this record of what I did see and hear, with deep gratitude to Mechmed Hamdi of Bagdad, who by his previous acquaintance with Mir Said Beg made even this much possible.

PSYCHIC EXPERIENCES OF FAMOUS PEOPLE

by IDA CLYDE CLARK

WASHINGTON and Lincoln were not the only Presidents with whom stories of the supernatural have been associated. General Garfield believed that he saw and conversed with his father after his death. But if, like Lincoln, he had any premonition of the untimely fate that befell him, the story has not been preserved.

Several members of President Grant's family believed that spirits of the dead communicate with the living. Mrs. Mary Grant Cramer, President Grant's sister, said that the death of the President's wife was foretold to her in a dream.

Mrs. Cramer was living in East Orange, New Jersey, with her sister, Mrs. Virginia Grant Corbin, when she had the dream. She said: "The dream was exceedingly vivid. I thought that Mrs. Grant came to my bedside and—placing her hand on my shoulder—said impressively: 'Mary, I have come to talk with you and to say goodbye, because I am not going to be with you much longer.' "

Mrs. Cramer told her dream at the breakfast-table the next morning and—to her astonishment—a friend of the family, Mrs. Katherine Lawrence, who was visiting her at the time, said that she, too, had had a singular dream the previous night. She thought that she, Mrs. Cramer and Mrs. Corbin were standing together at the portal of Grant's tomb on Riverside Drive, New York City, and that there appeared to be a large crowd of people outside awaiting the arrival of a cavalcade of some kind.

Mrs. Grant died eight days later, and the *New York Sun* and other papers of the day carried the stories of the prophetic dreams.

Many famous statesmen and publicists have recorded psychic experiences. Among them was Lord Balfour, Prime Minister of England, 1903–5. He was called "the Statesman clairvoyant".

One of Lord Balfour's earliest recorded experiences was with a crystal ball. His sister had said that she had seen a piece of old furniture in the ball. Her brother laughed at her and took the ball into his study. When he returned to her he was perplexed. He said he had seen in the ball a person whom he knew, making tea near a lamp. This was about five o'clock on Sunday evening at St. Andrews. On the following Tuesday he met a Miss Grant, whom he had known, at a ball in Edinburgh.

"On Sunday, at five o'clock," he told her, "you were sitting under a standard lamp making tea. A man in blue serge was beside you; his back was towards me. I saw the tip of his moustache."

He also described the dress she was wearing, which he had never seen. Every detail of his vision was confirmed by the lady. She and Lord Balfour wrote out and signed a report of the incident.

On another occasion Lord Balfour saw a house in a bowl of water. He had never seen this house, yet he described it perfectly, and said a white Persian cat was walking down the stairs. Though the light in the room was changed several times, the picture remained for some time. He afterwards met the lady who lived in the house and who owned the white Persian cat. She said the picture he had seen was accurate in every detail.

Lord Balfour writes:

> I suppose everybody would say it would be an extraordinary circumstance if, at no distant date, this earth on which we dwell were to come into collision with some unknown body travelling through space, and—as a result of that collision—be resolved into the original gases of which it is composed. . . . I have constantly met people who will tell you, with no apparent consciousness that they are saying anything more out of the way than an observation about the weather, that by the exercise of their will they can make anybody at a little distance turn round and look at them. Now such a fact (if fact it be) is far more scientifically extraordinary than would be the destruction of this globe by some such celestial catastrophe as I have imagined. How profoundly mistaken, then, are they who think that this exercise of "will-power", as they call it, is the most natural and the most normal thing in the world, something which everybody should have expected, something which hardly deserves scientific notice or requires scientific explanation. In reality it is a profound mystery, if it is true, or if anything like it is true; and no event,

however startling, which easily finds its appropriate niche in the structure of the physical sciences ought to exercise so much intellectual curiosity as this dull and at first sight commonplace phenomenon.

Chauncey M. Depew had a psychic experience just before he was to place Mr. Theodore Roosevelt in nomination for Governor of New York, in the Republican Convention at Saratoga. He had been asked by Mr. Roosevelt to make this speech, and he had little time in which to prepare it.

On Saturday afternoon, before the convention met on Monday, Mr. Depew sat on the piazza of his home at Ardsley-on-the-Hudson, dreamily contemplating the view across the river. Gradually the scene before him faded and in its place came a picture of the convention hall at Saratoga. He saw the delegates stroll in. He looked at the presiding officer, whose name he did not know, as he called the convention to order. He heard the speeches as clearly as if the speakers were before him. He heard Mr. Quigg, whom he had never known, introduce him; he saw himself rise and address the chair, heard himself deliver the speech, and felt the glow of satisfaction at its reception.

Then the picture of the convention hall faded and again he was looking at the scenery along the Hudson.

He got up, went to his study and wrote out with his own hand the exact speech he had just heard himself make. And two days later he delivered that speech, word for word. Furthermore the scene was precisely as he had seen it and people said the words he had heard them say two days before, while sitting on his piazza on the bank of the Hudson.

When the story was published and sent to Mr. Depew, he said of it: "This story is substantially true as written." Mr. Depew spoke of the occurrence as a strange mental phenomenon, and he did not attempt to explain it.

Mrs. Elizabeth Cady Stanton recorded in her diary an experience of Susan B. Anthony. The physician had ordered Miss Anthony from Philadeliphia to Atlantic City for her health. A few nights after she arrived she had a vivid dream. She thought she was being burnt alive in one of the hotels, and when she arose in the morning she told her niece of her dream.

"We must pack at once and go back to Philadelphia," she said.

This was done, and the next day the hotel in which they had been staying, ten other hotels and miles of boardwalk, were destroyed by fire.

Mrs. Stanton herself had a number of similar experiences. Arriving in a hotel at Springfield, Illinois, she was told there was no room available. The clerk, seeing her dismay, finally said if she would wait half an hour, he thought he could arrange for her to have a small room on the sixth floor. It was a small, plainly furnished room, but it had to serve for the night.

Mrs. Stanton went to bed early and slept soundly till she was awakened by the sensation of a hand touching her face, and a voice cried, with piteous accent, "Oh, Mother! Oh, Mother!" She was profoundly startled, but argued with herself that it was only a dream, and finally she slept again.

Once more she was awakened by a hand nervously stroking her face and a blood-curdling cry, "Oh, Mother! Oh, Mother!"

She then gave up trying to sleep, got up, put on a dressing-gown and lit a candle. Until daybreak she sat in an armchair, trying to read a book. As soon as she heard the servants stirring she rang. The chambermaid came in with a startled look, and when she heard Mrs. Stanton's story she said:

"Yes, marm. I told them not to put you in this room. The young man was carried out an hour before you came. He died, stretching out his hands, feeling for something, and crying in a heartbreaking voice, 'Oh, Mother! Oh, Mother!' "

Frances E. Willard's sister, Mary, had been dead some years when she appeared to her dear friend, Miss Milner. Miss Frances E. Willard wrote the story which was published in 1885.

Miss Milner was sitting in her room one morning when she saw a shadow, and she thought someone had come into the room. She looked up and there, at a distance of about four feet, stood Mary Willard in a light salmon-coloured dress. It was soft and beautiful.

"She was dressed just as she was when Miss Milner knew her," Miss Willard wrote. "Her hair was combed low on her forehead as the custom was. Miss Milner even saw her shoes; and said she did not look sick, but she made the same impression that she did when a schoolgirl, so bright and cheery, and came to school with something pleasant to tell. She remained about ten minutes, and Miss Milner said she smiled and looked exceeding pleasant; that they communicated but not by words.... She watched carefully, and Mary 'dimmed out', while she looked—faded from sight without moving from where she stood."

At the time she saw the apparition Miss Milner was ill, and she never expected—after seeing Mary—that she would get well. Miss Willard said she always spoke of the incident as "when I saw Mary". She lived but a short time after the occurrence.

On May 30, 1863, Charles Dickens wrote:

On Thursday in last week, being at my office here, I dreamed that I saw a lady in a red shawl with her back towards me (whom I supposed to be E.). On her turning I found that I didn't know her, and she said, "I am Miss Napier". All the time I was dressing next morning I thought: What a preposterous thing to have so very distinct a dream about nothing! And why Miss Napier? For I had never heard of any Miss Napier. That same Friday night I read.... After the reading came into my retiring room Mary Boyle and her brother, and *the lady in the red shawl*, whom they presented as Miss Napier. These are all the circumstances exactly told.

Sir Rider Haggard tells a story of a dream he had. He was startled from sound sleep by seeing Bob, his daughter's dog, lying on his side in great agony. The dog seemed trying to speak to him, and he was evidently dying.

He awakened his wife and told her his dream, which he also told to other members of the family next morning. Two days later the dog was missing, and they learned later that it had been run over by a train and killed the day following the dream.

Julian Hawthorne, son of the great novelist, said:

"My mother always affirmed that she was conscious of her

mother's presence with her on momentous occasions during the remainder of her life—that is—following her mother's death."

Sir Gilbert Parker, Sir Arthur Hayter, and others, testified to a strange case of a "double".

Major Sir Carne Rasch had been gravely ill, and was not able to attend the House of Commons. Sir Gilbert Parker related:

"My eyes fell on Sir Carne Rasch, seated in his accustomed place. As I knew that he had been ill I made a friendly gesture and said, 'I hope you are much better'. But he gave me no sign of response, which surprised me much. His countenance was very pale. He was seated, his head quietly supported by one hand; his face was impassive and severe. I pondered a moment what I had better do; when I looked in his direction again he had disappeared."

In the *Daily News* of May 17, Sir Arthur Hayter added his testimony to that of Sir Gilbert Parker. He declared that he, also, had seen Sir Carne Rasch and that, moreover, he had called the attention of Sir Henry Bannerman to his presence.

When his two friends congratulated Sir Carne Rasch on not being dead, he told them that he himself did not doubt that he had really gone in spirit to the House, for he had been very anxious to be present at a debate which particularly interested him.

The following story of the inception of *Uncle Tom's Cabin*, in the mind of Harriet Beecher Stowe, is told by C. E. Stowe and L. B. Stowe in their biography of the author.

> Mrs. Stowe was seated in her pew in the college church at Brunswick during the communion service.... Suddenly, like the unrolling of a picture scroll, the scene of the death of Uncle Tom seemed to pass before her. At the same time the words of Jesus were sounding in her ears: "Inasmuch as ye have done it unto the least of these my brethren, ye have done it unto me!" It seemed as if the crucified, but now risen and glorified, Christ were speaking to her through the poor black man, cut and bleeding under the blows of the slave whip. She was affected so strongly that she could scarcely keep from weeping aloud.

That Sunday afternoon she went to her room, locked the door, and wrote out—substantially as it appears in the published edition—the chapter called "The Death of Uncle Tom".... It seemed to her as though what she wrote was blown through her mind as with the rushing of a mighty wind.

The Reverend John Watson, "Ian Maclaren", was the subject of many experiences of the type usually regarded, and by him regarded, as telepathic. He called the power which he seemed to have to become conscious of events taking place at a distance, "Christian Telepathy", because of his belief that it sprang from the fellowship existing among the brotherhood that is centred in Christ.

Edward W. Bok related an incident that occurred during a luncheon of editors and publishers at the home of his father-in-law, Cyrus H. Curtis. Mr. Bok said:

"An editor sitting at my right leaned over to a publisher sitting at my left and suggested that the latter explain to me a quesion of editorial ethics which they had been discussing and upon which they had failed to agree.

"The publisher began his story, when suddenly there appeared before me, as plainly as if she were in the flesh, my wife's mother, who had passed away two years before. It was just such a gathering as she would have enjoyed and—radiant in smiles—she began a series of questions to which I gave answer, and began describing her state of wonderful happiness. The next thing I knew, I felt a hand on my shoulder and I heard: 'Well, what about it?' and I discovered the editor and publisher looking at me.

"I experienced the severest mental reaction as I readjusted myself to my surroundings, and I could only stammer: 'How about it? How about what?' I then recalled that I had been supposed to have listened to the question under argument. I felt sensibly dazed at the sudden transmigration of self that had occurred, and need hardly add that my friends were so with what they called my 'preoccupation'.

"I apologized and pleaded a period of abstraction.

"'You didn't seem to be here,' said the editor.

"That was true. I had not been there. But where had I been? I learned afterwards that the publisher's explanation lasted fully five minutes."

Robert Browning, who differed from his wife, Elizabeth Barrett Browning, concerning spiritualism, made record of a psychic experience. Mr. Browning was in Florence and Count Giunasi of Ravenna, with whom he was entirely unacquainted, was brought to his house by an intimate friend of the Brownings. The conversation turned upon the supernatural, and the Count claimed to have some sort of power. In answer to Mr. Browning's avowed scepticism, he offered to try an experiment, and asked for something personal, some relic or memento of the poet's that he might hold in his hand.

Mr. Browning was averse to wearing any sort of trinket or ornament—even a watch guard. But it so happened, by a curious accident—he said by the mistake of a seamstress—he was wearing some gold cuff-links. He had never before worn these links in Florence or elsewhere. He had found them that day in some old drawer where they had lain forgotten for years. One of the links he gave to the Count.

For some minutes the Count was silent, and then he said:

"There is something here which cries out in my ear, 'Murder! Murder!' "

"And truly," said Mr. Browning, "those very links were taken from the dead body of a great-uncle of mine who was violently killed on his estate in St. Kitts, nearly eighty years ago. These, with a gold watch and other personal objects of value, were produced in a court of justice, as proof that robbery had not been the purpose of the slaughter, which was effected by his own slaves. They were then transmitted to my grandfather, who had his initials engraved on them, and wore them all his life. They were taken out of the nightgown in which he died and given to me.... The occurrence of my great-uncle's murder was known only to myself, of all men in Florence, as certainly was also my possession of the links."

Shelley saw ghosts twice shortly before his tragic death. In the spring of 1822 the Shelleys occupied a residence on the shore of the Bay of Spezzia. Their friends, the Williams family, were with them.

One night they heard the poet crying loudly, as if in great fear in the *salon*. The Williams' rushed from their room and Mrs. Shelley also tried to reach the *salon*, but she fainted at the door.

Shelley stood in the middle of the room, staring as if in a trance, a look of horror on his pale face. He insisted that a figure wrapped in a mantle came to his bedside and beckoned to him, crying "Are you satisfied?"

One evening a short time later he stood looking from his terrace down at the surf when suddenly he cried out in terror. He was sure, he said, that he had seen the ghost of Allegra, the daughter of Lord Byron, who had recently died. She seemed to rise from the sea and clasp her hands, and she smiled at him as if in great joy.

Not long after this Shelley was drowned in that same bay.

Alice and Phœbe Cary believed in supernatural appearances before modern spiritualism was talked of. In the autumn of 1832 a new house was built for the family, and in a few days they were to move into it. It stood in full view of the old house. Late one afternoon a sudden thunder shower brought the father, Robert Cary, in from the fields. But soon the shower was over and the sun was shining brightly.

A member of the family, looking across at the new house, saw a woman with a child in her arms, standing in the doorway, as other members of the family saw them, asked why the door had been left open and what Rhoda and Lucy were doing there. Rhoda was the fifteen-year-old daughter, and Lucy was a child of two. But even as they were talking Rhoda joined them and Lucy was found to be playing within. The whole family gazed at the apparition for some time, and finally the figures seemed to go back into the house and disappear. Diligent search, upstairs and down, revealed no footprints or other signs of human presence.

Within the first year of their occupancy of this house Rhoda and Lucy died. For many years the ghost of little Lucy was reported flitting about the old farm-house. A little boy, whose family had moved into the old house, and who had been carefully guarded from the story, ran to his mother with a scared face, crying: "There's a little girl upstairs in a red dress!"

Goethe was more interested in psychic phenomena than most able thinkers of his period. He believed very strongly in the gift of prophecy because he knew his grandfather possessed such a gift. In *Wanrheit und Dichtung* he relates one of his own psychic experiences—of which he had many.

He wrote: "I now rode on horseback over the footpath to Drusenheim, when one of the strangest experiences befell me. Not with the eyes of the body, but with those of the spirit, I saw myself on horseback coming towards me on the same path, dressed in a suit such as I had never worn, pale grey with some gold. As soon as I had shaken myself out of this reverie the form vanished. It is strange, however, that I found myself returning on the same path eight years afterwards to visit Fredericka once more, and that I then wore the same suit I dreamt of, and this not by design but by chance."

Oliver Wendell Holmes relates an interesting experience of his own in *Over the Teacups.*

While at dinner with two ladies of his household he told them of a case of "trial at battel", offered by Abraham Thornton in 1817. He mentioned his throwing down his glove, which was not taken up by the brother of his victim, and so he had to be let off, for the old law was still in force. He said that Abraham Thornton had come to America, and that he might be living near them at that moment for aught they knew.

Upon leaving the table he was handed a letter that had arrived while he was at dinner. The letter was from Frederick Rathbone in London, who wrote: "In travelling the other day I met with the reprint of the very interesting case of Thornton for murder. The prisoner pleaded successfully the old Wager of Battel. I thought you might like to read the account." The clipping was enclosed.

Mr. Holmes said:

"Mr. Rathbone was a well-known London dealer in old Wedgwood and eighteenth-century art.... I was not expecting any communication from him.... I had long been familiar with this celebrated case, but had not referred to it, so far as I can remember, for years. I know of no train of thought which led me to speak of it on that particular day. I had never alluded to it in that company nor had I ever spoken of it to Mr. Rathbone....

"The case I have given is, I am confident, absolutely free from every source of error.... My knowledge of the case came from Kirby's *Wonderful Museum*, a work presented to me at least thirty years ago. I had not looked at the account, spoken of it, nor thought of it for a long time. I consider the evidence of entire independence, apart from possible 'telepathic' causation, completely waterproof, air-tight, incombustible and unassailable."

Stephen Phillips once leased a house in Egham near Windsor. He says he went there for peace and quiet, but no sooner was the family installed than they began to hear all kinds of uncanny noises.

He wrote:

"There were knockings, rappings, footfalls, soft and loud; hasty, stealthy hurryings and scurryings and sounds as of a human creature being chased and caught, then strangled or choked. Doors banged and were opened and closed unaccountably as if by unseen hands. I would be sitting quietly in the study writing when the door would be opened soundlessly. That in itself is enough in the dead of night to a man with his imagination aflame.... 'It is only a bit of a draught,' I would say to myself, as I held my breath and watched, but draughts do not turn door-handles, and on my life, the handle would turn as the door opened and there was no hand visible.

"My little daughter reported having seen an old man creeping about the house, but there was no such person to be found.... According to a common report and local tradition, an old farmer strangled a child there fifty years ago.... If there really is a ghost on the prowl it explains a lot."

Mr. Phillips says they gave up the lease and "got out of the house like a shot. The servants left so precipitately that they did not take their boxes. The house had not had a tenant for many years before now, nor has anyone lived in it since."

Mr. Phillips concluded his story as follows:

"As a man of reasonable intellect, I am open to accept any

feasible explanation of our experiences. Indeed, as the house continues 'To Let', and is still reported to be haunted, I shall be quite glad if some respectable body, such as the Psychical Research Society, would endeavour to clear the matter up."

Lord Tennyson once remarked:

"A kind of waking trance I have frequently had, quite up from boyhood, when I have been all alone. . . . All at once, as it were, out of the intensity of the consciousness of the individuality, the individuality itself seemed to dissolve and fade away into boundless being; and this is not a composed state, but the clearest of the clearest, the surest of the surest, utterly beyond words, where death was an almost laughable impossibility, the loss of personality seeming no extinction, but the only true life. I am ashamed of my feeble description. Have I not said the state was utterly beyond words?"

Dante, son of the poet, was visited in a dream by his father, who conversed with him and told him (correctly) where to find the missing cantos of the *Commedia.*

Victorien Sardou, the most famous French dramatist after Victor Hugo, was a spiritualist, and believed that he wrote his plays under spirit guidance. He related this remarkable experience of an exquisite engraving he made of Molière's house on copper:

"Seated one day at my table I fell into a reverie. Unconsciously I took up the graver and, impelled by secret influence, let my hand follow its own direction over the plate. The engraving you see is the result of several hours of purely mechanical toil. I could not of my own will make such a picture to save my life."

Victor Hugo, Captain Marryat, Sir Walter Scott, Henry Holt, William Lyon Phelps, John Ruskin and many other well-known writers have recorded remarkable psychic experiences.

Among explorers and scientists who have encountered supernatural phenomena are Henry M. Stanley, Ernest Seton Thompson, Hudson Maxim and Luther Burbank.

Mr. Burbank said:

"I inherited my mother's ability to send and receive communications. So did one of my sisters. In tests before representatives of the University of California she was able—seven times out of ten—to receive messages sent to her telepathically. My mother, who lived to be more than ninety-six years of age, was in poor health the last years of her life. During these years I often wished to summon my sister. On such occasions I never had to write, telephone or telegraph to her. Instead, I sent her messages telepathically, and each time she arrived in Santa Rosa, California, where I live, on the next train."

Hiram Powers was one of the greatest of the early American sculptors. His own country being unready for his work he made his home in Florence, Italy, for many years before his death in 1873. His statue of *Eve* was pronounced by Thorwaldsen, greatest of Danish sculptors, a masterpiece. The *Greek Slave* is the most widely known of his works, and many marble replicas of it are in existence.

From the time he was a little boy Mr. Powers was haunted by a dream. He explained:

"I used to dream of a white figure standing upon a pillar over the river, which I longed to get near but could not for the water—it was too deep to wade through. This dream haunted me for years afterwards in Ohio, and it ceased when I began to model in clay. It was a female figure and naked, but it did not seem alive. At that time I had never seen nor heard of anything in the way of sculpture."

Cellini tells in his autobiography of his supernatural visions and the protection of his "angels". There is a story that he was dissuaded from suicide by the ghost of a young man who frequently visited and comforted him.

Ben Jonson was visited by the ghost of his eldest son with the mark of a bloody cross upon his forehead, at the moment of his death, many miles away, from the plague.

Saint-Saens recorded this experience:

"When, for the first time, I made application as a candidate for the Académie des Beaux-Arts, I was not nominated. This rather provoked me, and I told myself mentally, looking at the Egyptian lions that adorn in such bizarre fashion the façade of the Institute: 'I shall present myself again *when the lions turn around!*' Some time afterwards *the lions were turned!*"

His friend, Camille Flammarion, was much interested in this incident, which the composer was inclined to treat lightly.

Flammarion wrote to him: "You are the most delightful of friends, the mightiest of musicians, the glory of the Institute, one of the profound thinkers of our era, but you are not logical. How could any collection whatsoever of chemical molecules beneath your skull have been able to 'secrete' this bizarre premonition? An *idea* cannot be produced by a material mechanism. Your mind saw an aspect of the future without suspecting it."

Later Saint-Saens testified to a number of interesting psychic experiences.

Robert Schumann tells how he was "obsessed" to compose a funeral fantasy. David Bispham had several interesting experiences with the supernatural. Tito Schipa, lyric tenor of the Chicago Opera Company, when a boy, saw the ghost of a woman with a Spanish veil and fan. Years later when in Spain he was glancing through an old photograph album, when he saw a photograph of this lady, a great-aunt of his whom he had never seen.

On a wild blustery night in St. Petersburg Anton Rubinstein sat talking with his pupil, Lillian Nichia. He asked her what the sound of the wind represented to her.

She replied: "The moaning of lost souls."

"There may be a future," he said.

"There is a future," she cried, "a great and beautiful future; if I die first I shall come to you and prove this."

He turned to her with great solemnity and said: "Good, that is a bargain. And I will come to you if I die first."

She wrote:

> Six years later in Paris I woke one night with a cry of agony and despair ringing in my ears, such as I hope may never be duplicated in my lifetime. Rubinstein's face was close to mine, a countenance distorted by every phase of fear, despair, agony, remorse and anger. I started up, turned on all the lights, and stood for a moment shaking in every limb. I had for a moment completely forgotten our compact. News is always late in Paris but *Le Petit Journal* next day published the first account of his sudden death.

She learned afterwards that Rubinstein died with a cry of agony impossible to describe.

Mme. Galli-Marie was the creator of the character of Carmen in Bizet's opera of that name. On a June evening in Paris she was on the stage singing this role. Suddenly she ceased to sing. She had felt in her side a shooting pain, "like a blow of a hammer in her heart". She regained possession of herself and finished the act. On reaching her dressing-room, she said to those about her: "Some misfortune has happened to our Bizet. As the blow seemed to strike me, I saw his face in front of me for just a second.... My God! My God! How pale he was!"

It was later ascertained that he had been stricken with a heart malady at the time Mme. Galli-Marie had the vision. He died shortly after the incident.

In February, 1772, when the remarkable psychic powers of Emanuel Swedenborg were being talked of all over the world, John Wesley received the following letter from him, dated at Stockholm:

> SIR:
>
> I have been informed in the world of spirits that you have a strong desire to converse with me. I shall be happy to see you, if you will favour me with a visit. I am, sir,
>
> Your humble servant,
>
> EMANUEL SWEDENBORG

Mr. Wesley received and read the letter in the presence of some of his preachers, and frankly acknowledged to the company that he had been very strongly impressed with a desire to see and converse with Swedenborg, and that he had never mentioned that desire to anyone.

He wrote in reply that he was closely occupied in preparing for a six-months' journey, but would do himself the honour of waiting upon Mr. Swedenborg soon after his return to London.

In reply to this letter Mr. Swedenborg wrote that the visit proposed by Mr. Wesley would be too late, as he, Swedenborg, "would go into the world of spirits on the 29th day of the next month, never more to return".

He died on March 29, 1772.

THE SPECTRE BRIDEGROOM

by WASHINGTON IRVING

"He that supper for is dight,
He lyes full cold, I trow, this night!
Yestreen to chamber I him led,
This night Gray-steel has made his bed!"
—*Sir Eger, Sir Grahame* and *Sir Gray-steel*

ON the summit of one of the heights of the Odenwald, a wild and romantic tract of Upper Germany that lies not far from the confluence of the Main and the Rhine, there stood, many, many years since, the Castle of the Baron von Landshort. It is now quite fallen to decay, and almost buried among beech trees and dark firs; above which, however, its old watch-tower may still be seen struggling, like the former possessor I have mentioned, to carry a high head, and look down upon a neighbouring country.

The Baron was a dry branch of the great family of Katzenellenbogen, and inherited the relics of the property and all the pride of his ancestors. Though the warlike disposition of his predecessors had much impaired the family possessions, yet the Baron still endeavoured to keep up some show of former state. The times were peaceable, and the German nobles, in general, had abandoned their inconvenient old castles, perched like eagles' nests among the mountains, and had built more convenient residences in the valleys; still the Baron remained proudly drawn up in his little fortress, cherishing with hereditary inveteracy all the old family feuds; so that he was on ill terms with some of his nearest neighbours, on account of disputes that had happened between their great-great-grandfathers.

The Baron had but one child, a daughter; but Nature, when she grants but one child, always compensates by making it a prodigy; and so it was with the daughter of the Baron. All the nurses, gossips, and country cousins, assured her father that she had not her equal for beauty in all Germany; and who should know better than they? She had, moreover, been brought up with great care, under the superintendence of two maiden aunts, who had spent some years of their early life at one of the little German courts, and were skilled in all the branches of knowledge necessary to the education of a fine lady. Under their instructions, she became a miracle of accomplishments. By the time she was eighteen she could embroider to admiration, and had worked whole histories of the saints in tapestry with such strength of expression in their countenances that they looked like so many souls in purgatory. She could read without great difficulty, and had spelled her way through several church legends, and almost all the chivalric wonders of the Heldenbuch. She had even made considerable proficiency in writing, could sign her own name without missing a letter, and so legibly that her aunts could read it without spectacles. She excelled in making little good-for-nothing ladylike knick-knacks of all kinds; was versed in the most abstruse dancing of the day; played a number of airs on the harp and guitar; and knew all the tender ballads of the *Minnelieders* by heart.

Her aunts, too, having been great flirts and coquettes in their younger days, were admirably calculated to be vigilant guardians and strict censors of the conduct of their niece; for there is no duenna so rigidly prudent, and inexorably decorous, as a superannuated coquette. She was rarely suffered out of their sight; never went beyond the domains of the castle, unless well attended, or, rather, well watched; had continual lectures read to her about strict decorum and implicit obedience; and, as to the men—pah! she was taught to hold them at such distance and distrust that, unless properly authorized, she would not have cast a glance upon the handsomest cavalier in the world—no, not if he were even dying at her feet.

The good effects of this system were wonderfully apparent. The young lady was a pattern of docility and correctness. While others were wasting their sweetness in the glare of the world, and liable to be plucked and thrown aside by every hand, she was coyly blooming into fresh and lovely womanhood under the protection of those immaculate spinsters, like a rosebud flushing forth among guardian thorns. Her aunts looked upon her with pride and exultation, and vaunted that though all the other young ladies in the world might go astray, yet, thank Heaven, nothing of the kind could happen to the heiress of Katzenellenbogen.

But however scantily the Baron von Landshort might be provided with children, his household was by no means a small one, for Providence had enriched him with abundance of poor relations. They, one and all, possessed the affectionate disposition common to humble relatives; were wonderfully attached to the Baron, and took every possible occasion to come in swarms and enliven the castle. All family festivals were commemorated by these good people at the Baron's expense; and when they were filled with good cheer, they would declare that there was nothing on earth so delightful as these family meetings, these jubilees of the heart.

The Baron, though a small man, had a large soul, and it swelled with satisfaction at the consciousness of being the greatest man in the little world about him. He loved to tell long stories about the stark old warriors whose portraits looked grimly down from the walls around, and he found no listeners equal to those who fed at his expense. He was much given to the marvellous, and a firm believer in all those supernatural tales with which every mountain and valley in Germany abounds. The faith of his guests even exceeded his own. They listened to every tale of wonder with open eyes and mouth, and never failed to be astonished, even though repeated for the hundredth time. Thus lived the Baron von Landshort, the oracle of his table, the absolute monarch of his little territory, and happy, above all things, in the persuasion that he was the wisest man of the age.

At the time of which my story treats there was a great family gathering at the castle, on an affair of the utmost importance: it was to receive the destined bridegroom of the Baron's daughter. A negotiation had been carried on between the father and an old nobleman of Bavaria, to unite the dignity of their houses by the marriage of their children. The preliminaries had been conducted with proper punctilio. The young people were betrothed without seeing each other, and the time was appointed for the marriage ceremony. The young Count von Altenburg had been recalled from the army for the purpose, and was actually on his way to the Baron's to receive his bride. Missives had even been received from him, from Wurtzburg, where he was accidentally detained, mentioning the day and hour when he might be expected to arrive.

The castle was in a tumult of preparation to give him a suitable welcome. The fair bride had been decked out with uncommon care. The two aunts had superintended her toilet, and quarrelled the whole morning about every article of her dress. The young lady had taken advantage of their contest to follow the bent of her own taste; and fortunately it was a good one. She looked as lovely as the youthful bridegroom could desire; and the flutter of expectation heightened the lustre of her charms.

The suffusions that mantled her face and neck, the gentle heaving of the bosom, the eye now and then lost in reverie, all betrayed the soft tumult that was going on in her little heart. The aunts were continually havering around her; for maiden aunts are apt to take great interest in affairs of this nature: they were giving her a world of staid counsel, how to deport herself, what to say, and in what manner to receive the expected lover.

The Baron was no less busied in preparations. He had, in truth, nothing exactly to do; but he was naturally a fuming, bustling, little man, and could not remain passive when all the world was in a hurry. He worried from top to bottom of the castle, with an air of infinite anxiety; he continually called the servants from their work to exhort them to be diligent, and buzzed about every hall and chamber, as idle, restless, and importunate as a bluebottle fly on a warm summer's day.

In the meantime, the fatted calf had been killed; the forests had rung with the clamour of the huntsmen; the kitchen was crowded with good cheer; the cellars had yielded up whole oceans of *Rhein-wein* and *Ferne-wein*, and even the great Heidelberg Tun had been laid under contribution. Everything was ready to receive the distinguished guest with *Saus und Braus* in the true spirit of German hospitality—but the guest delayed to make his appearance. Hour rolled after hour. The sun that had poured his downward rays upon the rich forests of the Odenwald, now just gleamed along the summits of the mountains. The Baron mounted the highest tower, and strained his eyes in hopes of catching a distant sight of the Count and his attendants. Once he thought he beheld them; the sound of horns came floating from the valley, prolonged by the mountain echoes: a number of horsemen were seen far below, slowly advancing along the road; but when they had nearly reached the foot of the mountain they suddenly struck off in a different direction. The last ray of sunshine departed—the bats began to flit by in the twilight—the road grew dimmer and dimmer to the view; and nothing appeared stirring in it but now and then a peasant lagging homeward from his labour.

While the old castle of Landshort was in this state of perplexity, a very interesting scene was transacting in a different part of the Odenwald.

The young Count von Altenburg was tranquilly pursuing his route in that sober jog-trot way in which a man travels towards matrimony when his friends have taken all the trouble and uncertainty of courtship off his hands, and a bride is waiting for him, as certainly as a dinner, at the end of his journey. He had encountered at Wurtzburg a youthful companion in arms, with whom he had seen some service on the frontiers: Herman von Starkenfaust, one of the stoutest hands and worthiest hearts of German chivalry, who was now returning from the army. His father's castle was not far distant from the old fortress of Landshort, although hereditary feud rendered the families hostile and strangers to each other.

In the warm-hearted moment of recognition, the young friends related all their past adventures and fortunes, and the Count gave the whole history of his intended nuptials with a young lady whom he had never seen, but of whose charms he had received the most enrapturing descriptions.

As the route of the friends lay in the same direction, they agreed to perform the rest of their journey together; and, that they might do it more leisurely, set off from Wurtzubry at an early hour, the Count having given directions for his retinue to follow and overtake him.

They beguiled their wayfaring with recollections of their military scenes and adventures; but the Count was apt to be a little tedious, now and then, about the reputed charms of his bride, and the felicity that awaited him.

In this way they had entered among the mountains of the Odenwald, and were traversing one of its most lonely and thickly wooded passes. It is well known that the forests of Germany have always been as much infested with robbers as its castles by spectres; and at this time the former were particularly numerous, from the hordes of disbanded soldiers wandering about the country. It will not appear extraordinary, therefore, that the cavaliers were attacked by a gang of these stragglers in the midst of the forest. They defended themselves with bravery, but were nearly overpowered when the Count's retinue arrived to their assistance. At sight of them the robbers fled, but not until the Count had received a mortal wound. He was slowly and carefully conveyed back to the city of Wurtzbúrg, and a friar summoned from a neighbouring convent, who was famous for his skill in administering to both soul and body. But half of his skill was superfluous; the moments of the unfortunate Count were numbered.

With his dying breath he entreated his friend to repair instantly to the Castle of Landshort, and explain the fatal cause of his not keeping his appointment with his bride. Though not the most ardent of lovers, he was one of the most punctilious of men, and appeared earnestly solicitous that his mission should be speedily and courteously executed. "Unless this is done," said he, "I shall not sleep quietly in my grave!" He repeated these last words with peculiar solemnity. A request, at a moment so impressive, admitted no hesitation. Starkenfaust endeavoured to soothe him to calmness; promised faithfully to execute his wish, and gave him his hand in solemn pledge. The dying man pressed it in acknowledgement, but soon lapsed into delirium—raved about his bride—his engagements—his plighted word; ordered his horse, that he might ride to the castle of Landshort, and expired in the fancied act of vaulting into the saddle.

Starkenfaust bestowed a sigh and a soldier's tear on the untimely fate of his comrade; and then pondered on the awkward mission he had undertaken. His heart was heavy, and his head perplexed; for he was to present himself an unbidden guest among hostile people, and to damp their festivity with tidings fatal to their hopes. Still there was certain whisperings of curiosity in his bosom to see this far-famed beauty of Katzenellenbogen so cautiously shut up from the world; for he was a passionate admirer of the sex, and there was a dash of eccentricity and enterprise in his character that made him fond of all singular adventure.

Previous to his departure, he made all due arrangements with the holy fraternity of the convent for the funeral solemnities of his friend, who was to be buried in the cathedral of Wurtzburg, near some of his illustrious relatives; and the mourning retinue of the Count took charge of his remains.

It is now high time that we should return to the ancient family of Katzenellenbogen, who were impatient for their guest, and still more for their dinner; and to the worthy little Baron, whom we left airing himself on the watch-tower.

Night closed in, but still no guest arrived. The Baron descended from the tower in despair. The banquet, which had been delayed from hour to hour, could no longer be postponed. The meats were already overdone, the cook in an agony, and the whole household had the look of a garrison that had been reduced by famine. The Baron was obliged reluctantly to give orders for the feast without the presence of the guest. All were seated at table, and just on the point of commencing, when the sound of a horn from without the gate gave notice of the approach of a stranger. Another long blast filled the old courts of the castle with its echoes, and was answered by the warder from the walls. The Baron hastened to receive his future son-in-law.

The drawbridge had been let down, and the stranger was before the gate. He was a tall gallant cavalier, mounted on a black steed. His countenance was pale, but he had a beaming, romantic eye, and an air of stately melancholy. The Baron was a little mortified that he should have come in this simple, solitary style. His dignity for a moment was ruffied, and he felt disposed to consider it a want of proper respect for the important occasion, and the important family with which he was to be connected. He pacified himself, however, with the conclusion that it must have been youthful impatience which had induced him thus to spur on sooner than his attendants.

"I am sorry," said the stranger, "to break in upon you thus unseasonably—"

Here the Baron interrupted him with a world of compliments and greetings; for, to tell the truth, he prided himself upon his courtesy and his eloquence. The stranger attempted, once or twice, to stem the torrent of words, but in vain; so he bowed his head and suffered it to flow on. By the time the Baron had come to a pause they had reached the inner court of the castle; and the stranger was again about to speak, when he was once more interrupted by the appearance of the female part of the family, leading forth the shrinking and blushing bride. He gazed on her for a moment as one entranced; it seemed as if his whole soul beamed forth in the gaze, and rested upon that lovely form. One of the maiden aunts whispered something in her ear; she made an effort to speak; her moist blue eye was timidly raised, gave a shy glance of inquiry on the stranger, and was cast again to the ground. The words died away; but there was a sweet smile playing about her lips, and a soft dimpling of the cheek, that showed her glance had not been unsatisfactory. It was impossible for a girl of the fond age of eighteen, highly predisposed for love and matrimony, not to be pleased with so gallant a cavalier.

The late hour at which the guest had arrived left no time for parley. The Baron was peremptory, and deferred all particular conversation until the morning, and led the way to the untasted banquet.

It was served up in the great hall of the castle. Around the walls hung the hard-favoured portraits of the heroes of the house of Katzenellenbogen, and the trophies which they had gained in the field and in the chase. Hacked corselets, splintered jousting spears, and tattered banners were mingled with the spoils of sylvan warfare: the jaws of the wolf and the tusks of the boar grinned horribly among crossbows and battle-axes, and a huge pair of antlers branched immediately over the head of the youthful bridegroom.

The cavalier took but little notice of the company or the entertainment. He scarcely tasted the banquet, but seemed absorbed in admiration of his bride. He conversed in a low tone, that could not be overhead—for the language of love is never loud; but where is the female ear so dull that it cannot catch the softest whisper of the lover? There was a mingled tenderness and gravity in his manner that appeared to have a powerful effect upon the young lady. Her colour came and went, as she listened with deep attention. Now and then she made some blushing reply, and when his eye was turned away she would steal a sidelong glance at his romantic countenance, and heave a gentle sigh of tender happiness. It was evident that the young couple were completely enamoured. The aunts, who were deeply versed in the mysteries of the heart, declared that they had fallen in love with each other at first sight.

The feast went on merrily, or at least noisily, for the guests were all blessed with those keen appetites that attend upon light purses and mountain air. The Baron told his best and longest stories, and never had he told them so well, or with such great effect. If there was anything marvellous, his auditors were lost in astonishment; and if anything facetious, they were sure to laugh exactly in the right place. The Baron, it is true, like most great men, was too dignified to utter any joke but a dull one: it was always endorsed, however, by a bumper of excellent Hoch-heimer; and even a dull joke, at one's own table, served up with jolly old wine, is irresistible. Many good things were said by poorer and keener wits that would not bear repeating, except on similar occasions; many sly speeches whispered in ladies' ears that almost convulsed them with suppressed laughter; and a song or two roared out by a poor, but merry and broad-faced cousin of the Baron, that absolutely made the maiden aunts hold up their fans.

Amid all this revelry, the stranger-guest maintained a most singular and unseasonable gravity. His countenance assumed a deeper cast of dejection as the evening advanced, and, strange as it may appear, even the Baron's jokes seemed only to render him the more melancholy. At times he was lost in thought, and at times there was a perturbed and restless wandering of the eye that bespoke a mind but ill at ease. His conversation with the bride became more and more earnest and mysterious. Lowering clouds began to steal over the fair serenity of her brow, and tremors to run through her tender frame.

All this could not escape the notice of the company. Their gaiety was chilled by the unaccountable gloom of the bridegroom; their spirits were infected; whispers and glances were inter-changed, accompanied by shrugs and dubious shakes of the head. The song and the laugh grew less and less frequent, there were dreary pauses in the conversation, which were at length succeeded by wild tales and supernatural legends. One dismal story produced another still more dismal, and the Baron nearly frightened some of the ladies into hysterics with the history of the goblin horseman that carried away the fair Leonora—a dreadful, but true story, which has since been put into excellent verse, and is read and believed by all the world.

The bridegroom listened to this tale with profound attention. He kept his eyes steadily fixed on the Baron and, as the story drew to a close, began gradually to rise from his seat, growing taller and taller, until, in the Baron's entranced eye, he seemed almost to tower into a giant. The moment the tale was finished, he heaved a deep sigh, and took a solemn farewell of the company. They were all amazement. The Baron was perfectly thunder-struck.

What! going to leave the castle at midnight? Why, everything was prepared for his reception; a chamber was ready for him if he wished to retire.

The stranger shook his head mournfully and mysteriously: "I must lay my head in a different chamber tonight!"

There was something in this reply, and the tone in which it was uttered, that made the Baron's heart misgive him; but he rallied his forces, and repeated his hospitable entreaties.

The stranger shook his head silently, but positively, at every offer; and, waving his farewell to the company, stalked slowly out of the hall. The maiden aunts were absolutely petrified—the bride hung her head, and a tear stole to her eye.

The Baron followed the stranger to the great court of the castle, where the black charger stood pawing the earth and snorting with impatience. When they had reached the portal, whose deep archway was dimly lighted by a cresset, the stranger paused, and addressed the Baron in a hollow tone of voice, which the vaulted roof rendered still more sepulchral. "Now that we are alone," said he, "I will impart to you the reason of my going. I have a solemn, an indispensable engagement."

"Why," said the Baron, "cannot you send someone in your place?"

"It admits of no substitute—I must attend it in person—I must away to Wurtzburg cathedral—"

"Ay," said the Baron, plucking up spirit, "but not until tomorrow—tomorrow you shall take your bride there."

"No! no!" replied the stranger, with tenfold solemnity, "my engagement is with no bride—the worms! the worms expect me! I am a dead man—I have been slain by robbers—my body lies at Wurtzburg—at midnight I am to be buried—the grave is waiting for me—I must keep my appointment!"

He sprang on his black charger, dashed over the drawbridge, and the clattering of his horse's hoofs was lost in the whistling of the night-blast.

The Baron returned to the hall in the utmost consternation, and related what had passed. Two ladies fainted outright; others sickened at the idea of having banqueted with a spectre. It was the opinion of some that this might be the wild huntsman famous in German legend. Some talked of mountain sprites, of wood-demons, and of other supernatural beings, with which the good people of Germany have been so grievously harassed since time immemorial. One of the poor relations ventured to suggest that it might be some sportive evasion of the young cavalier, and that the very gloominess of the caprice seemed to accord with so melancholy a personage. This, however, drew on him the indignation of the whole company, and especially of the Baron, who looked upon him as little better than an infidel; so that he was fain to abjure his heresy as speedily as possible, and come into the faith of the true believers.

But, whatever may have been the doubts entertained, they were completely put to an end by the arrival, next day, of regular missives confirming the intelligence of the young Count's murder, and his interment in Wurtzburg cathedral.

The dismay at the castle may well be imagined. The Baron shut himself up in his chamber. The guests who had come to rejoice with him could not think of abandoning him in his distress. They wandered about the courts, or collected in groups in the hall, shaking their heads and shrugging their shoulders at the troubles of so good a man; and sat longer than ever at table, and ate and drank more stoutly than ever, by way of keeping up their spirits. But the situation of the widowed bride was the most pitiable. To have lost a husband before she had even embraced him—and such a husband! If the very spectre could be so gracious and noble, what must have been the living man? She filled the house with lamentations.

On the night of the second day of her widowhood, she had retired to her chamber, accompanied by one of her aunts, who insisted on sleeping with her. The aunt, who was one of the best tellers of ghost stories in all Germany, had just been recounting one of her longest, and had fallen asleep in the very midst of it. The chamber was remote, and overlooked a small garden. The niece lay pensively gazing at the beams of the rising moon, as they trembled on the leaves of an aspen tree before the lattice. The castle clock had just tolled midnight, when a soft strain of music stole up from the garden. She rose hastily from her bed and stepped lightly to the window. A tall figure stood among the shadows of the trees. As it raised its head, a beam of moonlight fell upon the countenance. Heaven and earth! She beheld the Spectre Bridegroom! A loud shriek at that moment burst upon her ear, and her aunt, who had been awakened by the music, and had followed her silently to the window, fell into her arms. When she looked again, the spectre had disappeared.

Of the two females, the aunt now required the most soothing, for she was perfectly beside herself with terror. As to the young lady, there was something, even in the spectre of her lover, that seemed endearing. There was still the semblance of manly beauty; and though the shadow of a man is but little calculated to satisfy the affections of a lovesick girl, yet, where the substance is not to be had, even that is consoling. The aunt declared that she would never sleep in that chamber again; the niece, for once, was refractory, and declared as strongly that she would sleep in no other in the castle : the consequence was that she had to sleep in it alone; but she drew a promise from her aunt not to relate the story of the spectre, lest she should be denied the only melancholy pleasure left her on earth—that of inhabiting the chamber over which the guardian shade of her lover kept its nightly vigils.

How long the good old lady would have observed this promise is uncertain, for she dearly loved to talk of the marvellous, and there is a triumph in being the first to tell a frightful story; it is, however, still quoted in the neighbourhood, as a memorable instance of female secrecy, that she kept it to herself for a whole week; when she was suddenly absolved from all further restraint by intelligence brought to the breakfast-table one morning that the young lady was not to be found. Her room was empty—the bed had not been slept in—the window was open—and the bird had flown!

The astonishment and concern with which the intelligence was received can only be imagined by those who have witnessed the agitation which the mishaps of a great man cause among his friends. Even the poor relations paused for a moment from the indefatigable labours of the trencher; when the aunt, who had at first been struck speechless, wrung her hands and shrieked out, "The goblin! the goblin! She's carried away by the goblin!"

In a few words she related the fearful scene of the garden, and concluded that the spectre must have carried off his bride. Two of the domestics corroborated the opinion, for they had heard the clattering of a horse's hoofs down the mountain about midnight, and had no doubt that it was the spectre on his black charger, bearing her away to the tomb. All present were struck with the direful probability; for events of the kind are extremely common in Germany, as many well-authenticated histories bear witness.

What a lamentable situation was that of the poor Baron! What a heartrending dilemma for a fond father, and a member of the great family of Katzenellenbogen! His only daughter had either been rapt away to the grave, or he was to have some wood-demon for a son-in-law, and, perchance, a troop of goblin grandchildren. As usual, he was completely bewildered, and all the castle in an uproar. The men were ordered to take horse and scour every road and path and glen of the Odenwald. The Baron himself had just drawn on his jack-boots, girded on his sword, and was about to mount his steed to sally forth on the doubtful quest, when he was brought to pause by a new apparition. A lady was seen approaching the castle, mounted on a palfrey attended by a cavalier on horseback. She galloped up to the gate, sprang from her horse, and falling at the Baron's feet, embraced his knees. It was his lost daughter, and her companion—the Spectre Bridegroom! The Baron was astounded. He looked at his daughter, then at the spectre, and almost doubted the evidence of his senses. The latter, too, was wonderfully improved in his appearance, since his visit to the world of spirits. His dress was splendid, and set off a noble figure of manly symmetry. He was no longer pale and melancholy. His fine countenance was flushed with the glow of youth, and joy rioted in his large dark eye.

The mystery was soon cleared up. The cavalier (for, in truth, as you must have known all the while, he was no goblin) announced himself as Sir Herman von Starkenfaust. He related his adventure with the young Count. He told how he had hastened to the castle to deliver the unwelcome tidings, but that the eloquence of the Baron had interrupted him in every attempt to tell his tale. How the sight of the bride had completely captivated him, and that to pass a few hours near her he had tacitly suffered the mistake to continue. How he had been sorely perplexed in what way to make a decent retreat, until the Baron's goblin stories had suggested his eccentric exit. How, fearing the feudal hostility of the family, he had repeated his visits by stealth—had haunted the garden beneath the young lady's window—had wooed—had won—had borne away in triumph—and, in a word, had wedded, the fair.

Under any other circumstances the Baron would have been inflexible, for he was tenacious of paternal authority and devoutly obstinate in all family feuds; but he loved his daughter; he had lamented her as lost; he rejoiced to find her still alive; and, though her husband was of a hostile house, yet, thank Heaven, he was not a goblin. There was something, it must be acknowledged, that did not exactly accord with his notions of strict veracity, in the joke the knight had passed upon him of being a dead man; but several old friends present, who had served in the wars, assured him that even stratagem was excusable in love, and that the cavalier was entitled to especial privilege, having lately served as a trooper.

Matters, therefore, were happily arranged. The Baron pardoned the young couple on the spot. The revels at the castle were resumed. The poor relations overwhelmed this new member of the family with loving kindness; he was so gallant, so generous—and so rich. The aunts, it is true, were somewhat scandalized that their system of strict seclusion and passive obedience should be so badly exemplified, but attributed all to their negligence in not having the windows grated. One of them was particularly mortified at having her marvellous story marred, and that the only spectre she had ever seen should turn out a counterfeit; but the niece seemed perfectly happy at having found him substantial flesh and blood—and so the story ends.

WITCHCRAFT THE RELIGION

by RAYMOND BUCKLAND, PH.D.*

WITCHCRAFT is a religion. This simple statement comes as a great surprise to many people, yet it is a fact; Witchcraft *is* a religion. Furthermore it is one of the oldest religions, if not the oldest, known to man.

The god of witchcraft first appeared in Paleolithic times as the God of Hunting. As such he was naturally depicted as being horned, like the animals hunted. In those days in order to survive man had to have success in the hunt. There had to be food to eat, skins for warmth and shelter, bones to fashion into tools and weapons. One of the earliest illustrations of a priest representing this God is to be found in the Caverne des Trois Freres, Ariege, and known as *The Sorcerer*. This shows a man dressed in the skin of a stag and wearing a mask and horns. He is performing some sort of ritual to ensure success in the hunt. In Dordogne is found another, lesser known, cave-painting of a man again dressed in a skin, this time wearing the mask and horns of a bull. He is playing some form of musical instrument while, again, leading a ritual.

It is interesting to see how this form of sympathetic magic, to ensure success in the hunt, has survived right through to the present day. The American Penobscot Indians, for example, wear a deer mask and horns when performing a ritual for the same purpose. The Mandan Indians' Buffalo Dance is another excellent example.

Magick played an important part in the life of Neanderthal Man, as it does today in the lives of many men throughout the world. Two interesting forms of this sympathetic magick are to be found in the Ariege caves. Sympathetic magick is the belief that like attracts like. The most common example of this type of magick is the "waxen image", which has been used for thousands of years.

* The author is a Satan Church leader in New York. Dr. Buckland worships the Devil and tells why he and his many followers believe in Satan Worship.

It was a means of working evil against one's enemies. A model of the enemy was made in clay, or beeswax, or some similar substance. While making it, however crude the likeness in itself, the operator had to have a clear picture of the victim in his mind all the time. If something belonging to the intended victim could be mixed in with the wax, all the better. Preferably were actual parts such as nail-parings or locks of hair. Some of the extant examples of these figures are beautifully made; every feature worked in. Others are crude, simple little "gingerbread" forms. When made the figures would be given the victim's name and then be either stuck with pins or slowly melted over a flame. As the figure slowly melted, so would the actual person sicken and waste away. In the case of the pins he would feel sharp pains until, finally, a pin through the heart would finish him! This was supposed to be a most potent form of magick.

The ancient Egyptians were known to have used it. It is also to be found with the American Indian—the Modoc tribe, for example—the Australian Aboriginal, and many countries around the world. The Berwick Witches in their plot with Francis, Earl Bothwell, against King James VI, was a famous example of the "making of a waxen image".

The examples of sympathetic magick at Le Tuc d'Audoubert, Ariege, are probably the oldest. The first is a large, clay model of a bison—very realistic—on the floor of the cave. This model is pock-marked with dozens of holes where it was literally attacked with spears, javelins, arrows, by the Neanderthal hunters acting out the hunt before going out to the real thing.

The second example is of sympathetic magick being used this time not to injure but to bring about fertility. It is another large, clay model, this time of a male bison mounting a female. Fertility amongst the animals was as important, at this time, as fertility amongst men. There had to be sufficient numbers of animals to be hunted for food, clothing, etc., and there had to be sufficient children in the tribe to survive the many perils of the age and carry on the tribes' existence.

Although the first cave paintings representing a Deity were of the Horned God, the first carvings were of the Mother Goddess. There are a number of early examples of these carvings in existence, known generally as Venus figurines. The Willendorf Venus is perhaps one of the best known; another similar one being the

Venus of Sireuil. The Venus of Laussel is another very fine example, though it is not a complete figure in itself, being carved in relief in the rock wall of the cave.

These mother goddess figures have several things in common. The main points being the emphasis of the feminine attributes—heavy, pendulus breasts, big buttocks, pregnant-like belly, exaggerated sex organs—and the complete lack of identity with the face. In many examples the arms and legs are either non-existent or at least barely suggested. The reason for this style was that man was only concerned with the fertility aspect. Woman was the bearer and nurser of the young; the Goddess was her representative as the Great Provider and Comforter: Mother Nature or Mother Earth.

At a later stage, when agriculture was introduced and established the Goddess came more to the fore. When man had relied exclusively on hunting it was the God who was the more important but later, with her fertility aspect—for crops as well as for man and beast—it was the Goddess. This relationship has stayed in Witchcraft right through to the present day. Of the two main deities the Goddess is more important than the God.

As man developed so his religion—for that is what it had become—developed. Slowly and naturally. Man spread across Europe taking his Gods with him. In different countries the Gods would perhaps be known by different names, but they were essentially the same gods. The Horned God, originally of hunting, now looked upon more as the God of Death and what comes after; and the Goddess, of Fertility and Rebirth. Not only would the Gods have different names in different countries but the same was true in different areas of one country. A good example is to be found in England where, in the South, is found the God *Cerunnos* (the Horned One). A little further North is found the same horned God, this time known as *Cerne*. In another area still the name has become *Herne*.

It has been shown that the "Old Religion" was a natural one, developing gradually and easily as man developed. It was basically a very simple, uncomplicated religion, as can be seen from Witchcraft as it is today. The priests and priestesses of the Old Religion were known as the *Wica* (or *Wicca*), an Anglo-Saxon word meaning "the Wise Ones". It is from this word *Wica* that the word *Witch* is derived. These people really were the Wise Ones. They invariably had a great knowledge of herbs and acted as doctor as much as priest. They would lead the simple rituals, know all the magicks and on the Great Festivals would be, to the people, the living embodiment of the God and Goddess.

With the coming of Christianity there was *not* the immediate mass conversion that is often suggested. Christianity was a "man-made" religion as opposed to the natural, gradual development we have seen with the Old Religion. Whole countries were classed as Christians when it was only the rulers who had, often superficially, adopted the new religion. In Europe generally the Old Religion was still in prominence for the first thousand years of Christianity. It is still alive today and beginning to grow again as people, thinking for themselves, find how much more attractive it is than the artificiality of the general forms of Monotheism.

When the first Christian churches were being built the only craftsmen available—stone-masons, wood-carvers—were pagans. When these artisans were made to build the churches they very cleverly put figures representing their own Gods in with the other, often ornate, decorations in wood and stone. Many of these figures can still be seen today, on old English churches. The Goddess fertility figure was usually depicted with her legs spread wide, displaying greatly enlarged genitalia. The God was shown as a God of Nature, with his horned head surrounded by—or even entirely composed of—foliage, fruit, etc. For this reason these old carvings of the God are called "Foliate Masks" or "Jack of the Green" or "Jack 'o the Woods". Examples of these heads can be seen at the Buckland Museum of Witchcraft and Magick, on Long Island, New York. It is a motif which has retained its popularity right through to the present day. Comparatively modern buildings are often decorated with various forms of the old pagan foliate mask—though it is doubtful if many of the architects are aware of its derivation!

If the old pagan artisans were clever in putting their old Gods in the new churches the early Christians were equally clever in their choice of sites for these churches. The orders of Pope Gregory to his Priests in England contained a section telling them that, whenever possible, they should build their churches on the sites of the pagan temples and meeting places, so that people would, out of habit, continue to come there.

In those days, when Christianity was slowly growing in strength, the old pagan religion was its rival. It is only natural to want to get rid of a rival and the Church pulled no punches to do just that. The God of the Pagans had horns. So, apparently, had the Christians' Devil. Obviously then, reasoned the Church, the Pagans were Devil-worshippers! This type of reasoning is used by the Church even today. Missionaries were particularly prone to label all primitive tribes, upon which they stumbled, as "Devil-worshippers", just because the tribe worshipped a God or Gods other than the Christian one. It did not matter that the people were good, happy, often morally and ethically better-living than the vast majority of Christians—they had to be "converted"!

The charge of devil-worship, so often levelled at witches, is ridiculous. The Devil is a purely Christian invention; there being no mention of him, as such, before the New Testament.* Since the Old Religion stems from long before the start of Christianity obviously witches do not even believe in the Devil, let alone worship him!

As Christianity gradually grew in strength so the Old Religion was slowly pushed back. Back until, about the time of the Reformation, it only existed in the outlying country districts. The word "pagan" comes from the Latin *pagani*, meaning "people who live in the country". The word "heathen" simply means "people who live on the heath". Since this now inferred people following the Old Religion such followers were dubbed "pagans" and "heathens". The words are often used today in a derogatory sense, which is incorrect.

As the centuries passed the "smear campaign" against the Wica intensified. Everything they did was reversed and used against them. They did magick to promote fertility and increase the crops; the Church therefore claimed that they made women and cattle barren and blighted the crops! No one, apparently, stopped to think that if the witches really did that they would suffer equally themselves, since they too had to eat and live! An old act of fertility was for the villagers to go to the fields, in the light of the full moon, and dance around the field astride pitchforks, poles, brooms, etc.—riding them like hobby-horses. They would leap high in the air to

* It is interesting to note that the whole concept of Evil associated with the Devil is due to an error in translation. The original Old Testament Hebrew *Ha-satan* and the New Testament Greek *diabolos* simply meaning "opponent" or "adversary".

show the crops how high to grow. A harmless enough form of sympathetic magick. But no! The Church claimed that they were actually flying through the air on their pitchforks and broom-sticks! Surely an act of the Devil! In 1484 Pope Innocent VIII produced his Bull against "Witches", and two years later two infamous German monks, Heinrich Institoris Kramer and Jacob Sprenger, produced their incredible concoction of anti-witchery, the Malleus Malleficarum. Definite instructions were given, in the book, for the prosecution of witches. When, however, the book was submitted to the Theological Faculty of the University of Cologne—the appointed Censor of books at that time—the majority of the professors refused to have anything to do with it. The office of censoring books was shortly removed from the University by Papal order and given to the bishops, while Kramer and Sprenger, nothing daunted, forged the Approbation of the whole Faculty. This forgery was exposed in 1898 by the Cologne archivist.

Gradually the hysteria kindled by Kramer and Sprenger began to spread. It spread like a fire—flashing up suddenly in unexpected spots; spreading quickly across the whole of Europe. For nearly three hundred years the fires of the persecution raged. Mankind had gone mad. In 1586 the Archbishop of Treves "discovered" that the local witches had "caused" the severe winter of 1585! By dint of frequent torture a "confession" was obtained and one hundred and twenty men and women were burned on his charge that they interfered with the elements. The inhabitants of entire villages where one or two witches were suspected of living would be killed with the cry "Destroy them all! The Lord will know his own!"

A rough estimate of the total number of people burned, hanged or tortured to death, on the charge of witchcraft, is nine million. Obviously not all of these were really followers of the Old Religion. This had been a wonderful opportunity to "get rid of" anyone against whom one bore a grudge! Just to murmur "Witch!" was enough.

An excellent example of the way in which the hysteria developed and spread is the case of the "witches" of Salem, Massachusetts. It is doubtful if any of the victims hanged* there were followers of the Old Religion. Just possibly Bridget Bishop and Sarah Good, but of the others they were nearly all pillars of the local church

* In New England the law was as in England; witches were hanged not burned. In Scotland and on the Continent burning was the usual penalty.

up until the time the hysterical children "cried out" on them. The whole case is dealt with extremely well by Miss Marion L. Starkey in her book *The Devil in Massachusetts.*

In 1604 James I passed his Witchcraft Act but this was repealed in 1736. It was replaced by an Act which stated that there was no such thing as witchcraft and to pretend to have occult powers was to face being charged with fraud!

By the late seventeenth century the surviving members of the Wica had gone "underground". Christianity had shown its new strength in no uncertain terms—those it could not convert it would destroy! For the next three hundred years to all appearances witchcraft was dead. But a religion which had lasted twenty thousand years or more did not die so easily. In small groups—surviving covens, oftimes consisting only of family members—the Craft continued.

In the literary field Christianity had a heyday. Until the early part of the twentieth century everything written about witchcraft was written from the Church point of view. It was not until Dr. Margaret Murray, in 1921, produced *The Witch Cult in Western Europe* that anyone looked at witchcraft with anything like an unbiased light. From studying the records of the trials of the Middle Ages, Dr. Murray, an eminent folklorist and Professor of Egyptology at London University, picked up the clues that showed there was a definite organized, pre-Christian religion behind all the "hogwash" of the Christian allegations. She enlarged on this in her book *God of the Witches* (1931) and actually traced the Cult back to its Paleolithic origins.

In 1954 Dr. Gerald Gardner, in his book *Witchcraft Today** said, in effect, "What Margaret Murray has theorized is quite true. Witchcraft *was* a religion and, in fact, still is. I am a witch myself." He went on to tell how the Craft was still very much alive, though underground. He explained, so far as he was allowed, just what witches did and what they believed; as opposed to what—thanks to the Church's lengthy propaganda—it was generally thought that they did and believed. Since the Wica is a Mystery Religion, similar to the old Greek and Roman ones, with an oath of secrecy taken at the Initiation, Gardner was not able to tell everything.

* *Witchcraft Today* is *the* book on the Craft for anyone at all interested in the subject. Unfortunately out of print, but still to be found in the second-hand book world.

But he certainly told a great deal, and enough to show what nonsense was the "information" previously obtainable.

At the time of Gardner's writing it seemed, to him, that the Craft was only just alive. He was greatly surprised when, as a result of the circulation of his books, he began to hear from many covens in all parts of Europe still happily practising their beliefs. It is now known that there are covens in England, Scotland, Wales, Ireland, Isle of Man, France, Belgium, Holland, Germany, Spain, Italy, Lebanon, South Africa, Australia and the United States of America. This list is certainly not complete.

In only recent years did the Craft come to America. This is understandable when it is considered that the time that this country was first being populated was the time of the fierce prosecutions of the witches in Europe. One or two individual witches may have come here but it is doubtful if complete covens did. The individual witch family in all probability died out, so there is no long background of true Witchcraft in the United States. As of the time of writing there are now Covens in New York, New Jersey, Kentucky, California, Washington, D.C., Ohio, and one in Ontario, Canada. All of these covens are "descended", through the New York one, from the coven to which Dr. Gerald Gardner belonged.

A *Coven* is a single group of Witches, who meet together regularly at a place known as a *Covenstead*. This group is lead by a High Priest and a High Priestess—the High Priestess, representing the Goddess, being the more important. Without the High Priestess no ceremonies may be held. Being a religion very close to nature witches always work in pairs—male and female. A Coven may actually consist of any number of couples—from one couple to a thousand or more. What, however, controls the actual number is the size of the "Magick Circle" in which they hold their ceremonies. This Circle is, by tradition, nine feet in diameter. Having an altar in the centre it can be seen that the number of couples will be limited. In fact the maximum number that can fit comfortably into the Circle is twelve—six couples. With a High Priestess this would give a total of thirteen witches; the "traditional" coven.

A question frequently asked is "How can there be thirteen witches in a Coven if you always work in pairs?" Within the Craft there is a system of Degrees of advancement similar, perhaps, to the better-known Degrees of Freemansonry—except that where the Masons have thirty-three degrees Witches have only three. A Witch should spend at least a year and a day between each degree. When the Third Degree is reached he, or she,* is ready to become a High Priest or High Priestess, and is classed as an Elder of the Coven. In the old days there might have been several male Elders in the Coven and so the High Priestess could choose a different one at each meeting to act as her High Priest. The female partner would then sit outside the Circle for the particular Rituals so that there would be equal couples. These days there are rarely "full" covens since witches, on reaching requisite rank, are encouraged to break away and form a new coven. Consequently the High Priestess has a permanent High Priest—usually her husband or fiance—and the Coven totals an even four or five couples.

When a female witch reaches the highest degree and breaks away to start her own Coven the High Priestess of the original Coven is then a Witch Queen, and her High Priest is known as a Magus. Obviously there are several Witch Queens within the Craft—High Priestesses ruling over more than one Coven—but it should be noted *there is no such title as "Queen Witch" or "Queen of All the Witches"*. The only possible ruler of *all* Witches is the Goddess herself. Spurious claims, to such titles as the above, are often made by "non-witches" who, for some reason—perhaps purely self-publicity—claim to be "England's No. One Witch" or some such! If they only knew what figures of fun they appear to true Craft members perhaps they would feel the "gimmick" was not worth it—though the lure of the dollars often available to these "professional witches" is probably too strong. There is also no such title, in Witchcraft, as "King", so claims to the title of "King of All the Witches" are as valid as the above! By the Craft Law no true Witch may accept money for work done through the Craft. One should therefore be very, very wary of the much-publicized, fee-charging "witch"!

Within the circle a female witch must always wear a necklace. The reason for this is that it symbolizes the Circle of Rebirth—one of the tenets of Witchcraft being a belief in Reincarnation. As a badge of rank a High Priestess will wear a large, silver bracelet with certain signs engraved on it. The High Priest, too, will wear a bracelet though of a different type from that of the High Priestess.

* The word *Witch* is used for both male and female. The more specialized word *warlock*, for a male, is not wrong *but is* never actually used with the Craft.

The only other distinguishing signs are those worn by a Witch Queen. She will wear a silver crown—a thin band of silver with a crescent moon at the front—and also a garter. The garter is traditionally of green leather, lined with blue silk, and has on it a silver buckle for every coven over which the Queen rules. In "ruling" other Covens the Witch Queen would never actually interfere with the High Priestess' running of her Coven. The Queen is really there to give the newer High Priestess help and advice when needed. Every Witch has someone to turn to. The Witch can always turn to her High Priestess; the High Priestess to her Queen; the Queen in turn to her Queen.

Other than the jewellery mentioned a Witch wears nothing—literally. Witches always work naked or, as they call it, *skyclad*. There are definite reasons for this. One is that it is a sign of freedom, but the most important reason is because of the power which emanates from a person's body and which the Witches use to do their *magick*. That a power does come off from the body has been proved in recent years though Witches have held the belief for centuries. Professor Otto Rahn, of Cornell University, did many experiments with yeast cells to show that they could be killed by a person merely looking or pointing at them. The "rays" were not always harmful; for some they are beneficial to tiny plants.

He experimented further to show that certain parts of the body produced these rays far more strongly than others (e.g. the palms of the hands, soles of the feet, armpits, genital organs, breasts of women). Witches have ways of making this power come off very strongly. This is why they work naked. Obviously clothing would impede the power which they can "collect" and use.

The naturalness and simplicity of the religion have already been mentioned. This is obvious in the rituals and in the instruments, or *working tools*. For instance, the Circle itself. This may be a chalk circle drawn on the floor, or a circle of string laid out on the rug. At the time of the persecutions it was often signified by placing pots and pans around the floor as guide points, so that if disturbed they could be quickly kicked away. In this and other respects is seen the major difference between Witchcraft and Ceremonial Magick.

When burning incense some Covens use beautiful censers but they are not necessary. The incense could be, and in many Covens is, burned in an ordinary saucer. Most of the working tools belong to the Coven as a whole, but there is one tool every witch must have and that is the *Athame*, or black-hilted knife. This has certain signs carved on the handle and is, as are all the tools, consecrated in a special manner before use. The ceremonial sword has a hilt of traditional design; the same in Covens all over the world.

The ceremonies themselves vary depending on the time of the year. There are eight Main Festivals in the Witch year—four Greater and four Lesser. The four Greater are: Hallowe'en (the most important), February Eve (Candlemas), May Eve (Beltane), and August Eve (Lammas). Such a division of the year points out the antiquity of the Craft. Division at May and November, with two cross-quarter days, predates agriculture—having no connection with sowing or reaping—marking the opening of the two breeding seasons of both wild and domestic animals. The four Lesser Festivals are the Spring and Autumn Equinoxes and the Summer and Winter Solstices. In addition to these *Sabbats* there are the *Esbats*. These are the full moons throughout the year. As it is written in the "Book of Shadows" (the Coven's book containing all their Rites and Rituals, Spells, Charms, Cures, Chants) "once in the month. and better it be when the Moon is full, gather in some secret place and adore Me who am Queen of all the Witcheries . . ." i.e. the Goddess. And this is exactly what is done at the meetings—an adoration of the Goddess; a worshipping of the Old Gode. No black masses; no black magick; no devil-worship, or kissing the buttocks of a goat; pacts with the Devil or sacrificing children! All this belongs to Satanism or Diabolism, or the fairy-tale world of the Christian Church. Many people are disappointed when they find what Witchcraft really is—just another religion. They feel somehow cheated that there is no sensationalism after all.

The initiation into witchcraft can be roughly divided into four parts: the "frightening"; the ordeal; the oath; and the presentation of the working tools. The Oath is an oath of secrecy. The Craft, being a Mystery Religion, has its members take an oath that they will always keep the secrets of the Craft. There is not, however, any renunciation of a previous faith—no crosses to break, or spit upon!

The similarity to the Greek and Roman mysteries has been mentioned. In Italy, at Pompeii, is the Villa of Mysteries. This was the place where everyone in the country would go to be initiated into the Dionysian Mystery. Around the walls of the Initiation Room are beautifully painted frescoes showing a woman going through the various stages of the initiation. A Witch can look at these scenes and see many similarities to her own initiation. There are also many similarities to be found in Initiation and Puberty Rites of different tribes today, the world over. The recurring theme of Death and Rebirth is perhaps the most common. In Witchcraft there is a symbolical Death and Rebirth, and at the Rebirth there is taken a new name. Some examples of Witches' names are : Gerald Gardner's "Scire"; the Lady Rowen (High Priestess of the original New York Coven); Robat, her High Priest; Jonet, Skyld, Morven; Morag; Oonagh; Theo; Thain; Froniga; Diedra.

Witches do not go out looking for converts. It is felt that anyone who really "belongs" to the Craft, as the Witches put it, will eventually find it. Many people would come across Gerald Gardner's books and would write to him, when he was alive, or to his home on the Isle of Man. They still write there, or to the Buckland Museum of Witchcraft and Magick. Their letters are then forwarded to the High Priestess of the Coven nearest them. It is then up to the High Priestess to follow up on the letter, if she feels it is warranted.

Today more and more people are turning to the Wica, finding there the answer to their religious needs. Many things attract them : the love of the Old Gods; the smallness of the Coven—making for *participation* in the religion, rather than being just another body in a row at the back of a large, cold building; the lack of pomp and ceremony; just the feeling of "belonging".

If this account has helped in any way to straighten out some of the popular misconceptions of Witchcraft and to show the Wica for what it is—a religion, pure and simple—it has done its job.

The author welcomes any questions or comments, and parts with the Witches' traditional salutation : *BLESSED BE.*

THE TRUTH ABOUT VOODOO

by HARRY SAUBERLI

VOODOO rites are performed openly today in the streets of Port-au-Prince and in the jungle glades of the Haitian countryside.

You can watch frantic dancing, mass hypnosis, blood sacrifice, sexual orgies. By day some Haitians dismiss Voodoo and call it primitive and superstitious. *But by night these same sceptics are seen in the Voodoo temples, consulting the Voodoo priests and sacrificing to the Voodoo gods.*

Many writers have described this dark, strange Negro cult of the Caribbean. Most have been drawn to it by the occult powers apparently possessed by its priests, called *hungans,* and priestesses, called *mambos*—by their apparent knowledge of certain evil forces unknown to civilized men—power to inflict disease or death on enemies; the power to create the living dead, called *zombies*; the power to turn women into werewolves. Other writers have tried to explain the apparently unshakeable attraction Voodoo has for its followers. Still others have denounced it as brutal and barbaric and labelled these followers "blood-crazed, sex-crazed savages".

For three hundred years the white man has tried to exterminate Voodoo. But it has persisted. It flourishes today.

What is Voodoo? Very simply, it is a pagan religion. It has incorporated certain practices and beliefs of the Roman Catholic religion, but it remains, basically, paganism. It is practised today by most of the population of the Negro republic of Haiti. It is not too dissimilar from many other contemporary heathen religions—for example, those of the South Sea islanders which have been so extensively studied by anthropologists—or from the great pagan religions of the past—those of the Greeks, the Romans, the Germans.

Voodoo is a first cousin to other modern Latin American Negro religions, *Santeraia* or *Nanigo* in Cuba, *Obesh* in Jamaica, and *Orisha* in Brazil. It was introduced to the United States by West

Indians living in New Orleans and became a considerable force in Louisiana in the years before the Civil War. Today Voodoo is outlawed in the United States. *But in the outskirts of Memphis, the slums of New Orleans, the back alleys of Harlem, its secret practice continues.*

Where does Voodoo come from? To look for the origin of Voodoo we need only to examine the word itself. It comes from the Creol word "*vaudou*". Creol is a comparatively recent language derived from French just as French is derived from Latin. It preserves phonetic habits and grammatical structures which, in origin, are clearly African. And so it is not surprising to discover that "vaudou" is merely a corruption of "vodu", a word of the Fon language group of West Africa. In West Africa "vodu" means a god or spirit, or a sacred object or fetish. Hence we deduce that Voodoo comes from West Africa and is the worship of various West African gods or spirits. And investigation has revealed that the Voodo gods, or loa, and rites attending their worship, and the gods and rites of the pagan religions of West Africa, are practically identical.

To trace the history of Voodoo it is necessary to go back to a dark and cruel time. For the story of Voodoo is meshed inexorably with the tragic history of that island of which Haiti forms the western half.

This island, called Hispaniola, was discovered by Christopher Columbus on the morning of December 6, 1492. It was a beautiful, semi-tropical place with mountain peaks jutting above the verdant forest and a native people who were gentle and peace-loving. Looking at this island, Columbus must have reflected on the happiness which would be the lot of all who might settle.

But this happiness was not to be. The Spanish settlers who followed Columbus soon discovered that the rich soil of Hispaniola could be turned to profit by creating huge plantations. To work these plantations the native population was forced into slavery. And by 1600 most of these natives were dead—either killed by the Spanish in battle or killed by the grinding labour they were forced to perform on the slave plantations.

Today, no trace remains of these gentle people. Spanish greed had exterminated an entire race of men.

Meanwhile, French buccaneers had established a settlement on the sparsely populated western end of the island. In 1664 they founded the town of Port-au-Paix. These Frenchmen were squatters, but since the Spanish could not dislodge them, they finally recognized them in the Treaty of Ryswick, 1697. The western part of the island became the French crown colony of Saint-Domingue.

During the next hundred years Saint-Domingue grew into one of the richest colonies of the New World. Its huge plantations produced sugar, coffee, indigo, cotton, cacao, and dyewoods for France. This prosperity was the result of one thing—*Negro slaves, imported* continuously and in massive numbers from Africa.

The African slave trade is one of the most inhuman chapters in the history of civilization. It began almost by accident some fifty years before Columbus. A group of Portuguese sailors, exploring the Atlantic coast of Africa under the banner of Prince Henry the Navigator, captured small bands of Moors. These Moors directed the Portuguese to carry them to the African coast. The Portuguese did so and were surprised to receive ten Negro slaves and a quantity of gold dust in exchange for their Moorish prisoners. Soon the Portuguese were buying more Negroes from the Moors and selling them to Spain.

When the first Spanish Governor of the new colony of Hispaniola set sail for the Caribbean he took with him a group of Negro slaves born in Seville. The Spanish soon discovered that the Negroes performed the hard work of the hot Haitian plantations much more satisfactorily than the Indians of the island. And as the Indians died off, the demand for Negro slaves increased.

There is an area on the Gulf of Guinea, on the western coast of Africa, which until quite recently was shown on maps as the Slave Coast. Here the native population was (and is today) extremely dense. Two principal nations, Dahomey and Nigeria, both have a long history of slavery and include in their religion the sacrifice of human beings.

Dahomey was infamous for its customs of sacrificing thousands of people on the death of its kings. After an elaborate ceremonial, featuring much dancing and feasting, the sacrificial victims were dressed in special costumes, put into large baskets, and lifted to the top of a platform. There the new king would make a speech explaining that the victims were sent to testify to the greatness of the dead king in the spirit land. Then the victims were hauled down into the middle of a surging crowd and butchered. So many people were killed in this fashion that skulls adorned the royal palace and the king's sleeping chamber was paved with the heads of his enemies.

The city of Benin in Nigeria was notorious for its wholesale human sacrifices. Europeans called it "the city of blood". When the King of Benin assassinated the acting British consul-general in 1897, the British Navy occupied the city and found hundreds of altars covered with human blood, bodies crucified on trees, and the remains of innumerable human sacrifices.

The victims for these sacrifices were generally prisoners of war. The European traders who flocked to the area once the slave trade became profitable found it simple to persuade the various kings and chiefs to sell part of their prisoners in exchange for European products. In time, payment was made more and more often in liquor, arms, and ammunition, which further encouraged inter-tribal warfare and thus increased the number of prisoners available for sale as slaves.

In the kingdom of Dahomey the slave trade soon became the national industry. Its whole economy was based on annual expeditions against neighbouring peoples. The King of Dahomey maintained a monopoly on prisoners of war and sold most of them to the white traders, keeping back only those due for sacrifice to his ancestors and those needed as agricultural labourers. Because of its success in these annual wars, Dahomey became during the 1700's one of the most powerful nations in Africa. In 1727 it smashed the neighbouring kingdom of Whydah and turned its capital city into a huge slave emporium which remained popular with slavers up to a hundred years ago. It has been estimated that over 1,000,000 people were sold into slavery at this single market place. Such was the legacy of the Old World to the New.

Officially, the Negroes brought to Saint-Domingue were baptized and made Christians. Article Two of the Code Noir, published by the French in 1685, made baptism and instruction in the Catholic religion mandatory for all slaves in the French colonies of America. The King of France considered this law very important since the only moral justification for France's expanding slave trade was the conversion of the Negroes.

In practice, however, the colonists concerned themselves little with the religious life of their Negroes. The only part of the Code Noir which was properly observed was the one relating to baptism. As soon as the newly-arrived slaves were baptized, slave owners felt acquitted of their duty to God and King.

The life of a slave in the 17th and 18th centuries was incredibly harsh. The Negroes were herded into the cramped slave ships like cattle. With little food and no sanitation, half of them died on the voyage across the Atlantic. Once in Saint-Domingue they were quickly sold and put to work in fields. The over-exertion was so crushing that the life of the average Negro sold to a plantation was reckoned at about ten years.

Religion for slaves was considered a waste of time. No religious instruction was given. Few planters allowed priests on their land since they feared that the priests would censure them for their treatment of the slaves. The only Negroes who acquired even a veneer of Christianity were the house slaves who lived with the white family, went to mass with them, and took part in family prayers every evening.

The hard work and cruel treatment ought logically to have crushed the spirit of the Negroes on Saint-Domingue, as they had crushed the spirit and indeed the lives of the original inhabitants of the island. But they did not. For the Negroes contrived to re-establish religion as they had known it in Africa.

Despite certain linguistic differences and very deep antagonisms, the various ethnic groups of the Gulf of Guinea have basically a common culture and religion. They had little difficulty in combining their respective traditions to build up a new syncretic religion. And the one thing which sustained the Negro throughout this era of harsh oppression was the worship of his native gods, called loa, and the magic surrounding such worship. Records of the colonial plantation owners reveal that late at night the slaves would disappear into the jungle and engage in mysterious rites. Mere physical exhaustion should have prevented this. And the punishment meted out to those caught practising what the colonists labelled "sorcery" was severe. The mere fact that such rites were held testified to the hardiness of these Africans and the power of their religion.

For many years certain apologists for the slave trade propounded the theory that slave cargoes were made up of the dregs of African society and that the Dark Continent was all the healthier for being rid of them. Actually, since the slaves were originally prisoners of war the slave ships held representatives of all classes of West African society. The formation of Voodoo can be explained only by the presence in the slave gangs of priests, or "servants of the gods", who knew the sacred rites and mysteries of Africa. Otherwise, in Saint-Domingue the Negroes could have evolved little more than incoherent practices and simple rites of black and white magic. But instead, by the late 1700's, documents reveal the existence of temples, an organized clergy, a complicated ritual, and sophisticated dances and rhythms. Among the slaves there must have been bokono (magicians) and vodu-no (priests), trained in Africa, who taught the following generation, born in slavery the names and characteristics of the gods and the sacrifices required.

The pantheon of the Voodoo religion is made up of many gods. Some are worshipped by everyone, and some are private, hereditary gods, usually ancestors who have become deified and who are worshipped by their particular family. By tracing the various gods to their African origin anthropologists have been able to discern the origin of the present-day Haitian people. Most of them came from Dahomey and the area immediately surrounding that country, a large minority came from Nigeria, and certain others came from Guinea, Angola, and the Congo. One of the more important discoveries is the worship in Haiti of gods belonging to the royal family of Dahomey, suggesting that members of the royal family itself were reduced to slavery and transported across the sea. For no one else would have been qualified or even concerned to establish the worship of these royal household gods.

As the white colonists of Saint-Domingue grew prosperous and the oppression of their Negro slaves grew more severe, a strange uneasiness spread over the island. *Slowly the colonists became aware of Voodoo.*

As time passed this knowledge grew into a deadly fear. The more the master mistreated his slaves the more he feared their hatred and the more he dreaded the occult powers which he came to feel his slaves possessed.

The records of the 18th century reflect a ubiquitous terror which solidified in an obsession with poison which was undoubtedly used by many slaves to revenge themselves on tyrannical masters. But the fear which reigned in the plantations had its real source in the deeper recesses of the soul. It was the witchcraft of remote and mysterious Africa which troubled the sleep of the people in the "big house". Any slave even suspected of belonging to the dreaded sect called the "Voodoos" was branded and tortured.

In the late 1700's a Frenchman, Moreau de Saint-Mery, in his book *Description of the French Part of Saint-Domingue*, gave the white man the first detailed account of the Voodoo religion.

Saint-Mery translated the word voodoo quite correctly as "an all-powerful and supernatural being". He identified it as "the snake under whose auspices gather all who share the faith". Here he was identifying the popular Voodoo god Damballah-wedo, the snake god, who is, although Saint-Mery did not realize it at the time, but one of many Voodoo gods.

Voodoo gatherings, said Saint-Mery, take place secretly at night in "a cloistered place shut off from the eyes of the profane". The priest and priestess take up their positions near an altar containing a snake in a cage. After various ceremonies and a long address from the priest and priestess, all initiates approach in order of seniority and entreat the snake, telling it what they most desire. The priestess stands on the box in which the snake lies and, said Saint-Mery, "modern Pythoness—she is penetrated by the god; she writhes; her whole body is convulsed and the oracle speaks from her mouth". The snake is then put on the altar and each person brings it an offering. A goat is sacrificed and its blood, collected in a jar, is used "to seal the lips of all present with a vow to suffer death rather than reveal anything, and even to inflict it on whoever might prove forgetful of such a momentous pledge".

Then begins what Saint-Mery called the "danse vaudou". This is the moment when the new initiates are received into the sect. Possessed by a spirit, the novices go into a trance, and do not come out of their trance until a priest hits them "on the head with his hand, wooden spoon or, if he thinks necessary, ox-hide whip". The ceremony ends with a collective delirium which Saint-Mery believed to be the result of magnetic emanations. As proof he cited the paroxysms of whites who had merely come as spectators. Saint-Mery described this collective trance as follows: "Some are subject to fainting fits, others to a sort of fury; but with all there is a nervous trembling which apparently cannot be controlled. They turn round and round. And while there are some who tear their clothes in this bacchanal and even bite their own flesh, others merely lose consciousness and falling down are carried into a neighbouring room where in the darkness a disgusting form of prostitution holds hideous sway."

The sexual aspect of Voodoo has been tamed somewhat, but this description leaves no room for doubt that there existed in Haiti at the end of the 18th century rites and practices which have changed little up to modern times. It is not a normal custom now, however, to represent Damballah-wedo by actual living snakes. In fact that god is most commonly represented today by a picture of Saint Patrick driving the snakes out of Ireland. It is also interesting to note that to this day in Whydah there is a large temple of snakes and that the snake god is the principal deity of the place.

Voodoo gods are divided into two groups: *the rada and the petro*. The origin of the word "rada" is easily found. It comes from the town Arada in Dahomey, a name which in the 18th century covered all Dahomeans. On the other hand the name "petro" comes from the name of a man, Don Pedro. Saint-Mery describes how, in 1768, a Negro of Le Petit-Goave, a Spaniard by birth, introduced a new set of gods and dances to Haiti. The petro rites are extremely complicated and few today feel that they could have possibly been introduced by one man. Although not Dahomean, they are none the less African in origin. In contemporary Voodoo, Dompedre is a powerful god who is normally greeted by the detonation of gunpowder. And so it seems certain there must have once been a hungan, or priest, whose impact was so profound that his name took the place of African tribes who today worship gods bearing his name, petro, and not theirs. But unless we discover documents telling us more about this Don Pedro, his deification and powerful effect on Voodoo will remain a mystery.

By 1789, the year of the French Revolution, Voodo in Haiti was an organized religion different from the Voodoo of today only in that it bore a more distinctly African character. It was beginning to adopt certain Christian elements, but at this stage it had not been invaded, as it is today, by Catholic liturgy. With the Revolution, and the subsequent War for Haitian Independence, Voodoo entered a new era. The importing of slaves ended abruptly, and with all ties to Africa thus cut, Voodoo was free to evolve as a purely Haitian institution.

The French Revolution aroused the whites in Saint-Domingue because they wanted greater independence from the King of France. It aroused the free mulattos because they wanted equality as citizens. With a population of 30,000 whites, 40,000 mulattos, but over 500,000 Negro slaves, it is hardly surprising that this fervour for freedom should spread to the slaves.

On the night of August 14, 1791, a great number of slaves met in a glade of the Bois Caiman. A pig was sacrificed according to Voodoo custom and with its blood the Negroes swore themselves to the destruction of their white masters. A few days later thousands of whites were massacred and their plantations reduced to ashes. Thus began a war which was to last twelve years.

Most slave rebellions of history have ended in dismal failure. The institution of slavery does not tend to produce leaders clever enough or a revolutionary spirit gallant enough to galvanize a downtrodden people into an effective army. But miraculously the slaves of Haiti were provided with both. *Voodoo gave their cause a spiritual substance and from their ranks emerged leaders of considerable ability.*

The first of these leaders was Pierre-Dominique Toussaint-L'Ouverture. As a slave Toussaint had practised the art of healing with herbs, and it was as a herb-doctor that he began his military career with the guerrilla bands of Jean Francois. Toussaint rose to the position of general, defeated the white men, proclaimed a constitution in May, 1801, and made himself Governor-General of Haiti for life.

Napoleon, having established himself in France, dispatched an army under General Charles Leclerc to crush this "First of the Blacks". On the very day this army landed in Haiti, Toussaint visited in the fort of Crete-a-Pierrot a Voodo priest famous for his ability to foresee the future. The priest predicted that Toussaint would be betrayed and handed over to the French by his most trusted and senior general, Jean-Jacques Dessalines. Toussaint soon developed an obsession that the "vodoos" had cast on him an evil spell. This obsession proved to be justified. Toussaint was captured by the French and sent to France in irons where he died a year later.

Dessalines, a Voodoo practitioner who was said to have the power to judge a man's intentions by examining the humidity of the tobacco in his snuff-box, quickly decided that Napoleon planned to restore slavery and so, together with another Negro general, Henri Christophe, he renewed the war against the French. Dessalines was said to have made great use of Voodoo to arouse his followers. Finally, on November 8, 1803, the French army, decimated by yellow fever, surrendered.

On January 1, 1804, Dessalines declared the independence of Haiti and made himself Emperor of the entire island. Once in power he lost his sympathy for Voodoo. He relentlessly hunted down what he now labelled "secret societies", prohibited Voodoo services, and shot all Voodoo adherents. This, combined with other tyrannical acts and the general poverty into which the island had sunk, led to his assassination in 1806.

Henri Christophe then declared himself Emperor of the North, while in Port-au-Prince, Alexander Petion, a mulatto general, was elected president. Christophe had little sympathy for Voodoo or for the laziness of the common people who had stopped working at the beginning of the revolution. Christophe herded his people into forced labour gangs, restored the Haitian economy, and built his magnificent palace of San Souci. But in doing this he became hated as a tyrant. His people revolted in 1820, hounded the Emperor to his supposedly impregnable mountain-top retreat, and there, on hearing the approach of the rebels, Henri Christophe hurled his own body into a pit of lime.

From the downfall of Christophe until 1915, Haiti was ruled by a succession of twenty-three dictators. Eighteen of these were ejected from office by violence.

The most notable of these rulers was Faustin Soulouque, an illiterate but crafty soldier who seized power in 1847. Soulouque revived the practice of the founders of Haiti and set himself up as Emperor. Under his rule Voodoo became almost the established state religion. Soulouque believed implicitly in the Voodoo gods.

As soon as he became Emperor, Soulouque began to feel that evil powers were at work against him. He consulted a mambo who declared that President Boyer, overthrown in 1843, had hidden a charm in the palace garden. This charm, said the mambo, prevented any presidential successor from staying in power longer than thirteen months. Soulouque ordered a search of the garden and the charm was found in the place indicated. And so, instead of thirteen months, Soulouque ruled for twelve years. In the end, however, he was overthrown by Fabre Geffrard who signed a concordat with the Vatican in 1860 and tried to re-establish conventional Catholicism as the religion of the country.

Of the later presidents, Antoine Simon enjoys the greatest reputation as a Voodooist. This former rural constable was swept to power by revolution in 1908. His daughter, Celestina, was a mambo with reputedly marvellous knowledge. She was often seen on the grounds of the presidential palace going through various rituals to counter the traps laid by those who were plotting against her father. Her success was temporary, however. After two and a half years of dictatorship, Simon was overthrown by another revolution.

In 1915, after a mob had seized and brutally butchered President Vilbrum Sam, Haiti was occupied by the United States Marines. The country was kept under American jurisdiction until 1934. Since that time Haiti had achieved something closer to political stability.

The current President of Haiti, Dr. Francois Duvalier, maintains a life-long interest in Voodoo and has published many articles on the subject. He is known to the common people of his country as "Pappa Doc". His rivals have denounced him as a chief hungan, and have accused him of using Voodoo for his own political ends.

Today Voodoo is officially tolerated, and its practice is as popular as ever. For despite the sincerity of their attachment to the Church, most Haitians are reluctant to give up their loa and their magic. They believe that Voodoo contains supernatural truths of which the Catholic hierarchy is ignorant, or at any rate, will not concern itself. Haitians believe in the power not only of white magic but of black magic.

In Haiti today, even the sophisticated collect their cut hair at the barber shop and carefully destroy finger-nail parings to prevent these from falling into the hands of enemies who might use them to create evil curse-charms.

Today Voodoo is appreciated by those who have studied it not as merely witchcraft but as one of the faiths men live by. Studies in hypnotism at Duke University have confirmed hypnotic principles which Voodooists knew and practised centuries ago. Voodoo music, such as the mambo, is now popular throughout the world. Sophisticated audiences fill concert halls to hear the rhythms of Voodoo drums.

Now medical authorities are beginning to study the astonishing knowledge of ancient herbs long common to Voodoo. Who can say that the Voodoo belief in spirits—good and bad—which control men's destinies is not as much a part of supernatural truth as the beliefs of established, civilized religions?

The people of Haiti believe that there is nothing in the teaching of Christianity which conflicts with Voodoo as practised today, that their spirits, derived from the ancient gods of Africa, are but a part of a spiritual whole.

To the Haitians, Voodoo explains Christianity and gives it meaning.

I WALKED ON FIRE

by WILMON MENARD

MY interest in man's strange experiments in fiery tortures was aroused some years ago when the late Robert Ripley, of "Believe It or Not" fame, sponsored a fire-walking Hindu mystic by the name of Kuda Bux in a public demonstration. Bux strolled barefooted across two separate fire pits in a parking lot at Rockefeller Center in New York City. It is a matter of official record that three cords of oak and five hundred pounds of charcoal burned for eight hours before Kuda Bux made the walk across the two separate ovens, whose temperature a pyrometer registered at 1,220° F. Attending physicians peered and smelled at the soles of the fire-walker's feet, but found only one small burn, where a coal had stuck to his instep. But their nostrils detected no odour of burned flesh. I was one of the astounded spectators, and I was deeply impressed.

Just a short time ago, I was in Papeete, Tahiti, when word reached me that an *umuti* (firewalk) was to be held on the island of Raiatea, one hundred and thirty-five miles away. I lost no time in booking passage on an inter-island trading schooner. But, for all my eagerness, I didn't realize then that I myself would take part in the ceremony.

A native friend took me at dawn to the valley where the oven, heaped high with large rocks, was blazing. It was thirty feet long, fifteen feet wide and four feet deep. It had been burning for two days. The huge rocks, which were settling to the level of the ground, glowed bright red in the faint light of the South Pacific dawn. Now and then, between us and the oven, the coconut-oil smeared bodies of the Polynesian fire tenders passed briefly, as they raked out the last of the log cinders and levelled the hot rocks. It was not unlike a scene from Dante's *Inferno*.

Now as I watched, holding my hand in front of my face to shield it from the intense heat radiated from the *umu*, or oven, I thought of man's superstitious dread and awe of fire, coupled with his instinctive, practical usages, which have combined to produce so many fantastic fire ordeals. The American Indians, during certain rites, danced in the lives coals of their camp-fire; devotees of the Sinsyu Shinto sect of Japan walk barefooted over glowing coals. In Hawaii in the early days, the priests and priestesses of the fire goddess Pele strode across the molten lava on the broad bosom of Kilauea Volcano. In some parts of Africa, new-born children are held briefly over a flame. In India cremation of the corpse is supposed to be the soul's only passport to life beyond death.

Now the Firewalk of Polynesia was to be performed before my eyes. Chief Terii-Pao, the young and hereditary firewalker of Raiatea, had suddenly decided to call an *umuti*, primarily, of course, to pay homage to the two great goddesses of ancient days—Hina-nui-te'a'ara, the Goddess of the Moon, and Te-Vahine-nui-tahu-ra'i (The-Great-Woman-Who-Set-Fire-to-the-Sky)—but also to earn a few francs with which to buy a bottle of rum and a few yards of calico cloth for his woman.

As I watched, Terii-Pao stepped from his nearby coconut-palm temple, and several attendants, similarly garbed in native *preu* and sacred *ti*-leaves, followed. I could feel the crackling excitement that swept the clearing upon his appearance. The laughter, singing and loud talking ceased instantly. All eyes were fixed upon the handsome chief, a splendid figure standing at the head of his assistants. He turned, caught my eyes and smiled. Once we had sailed aboard a trading schooner to the pearl-diving atoll of Anaa in the Dangerous Archipelago; I had given him a case of foodstuffs, and we were friends.

The many tourists who had voyaged on the inter-island schooner from Papeete surrounded Terii-Pao and began a careful inspection of his feet. He submitted indulgently, grinning broadly at their thorough examination. I saw one of the tourists turn, walk to the edge of the fiery pit, and look full into the centre of the oven for a few seconds. With a groan he backed away as he clapped his hands over his face. I could see that his neck and face were badly seared and tears streamed from his glazed eyes. Another visitor, with the aid of a long stick, dropped a handkerchief upon the rocks and it turned almost instantly to a grey powder. The oven was certainly hot! The tourists withdrew from Terii with baffled expressions.

Chief Terii, his head held high and his eyes uplifted to the opalescent sky, walked towards the end of the oven, a branch of *ti*-leaves in his hand. There he stopped, striking the rocks three times with the *ti*-wand. He began to chant in Tahitian the ancient fire-walking prayer. I know the language, and I listened closely.

These were the words:

"O Being who enchants the oven, let it die out for a while! O dark earthworms! O light earthworms! Fresh water and salt water, heat of the oven, darkening of the oven, hold up the footsteps of the walkers and fan the heat of the bed. O cold host, let us linger in the midst of the oven. O Vahine-nui-tahu-ra'i, hold the fan and let us go into the oven for a little while!"

Finally came Terii's loud and exultant shout of: "*O Vahine-nui-tahu-ra'i-e!* All is covered!"

I shall never forget the great sigh and then the hush that followed the chief's first step upon the pit. He hesitated a moment as if to be sure that the stones would not shift under his weight, and then, with an almost hypnotic expression, he walked on to the glowing bed of rocks. The tourists gave a gasp of dismay; the natives sat stiffly, unmoving, as if mesmerized. I watched wonderingly. This was no sham. A human being was walking on to an oven of rocks sufficient to roast him! Terii crossed the pit and then turned and retraced his steps. Upon his return, his assistants formed in a straight line behind him. Again Terii struck the edge of the glowing rocks with his *ti*-wand; then he and his followers marched with firm steps across the *umu*.

I could see the heat waves rippling above their heads, but there was no odour of seared flesh, as one might expect. I stared fixedly until they had traversed the oven, expecting every second that one of them would leap with a scream of agony from the line. But each one passed safely. The last firewalker stepped from the oven, and Terii raised his *ti*-leaves, took his place at the head of the column, and led them back across the fiery expanse. This was repeated three times.

With the third crossing, Terii raised his *ti*-leaves and cried: "*Atira!* Enough!" Then, unexpectedly, he turned quickly and *crawled across the thirty-foot oven of rocks on his stomach!*

At the far side he stood up, grinned and beckoned to the tourists to make their inspection. One of them placed his palms to the soles of Terii's feet and then turned a baffled face to the other's, crying: "They're not even warmed!" I also moved forward to examine his feet. They were not even marked by the crossing of the fiery furnace! The examination over, we withdrew, our amazement plain in our faces.

Terii then turned to the assembled natives and exhorted those who were afflicted with any physical or mental taints, who were in need of spiritual purification, or who wished to test their courage with fire, to walk behind him over the hot rocks. Passing close to me, he caught my eye again, grinned, and stopped. "Perhaps you would like to walk behind me across the *umu.* You have lived long in our islands and understand our customs and ceremonies. But if you are afraid, it would be dangerous to attempt the fire-walk."

It was his last remark that compelled me to kick off my sneakers, remove my socks and cry: "*Haere outou!* Let's go!"

A loud chorus of "*Maitai!* Good!" rose from the native onlookers. A comic among the tourists yelled: "You're going to be sorry, chum!"

I stepped into the column of walkers forming behind the chief. Now my bravado was on the ebb. I was experiencing the first symptoms of fright, and I cursed the impulse that had made me accept Terii's invitation to walk behind him over the *umu.* There was the customary taut feeling in my throat, and my stomach felt as if it had suddenly been invaded by crazed butterflies. My heart started to pound violently; my head ached, and I wanted very badly to step out of line. I have always had an uncommon fear of fire, since the day in my childhood when I fell into a burning bonfire. Now that memory was intensified. The stalwart *tahua* (priest) behind me gave me a light push. Terii had started towards the fire pit!

I clamped my teeth hard, inhaled deeply, and gave a belly-depth groan. Mechanically I started to walk, and I felt not unlike a somnambulist proceeding towards a portentous fate. My legs felt numb and leaden; my heart was now thudding with jarring impact against my ribs. Then my bare feet touched something uneven and elevated. This is it, I told myself; you'd better step out of line before it's too late! Another firm shove on my shoulders, and in the next instant countless tiny electric shocks pricked the bottom of my feet.

It was not unlike the sudden jabbing of the skin with sharp

needles. Smothering heat waves shimmered before my steadfast gaze, compelling me at last to half close my eyes. It was like the sudden rush of heat that explodes from the widely flung doors of a huge blast furnace. The heat of the oven all but suffocated me. My lungs became filled with superheated air, and I felt I would collapse if I did not breathe pure cool air quickly. As if from a great distance, through a long windswept tunnel, I heard the murmuring of the spectators. And as I walked I felt that I must surely present an abject figure treading behind Terii, if my physical aspect matched my mental unrest.

Then, suddenly, the tingling sensation on the bottom of my feet ceased, and I knew that I had crossed the oven. I glanced down at my feet. They were untouched! I had half-expected to see burn-blisters erupting between the toes, and the flesh bursting under intense roasting. Every pore of my body filtered rivulets of sweat, and I could see that Chief Terii's broad back was glistering with globules of body moisture. Terii abruptly lifted his wand of *ti*-leaves, a recognized signal that the last in line had passed over the *umu*, and now everyone was to right-about-face for the return transit. I knew that I could not undergo another walk upon the hot stones, so I stepped quickly out of line. Terii grinned and gave me an understanding slap on my shoulders. Then he led his followers back across the oven.

Quickly I was surrounded by the tourists, who lifted my feet and wiped away the dirt to search for burn marks. There were none! The natives shook my hand, and gave complimentary shouts of "*Maitai-roa!* Very good!"

Several white men have walked barefooted across the fiery ovens of Polynesia, among them Dr. William Craig and his brother, former British resident agents of the Cook Islands, and they made a safe crossing. Some, voicing flippant or sceptical remarks, were horribly burned during an *umuti*, necessitating hospitalization; others, believing in the strange ceremonies of the islands, have made the walk unscathed. The reasons for the different experiences I cannot explain.

Some assayers of human immunity to fireburn have made interesting observations. A writer and traveller in Japan, John Hyde, noticed that the priests, before walking over their herb-strewn fire pits, rubbed the soles of their feet with salt. He experimented similarly, and after a walk across an oven, he remarked: "My confidence was not misplaced. In my feet I felt only a sensation of gentle warmth, but my ankles, to which no salt was applied, were scorched."

Some years ago, the astute magician and escape artist Harry Houdini, an avid debunker of performances of the so-called supernatural, blasted demonstrations of fire-eaters and firewalkers in his book *Miracle Mongers and Their Methods.* He took particular exception to a "roasting alive" act performed by a young man garbed only in bathing trunks, inside a heated glass enclosure, a steak dangling from his arm. The idea was for the exhibitionist to remain inside the booth, exposed to a high register of heat, until the steak was thoroughly cooked. Houdini pointed out that the young man protected his hair with a bathing cap and had smeared clay over his eyebrows, so that the hair would not retain the heat longer than skin cells. That, Houdini maintained, with the tempering effect of excreting perspiration, was the solution to this heat-torture act. However, the magician explained, if the man had stayed in the over-heated enclosure beyond a certain period of time, his body would have become dehydrated and serious heat prostration would have resulted. Precise timing was the explanation of this trick, according to Houdini.

Some debunkers of firewalking have suffered severe penalties—just recently, in the case of one William Spaeth of Hollywood, California, who dabbles in fiery rites in his stage shows. One of his tricks was to walk over burning charcoal scattered over a sandy bed. He decided to use larger chunks of charcoal, but at a rehearsal the performance backfired, and Spaeth was hurried to the Georgia Street Receiving Hospital in an ambulance, suffering first and second degree burns. He had to learn to walk on his hands for a while.

At a jungle shrine in Ceylon, just a short time ago, a group of local *sadhus* celebrated a rite of Hindu holy men: walking barefoot over a bed of glowing coals. This was good news to Reverend Eric Robinson, a British Methodist missionary, who decided to debunk the *sadhus.* He kicked off his shoes, tore off his socks, and headed for the fire pit. He stepped on to the coals and, before the holy men could stop him, marched the entire length alone. The doctor's verdict: horrible burns on the feet, which kept the Reverend Mr. Robinson from his missionary work for some weeks.

A more sober experiment in heat and its effects on the human body was conducted at the University of California in Los Angeles. The study was supervised by Dr. Craig Taylor, physiologist and engineer, at the request of the United States government. It was not simply a considerataion of pyrolatry, or worship of fire.

The government wanted to know one very important thing: was there a possibility that Army, Navy, and Marine jet pilots would be roasted alive in the friction-heated cockpits of their supersonic crafts? These jet planes need refrigeration systems to keep their cockpits comfortable and bearable. What would happen to a pilot if the cooling equipment failed as a runaway jet screamed through the sky? Would the pilot collapse at the controls? Would he succumb to heat prostration? Would he have to bail out in the stratosphere, or would he be literally baked alive in the cockpit? Could he stay at the controls, enduring the terrific heat, until he could slow the plane down?

This was a big order, but Professor Taylor was determined to find out what would happen to a human in a jet plane in flight if the cooling system faulted. With the help of his assistants, he made a testing furnace out of a huge steel cylinder, and provided a strong fan to suck in dry air across an outside battery of white-hot electric grids. The first human guinea pigs remained in this hot-box until the heat passed the boiling point of water (212° F.). These student volunteers in the heat experiment came out a little groggy and florid-faced, but quite "uncooked".

Professor Taylor reserved the final and decisive tests for himself. His hands, feet and neck were protected before he was wheeled into the cylinder, whose temperature upon entrance in this supreme experiment read 230° F. He remained in this overheated atmosphere for 15¼ minutes, as the heat climbed to 262° F. While he was in the cylinder, an egg fried on a metal frypan in front of him. His face became fiery red when the hot blasts of air hit it, and his nasal membranes contracted, but apart from these discomforts he experienced no physical or mental agony.

His answer was simple and to the point: The human body's resistance to heat is in its own cooling system, which nature has so thoughtfully provided—perspiration and mucous secretions. He proved that the moisture evaporating from the skin provides part of the body with a layer of cool air—just as a "desert waterbag" hanging on the outside of a car travelling through hot wasteland keeps the water cool from its own evaporation of moisture through porous canvas.

While inside the hotbox, Professor Taylor learned that at one time, when the register of heat was at 236° F., the air three-quarters of an inch from his nose was 226° F. The skin of the nose itself registered a safe 119.5° F.—over 100 degrees cooler. Air drawn into the nostrils was cooled down to 100° F., which certainly could not injure the lungs. The general temperature of his body rose only a couple of degrees.

But what the Professor did emphasize as a danger to jet pilots in overheated cockpits was the raised temperature of the blood conveyed to the brain cells. This would give pilots of jet planes the surest indication of approaching heat prostration should cooling equipment break down. He pointed out that man's fear of heat is chiefly a mental torture. Humans, no matter if they are pilots in friction-heated cockpits of jet planes or unfortunate victims trapped in burning buildings or ships, can overcome high registers of heat by rational, well-organized attitudes of self-preservation. Fright or over-excitement can raise the temperature of the blood many degrees.

Later, another test was made to learn the effects of heat on the minds and bodies of GI infantry troops in desert fighting, where the daytime temperature averaged 116 degrees. An experimental station, comparable to heat and humidity conditions of other deserts in the world, was set up at the Yuma Test Station in Arizona, where stress and strain on the men under intolerable heat could be gauged on a treadmill, which, housed in a hotbox, was promptly labelled "The Idiot Box". Eighteen GIs were put in relays on the squirrel run, with the heat well above 116 degrees. After a long session on this getting-nowhere hike, the GIs were taken out and urged on a double-time march, with and without packs, and ordered to grub out foxholes and perform experimental tactical problems. During this period, their pulses, weights and temperatures were taken regularly.

The findings were illuminating: the body took from five days to two weeks to adapt itself to the heat. During this time, the skin became accustomed to perspiring more advantageously, losing a minimum of salt; more blood circulated to the skin and thereby cooled itself; and the men learned to move slowly and retain energy. It was found, too, that a man subjected to this heat can sweat more than two quarts of water an hour, which is about forty-eight times more than the average loss in a temperate climate. It was recommended that infantry troops exposed to desert heat should drink as much water as they wanted, notwithstanding the old campaign concept of "water discipline", which permitted only a rare, maddening swallow. Also, salt tablets were abandoned in the Yuma test in preference to having a normal amount of salt with meals.

The GIs expended much of their body heat upwards to the open sky. They were cooler on the open desert than in a wash or in the bottom of a ravine, or even in their tents. The standard weight of the pack was too heavy for desert operations. The men became 24-carat moaners about their chow, refusing such popular items as greasy pork chops and oil-soaked, mayonnaise-smeared salads. Some demanded more fruit juices and light foods, and many lost their appetites altogether. Most of the GIs slept poorly during the constant heat, and became cranky, argumentative, complaining, and hard to handle.

The firewalkers of Raiatea, Japan, Fiji, India, and Africa have had no indoctrination as to the scientific principles of heat, and, therefore, it is quite understandable that they would look to a psychic or supernatural source to explain their safe walks across fire pits. Certainly, the *umuti* of Raiatea is a remarkable feat. You must bear in mind that hot rocks and not hot air come into contact with the flesh of the participants. I think Professor Taylor would have to admit that Chief Terii's ceremony is quite different from the study he conducted.

And I have to remind myself that no scientist has completely explained to my satisfaction how I crossed the fiery pit at Raiatea without so much as a blistered toe.